Acclaim for
THE WOMAN WHO PAINTED HER DREAMS:

'The power of Dewar's highly visual imagination brings off this tender, uncompromising story with panache and feeling'

Glasgow Herald

'An accomplished and beautifully written novel'

Real magazine

'I have loved Isla Dewar's novels right from the start; she manages to combine humour with beautiful writing and wonderful characterisation. THE WOMAN WHO PAINTED HER DREAMS is her best yet'

Sarah Brown

'The feisty character of Madeline carries this charmingly written story of conflicting desires'

Family Circle

'She knows just what will move us'

Scotsman

'Isla Dewar is remarkably good at setting a period. The perplexities of being a small only child in a house of adults circa 1959 is beautifully captured'

The List, Glasgow

'You will wish that this magical, poignant and funny story never has to end'

Glasgow Evening Times

'Wry humour, beautifully evoked landscapes and skilful characterisation'

Bookseller

'Isla Dewar is not just a fine craftswoman; like Madeline Green, she too is an artist'

Sunday Herald

'[Isla Dewar's] sixth book, THE WOMAN WHO PAINTED HER DREAMS, is her best yet'

Scotland on Sunday

'Isla Dewar's true skill is in her eye for detail and character development . . . Dewar writes touchingly but not too sentimentally'

Aberdeen Press & Journal

'Funny, sad and poignant, this is a brilliant observation of family life and childhood . . . Isla Dewar paints a picture with words, sights, sounds and smells and such warmth in an incredibly evocative novel'

Yorkshire Evening Press

'Such a compelling read . . . you won't be able to put it down'

Newcastle Journal

'It's the way that Isla Dewar develops her characters that gives her writing such extraordinary strength . . . Dewar has the ability to conjure up the most delightful cameo scenes, and the power to keep the story moving towards its inevitable end'

Oxford Times

Also by Isla Dewar

Keeping Up With Magda
Women Talking Dirty
Giving Up On Ordinary
It Could Happen To You
Two Kinds Of Wonderful

THE WOMAN WHO PAINTED HER DREAMS

Isla Dewar

review

First published in 2002
by HEADLINE BOOK PUBLISHING

First published in paperback in 2003
by HEADLINE BOOK PUBLISHING

A REVIEW paperback

10 9 8 7 6 5 4 3 2 1

ISBN 0 7472 6158 X

Typeset by Avon Dataset Ltd, Bidford-on-Avon, Warks

Printed and bound in Great Britain by
Clays Ltd, St Ives plc

HEADLINE BOOK PUBLISHING
A division of Hodder Headline
338 Euston Road
London NW1 3BH

www.reviewbooks.co.uk
www.hodderheadline.com

To Bob in undying chumship,
and with love.

Grateful thanks to my editor, Marion Donaldson,
for her care, encouragement and enthusiasm.
And to Yvonne Holland for meticulously looking
things up, pointing things out above and beyond
the call of duty.

Discovering Ted

When Madeline Green was three she made a discovery. Her father was a Ted. Thus far she had thought of him as Daddy. Though she knew some people – the milkman and Mrs Turner along the road, for example – called him Mr Green. But this Ted thing was a revelation.

'You're not Ted,' she almost scolded. 'You're Daddy.'

'I'm only Daddy to you,' he told her. 'You're special. My daughter. My friends call me Ted. That's my name. Like your name is Madeline.'

He had noticed of late that the little bundle of humanity he washed, fed, helped dress, then left each weekday morning with Mrs Turner three doors down was becoming very vocal. As if, from nowhere, she had opinions: 'Tomatoes aren't very nice.' Questions: 'Do frogs have teeth?' Ted didn't think so. He wasn't sure. He noticed that the child, once given to small remarks on the obvious, pointing to things, stating what they were – dog, moon, yellow flower – had started stringing words together in small strident sentences. She had learned to speak. And, now that she had mastered the art, it seemed she would never stop.

Ted would waken to the sound of her chattering to herself in the grey dawn light, and would fall asleep to the childish mutterings each evening at seven when he put her to bed. He'd be reading to her, and would often slip into a pleasant slumber himself, book open on his knee whilst Madeline lay abed, blanket comforter pressed to her cheek, chattering, disagreeing with the events in the storybook.

It had happened, this Ted revelation, at one of his little gatherings. Three years a widower, he was slipping back into the world. Making friends. Recovering. He was a prominent and very active member of a watercolour society. It was 1959.

1

On Sundays, Ted often invited his fellow artists round for lunch. They'd talk, drink wine, and softly, in the background, Mahler would sift through the conversations, filling the silences. Swelling riffs of joy and sorrow. Ted always supplied a buffet. Open sandwiches which, at the time, were thought avant-garde.

It was always the same crowd. Madeline knew them mostly by their knees, and the faces that loomed down at her. Some of the faces – Tom's, Bill's – were hairy. Some had pipes in their mouths. Some faces were painted, and some smelled of flowers and oranges. Some knees were corduroy, some were flannel. Janet's knees were black, encased in tight trousers that stopped midway down her calves. She wore a tight black, slash-necked top and a red scarf at her throat. Her lips and fingernails matched the scarf. And once, when Madeline was lining up her dolls under the kitchen table, she'd seen Janet slip her foot from her black pump, and noticed that her toenails matched the scarf, too. Madeline had stared at those toes in wonder.

Marie wore a full flared skirt with a wide, tight belt. She wore high heels. And a blouse with the collar pulled up. Her lips weren't as red as Janet's and her nails were shiny, but not coloured. Madeline thought she smelled pink, of pinky things. Whilst Janet's smell was more purple.

The men with hairy faces both laughed a lot. One smoked a pipe and wore a blue jumper with his shirt collar flapped over the neck. He thought Turner was a genius. Janet said he was stuffy. She said Van Gogh made her weep – such tragedy, such vibrancy. Madeline didn't understand a word of it. But once she'd heard Janet saying to Marie that she liked Mars Bars. Madeline liked Mars Bars, too. And puzzled over this information that one of these people who spoke about things she didn't understand and painted her face and toenails could like something she liked.

Still, there was the Ted thing. 'If all these people call you Ted, why can't I?' she said. 'Why do I have to be the only one calling you Daddy?'

'Because I am your daddy. I'm not anyone else's daddy.'

'She's got a point, though,' said Janet. 'She's a bright little thing.'

Madeline looked at her. This woman gave her a funny feeling in her tummy. She was always touching Ted, and looking at him and laughing at his jokes. Madeline didn't like that. He was her Ted. And his funny jokes were for her.

Small though she was, she knew a rival when she met one. Though she sat on other knees, she never sat on Janet's. And she would call her daddy Ted, like Janet did. To show her who Ted belonged to. When Janet or Marie spoke to Ted, standing close, smiling, looking into his eyes, Madeline would stand beside him, take his hand and stare unblinkingly up at her rival. She didn't plan this, just found herself doing it. She never liked to share Ted. Of course, Ted was too involved in the arty talk to notice. But the stare had an effect on Janet and Marie, who would often forget what they were talking about, or start to mumble. Guiltily. The child *knew* what they were up to. *Knew* that they were after her father.

Usually, after one of Ted's lunches, Madeline would dream. She dreamed of painted faces. And of Ted being gone. She was alone in the house, and couldn't find him anywhere. She would wake up crying, and he'd come to her. Tuck her up, and tell her to go back to sleep. He'd make sure she had good dreams this time.

'It's a phase,' Mrs Turner from three doors down told Ted when he complained about the Ted business. The sudden use of his first name. 'It'll pass.'

It didn't. 'Bye-bye, Ted,' Madeline shouted every morning when he left her with Mrs Turner. And 'Hello, Ted,' when she rushed towards him, arms wide, sandalled feet scudding over patterned carpet, when he collected her again at six o'clock.

Mrs Turner was a comfortable woman. Large, with a personality and voice to fit her body. When speaking on the phone, she roared as if she did not trust this method of communication. Better shout to make yourself heard. The further away her caller was – Liverpool, Inverness, Nova Scotia, when she was in Edinburgh – the louder she yelled. Though it was 1959, she was entombed in a distant era, prewar. She wore twinsets that stretched, fascinatingly, over her hefty bust; a straight, tweed, no-nonsense skirt, and low-heeled beige shoes that just, and no more, encased her water-logged feet.

3

She was of the opinion that what Madeline needed was a good hard smack. Indeed, several good hard smacks on the backside. She threatened often: 'I'll take the back of my hand to you.' Or: 'Any more of that and I'll put you across my knee and give you a damn good hiding.' But never delivered.

Madeline would stand her ground. 'I'll tell Ted,' she'd threaten back. 'And he'll give you a smack, too.'

It was enough. 'You can hit your own,' she'd tell Babs from upstairs, 'but you have to leave other folks to sort out theirs.'

Every morning, five to ten, Mrs Turner would put on the kettle, lay out a plate of bourbon biscuits. Then she'd bang on the ceiling with a broom handle (this had been going on for so many years the paintwork was pockmarked with small round dents), summoning Babs down. Tea was brewing.

Babs Todd lived upstairs with her husband, Jim Todd, and Sandy Todd. Sandy was a cat, but he always got his full name. The Todds had the top half of the garden, the Turners the bottom.

Babs would clatter down the stairs. And she, and Mrs Turner, would sit either side of the fake coal fire in the living room and talk. And talk. And talk.

Madeline liked the fire. Red plastic, blackened here and there, giving the impression of plastic coal, and lit from below by a red bulb, on top of which sat a metal whirly thing that moved with the heat of the bulb, making an effect of actual flames. She would sit, listening to the drone of conversation, palms spread before the fake embers, though the heat came from the two electric bars above the plastic.

The talk fascinated her. Though it seemed senseless. Babs and Mrs Turner spoke about the price of electricity, Mrs Smith's daughter across the road who wore drainpipe jeans and, as Mrs Turner put it, left nothing to the imagination.

'Men don't like that,' she said. 'Let them wonder,' she said. 'Keep them guessing.'

Babs would nod. 'Absolutely.'

Madeline would stare at Mrs Turner's formidable bosom and wonder what men would guess about.

They discussed recipes. 'I just used a tin of mushroom soup for the sauce, and it turned out lovely.' What their husbands said, or did not say. 'I asked him what he thought of the new curtains. But you know Jim, he never says nothing.'

Madeline wondered, since Jim never said nothing, why bother to ask him? They talked about such things with such authority, Madeline thought they must be important. 'I got a steak pie from the butcher's last week and it went down a treat. Lovely. Nice pastry. I wasn't going to buy it, because, you know me, I don't trust pastry.'

Madeline wondered what there was about pastry that you should not trust. It was all so puzzling. She decided, in her little way, that she'd come to it all when she grew up. Then she'd understand. Maybe she'd one day be as old as Mrs Turner, and she'd talk about pastry too. She didn't want that.

In the background, the wireless would be on, softly; songs of the day would drift out. Ella Fitzgerald sang 'Paper Moon'. Madeline loved that. There were other songs she liked, secret ones that Mrs Turner hated. Jerry Lee Lewis singing 'Great Balls of Fire' – 'Goodness gracious . . .' She sang it for Ted whilst he was preparing her tea. Two eggs, soft-boiled, runny yolks and toast soldiers. ' "Goodness gracious" ' Big shrug. Eyes wide.

Ted scooped the eggs, three minutes in boiling water, from the pan. Told her she was a whiz. And gave her a swift blast of Buddy Holly. ' "Rave on . . ." ' he sang. Little hiccups in his voice.

A few Sundays before, Ted had been passing his radio when *Family Favourites* swirled out . . . 'Corporal Thomson with British Forces in Germany wants to say hello to Mum, Dad, Aunty Peggy, Flora the dog, and deepest love to Fiona who he's going to marry when he gets home in September. He's asked for Buddy Holly.' And the voice came on. '*Wellawellawella . . .*' A roll of drums. Ted was hooked. He'd bought several records – 'Peggy Sue', 'Raining In My Heart', 'Oh Boy'. He and Madeline were practising their jive.

Looking up at him, listening to the song, watching his gentle face, Madeline was swamped with love. She vowed that Janet person would never steal him from her. She'd never get to be his best pal. He was hers.

Mornings, bored with the living-room gossip, Madeline would wander into the garden. If she climbed on to the lower branches of the sycamore tree she could see over into next-door's garden and the garden beyond, and beyond that the park where Mrs Turner sometimes took her to feed the ducks. She'd stare into the distance and vow that she'd never grow up and talk about pastry and curtains and making sauces from tinned mushroom soup. When she climbed down, she would play with Sandy Todd, who was unwilling, but suffered. He was scolded. Told he needed a good hard smack. Dressed in a woolly hat and scarf and told to watch not catch his death.

Mrs Turner was very firm on the matter of catching your death. Children needed to be well wrapped up. She'd dress Madeline, on days when it wasn't terribly chilly, in a vest, a liberty bodice – 'A liberty bodice,' Madeline was to say to Annie, years later. 'What the hell kind of garment was that? All fleecy lined and, Christ, it made you sweat' – a jumper, a pinafore skirt, knee-high grey socks held up with elastic garters that bit cruelly into Madeline's leg and left a red weal. After that, if she was going out, there was a long scarf crossed over her chest and secured at the back with a safety pin, then a coat, hat, and gloves, made safe by a length of elastic that stretched up one arm and down the other.

'My God,' Madeline said to Annie, when they were having one of their nostalgia conversations, 'how did I move? No wonder we all grew up to throw away our bras and wear as little as possible. It was those woolly layers did it. The aftereffects of the trauma of being happed up.'

Sometimes Mr Turner, who worked shifts on the railway, was home. He was Archie. Madeline was allowed to call him that. Mrs Turner was always Mrs Turner. If Ted was her love, Archie was her first real pal. He had time for her. He'd bend down so that his face was close to her face. 'How's my girlfriend, then?'

'I'm fine.'

Then he'd put his hand in his pocket. 'What's in here?'

Madeline would, on tiptoe, feel into the pocket. Pull out a toffee, or a sixpence. 'Thank you.'

6

He had time for Madeline's endless questions: 'Where is that man going?' pointing to some innocent person who happened to be walking in the street at the same time they were. They'd spend happy hours making up stories about the man. Giving him a name. A home. A family. A reason, usually preposterous, for walking along the street.

Archie would let Madeline help him polish his shoes. They'd line them up on an old newspaper. A brown pair with holes along the toe. And two black pairs. He would put on the polish. Madeline would put her tiny hand inside, hold up the shoe and brush till the shoe was shiny.

'A gentleman,' Archie told her, 'always polishes his shoes. That's how you can tell if a man is a gentleman. Look at his feet. Shiny shoes, and you'll know he's all right.'

'Ted hasn't got shiny shoes,' Madeline told him.

'That's because they're suede.'

'Suede,' said Mrs Turner, lifting slices of cod's roe from the frying pan on to warmed plates. 'Suede shoes.' And she tutted. She would never trust a man who wore suede shoes. That was how she knew Ted was not a gentleman – his shoes.

Archie would take Madeline to the park, where they'd play cricket. Madeline would bat. Archie would rub the ball on his trouser leg. Then thunder towards her, hefting the ball high. And bowl the gentlest of shots. Which Madeline would swipe mightily. Archie would look as if he was running hard. But he took his time, letting Madeline get several runs. When she tired, he'd carry her home on his shoulders. Chatting till he felt her head slowly slump on to his head. She'd sleep.

Home, he'd lay her on the sofa. Cover her with an eiderdown that smelled of lavender. Through the melting haze of near slumber, Madeline would hear Archie and Mrs Turner talk about her.

'Poor wee soul,' she'd say.

On an intake of breath, Archie would agree. 'Aye. She's that.'

'She needs a proper home. Proper life,' Mrs Turner would say. Then, a deep and savage breath. 'That man.'

Madeline knew she meant Ted. But said nothing because she

wanted to find out why she was a poor wee soul, and why Ted was *that man*. But sleep always took her.

Ted was a quiet man. Tall. Soft-spoken. A dental mechanic. He made false teeth. Mrs Turner was impressed by that. It was almost as good as being a dentist. 'Good with his hands,' she'd say. This pleased Madeline, though when Mrs Turner said it she looked at her and told her she knew that already.

'Important,' Mrs Turner would add. 'We all need false teeth.'

Ted worked in a lab with half a dozen other mechanics and wasn't really that important at all. Except to Madeline. Who loved him.

Ted had been married to Jem, short for Jemima. A florist. She owned a little shop, Bloomers, where she made up elaborate arrangements and delivered them by bicycle in the evenings after she closed. She could not afford a van, far less an assistant to mind the store whilst she did her rounds in the afternoon. After work, and at weekends, if he was not making an emergency dental plate or bridge, Ted would help. He'd cycle across town, flowers pouring from the wicker basket at the front. He'd whistle as he went. His coat flapping behind him. The wind at his throat, which was uncovered. Ted hated ties, and rarely wore one. Which was another thing that Mrs Turner did not approve of. As was Ted's choice of shirts – wide blue and white stripes, or red; one was ochre. Mrs Turner thought shirts, all shirts, should be white.

Ted and Jem had been exquisitely happy. They'd met at a concert in a church hall not far from the West End, just after the war. A string quartet had been playing Bach. He'd secretly watched her from across the aisle. And during the interval had approached her, shyly. Did she like Bach?

'Oh yes,' she enthused. 'Though,' small apologetic smile, 'I prefer Schubert. I know Bach's music is as near perfection as anything could get. But Schubert . . . It's the tunes. The passion.' She looked at her feet, feeling foolish. Passion. A woman didn't mention such a thing to a stranger. But Ted nodded his head, agreeing. Passionately. Though, in fact, he was a jazz man. He loved Charlie Parker and Louis Armstrong. He'd only gone to the concert because he'd been passing and it had started to rain. But right now, looking at Jem, he was prepared to love Bach. And Schubert, too. Whatever it took.

He took her to dinner at a tiny humming Italian place. Neither of them was expert at eating pasta. They wrapped it slowly round their forks, stuffed it, dripping, into their mouths. For them both, back then, all those years ago, wine was an adventure. They got flushed and heady.

Next day he took her for a walk through Princes Street Gardens. They watched the trains speeding out of and into Waverley. He knew them all – where they'd been, where they were going. He loved trains almost as much as he loved painting watercolours. He held her hand, which was cool. Her hands were always cool, as if her blood never reached them. Ted thought her pale and fragile. He wanted to protect her, keep her safe. And warm.

Within six months they were married. Ted was forty-two, Jem thirty. Ted wanted a family. He thought he was getting old. By the time his child was twenty, he'd be sixty-two. At the time that seemed ancient. A baby didn't happen. They hardly spoke about it. If anyone asked, they'd shrug. They didn't mind. A baby would be lovely. But if it wasn't meant to be, they were happy.

Meantime they worked on their house in Ogilvy Avenue. They stripped and polished the floors, put paper shades on the ceiling lights. Painted their walls. One red, the other three white.

Mrs Turner, passing one evening when the light was on and the curtains open, noticed this; told Archie: 'That's not right. It looks all funny. A room should all be the same colour. I don't know about these folks.'

Ted and Jem put Van Gogh and Degas prints on their walls. By the window they placed a wicker chair that had three stainless-steel legs and a red cushion that matched the wall. They bought a large sofa, and a single armchair. They scoffed at three-piece suites. They had style, they thought. Sundays, wearing matching dressing gowns, they'd drink freshly made coffee and read *The Sunday Times* and the *Observer*. They were happy. They were set. They didn't need a child.

But a child came. Nine years later, when they'd given up on the notion, Madeline came along. Jem had an easy pregnancy. She glowed. She knitted. She planned. She worked in the garden, planting delphiniums, foxgloves, lupins, which she loved. She collected nappies, little blankets and clothes. Ted bought and restored an old wooden rocking horse. He painted watercolours to put in the nursery – a train, its carriages filled with merrymaking cats; an elephant standing quietly in the queue at the bus stop. Soon he and Jem would be a family.

At thirty-six weeks, Jem went into labour. Anxious and pale, they turned up at the hospital. Jem, belly heaving, waddling up to the desk, looking fraught. He, in a pale sweat, hair on end, carrying a small black case. Ted thought their plight looked so obvious, he wanted to laugh. They were going to have a baby. Jem was whipped away. Shaved. Given an enema. And wheeled into the delivery room. The nurse told Ted he might as well go home. 'It might be a while,' she'd said.

But Ted wouldn't leave. He paced. He smoked Senior Service. He fretted.

And, when, six hours later, Madeline was born, he cried. There she was, tiny and bawling. Six pounds four ounces. 'Small but noisy,' the midwife said. 'Four weeks early. Too keen to get going. Couldn't wait.' Even then, she looked astonishing. She was born with a mane of black hair. Jem and Ted wondered at it. Where had she come from? So little, so assured. They weren't like that. Ted was tall, fair. Jem, pale, mousy. They knew they'd done something irrevocable with their lives. Two hours into her life, her parents could tell Madeline was a *tour de force*.

Ted couldn't contain his joy. He was a father. He had a daughter. He took a taxi to the end of Ogilvy Avenue, and ran the rest of the way home. He opened the windows, played Rossini. He drank Chianti. He sang along with *The Barber of Seville*. Swinging his glass. He had a girl. And she was beautiful. He would read her poems. He would open her ears to music, her eyes to art, her heart to song. She was perfect.

It always plagued him. It always made him keel over with pain, guilt. The phone rang, and rang. And he didn't hear it. He was lost in opera. '*Figaro, Feegaro, Feeegaro . . .*' he sang. He downed glass after glass of wine. Overjoyed. Singing, and laughing and drinking. That was what he was doing when his beloved Jem died.

Madeline was born at ten o'clock. Ted left her and Jem just before midnight. Jem was looking pale, tired but triumphant, and, to Ted, more beautiful than he'd ever seen her before. And she always looked beautiful to him. He loved her face. At two in the morning that face curled into horror. She haemorrhaged.

That hospital rush and clatter. The screens hauled round her bed. Doctors running up the ward. Jem slipped from the world apologising for all the fuss she was causing. Apologising to Ted for leaving him. And to her daughter for not being around to look after her.

Ted went into shock. He could hardly speak. He took Madeline home, and when the health visitor called she'd check the baby, weigh her, coo over her, tell her she was just a gorgeous little thing, so she was. Then packing her neat black case, she'd turn to Ted: 'Will you be all right, Mr Green?' He'd stare at her, mouth slightly open, eyes agape, Adam's apple trembling. Saying nothing. And she'd leave it at that. Saying out loud that of course he would be. Knowing he wouldn't.

Mornings, Ted would wake to the howls of little Madeline needing fed. Needing changed. Needing human comfort, cuddled, touched, crooned to. He'd have a second, a fleeting moment of relief, joy. 'I have a daughter.' And his heart would ache. 'Why is that?' Then he'd remember. His Jem. His lovely, lovely Jem was no more. He'd never wake to find her sleeping beside him. Never share the Sunday papers with her. Never listen to the morning radio with her. Never cycle across town with her flowers. Never anything with her again. She was gone.

He started to walk with a stoop, as if the pain he felt was a physical weight on his shoulders. He shuffled into each day, stiffly, fearing the slightest knock, rebuff or slight. He could bear nothing more. The smallest disasters made him weep. With only the tiniest movement of her curtain, the woman across the road saw Ted bend over a broken lupin, and sob.

'It's not the lupin he's grieving,' said Mrs Turner from three doors down when the matter was discussed at the newsagent's next morning. 'Sometimes it takes your mind off the main thing to cry over a lupin when your wife's gone and died, and left you with a bairn to care for.'

Thinking of that house, and what was going on in there, the pain, the grieving, and the lust for life of little ones, new to the world, the stolid heart, beating in the depths of Mrs Turner, beneath the no-nonsense twinset and the sturdy heavy-duty bra, stirred.

It was a Tuesday and Mrs Turner had just had the lupin conversation with the neighbour from across the road. Walking home, she glanced furtively through Ted's window. The man was standing in the middle of the room, hands by his side and looking bewildered, lost, alone. The child was crying. Howling would better describe the racket coming from the house. Mrs Turner walked on, contemplating this. She stopped. Stood with her brown shopping bag dangling at her side. It contained a pint of milk, a copy of the *Daily Mail*, a packet of bourbon biscuits and three pounds of potatoes. She stared ahead. Thinking. She was not the interfering sort. But . . . sometimes. Sometimes interfering was called for. Even if the man whose life you were about to step into had one wall painted a different colour from the other three. She turned. Walked back, stood watching Ted gasping sorrow in his living room. She opened the gate, walked up the path and rang the bell.

'It strikes me,' she said to Ted when he answered the door, 'that you need a hand. With the little one, like.'

Ted looked at her. Silently. In years to come, when he recalled this moment, he thought he opened and shut his mouth, fishlike.

'Now,' said Mrs Turner, 'human beings I'm not good with. I have no idea what they are on about. But babies – babies I know. I've had four and I can do babies. It strikes me, Mr Green, and just tell me to go away if you think I'm sticking my nose in, but it strikes me that right now, the state you're in, you could do with a hand.'

Ted nodded. Somewhere in the house Madeline bawled. And bawled.

'Like I said, babies I can do. Feeding, changing, wiping. All that.'

Ted nodded again. And stood.

And Mrs Turner knew that if, right now, she did not take matters in hand, terrible things might happen. The child might go unfed, might choke, might cry herself to death. If such a thing ever happened to babies. She handed her brown shopping bag to Ted – who took it mildly – and walked past him. Straight into the nursery she went. Though she had never before crossed the threshold of Ted's house. It was homing instinct, she would say later. 'I have a feel for little ones.' She found Madeline in an infant rage. Screaming, red-faced, sweating, small fists clenched.

'Oh my,' said Mrs Turner. 'Oh my, the poor wee soul.' She scooped up the child. Held her close. Stroked her, patted her back. Kissed the tiny damp forehead. 'Wee soul, wee soul,' she repeated. She rocked gently back and forth. And heaving, sobbing, the child silenced. 'She just needs a wee cuddle,' Mrs Turner scolded Ted, but softly, for the man was suffering. 'She just needs you to touch her, hold her. Let her know she's not alone. She's only little.'

And Ted nodded again. Tears rolling down his unshaven cheeks.

Mrs Turner from three doors down reached out and touched the sodden face. 'It'll be fine, Mr Green. You'll see. We'll get by.'

This surprised her for, as she was to tell Archie, 'I'm not the touching sort. I don't usually touch people I don't really know. And I certainly wouldn't want to go touching a man like that. Who wears them kind of clothes and has funny pictures on his wall.'

Mrs Turner came every morning to care for Madeline. She bathed the child, fed her, trundled her out in her pram every afternoon, rain or shine, to let the fresh air into her little lungs. And to let Ted get on with his grieving.

'I love babies,' she told Ted. 'Had four of my own. All flown the nest now. To tell the truth,' putting Ted's kettle on Ted's stove to make herself a cup of tea, 'I can't be doing with children. When they get up a bit they've got minds of their own. Answer you back, set about doing things without asking first. They're never where you put them down. Crawl off exploring. But babies are lovely. As human beings go, in categories, like, I'd say babies were top of my list.' Men, especially men like Ted, were bottom.

Four weeks later, Ted went back to work. Mrs Turner took Madeline every morning at half-past eight. And handed her back at six when Ted got home. At first it suited them both. But in the years to come, Ted was to say that if Mrs Turner claimed she was not the interfering sort, then she'd found her calling. Interfering came to her naturally. She was born to interfere. She read Ted's mail. Checked his bank statements. Leafed through his watercolours, and voiced opinions about them: 'You haven't got the hands right here.' Or: 'I don't like the colours of the sky on this one.' Or: 'It's just not right, you painting nudes. At your age and with a little one about. She might see that.' Then a sudden and deeply shocking thought: 'I hope none of these women posed for you. Not here. Not in this very living room.'

Ted would shake his head and shuffle his feet and look away. He never was one for confrontations.

As Madeline grew, people, including Ted, wondered where she'd come from. She continued to bear no resemblance to either him or Jem. Madeline was a sturdy child, with a tumbling mass of black curls. Ted, to Mrs Turner's endless scorn, dressed her in denim or corduroy dungarees.

'That's no way to dress a girl,' she complained. 'She'll grow up with a complex.'

She usually gave Madeline a morning bath, thinking it not right at all that a man bath a little girl, and would afterwards change the child into clothes more suitable for a girl. Dresses that tied with a bow at the back. White socks. A kilt in winter.

Then there were Ted's ladies. About three years after Jem died, Ted joined the living again. He had lady friends.

At first, to Mrs Turner's mortification, when Ted went calling on his ladies, he took Madeline with him. Bundled in blankets, she'd lie in the back of his little Renault. When they arrived at Janet's or Marie's, or whoever's (Ted had no intention of settling down again, and enjoyed the company of many women), she'd be put to bed in a spare room. She'd lie in the dark, listening to distant laughter and music pouring in from other parts of the house. A sliver of light slipping along the bottom of the door. And, thinking Ted was being stolen from her, she'd call his name. Tell him she had a sore tummy. Sometimes, in her pink pyjamas, she'd come through to the light, the music and laughter. Sit on Ted's knee and glare at Marie, or Janet, or whoever. He's mine.

At two or three in the morning, Ted would carry her back out to his car. Place her on the back seat. Drive home. Madeline always woke. Nights were cool. Still. Quiet. Madeline always loved that time of night. And the malty smell of whisky on a man's breath made her think of Ted.

By the time Madeline was five Ted had, in Mrs Turner's opinion, far too many women friends. She gave him a ticking off.

'You have to stop all this womanising. You can't go taking a child out all times of the night. She's at school now. She needs her proper sleep.'

Ted hung his head, and agreed.

After that, Ted's ladies came to him. They arrived at the house after Madeline was in bed. She only saw them if she got up in the night for a drink of water or to visit the lavatory. She knew them by the scents that drifted into her room when they went past her door. Or by their voices that spread up from the kitchen where Ted would serve them moussaka with rich red wine. And talk about art, and life and love. Madeline would smell strange herbal scents. And alcohol. Hear laughter. Music. And soft moans.

Saturdays and Sundays, Ted was Madeline's. And Madeline Ted's. They would wander through Princes Street Gardens. They'd stand on the bridge, watching trains. Ted still knew them all. Where they'd been. Where they were going. He'd whisper names of distant places to Madeline. 'The fifteen forty-three stopping at Waverley, North Berwick, Carlisle, Doncaster, Newcastle . . .' Him, leaning over the railings. Her, no higher than his knees, clutching the iron bars, head pressed against them, infused with his excitement. Madeline loved trains. She'd play in the evenings outside the house. Skipping. Chanting, to the slap of rope on pavement, the names of the stations between Edinburgh and London.

When they'd finished watching trains, Madeline would play on the swings, heaving herself skywards, as Ted sat nearby painting. He did meticulous watercolours. Perfect things. Flowers, shrubs and trains. But if she looked at them closely, Madeline would see that in the lush green lurked little people. Fairies, angels, devils. In the evenings he would sit at the kitchen table with Madeline, teaching her tricks to do with inks and water. Keep your paper flat. A blob of water, now red ink. Drop it in the water. Watching as, tongue waggling out of the corner of her mouth, she did as she was told.

'Now,' he told her, 'pull the watery ink out of your little pool with the brush. In lines. Upwards. Downwards. Sideways.'

Thin spidery lines of red-pink ink spread across the page. Madeline painted a giant flower. Water. A blob of blue. Spreading out. Green stem. Another flower. Miles Davis's *Sketches of Spain* playing on the gramophone. Ted's cheek against hers. Even after he left her to make a cup of tea she could still feel the gentle scratch of his stubble, lingering.

When Madeline was ten, Ted started to grow his hair. Madeline thought it lovely. Mrs Turner was horrified.

'The man's a middle-aged hippie,' she said. 'That's not right.'

But Madeline thought Ted was a wonder. Ted was marvellous. Ted could draw flowers. Trains speeding along country tracks, spewing great billows of steam. Giant shrubs with secret little people hiding, waving. Ted grew orchids in the greenhouse at the bottom of the garden. Tending them, packing them in sphagnum and bark. Collecting rain in the barrel by the greenhouse door, to water them. Nothing else was pure enough. Whispering to them. And when the spike budded, then flowered, the place would fill with scents that made Madeline high, heady. Ted would sweep Madeline above his head, so she could touch the ceiling.

Beside the orchids, he grew his ssshh plants. He held his finger to his lips whenever Madeline mentioned them. 'Ssshh.' They were a secret. She must not tell anybody about them.

'Secret plants in our secret garden,' Ted told her.

And the magic of this pleased her. So she told nobody.

Ted knew all the words to 'Visions of Johanna' and 'Satisfaction', and would sing along, waving his arms. Now his shirts were covered with flowers. Ted would waltz Madeline round the living room. Ted could make moussaka. Ted could boil an egg, white perfectly firm, yolk runny, and toast soldiers, heavy with butter, to dunk in it. Ted was all a little girl could want in the world. He was hers. Pull the curtains, lock the door and they were in their own little world. She'd help him make supper, singing silly songs together. 'The Laughing Policeman', 'Shrimp Boats Are A Comin'. But Mrs Turner thought Ted a bad influence on his daughter.

'Hair,' she said to Archie, 'at his age. He must be past sixty. Heavens above, he's older than me. He'll soon be on the pension. What a way for a pensioner to behave.'

Children in the street followed Ted, shouting, 'Weirdo! Weirdo!' And Ted would turn to them and smile.

In school they taunted Madeline: 'Your dad's a weirdo. Weirdo.' She would fight for her father's honour. Came home bruised, cut, hair torn out. 'I fell,' she told Ted.

Mrs Turner agreed with the juvenile taunters. 'He's a weirdo. He shouldn't be in charge of a wee lass like Madeline.' She seemed to suck herself inward, hug her ordinariness and rightness to her. 'He's got weird pictures on the wall. He listens to weird music. His house is done up weird. Different coloured walls and no carpets. You need carpets. And it's a mess. Always dishes needing washed. And it smells funny. He wears weird clothes. Flowery shirts, for goodness' sake. What sort of a man wears them? And his hair. Well . . .' Words failed her. The thought of Ted's hair made her tremble. It was a disgrace. 'He's a man. Not just a man. An old man. He's going about like one of these hippie young ones. Free love and flowers. It's a scandal.'

Archie made his usual intake of breath agreement and said that Ted seemed to grow weird plants as well.

'Oh, them's just orchids.'

'No,' said Archie, 'the other ones.'

'Tomatoes?'

'They're never tomatoes,' Archie protested.

'Oh yes.' Mrs Turner was sure of this. 'I asked. And they're an exotic variety. Moroccan tomatoes.'

Archie looked at her long and hard. 'Well, just don't you go eating any of them.'

The hostility from three doors down was so thick, so deep, it was almost a tangible thing. It bothered Ted. But only a little. He was happy. He thought he was living through fabulous times. He saw only gentle days stretching ahead. Flowers and love. Oh, how Jem would have loved it all. The women he saw – and through the years there had been many – were a comfort. Now they were all younger than him. And younger by many years. They wore their hair long, and dressed in short skirts or long floating dresses. Often they were mistaken for his daughter. They were all beautiful. But they weren't Jem. He missed her. He had Madeline, of course. And she was a joy. A worry and a joy.

She brought home letters from school saying she was bright, but spent most of her time in class drawing. Her jotters were covered in sketches. Doodles. Sure signs of dreaming. She spent too much time with the folks three doors down. Ted feared for her.

And so did Mrs Turner. 'Poor wee soul,' she said to Madeline. 'You should have a mum. Girls need mums.' She was preparing a plate of beetroot sandwiches at the time. A speciality of hers. Sliced bread spread with marge, a layer of pickled beetroot that turned the whole treat deep and soggy red, then more bread.

Hearing this, Madeline raged. 'I do not need a mum. I have my Ted.'

'Ah,' said Mrs Turner, 'but what if something happened to Ted? What then?'

Madeline stared at her. What could happen to Ted? He could die. He could get run over on the way to work. A panic set up in her heart. Life without Ted was unthinkable.

'Look at me,' said Mrs Turner. 'I'm an orphan.' She spread her palm across her chest, looked out the window at the huge pink hydrangea growing in the border beyond the path. 'I have nobody.'

'You have Mr Turner,' Madeline told her. 'And your children. And me. And Ted.'

'I know. But my mother's gone, and my father. If tragedy strikes, where will I turn?'

Madeline, then ten years old, didn't know what to say to that. Up till now, she'd always thought orphans were children who wore leather shorts, and wandered the woods, looking forlorn and lost.

But ever since that conversation, she waited, secretly, for tragedy to strike. Sometimes she would turn around, looking for it. She never did trust happiness. She was always convinced that at the end of every sunny day, rain would come. At the centre of every silver lining, was a dark cloud. One day, she was sure, tragedy would strike.

Even then, Madeline had that walk. A stride. Knowing where she was going, what she was doing, a determination about her. She was considered a handful. A stroppy soul, moving through the world, opinionated, verbose and tiny. And outrageously bold.

Madeline, it was, who caused passers-by on the number twelve bus to reel in horror when she was spotted cycling along the parapet of a railway bridge. It was a bet. She won a Mars Bar for her derring-do. She took it home, shared it with Ted but never told him how she got it.

Madeline stood up in class at school and challenged the minister when he was telling the story of the loaves and fishes. 'I don't think so,' she said. 'If that's possible, why doesn't someone do that again. Now. So's we could feed the starving in Africa.' She knew there was starving in Africa. Mrs Turner told her often. Every time she did not eat up all her cabbage, or didn't finish a beetroot sandwich, Mrs Turner pointed out that there were starving in Africa who'd be glad of it.

Madeline was considered disruptive in class. Talking. Not paying attention. Drawing in school jotters that were reserved for maths or English. It was obvious from when she was five years high, fresh-faced, gap-toothed and argumentative, that she had a gift. She could draw, she had a way with shape and colour and light. When she was six she discovered that there were such places as art colleges where people went, and all they did was draw or paint and learn about drawing and painting, and artists whose paintings she and Ted stood before on Sunday afternoons when they visited the National Gallery.

'Why can't I go now?' she asked Ted. 'Why do I have to go to ordinary school?'

'Because you have to learn to read and write,' he told her. 'And to count. And what about geography and history?'

'I don't need to know how to count,' she protested. 'I won't ever do that. I want to go to art school.'

From when she was six, her mind was set. She would go to art college. And she would do whatever was necessary at ordinary school to get there.

As Madeline grew, her relationship with Ted changed. By the time she was seven, she'd stand on a chair every morning, sorting his shirt collar.

'There you go. You look pretty.'

'I don't think I want to look pretty,' Ted would say.

'Of course you do. There's two kinds of pretty. Ladies' pretty and men's pretty. You look like a pretty man.'

'Oh well,' Ted would say, 'that'll be fine, then.'

By the time she was ten, she had started to care for him. She shopped, she cooked. She fussed. She made him wear his overcoat when the world turned chilly. Wrapped his scarf round his neck, told him to eat his soup when he got home. He needed feeding up. There were starving children in Africa who'd be glad of a plate of hot soup, she told him. She was ten going on fifty-two.

When Madeline was fourteen, Ted retired. She felt she was losing him. He was slipping from her in the strangest way. It bewildered her. Though old for her years, she knew nothing of illness.

It started with little things. Ted forgot words. And raged frustration. Sometimes banging his head with his fist as if that would loosen the block, release the missing noun. He'd put ordinary things away in strange places – the keys in the fridge, the milk with the cleaning things under the sink – then deny doing it. Quite angrily: 'Of course I didn't do that. You must have done it. Don't accuse me of being silly.'

One morning Ted appeared in the kitchen wearing two shirts. Madeline quietly pointed out that if that was how he wanted to go out, perhaps it would be better to wear two that matched, rather than blue and white checks over green and brown checks. Ted looked down at himself, puzzled. 'I don't remember doing that.' Then he started to cry. 'I'm always doing things I don't remember.'

Often, of late, Madeline had seen Ted cry. It always set her off too. 'It's no big deal,' she comforted him. 'We all do silly things sometimes.' Sniffing. Wiping her eyes with the back of her hand. They stood in the morning kitchen, toast simmering to black under the grill, weeping.

Three days later, Mrs Turner found Ted wandering along the street wearing his pyjamas. Ten o'clock at night, November and bitter, he did not know where he was. He'd been putting the milk bottles out, and had stared out into the black, wondering what he was doing. And had set off. Without really knowing where he was going. And outside Mrs Turner's house had become confused. Lost his way. He didn't know where he was. Panic swirled through him. He tried to open her gate. But couldn't. This wasn't his gate. Someone had changed it. Who? Jem? Jem wouldn't do that. Not without telling him. And he was cold. He needed to get inside. 'Jem,' he wailed into the night. 'Jem? Why have you changed the gate?'

Across the road, curtains moved, faces loomed at windows. Mrs Turner's light went on. And, wrapping a giant tartan dressing gown round her, she came out.

'Mr Green,' she said, 'you've got all confused. This isn't your house. You live down there.' Pointing to Ted's front door.

Ted stared at her blankly. Who the hell was she? She wasn't Jem. 'You're not Jem,' he told her.

'No, I'm not. That's right,' said Mrs Turner. 'Let's get you home before you catch your death.' She took his hand, led him home. Rang the bell. Madeline, who'd been working on her portfolio for art school in her bedroom, unaware of what had been going on, appeared at the door.

Ted had been expecting Jem. He was thrust into hell. Who was this, answering his own door? 'You're not Jem either,' he shouted. Pointing at his daughter. 'Who are you? Where's Jem? What have you done with her?' He pushed past Madeline into the house, shouting, 'Jem. Jem.' Opening cupboards, staring in. Calling.

Madeline looked to Mrs Turner. 'What's wrong with him?'

'He's gone all confused,' she said. 'His mind's jumbled up.'

Ted was in the kitchen. Shouting for Jem. Madeline went to him. Touched his arm. He was cold. 'Jem's dead,' she said. 'Remember?'

Madeline would never forget Ted's response. His face contorted. Gone was the confused, frightened man. For a moment he hated her. He raged. Red with rage. 'You killed her,' he hissed.

'No. No.' Madeline was bewildered. Scared. What was happening? 'I haven't killed anyone.' With clenched fists she beat Ted's chest. 'What's got into you? Stop this.'

Mrs Turner pulled Madeline away. 'Now, now.' Calm voice. 'This won't do. Jem died years ago.' She led Ted to the table, sat him down. 'We'll have a wee cup of tea. We'll feel better after that.' She put on the kettle. Noticing the while that the sink could do with bleaching; there were bits of cauliflower blocking the drain. She cleaned them up. Couldn't help it. Cleaning was her forte. The whole house smelled of fish. And the cups were dark brown pottery.

'Dark brown pottery cups,' she said to Babs from upstairs next morning over tea and bourbon biscuits. 'I didn't like them. Arty. And the tea tastes funny. You need proper china for tea.'

'Oh, absolutely,' said Babs. 'Funny about the fishy smell.'

Mrs Turner had served tea. Each cup with two heaped spoons of sugar. 'Hot, sweet tea. That's the thing for shock. And we're all a little shocked, I think.'

Madeline drank, screwed her face. She never took sugar. Hated the sweetness.

'Now,' said Mrs Turner, 'what about tomorrow? Do you want me to pop in and mind your dad when you're at school?'

Madeline shook her head. She'd be fine. And, anyway, she wasn't going to school tomorrow. 'I have to wash all the towels and sheets,' she said. 'On account of the fish.'

Two weeks ago, Ted had bought cod for supper. On arriving home he'd absently put it in the airing cupboard and forgotten about it. It took a few days for the smell to seep through the house. 'Fishy smell,' Madeline would say. 'Where's it coming from?' She searched. But the airing cupboard didn't occur to her. It wasn't till she was getting fresh sheets that she discovered four, fetid rotting fish hidden behind a pile of towels. By then the whole cupboard, and everything in it, reeked.

Ted got worse. Madeline tried to persuade him to see a doctor. He refused. Insisting, in his lucid moments, that there was nothing wrong with him.

It was becoming clear to Madeline that she could not keep the world at bay. She hardly slept nights, for fear of what Ted might get up to. In a milder moment he took a plate of sausages out to feed his orchids. But at his most turbulent he could not be trusted with knives. He often put food on to cook, and forgot about it. Madeline was becoming adept at dousing fires. Before going to bed she would switch off the cooker, and hide anything that Ted might use to harm himself. Once, after slashing his palm with the vegetable knife, he looked at the wound and demanded to know, 'Who did that to me?'

When she eventually asked for help, it came. And quickly. She was caught sleeping in class, and after a severe scolding from her teacher, she broke down. Life was hell. And Ted, her father, was going mad. Her teacher told the headmistress, who phoned Madeline's doctor, who knew, even over the telephone, what was wrong with Ted.

'Dementia,' he said.

When Madeline got home from school, the doctor had called. Ted had been taken to hospital for tests. And she, not yet fifteen, went to stay with the Turners.

Ted was given drugs to stabilise his condition. Madeline came home to live with him. But Ted wasn't Ted any more. They no longer washed up together, singing silly songs. He'd forgotten the words. He didn't dance her round the living room. His watercolours were nightmare clashes of colour, the demons that plagued him. In the greenhouse, the orchids and the ssshh plants withered and died.

Looking after this new, disorientated Ted, Madeline made discoveries about the old Ted she had loved. Sometimes, as he sat alone amidst his confusion and swirling memories, he'd call out. 'Oh stop that, Janet. Not with the little one through the house.'

Madeline's heart would still. She'd remember waking in strange houses. Light filtering under the door, and her father's laughter and boozy scents drifting through the dark. She remembered when the women started to come to this house. How she'd sit in front of the television, turning up the volume, programmes that bored her. But she'd sit. Stiff, hostile. Back turned to some scented person, who tried to be friendly. Sit, though she needed to go to bed. Tired and hurting. She would not leave Ted and this woman alone. She might steal him away.

Listening to him, she felt ashamed of herself. If it hadn't been for her, he might have found a new love. Married again. Then he'd call for Jem: 'Make us a cup of tea, Jem.' Or: 'I see the delphiniums are coming up again.' Outside, the garden had run wild. The delphiniums and lupins long gone.

Madeline remembered all the meals she ate, a single plate in front of her. Ted at the table across from her, glass in hand, watching, drinking, smiling. He'd smoke. First thing he did when he came home from work. Carefully rolling a long cigarette. Leaning back. 'Ah.' A wicked grin. Evenings he would sit sideways on a chair, legs draped over the arm. Smoking, dreaming. Saying nothing.

'My God,' she said out loud. 'The ssshh plants!' Hand to mouth. Her father had been growing grass. Cannabis.

Next morning she threw all the withered, dried and now lifeless things out. With nurses and the doctor calling regularly they could get found. Ted could get into trouble. Ted, her Ted. A lady's man, pot smoker and drinker. But he'd been lovely. Madeline looked at him, sitting in the living room, lost from her, and ached to have him back.

Six months later, Ted was too ill for her to look after. On the doctor's advice he was put in a home. The strain of looking after him took its toll on Madeline. She failed all her exams. Her teachers said she could do resits. All was not lost. When the exam board heard of her circumstances, they would consider her case. But Madeline didn't care. She was drained, physically from looking after Ted, emotionally from losing him. Exhausted and lonely, sixteen years old, she left school. Took a job in a department store, selling shoes. It was work. It was money. 'Stuff art,' she said. A kind of defiance. She didn't really mean it.

She remembered Mrs Turner's words: 'What will you do if something happens to Ted? If tragedy strikes?'

Back then, she had shrugged. She didn't know. Now she still shrugged. Damned if she knew. Damned if she cared.

She was determined not to let anybody see how much she cared. She chewed gum, answered in a monotone when people spoke to her. She mastered the art of looking bored.

Only at night, when she slept, did her pain come to her. She dreamed lonely dreams. Once she dreamed that Ted lived high in some distant foreign mountains, in a huge white castle. His hair was in a ponytail, and he wore a dark aubergine shirt. He was sitting behind an old writing desk with a padded leather top. The curtains were aubergine, as was a chair in the corner. They matched the shirt. Though she'd come miles and miles to visit him, he paid her no attention. Did not look at her. He instructed a maid, dressed in black and white, to take her to her room. The room was white, cool, a bed in the corner. White bedspread. Looking through the open window, Madeline could see forest. Swaying treetops. Vividly coloured birds flying far beneath her. Suddenly she took a long white pole from the corner, ran top speed across the floor, and vaulted from the window. She was flying. High, high above the forest, holding on to the pole. Horizontal. All the forest sounds floated up. She looked round. The maid was standing watching, aghast. Her father was still sitting at his desk in his aubergine shirt. Not looking at her. Quite oblivious of her performance.

When she woke, she could hardly believe she was in Mrs Turner's spare room. She switched on the bedside light. Looked around. She could remember every sleeping moment. It astounded her. She called this her aubergine dream. And never forgot it.

25

Missing Ted

Mrs Turner took her in. 'Poor wee soul. She's as good as an orphan now.' And Archie drew in his breath, and agreed. He had a soft spot for Madeline.

But poor Mrs Turner, if babies were her favourite human being, if you put them in categories, like, children perplexed her. And teenagers drove her to fury.

Madeline, sixteen years old. A working girl with no real parents to keep her in line, discovered the night. And vodka.

'You be in by eleven o'clock,' Mrs Turner would say.

Madeline would solemnly nod. 'Right,' she'd say. And at the time, with Mrs Turner standing forbiddingly over her, she meant it. But once out in the world with half a dozen vodkas swirling inside her, and music thrumming, she forgot all her promises. In a heaving club, flirting and laughing, going home was never an option.

'Where have you been?' Mrs Turner would shout. She'd be standing in the hallway. Tartan dressing gown wrapped round her. Swollen feet wedged into a pair of pink furry slippers. 'We've been worried to death. I was on the verge of calling the police. I've been in such a state Archie had to give me brandy to soothe my nerves.'

'Sorry,' Madeline would say. 'I forgot the time.'

Mrs Turner would sniff the air. Head raised. Nostrils flared, taking in, sifting through the scents that came to them. 'HAVE YOU BEEN DRINKING?'

'I only had a Babycham,' Madeline would plead. 'Just the one.'

'I knew it,' Mrs Turner would crow. 'I have a very fine-tuned sense of smell. Nothing gets past my nose.' A pause whilst she congratulated herself on this attribute. Then, 'Where did you get it?'

Madeline knew better than to admit to having been in a pub. Mrs Turner loathed and mistrusted pubs. They were rude, noisy and crowded with shouty people, she claimed. That's how the last one she'd been in had been. But then it had been VE Day. Still, she was a woman who made an opinion and never changed it. 'I stick by my guns,' she said.

'I was at a party,' Madeline lied. 'The people there insisted I had some.'

'You just have to say no,' Mrs Turner told her. 'A little word. Easy to say. I hope you're keeping it in mind.'

Mrs Turner knew that drinking could lead to other things. That was how young girls got into trouble.

'I fear for the girl,' she told Babs from upstairs. 'She's been up to things. When they start messing with the other sex, you can tell. They change.'

'Does she know?' Babs asked.

'Oh, yes. I saw to that. I've had four of my own.'

When Madeline was twelve Mrs Turner had decided the time had come to tell her about womanly things. It was a conversation she'd had before. She considered herself expert at it. After all, none of her four daughters had got into trouble. She prided herself on that. Now they were all properly married, and living on the other side of the world. Two in Canada, one in Australia and one in New Zealand. But she had done right by them. Now she'd do right by Madeline. After all, that man, her father, couldn't be trusted.

She sat Madeline by the fire, on the chair Babs used, whilst she sat on the arm of the chair opposite. She thought this gave her more authority. 'Now,' she said, 'there's things you have to know. About life. And about being a woman, which you will be soon. Sooner than you think.'

'Yes,' said Madeline.

'Right,' said Mrs Turner. She gave Madeline a long, hard look. Silence. Then. 'You know, don't you?'

Not wanting to appear a fool Madeline said, 'Yes.' Though she didn't. She hadn't a clue what Mrs Turner was talking about.

Mrs Turner said, 'I thought you did. Well, that's it. You know.' She slapped her knees. That was it. Tricky job done. 'Let's have a cup of tea.'

At the Turners' Madeline slipped into herself. She let the new routine wash over her. There were rules here. Tea was served at five. Since the shop where she worked closed at six, she was never there. Her food was left in the oven. It was dried and flaccid by the time she got to it. She ate alone in the kitchen, listening to the radio. Mastered the art of swiftly scraping tasteless stew or chops on to a sheet of newspaper, wrapping it, shoving it outside into the bin. She ate fruit. Grew thin.

Mrs Turner put it down to shock. 'She's missing that man.'

Every night the television was switched off at ten. Lights out half-past. 'We're early bedders,' said Mrs Turner. 'And early risers.' She thought there was something almost holy about this. She'd noticed often the drawn curtains in Ted's house. Past nine in the morning and still closed. That was a sin.

Madeline was glad of the early nights. She could escape into her room. Shut the door. Put out the light. Crawl into bed. Pull the blankets over her head. And cry. She missed Ted. She hated staying at the Turners'. She wanted her old life back. Why had Ted become ill? It wasn't fair. Nothing was fair. Then there was work. She was about to get fired. She was sure of that.

It wasn't that she minded selling shoes. In fact, she loved shoes. It was feet she minded. Other people's feet. They'd be placed on the stool in front of her, whilst she struggled to push a new shoe over it. Wrestling with a long shoe horn, till the customer would tire, lean down and take over. 'I'll do it myself.' Madeline was careless. Put shoes back in the wrong boxes. Once a customer, who had spent some time deciding between a black pair and a navy pair, had gone home with one of each. Another with two, both fitting her left foot. And, Madeline was accused of dreaming. True, she agreed with that. She had often been caught staring idly out of the window whilst customers sat in impatient rows saying pointedly, 'Is anyone serving around here?'

Her latest sin was her worst. She kept a book in the stockroom. At the moment it was Doris Lessing. Every time she was sent to fetch something – 'A pair of brown slingbacks, size five, please' – the book would be there. Luring her. Enticing her. So she'd read a little bit. But she'd got engrossed. Sat on a stool, turning the pages avidly, forgetting about a woman who was sitting, stockinged feet at the ready, waiting for the slingbacks. Fifteen minutes, the woman sat. Twenty. Thirty. Then she snapped.

'For crying out loud, how long does it take to find a pair of size five slingbacks?'

Mrs Bateman, the buyer, had gone in search of Madeline. Found her, so caught up in what was happening between the covers of her book, she did not hear her coming.

'Madeline, what are you doing?'

The voice, the shrillness of it, cut into the world Madeline had entered. She started. Dropped the book. And looked at Mrs Bateman, flushed and guilty. There was no hiding her misdeed.

'Caught you red-handed,' hissed Mrs Bateman. 'I'll deal with you later.'

The customer was told the shoes had been put on the wrong shelf. And appeased with a five per cent discount. Madeline was reported to the shop manager, Mr Speirs. Ticked off.

As she was leaving his office, Mrs Bateman said, voice raised, so Madeline would hear, 'The girl's no use. She dreams all the time. Ignores the customers. She gets shoes mixed up. Puts them back on the wrong shelf. She has to go.'

The words shot through Madeline. Seemed to skip her brain, go straight to her stomach. Where they started a fire that simmered all afternoon. All evening. And blazed that night when she lay in the dark. She was scared. Soon she'd have no Ted. No job. Nothing.

Archie stood outside her door. Listening to her weep. When the staggered breathings and snufflings got too much for him to bear, he knocked gently. Eased open the door. You never knew with these young ones. She might be naked.

But she wasn't. She was wearing one of Ted's old pyjama tops. She switched on her bedside light.

'I thought that was what I heard,' said Archie. 'I thought I heard you crying.'

Madeline blew her nose on the sheet.

'What's the matter?' Archie wanted to know.

'Nothing,' said Madeline.

'Just like Mrs Turner. She often cries for nothing.'

'Mrs Turner?'

'Oh, yes.'

'Why do you call her Mrs Turner? Do you call her that in bed?' The words slipped out. She hadn't meant to be impudent. She was curious.

'I only call her Mrs Turner to other folks. She's a Mrs Turner sort of person. You'll agree. But she's Joanie to me when we're alone. Especially in bed. She still likes a cuddle.'

'Mrs Turner?' Madeline was horrified.

'Oh, yes. She may seem old to you, but she isn't to me. And she isn't to her. You'll find out when you get there.'

Madeline blew her nose again. It helped relieve the shock.

'There you go,' said Archie. 'A good blow always helps. I expect you're missing your Ted. And you'll be wondering what's happened to you. Suddenly finding yourself here with a fussy old couple like me and Mrs Turner.'

Madeline nodded. She had no intention of telling him about the job. That would lead to confessing about Doris Lessing. But the Ted bit was true. And she cried for him nightly.

She'd lost him. Lost the flat she shared with Ted, and now it was relet. It hurt to walk past it every morning and again every night, and see the new people moving about in it. She'd sold off the furniture and used the small sum it brought to buy treats for Ted. A cassette recorder to listen to his favourite operas, Buddy Holly, the Rolling Stones and Charlie Parker. Though *The Barber of Seville* made him cry and rage. Madeline didn't know why. She bought him several pairs of pyjamas and a dark blue silk dressing gown. 'All the ladies will be after you in that,' she told him. The rest of the money she kept in what she called her Ted fund. Should tragedy strike again, she'd be ready. At work when asked about her parents, she said they were both dead.

She felt guilty about this. But found it hard to tell anybody that her lovely Ted was now entombed in a home. She thought of him often. Imagined him sitting in his little room, a small single bed, a weary chest of drawers, television on and unwatched. His chair was by the window, and she made sure there were always flowers in the yellow vase he'd brought with him. He'd be in his own world, lost in his jumbled mind, waiting for Jem to come to him. Wondering where his orchids were. Alzheimer's was cruel, she thought. Cruel and vile. She visited Ted twice a week, though sometimes he didn't know she was there, and sometimes, when he did, he didn't know who she was.

'I told the people at work that my dad was dead,' Madeline confessed. 'Do you think that was terrible of me.?'

'Why did you do that?' asked Archie.

'I don't know. It just come out. I just couldn't say the truth. It seemed so hard.'

'Well, maybe in a way he is dead. The old Ted is gone from you. I don't think he'll come back.'

Madeline nodded. 'I miss him. I want him back.'

'Look at it this way,' Archie told her. 'Anybody looking at you, seeing you going about your business will know that you are special. Ted did that for you. You were loved. Not many of us can say that.' He patted her hand. 'You see, it'll all work out. Good things will come to you. I reckon it's your turn. You know what Mrs Turner always says.'

' "What's for you will not go past you",' chanted Madeline. Words that had fallen often from Mrs Turner's lips.

'You'll see,' said Archie. 'Something good is coming to you. Very soon.' He rose stiffly. 'And don't you let Mrs Turner see you wiping your nose on the sheet. She'll have something to say about that.'

Madeline lay in the dark. Archie had said she was special. She held the words close. A comfort. She wondered if he and Mrs Turner were cuddling. Usually such a thought would make her giggle. But, right now, she envied them.

Two days later Mr Speirs called her to his office. He'd been watching her. He thought she had a knack. A way with things. How to lay them out. The little beach display she'd done, with the shells, had been a treat. He offered her a job as a junior window dresser.

Madeline accepted. He smiled. Problem solved. Mrs Bateman rid of the dreamy assistant. And he hadn't had to fire the one the staff called 'the poor wee orphan girl'.

Madeline soared. She was a window dresser. That was special. Arty. She could wear jeans and soft shoes. She could walk about the shop carrying display materials. Make discount and sale signs. She could stand in the window and watch the world go by. Maybe Archie was right, after all. She was special.

She celebrated by buying a sketch pad and soft lead pencils. In her room that night, she started to draw Mrs Turner and Archie lying entwined in their big wooden bed with the pink candlewick bedspread. It pleased her. Drawing, forming shapes, planning the scene as a whole – the bed, the tumbling bedspread, the huge Mrs Turner – curlers in – and the thin, wiry Archie, the alarm clock – sent her mind racing. And she did not grieve for Ted. She thought she should have been doing this all along. The pleasure it gave her. In fact, though, she had never stopped. She was always drawing in her head. Noting things, deciding how to put them on paper. She drew on the table with her finger when alone in the Turners' kitchen not eating the dried meal that had been left warming in the oven for her. She drew shapes in the spilled sugar in the canteen at work. The counter of the shoe department had been covered with little sketches drawn on stray bits of paper. She didn't realise sometimes that she was doing them. She just liked to have a pen or pencil in her hand and watch the shapes in her mind appear. It made her feel complete.

A Friend

Maybe that's what Annie saw when she watched Madeline going about the store. She saw someone who had all the things she suspected she lacked. A certain inner confidence, a stride, a self-knowledge, a completeness. Without acknowledging it, Annie wanted all that. She befriended Madeline. Which, as she was to say later, and often, was not easy.

Annie was older than Madeline. Nineteen. She was underbuyer in the gents' department. The first career girl Madeline had ever known. Until Annie came into her life, Madeline hadn't considered a career. She wanted to paint. The ins and outs of it, the ifs and buts, the business of earning a living at it, didn't bother her. She had thought she'd get by – somehow. She just – and desperately – wanted to be good at it.

At break times, staff went to the canteen in the basement. In striking contrast to the plush and scented opulence of the sales floors, the canteen was dim, painted dark brown. It had scattered ancient tables and an assortment of even older chairs. On the walls were torn festival posters, and yellowing holiday rotas dating back to 1962. Coffee was instant, made with slightly off-the-boil water and a strictly measured level teaspoon of Nescafé. Tea came scaldingly hot from a dubiously ageing urn, the insides of which were the colour of thick varnish. Both were served in thick, heavy-duty white cups, no saucers. A limited selection of biscuits was available at trade price. Madeline never bought one; her budget didn't run to biscuits.

The store had a strict pecking order that was at its most bitter, and fiercest, at break times. Buyers sat with buyers and, if no other buyers were around, with underbuyers. Head salesmen and women sat with head salesmen and women. Juniors sat with juniors. The three window dressers sat apart. They were arty, and therefore not part of the main pecking body. It was considered acceptable, daring, even, to sit with them if there was nobody of your rank available.

It was also considered perfectly all right to sit with Madeline. Not only was she a window dresser, she was a poor wee soul with no mum or dad and probably in need of a spot of cheering up. In fact, sitting with Madeline was more than acceptable – it was downright benevolent, an act of kindness. And buying her a biscuit raised your ante with the others. Not that Madeline ever accepted the proffered Penguin or YoYo. This was, of course, regarded as absolutely the right thing to do. Accepting a biscuit that she could not return, however graciously she did it, would have been considered accepting charity in the workplace. And as every senior member of the staff knew, being beholden to your peers only led to grief. Being beholden to your elders and betters was, however, fine. But, none of Madeline's elders or betters had any intention of buying her a biscuit. They were old enough to know a misfit when they saw one, and wise enough, they congratulated themselves, not to get involved.

Annie knew Madeline's break times and, whenever she could, took the same twenty minutes to visit the unspeakable basement and drink the undrinkable tea. She'd sit with Madeline and attempt conversation. But Madeline was never willing. She'd give monosyllabic answers to Annie's questions, mistaking the invitation to chat for nosiness.

Annie: Crap weather.

Madeline: Suppose.

Annie: Hope it clears up for the weekend. What are you doing Saturday?

Madeline: Not a lot. Actually, I have to go.

And, she left.

With every advance Annie made, Madeline got more and more brusque. And the more brusque Madeline got, the more intrigued Annie became. She wanted to know this person, break down the defences. She tried every conversation opener she could think of – nights out, boyfriends, clothes, the weather, work, colleagues. Madeline, master of the disinterested shrug, would move her shoulders upwards and agree or disagree, as the mood took her. Annie hit on food quite by accident.

The Turners' house was half an hour's walk from the store. Madeline knew the walk well, did it twice a day. Bus fares were not on her budget, which revolved round vodka at weekends, cheap clothes and, mostly, art materials. When the weather was fine, she wandered, carefully avoiding restaurants. Otherwise the waft of cooking would engulf her, filling her with longing. It reminded her of Ted. And the food she'd once eaten. The wrapping of Mrs Turner's dried inedible cuisine in newspaper and throwing it into the bin left her constantly hungry.

When Annie, in one of her long, one-sided chats, mentioned that it was bloody stew for tea tonight – it was always bloody stew on a Thursday – she touched a nerve. Ted made lovely stew. Thick, garlicky, laced with baby onions, slivers of bacon and olives.

'Stew,' Annie said.

And something within Madeline stirred. 'Stew,' she said. Almost orgasmically. She repeated it, savouring it, 'Stew.'

'You like stew?' Annie was amazed that anyone could like stew.

Madeline regained her composure. 'Sometimes.'

'Well, come home with me. Have some. My mum loves feeding people.'

Madeline considered this. The pros and cons. She could phone Mrs Turner. Say she was going to have tea with a friend. Mrs Turner would approve of that. She was always nagging Madeline to make friends. Madeline thought she could eat the stew, and go. That this might be considered impolite, that she ought to linger and converse with her hosts, didn't cross her mind.

As she debated the invitation, Annie chattered. 'Of course, you'll have to put up with my family. But you know families – you don't pick them, do you?'

Madeline looked surprised. This was a new thought to her. But, of course, had she had the pick of fathers, she couldn't imagine a finer choice than Ted.

Annie mistook the look for hurt. Realising she'd made a derogatory remark about families, when she was under the impression Madeline no longer had one, she felt a fool, callous. Reached out, touched Madeline's hand and apologised.

Here were two things young Madeline hadn't had in a long time. Physical contact with another human being, and the offer of hot food that would be eaten with other eaters around her. Her reserves crumbled. 'I'd love to come for tea,' she said.

Annie's mother was what Madeline thought of as a mumsy woman. She worked part time doing accounts for a chain of garages. But her family was her life. Her freezer was filled to overflowing with soups, stews, lasagnes. Her house was clean, smelled of lavender wax and fresh coffee. Weighing up the new notion of choosing your relatives, Madeline decided, if she could choose a mother, it would be Annie's. She looked round at Annie's living room, fire glowing in the grate, brothers sprawled on the sofa, on the chairs, television beaming. She was enfolded in a new warmth. And she envied Annie even more than she envied Mrs Turner's cuddle from Archie.

The stew was served in the dining room. Lizzie Borthwick, Annie's mother, had strict rules about eating. In her opinion – the only one that, in her opinion, mattered in the household – eating was not something that one did in front of the television. Unless it was a takeaway. Takeaways were casual food, and could, therefore, be eaten casually.

Stew was not casual food. It was serious. They took their places round the table, Madeline, a guest, sitting where guests sat, on the right-hand side of Douglas Borthwick. A doctor, and jolly to the point of embarrassment as far as his children were concerned. He served.

'Guests first,' he said. Heaping a mound of meat swimming in a thick red wine sauce. It was topped with whole button mushrooms, tiny onions and thyme. Madeline thought of Ted.

'Potatoes, Madeline?' asked Douglas.

She nodded.

'Veg?'

Madeline nodded. Green beans tossed in olive oil and fresh mint, broccoli steamed gently, buttered and strewn with Parmesan were added. The plate placed in front of her. Hands neatly folded in her lap, she waited till everyone was served before picking up her knife and fork. Her eyes, though, never left her plate.

And when she started to eat, the world melted away. There was only food. She leaned over the table, fork moving from plate to mouth in perfect fluid motion. Later, remembering this meal – and cringing with shame – she thought she might have moaned with pleasure. She finished everything. And only after she'd wiped her plate to gleaming with a lump of bread broken from a French loaf, and leaned back, did she notice the silence.

She looked round. Everyone at the table had given up eating their food, and was instead watching her in awe. Every plate was politely touched, small mouthfuls taken, enjoyed. Hers was glaringly empty. 'Sorry,' she said. Quietly. 'I was hungry.'

'So we see,' said Lizzie. 'Doesn't your mother feed you?'

'Her mother's dead, Ma,' said Annie, as if her mother ought to have known this without being told. 'So's her dad.'

Lizzie considered this. She looked at Madeline and saw an orphan, a waif. Something should be done, she thought. This was but a child who needed mothering. And though she would have hotly denied it, mothering came to her naturally. It was an instinct. She scattered crumbs for sparrows. Weren't there two ex-stray cats lying right now stretched, replete and purring, before the Aga? She cooed into every pram she came across. Halloween, there were always sweets and coins for any children who knocked at their door. She smiled to Madeline, reached out for her plate, and refilled it. 'In that case, you'll no doubt be needing a wee bit more.'

Madeline nodded. A wee bit more sounded fine to her.

Art and Sex and Sherry

At the time, Annie was seeing Willie Melville. A huge bear of a man Annie secretly thought to be held together with hair that sprouted amazingly, profusely over his whole body. Evenings, after the pub, and before she had to get up and go home, she'd stroke it, declaring that she didn't know people grew hair there, and there.

It was commonly believed that beer, not blood, ran through Willie's veins. Such was his passion for the stuff. He was a builder. Lizzie had no time for him.

'A builder,' she scoffed. 'That one. He's the sort comes into your kitchen, takes it apart, knocks down walls, then disappears for ever. All he builds is piles of rubble. And,' warming to her theme, 'that's what he'll do to you, turn your life to rubble. And he's too old for you.'

Willie was thirty-two. This added to Annie's desire for him. The more Lizzie disapproved, the more alluring Willie was to Annie. She was a misfit at home. All her brothers had followed their father into medicine, and, though the same had been expected of her, she'd left school, rejected the offered university place to train as a buyer in retail. She was a disappointment. But Willie made her feel special. When in the pub his huge arm enfolded her, pulled her to him, and in front of all his friends he drunkenly nuzzled her neck, she felt like someone. Annie Borthwick, Willie's girl.

In time Annie would blame Lizzie for the relationship, complaining that if she hadn't made such a fuss, hadn't said at every possible opportunity what a rogue he was, how unsuitable he was, she, Annie, would never have bothered with him. It was, she said, the thrill of the clandestine romance. A passion like Romeo and Juliet's. Which, once they married, was no longer clandestine, and, of course, no longer thrilling.

Meantime, Lizzie took Madeline under her wing. She insisted the girl come eat with them a couple of times a week. Annie would go out, sneaking off to see Willie, saying she was going to night classes, leaving Madeline and Lizzie chatting in the kitchen.

They'd talk about art and food and Mrs Turner, while Annie was in Willie's bed, laughing, rolling herself up in his sheets, sprawling on top of him, singing along with his wild bawdy songs of love and lassies and drunkenness.

He made her feel like a woman. At ten o'clock, she would slip reluctantly from his arms and cross the room to where her clothes lay heaped on a faded velvet armchair.

He would lean out of the bed and pull her back to him. 'Don't go.'

'I have to. I told my mother I was at night school. Doing French.'

They sniggered.

'Tell her you went for a pint with some mates,' pleaded Willie.

'It's ten o'clock. The class finished at nine. I'll have to say that anyway. Though I'll tell her coffee. She wouldn't approve of a pint.'

He put his hand between her legs. 'You don't want to go. I can tell.'

She'd sigh. A rush of longing. Then turn from him. 'I'm going.'

Willie would lie, head propped on his arm, watching her dress. Then blow her a kiss as she went out the door. Down the long narrow hall, and out into the night. She'd catch the bus home, sit on the top deck, composing herself. Hoping she didn't smell of sex. Preparing her lies.

In Lizzie's kitchen Madeline spoke about her father, his orchids, how he sang to her, his meticulous watercolours. 'I wanted to paint too. But there you go. I didn't.'

'But you're young,' Lizzie cried. 'You can do anything you want.'

'I didn't go to art school. But I still draw. At night in my room. But art materials are expensive. I can't afford as much as I'd like. I'd like to paint more. But, you know, paints . . . Brushes . . . Brushes are fabulous.' She glowed enthusiasm. 'Just some sable, but you can do anything with them. The thickness of a line, the way it flows. How loaded it is with paint or water, how dry it is. You can say more with a brush than a million words in a dictionary.'

'Why not do it then?'

'I can't afford it. And . . .'

And painting was inevitably messy. And Mrs Turner had no time for mess. She didn't understand it. Madeline feared if she moved from sketching into painting, her room would fill with tubes and jars and brushes. The clutter would take over the room. In the Turners' she felt hemmed in. Compelled to comply with house rules. Lights out at half-past ten.

'And what?'

'I don't feel comfortable painting at the Turners'. They're so kind to me. But I don't think I could feel at ease painting there. You know, the stuff lying around. And I don't think Mrs Turner would like the things I'd paint. She wouldn't approve. I feel inhibited there.'

'Suppose.'

Madeline looked around Lizzie's kitchen. A shiny place. Glass-fronted cupboards filled with crockery. All those cups. She could not imagine what someone would do with so many cups. Lizzie's four tea sets on display. Forty-eight cups. Why, there were only six of them in the family; even if they had visitors they'd not need more than ten or twelve.

She had once discussed Lizzie's cup situation with Mrs Turner. 'Why would anyone want so many cups?' Madeline asked.

Mrs Turner leaned back in her seat, thinking about this. It was a tricky one. But she liked tricky problems. And she liked being asked for her opinion. She had a lot more opinions than Lizzie had cups. 'It's a show of wealth,' she decided. 'Like the lords of old who made a big display of owning land and peasants and horses and virgins. Your Lizzie displays her cups.'

Madeline nodded. This could be true. Though it was a bit strange hearing Mrs Turner say virgins. Madeline couldn't imagine Mrs Turner knowing about virgins. Though she supposed she must.

'See,' expounded Mrs Turner, 'Archie and me have ordinary china and good china. We put the good in the cabinet in the lounge. We're not poor. We're just not rich. But we're not so short of money as we can't afford good china which we keep for special. But your Lizzie has many, many cups. So she shows them off. That's how wealthy she is. What does her man do?'

'He's a doctor.'

Mrs Turner raised her hands. 'There you go. They're rich. Cups for all occasions.' Problem solved.

Now Lizzie leaned confidingly towards Madeline. 'If you have a gift, you must nurture it. You are blessed.'

'Blessed?'

Lizzie nodded. 'Yes. Blessed.' She loved the sound of that. She loved to hear herself dispensing love and wisdom. It felt so good. As if telling someone they were blessed made her blessed also. 'Blessed,' she said again, nodding.

Secretly, Madeline thought this ridiculous. She wasn't blessed, she was ordinary. In fact, less than ordinary. Except, Archie had said she was special. So she sucked this in and let it linger a while. Savouring it. To be blessed, if only for the few minutes she indulged in believing it, was lovely.

'I can't afford to paint,' she said. Was this true? She thought not. It was more a matter of not getting started. She'd stopped painting when Ted was moved into a home. Painting reminded her of him. And that hurt. And she felt guilty doing something he had enjoyed so utterly. Then there was the business of doing it without Ted, her mentor. He'd always been there advising, helping. She showed him everything she did, and he always had something to say, something to add. It had felt like a dance. As if he was holding her, leading her. Showing her she could do more than she'd thought she could. It had been exciting. Whenever she'd finished something, she'd shown it to Ted.

When she'd first started, her work had been immaculate, tight, controlled. She feared making mistakes, and worked painstakingly, slowly. Shyly, she'd put her latest work before him, the boys at her school gathered by the railings, wearing this year's interpretation of the uniform, ties loose, shirt collar open, sly cigarettes hidden in the curve of their palms. Ted would look at it, see the careful lines. The inhibition. 'Let go,' he told her. 'Just let go.' He was always telling her that. Let go.

She didn't think she could paint without Ted. She doubted herself. And, of course, the business of not being able to afford it wasn't true. She already had, in a box in the corner of the little bedroom in the Turners' house, tubes of acrylics and gouache, bottles of inks, brushes. Face it, she told herself, you're scared you can't do it without Ted.

So she pursued the poverty line. 'A junior window dresser doesn't earn much. I have a tight budget. Clothes. Bus fares, though only when it rains. I usually walk. Then I save a little.' She didn't mention nights out. Vodka. She counted on her fingers, indicating the hopelessness of her financial situation. Then waved her hands in the air. 'There's nothing left.'

Lizzie was impressed. A budgeter, like herself. And so young. She thought of her own children, always borrowing money. Never paying it back. Not that she would have taken it, just it would be nice, she thought, if they offered.

'I'll give you the money,' she said.

Madeline shook her head. 'I couldn't do that. I'd never be able to pay you back.'

Lizzie reached for the sherry bottle. She liked a drop of an evening, she said. It was good for you, she assured herself. Relaxing, and did wonders for the circulation. Definitely that. She poured a glass for herself and one for Madeline, who wanted to refuse, but didn't know how. She took a sip, then another, then a sip too many. She wasn't used to sherry. Until this moment, she thought it a silly old-woman's drink. Not at all strong. She was wrong. The sherry skipped her circulation, went straight to her cheeks, and her head.

Lizzie drained her glass. Refilled it. She'd already had a surreptitious two or three whilst preparing supper. Was feeling mellow. 'You don't have to repay me. You could give me your paintings. Not all of them. Just some. That's what they did in the olden days. Rembrandt and such like.'

She wasn't sure exactly which painters had been given money to subsidise their art. But was sure some had. 'Painters used to give their work for a meal, or a glass of wine.' She filled her glass again. 'Picasso, Monet, Matisse. All these chaps.' She nodded, enthusiastically. 'I'm sure.' She had no idea. 'Think of the favour you'd be doing me. I'd be patron of the arts. A benefactor. I've never been that before. I'd enjoy it. I know I would.' More sherry. 'Just think. You could become famous. Your work could be worth a fortune. And . . .' a sudden dazzling thought, '. . . if you died. Well . . .'

Madeline was shaken by this. She was approaching seventeen; dying wasn't on her to-do list. 'I'm not going to die.'

More sherry.

'No. No. Of course not. But if you did. The market value of your work could rocket. I could be sitting on a fortune. You must let me help you.'

She opened her purse. Removed two twenty-pound notes, which she pressed on Madeline.

Annie, lies lined up, ready in her head, burst into the kitchen. Shouting that she was home. And was there anything to eat? She saw her mother pushing money into Madeline's hands.

'What are you doing?'

Lizzie looked up. Drunkenly announced that she was now a patron of the arts. She was sponsoring Madeline. Art was everything. The only thing that mattered in the world. And one day, when Madeline's gift was recognised, she'd be rich.

Annie said, 'Jesus Christ, you're drunk.' Left, slammed the door. Into the living room. Was hit by a wall of airless heat, a flickering, blue television light. Her father and brothers were slumped, vacant-faced, eyes fixed on an LA car chase. The squeal of rubber, gunfire and outpourings of American oaths drowned her cheery hello. Nobody looked at her. She slammed the door. Stormed, stamping, up the stairs. Slammed her bedroom door. Dammit. Dammit. She had her story ready, and nobody asked. Anything could happen to her. Anything. And they wouldn't know. They wouldn't care. She could've been raped. Mugged. She kicked off her shoes. She could've stayed with Willie. More love. Warm in his bed. Dammit.

Madeline stiffened. Sat in her chair, alarmed.

Lizzie reached over, patted her arm. 'Don't let her little outburst bother you. She's mad at us 'cos nobody asked where she's been.

And how her night classes went. She's had her story primed, ripe for the telling, and nobody wanted to hear it. Infuriating, isn't it, when you've got your lies to perfection then don't get to tell them?'

More sherry.

'Suppose,' said Madeline.

Lizzie leaned over the table, confidingly. 'She's been with that man. Willie Melville. Stupid girl. Sleeping with him. In his bed. In that flat. Thinks I don't know. But I know. I know that look. The smirk. The glow. Sex does that to you. And secret sex makes you shine harder. Oh yes. I know that, too.'

'Goodness,' was all Madeline could think of to say.

'Sex,' said Lizzie. Slurring slightly. 'It's the reason for it all. It's to blame for everything. Sex and love and horniness. Rows of houses, all the same. Couples needing a place of their own, somewhere to make love. Shut the door, pull the curtains. There they are. Doing it. With nobody around to hear. All the stuff, privet hedges, shiny cars at the door. Going out on Saturdays to buy shoes – which let me tell you is as close to hell as you can get. It all started with a tingle – down there.' She pointed to her crotch. A part of Lizzie Madeline didn't really care to think about. 'Oh yes. Look at me. It started with sex. And now I have all this.' She opened her arms, indicating the kitchen. 'Spoons in the drawer, a great deal of crockery. Food in the freezer. Carpets everywhere. Linen on the beds. A family, noise all the time. And I'll tell you, Madeline, I'm lonely. I meet friends for lunch. I chat on the phone. And I love my family more than I can tell you. But I wanted more. Douglas didn't want me to work. I took my wee job anyway. But I wanted a career. I'm looking at sixty. Too late. And, to tell the truth, I've gone off sex. I'm so sad about that. Because I remember how I used to feel. I loved it. I loved to feel Douglas in my bed. The heat of it. Him in me. I couldn't get enough. Oh, it was lovely.'

Madeline blushed. And said, 'Goodness.' Again.

'I make secret lists. All the things I haven't done. Been to India. Made love outside in the open air. Ridden a horse.' She sighed. 'I won't do any of them now. And the list goes on and on. You don't want a list like that. And if you did, you wouldn't want your painting to be on it. Art, my girl, art is worth more than anything I can think of. It lives on. Pursue your art.'

'I think,' Madeline said slowly, wondering if she should really speak this out, 'you've had too much sherry.'

'My dear, when you feel like I feel, you can never have too much sherry.'

A Catfight, Alarm Farting
and a Proposal

For three weeks the money lay on the wooden chest beside Madeline's bed. She touched it, fondled it. But didn't spend it. She hadn't earned it. And, therefore, didn't merit it. Money from relative strangers was not to be trusted. Money from a drunken relative stranger was to be trusted even less.

Douglas Borthwick had driven her home that night. She'd clutched the notes, crumpled in her palm. She'd sat in his large Rover, purring through the Edinburgh night, puzzling about the Borthwicks. She was at a loss when she was with the Borthwicks, quite lacking in the social graces.

Life with Ted had been so different. They had eaten in front of the telly, a sin at the Borthwicks' (except, of course, for takeaways). There was always, at the Borthwicks', an undertow of politeness that unnerved Madeline. She and Ted had never been like that. With her, Ted had always been Ted. They laughed, they sang silly songs, they bickered, fought, made up. But there had been no barriers. There were barriers at the Borthwicks', but Madeline was too young to define them, understand them. She just knew they were there and tried to deal with them.

There were rules in the Borthwick household. But nobody spoke them out. You said 'Pardon' if you belched. Nobody ever farted. Ted had farted often, and laughed about it. Blamed Madeline's cooking. Mealtimes at the Borthwicks' were not so much about eating, as conversing. Everybody spoke, yet nothing was really said. They discussed their separate days, what they'd done, what they were going to do. Passed on a joke they'd heard, but only if it was acceptably clean. There was always two glasses per person on the table. One for water, one for wine. Madeline worried that she might fill the wrong glass. Eaters were expected to make slow progress with their food, stopping to savour the meal. Not stuffing yourself. Something Madeline longed to do.

Here were people who had never in their lives been cold or hungry or frightened. When Ted had been at home, and ill, raging, looking for Jem, Madeline had often been frightened, bewildered. Still, she sensed she had something the Borthwicks wanted. She didn't know what.

Watching the television, they spoke about the programmes. But if, God forbid, something unseemly came on, elephants mating in a nature series, or a couple setting steamily about one another, or gays kissing, then there was an uncomfortable silence. Lizzie would cough, say it was time they all had a cup of tea. And disappear. Yet, she had said these things about sex, how once she'd loved it, couldn't get enough of it. Now it embarrassed her. Madeline found it all very puzzling.

Douglas stopped the car in front of the Turners' house, leaned over the steering wheel and gazed up at it. 'Here we are.'

'Thank you,' said Madeline. 'It was kind of you to drive me home.' That's what you did. You didn't say, 'Thanks a bunch, Doug. See ya.'

'No bother,' said Douglas. Then, 'You like it here?'

She shrugged. 'Mrs Turner looked after me when I was little and my dad went out to work. Then she took me in.'

'Right.' He nodded.

Madeline paused. Hand on the door handle. 'Um . . .'

'Yes?' said Douglas.

'Your wife, Lizzie, gave me this.' She uncurled her palm, revealing the money. 'I don't think I can take it.'

'Why did she give you that?'

'I paint. I used to paint. I wanted to go to art school. But, you know, my dad . . . and everything. I didn't go. She thinks I have a gift. She wants to sponsor me. Give me money for my art. But I can't take this. I think she was drunk.'

'Sherry,' he said. Flatly.

Madeline nodded.

Douglas pressed the money back into Madeline's hand. Crushed her fingers over it. 'Take it. Do us proud.'

He meant it kindly. But how could she do that? The responsibility heaved in on her. These witty, sophisticated people – all of whom knew more about everything than she did – would look at her painting and see what she already suspected – that she was useless.

She watched the car move out of her street, then went inside.

Safe in her own room. Door shut. The Turners snoring in unison across the hall. She smoothed out the notes Lizzie Borthwick had given her, put them under her alarm clock. Took her clothes off, put on Ted's old striped pyjama top and crawled into bed. Pulled her duvet over her head. This was the moment in every day she liked best. The moment she looked forward to, when she could relax, let her feelings roll. Recently, the feeling had been anger.

It swept over her just after she'd plagued herself with what-ifs. What if she lost her job? What if the Turners tired of her, wanted the place back to themselves? She sensed sometimes, especially on Sunday mornings when she didn't go to work, that they wanted to sit at the kitchen table and chat. She thought she was in the way. What if they asked her to leave? Then what? Her imagination soared. She'd end up on the streets like the people she saw through the windows of the shop. They came early, spread their blankets on the pavement, propped their notices, written in felt-tip – 'Homeless Please HELP' – beside them. And sit. And sit, all day. That might be her. Except she'd do a better notice. She'd planned it. It would be bold, multicoloured with drawings of despair. That'd do the trick. That would win over icy hearts.

She thought about Ted. How dare he get ill, abandon her? 'Damn you for that,' she said, whispered rage under the bedclothes. And what if he suddenly got better? Found himself in a home? What would he think of her? Last week he'd been fine for a while. Madeline had been allowed to take him out for a walk. Then in the middle of the park he'd started shouting for Jem. Loudly. People stared.

Madeline had taken his hand. 'Jem's not here.'

'Who the hell are you?' he asked. Then he started singing 'The Laughing Policeman'. People sniggered. Madeline led him back to the home vowing never to take him out again. Thinking about it now, angry at Ted, 'I hate you. Hate you for getting ill. Spoiling everything,' she said.

Tonight she thought about the Borthwicks. They were in that big house. Lights out, door locked, big car outside. They had nothing to worry about. Drunken Lizzie had given her money. How dare she? 'Patronising old bag,' said Madeline. She vowed never to go there again. Except to deliver her painting – if she ever painted again. And there was another source of anger. Now that Lizzie had given her money for a painting, Madeline felt obliged to do one. 'Damn, damn, damn.'

Across town, Annie was also lying in bed cursing her lot. Her mother was a drunk. A sherry-swilling cow who obviously preferred Madeline to her – her own daughter. In fact, it was plain from the way they fussed round her, the whole family preferred Madeline to her. 'Bastards,' she breathed. She'd show them all. One day – somehow. Sooner or later. And furthermore she wouldn't bring that Madeline home again. For sure.

By the time they got to work next day, Annie and Madeline had fallen out. Privately, in the quiet and dark of their own rooms, each had decided she loathed the other. And had to let the other know. They exchanged clipped hellos. Bodies stiff. Lips tight. This wasn't enough. If war was declared, both Madeline and Annie vowed to win. To crush the other, have the last and deadly word.

The sudden hatred was obvious to all the other assistants working in the shop, and became the latest topic of gossip, pushing aside the affair between the manager, Mr Speirs, and Jenny Watson from the linen department, who was, everyone agreed, gorgeous. But as the clandestine romance had been going on for the past six months, the lingering looks between them were not nearly as thrilling and dangerous as the vicious glares that were passing between Madeline and Annie.

On day two of the battle, the glares and furious looks had worked up to include gestures. A stiffly raised single finger from Annie. A double, two-handed V-sign in retaliation from Madeline. Annie decided she'd won that round. The finger was infinitely ruder.

Day three, and the gestures gave way to insults.

Madeline to Annie: 'Cow.'

Annie to Madeline: 'Arsehole.' One of Willie's favourite words.

'Shitty little cow. Chancer.' Madeline to Annie.

'Moocher and scumbag.' Annie to Madeline.

'Liar and whore.' Madeline to Annie.

Excellent, thought Madeline. Liar and whore beat moocher and scumbag. Though, moocher and scumbag hurt. Considering all the food she'd eaten, remembering the silence as she'd solidly worked through a vast plate of stew, Madeline thought this might be true.

'Petted spoiled brat,' she hissed at Annie in the staff canteen.

'Redneck, white trash orphan,' said Annie. She was sitting at the time with Mrs Carmichael, head buyer of her department.

Mrs Carmichael was shocked. 'Annie!' she said. 'That was unnecessary. Thing to say.'

'She called me a petted spoiled brat,' Annie protested.

'Well, my dear,' said Mrs Carmichael, gathering her purse, pack of Silk Cut and shoving them into her handbag, 'the way you are carrying on she may be right. You are management stock. She is a trainee window dresser. We do not expect behaviour from her.'

Annie reddened, squirmed and vowed revenge.

By Friday, the battle was all. They had lost track of why they were fighting. The winner would be the one to have the last, and the foulest, word. Both were hellbent on having it. Dreamed up insults in secret. Had them ready for the next confrontation. And, if the actual words were obvious, a bit lame – neither of them had much experience of catfighting – the passion and wrath with which they were hurled hurt. There was a showdown in the offing.

It came on Friday. Five o'clock, the shop was teeming. The rush and bustle of evening people. Madeline and Annie came face to face with each other at the door, in front of the makeup counter.

Madeline was carrying a box of tiny yellow chicks and wooden eggs for an Easter display. Annie had been buying some eyeshadow; this being Friday, she was seeing Willie tonight. They glared. Nudged and jostled by the evening crowds, neither would stand aside for the other.

'Excuse me,' said Annie.

'Excuse *me*,' said Madeline.

Mrs Findlay, who thought makeup made the woman, and anyone who showed her face in the morning without a good coating of it had let herself go, was extolling the joys of Estée Lauder moisturiser to a woman who had, according to Mrs Findlay, combination skin and therefore needed a very special cream.

'Expensive, yes,' she said, 'but worth every penny.' Her voice drifted off. Her attention was drawn to the confrontation that was starting up right before her. 'Now, girls,' she warned.

They ignored her. Honour was at stake. The redneck orphan and the petted spoiled brat had a score to settle.

'Excuse me,' said Annie. Once more. Icily polite.

'Won't,' said Madeline.

'Eff off,' said Annie.

'You eff off,' said Madeline.

It seemed to Mrs Findlay that they were leaning into one another, hands clawed, ready for some serious scratching. 'Language, girls!' she shrieked. Then watched in amazement as Annie and Madeline let loose at one another. A small crowd was gathering. Watching women rage was always entertaining.

'Whore,' shouted Annie.

'Shite,' squealed Madeline. It was a reaction. Being a whore was so much worse than being a shite. Madeline felt she was losing the fight. She took a fluffy chicken from her box, hurled it at Annie. It landed neatly in the centre of her forehead. Madeline grinned. Proud of that.

Annie stood a second. It hadn't hurt. Well, only her dignity. And Madeline's grin infuriated her. She reached into the box, withdrew a chicken, threw it, with venom, at Madeline.

It missed.

Madeline laughed. 'Missed.'

The mockery was too much. Annie lost control. And she hated that. Hated herself for it. It happened to her face. Everything showed

– bewilderment, fear, self-loathing – and in the depths of her, she
hated that too. And Madeline was everything she wanted to be. Self-
contained, quietly confident, arty. She knew about music. Had read
all sorts of books. Furthermore, Annie was in a private panic. Her
period was a week late. Oh God, she might be pregnant – how could
she tell her family? All that and, in this horrible moment, the things
that were happening to her face, the way it was contorting, everyone
could see. And she was ugly. She hated that too.

'I hate you,' she shouted. And moved in on Madeline. Who backed
off.

'Oh, dear me,' screamed Mrs Findlay. This would not do. She
rushed from behind her counter shouting, 'Let me through. Let me
through. I'm an Estée Lauder consultant.' She shoved between the
watchers. Stood a moment, wondering. What to do? Getting caught
in a catfight wasn't seemly. It could mess the makeup. She was a
woman who hid all her thoughts, emotions behind a palette of
foundation, blusher, eyeshadow and mascara. The air around her
reeked of Youth Dew.

Should she grab Annie? Madeline? She knew for a fact Madeline,
when working in the shoe department, had gained a reputation for
being impudent to customers. She had no parents. Such a child with
such a background might know about biting and kicking. A well-
brought-up child like Annie would never resort to such unladylike
behaviour.

She was wrong. She gripped Annie round the waist, yanked her
away from Madeline. Annie, enraged, dug her elbow into Mrs
Findlay's ribs, turned and bit her on the shoulder. The second she
felt her mouth fill with silk shirt, and her teeth sink into flesh, Annie
knew she'd gone too far. She came reeling back to sanity and saw, as
she opened her eyes, Mr Speirs, the shop manager, standing, awed,
at the front of the crowd.

His office Madeline thought interesting. Most things backstage in
this glittering departmental store were dingy. This office, on its way
to dingy, had stopped at tired opulence. An overall mood of brown,
old brown. But polished old brown. Large brown desk covered with
letters, invoices, memos. A single shiny executive toy, steel balls that

clashed together in constant movement. By the window a dark green button-backed leather sofa.

Still, right now, Madeline, standing, hands behind her back, in front of the desk, turned to gaze at the sofa, wondering if Mr Speirs and Jenny Watson had done it there. On that sofa, moaning and sighing, and vowing eternal love to each other.

Mr Speirs put his head in his hands. He was balding on top. Until now Madeline hadn't known that.

'What the hell was that about?' he asked.

Madeline and Annie shrugged in unison. It didn't do to confess sins and heartaches to senior management.

Madeline noticed the painting on the wall behind Mr Speirs' back. It was in blues and greens, a washy sort of thing. A woman sitting in a café overlooking a river, staring dreamily out at the water. She didn't like it.

'I feel I shouldn't have to remind you of the standard of behaviour we expect from our staff. That customers should see such a disgusting spectacle is horrendous.'

Why, Madeline wondered, did she not like this print? And why was she not taking this moment more seriously?

'I don't think I need to impress the seriousness of what you've done on either of you. It's a sacking offence.'

Madeline shot him a glance. The sack for her would be devastating. He saw the panic in her eyes. He should fire them both. But he'd taken a shine to Madeline. The way she moved about the shop floor. She had an eye, he thought. Her windows made passers-by stop, stare. Then again, it would be hard to fire Annie Borthwick. Her father was a friend, and was, at the moment, seeing him through some embarrassing prostate problems.

'I should sack the pair of you.'

Should sack, Annie noted. Should. So he wasn't going to. Excellent. Relief swept through her. She would not now have to go home and tell her mother she'd been fired. 'By the way,' she could add, 'I think I'm pregnant, too. Just by the by, sort of thing.' She smirked.

'Are you smirking, Annie Borthwick?' Furious voice. 'This is not a smirking matter.'

'No, Mr Speirs.' Affected innocence. 'I always sort of smirk when I'm nervous. It's a reaction.'

Madeline looked out of the window. A spring evening out there, shiny sharp. She looked at her feet. She wished she could be cheeky, like Annie. Annie didn't care about anything. She looked again at the picture. Decided what she didn't like about it was the way the woman was looking away when she had a cup of rich dark bitter coffee and a golden pastry in front of her. She should be tucking in, Madeline thought. Eat first, dream later. She sighed.

'You, Annie, will apologise to Mrs Findlay, who is in such a state she has had to be driven home. What on earth possessed you to bite her?'

'I don't know. It was the passion of the moment. I've never bitten anyone before.' She looked helpless.

'I have never seen anyone in the state Mrs Findlay was in.'

Annie nodded. But if Mrs Findlay was surprised to be bitten, Annie was more surprised to find herself biting someone. She hadn't known she had such violence in her.

'I trust you will reimburse her for the shirt you ruined.'

Annie nodded. 'Yes, Mr Speirs.' She sucked in her cheeks. Willing herself not to giggle.

'Next time, there will be no hesitation. No second chances. You'll be out the door so fast you won't have time to fart in alarm. Now get out of my sight, the pair of you.'

They walked politely to the door. Shut it behind them. A swift walk down the corridor. Into the lift. They exchanged glances. Fetched their coats from the staff cloakroom, and went together into the sharp spring evening. Walking side by side, they turned to one another. And burst into explosive giggles.

'Cow,' said Madeline to Annie. Pleasantly.

'Moocher,' said Annie.

'Whore,' said Madeline.

It was a conversation they were to have often. Remembering.

'The pub.' Annie pointed at the first neon sign they came upon.

'Excellent,' said Madeline

They drank vodka and Coke till their cheeks flushed and eyes glazed. Every now and then, one or other would break the flow of conversation, 'Oh, excuse me. I'm going to have to fart in alarm.' And they'd fall about laughing.

It became a ritual. Friday nights, the pub, and the crack that always started with, 'Cow.' Then, 'Moocher.' And, 'Whore.' Then, 'Watch out, alarm fart coming.'

Madeline went drinking with Annie. Celebrating life, love, sex, vodka, men and the extremely late arrival of Annie's period. Madeline met Willie and all Willie's friends. Was there when they sang. And joked and laughed. Partied with them. And was there the night Willie, with shirt unbuttoned, large hand on hairy chest, a single red rose between his teeth, went down on one knee and asked Annie to be his wife.

Standing on the edge of the crowd, Madeline went quiet. Flooded with fear and envy. She wanted that: someone to kneel before her, declaring undying love. Then again, she would like that person not to be Willie Melville. But she sensed that if Annie married, things would never be the same again. Dammit, just when she was starting to enjoy herself.

But Annie was overjoyed. 'Yes,' she squealed. Clapping her hands. Nearly jumping for joy. She'd have a place of her own. No more getting up to go home. She could see only bliss ahead.

Lizzie Borthwick went into shock. Ashen, she sank into a dining-room chair. 'That man,' she breathed. 'That man. Anybody but him.'

Her horror delighted Annie. She wished she'd come up with this marriage thing sooner.

'When?' asked Lizzie. Hoping the big day would be at least a year from now, give Annie a chance to come to her senses.

'Six weeks,' Annie said gleefully.

'Oh my God, you're not . . .?'

'No,' said Annie. Momentarily regretting the late period. That kind of shock would have been worth what she imagined to be nine months of horror.

Annie didn't think of marriage, really. The wedding was everything. She threw herself into the arrangements. She booked the hotel, chose the menu, ordered invitations, selected a dress.

Through it all, her mother fretted. Every now and then, she'd sit Annie down, look at her tenderly. 'Are you sure about this?' she'd say.

Annie would nod. Aglow with enthusiasm. 'Yes, of course I am.'

As Annie left for the church, sailing down the garden path in her exquisite white frock, clutching her bouquet, beaming, her mother trailed behind her. 'It's not too late, you can change your mind,' she wheedled.

But Annie was sure. This was it. This was what she wanted. A man in her bed. A home of her own. And the kind of title she thought would bring respect. She'd be Mrs Melville.

A Red Velvet Dress

Briefly, whilst Annie was caught up in the thrill of her wedding. Madeline slipped away from her. They saw less of each other. It wasn't a deliberate thing. Annie was in thrall with the notion of a wedding, her wedding. A great excuse for a party. Madeline, never an enthusiastic party person, didn't understand any of it.

Weddings puzzled her. But then, never having been to one, she'd only viewed them from a distance. Passing glimpses of beaming brides emerging from churches. Photos in the newspaper. What was it all about? Why did someone want to dress up like a meringue, walk down the aisle and pledge undying love? A huge day, and then what? A life in a house in a row of houses? Putting on the kettle, making the supper, eating in front of the telly, having folks round for dinner, was that it?

'What are you going to do once you're married?' Madeline asked Annie.

And Annie laughed deeply. 'God, Madeline, don't you know? What do you think?'

'But you can do *that* anyway.'

For a second this silenced Annie. 'But it's not the same. We can stay in bed all morning, if we want. He'll be there every night. And he'll be mine.'

'But he's yours anyway. And is that it? You won't ever sleep with anyone else? And is legal sex more exciting? Or just safer?' Madeline wanted to know. And had a good few more questions lined up in her head, ready for the asking.

But it was too much for Annie. She patted Madeline's arm. 'One day you'll meet someone. Then you'll know. You'll see things differently.' She went moist with romance. 'There's someone out there waiting for you.' She waved her hand at the canteen window, and the grim wall beyond. Everybody had a somebody. She believed that. Only some people never met their somebody. And then again, not everybody knew their somebody when they came across them. 'He's looking for you. Calling your name.'

Madeline didn't think so. 'How does he know my name? If we haven't met?'

'Well, it won't be your actual name at the moment. He's just got a notion of you. But one day you'll meet. And all your questions will be answered.'

Madeline sneered. But Annie was too misty to notice. Love was wonderful, fabulous. And if you were in love, life was worth living. And if you weren't, it wasn't.

From a huge distance across the table, Madeline watched Annie go. Drift off into her rose-tinted world. Some sort of insanity had gripped her, Madeline thought.

Madeline found Annie's near-constant wedding talk bewildering. She could not join her friend in her enthusiasm. Was left cold by Annie's outpourings on bridesmaids' frocks, choice of hymns, flowers.

'I absolutely do not want lilies,' Annie said. And with such resoluteness, Madeline felt left out of some knowledge of the inappropriateness of lilies. Something she felt the whole world knew, and she didn't.

'What's wrong with lilies?' she asked.

Annie screw up her nose. 'Ugh, you can't have *them*.'

Madeline shrugged. 'I like them.'

'I want orchids. I want the church to be overflowing with orchids. A fragrant day.'

'My dad grew orchids,' said Madeline.

'Did he?' Annie said, mildly. Not in the least interested in anything other than her own wedding arrangements. Her passion. And continued to enthuse about her bridesmaids' frocks, which were to be dusty salmon pink.

Madeline shrugged again. Her friend's obsession was a mystery to her. Madeline found it all absurd. In the midst of it, she decided she didn't want ever to marry. Or if she did, she wouldn't have a wedding. Just some sort of quiet ceremony with as few people as possible. But the coldness she felt for all that Annie was excited about made her think she must be odd. She felt alone and passionless in a swirl of pink fluff.

Seeking comfort, and some distraction from her loneliness, Madeline took the money Lizzie had given her and bought a canvas, brushes and oils. She would paint, but only, she promised herself, when she was ready. Evenings, she sat, working on her life drawings. She found it hard to draw people. She'd pose for herself. Standing in the middle of her room working out angles of elbows, knees, neck, shoulders of human beings running, standing staring, leaning over shop counters.

She drew Mrs Findlay. Orange face, gleaming terrifyingly under the harsh shop lights. Madeline wanted to capture some of that fiercesome painted-on confidence, the people round her ashen. Strained and polite. Slightly scared. She drew Mr Speirs exchanging longing glances across the shop floor with Jenny Watson. She struggled with her figures. Could never get them fluid. They always stood stiffly on her page, lumpen.

By the time she started working on her impression of the shop canteen, she felt she was beginning to express what she was trying to say. She used tea to stain the walls, to get the feel of oldness, neglect. And now, at last, she had made the lumpenness of her people work. They were lumpen. The teacups looked huge, clumsy in their hands. As if what they contained wasn't worth drinking. Ashtrays over-flowed. Crumpled biscuit wrappings lay abandoned at empty tables. And the boredom was there. People made dowdy by the place they were sitting in, the clothes they were forced to wear. The air was silky blue with curls of smoke and, from the way people, lumpen though they were, leaned across the tables talking, alive with riffs of gossip.

Madeline was pleased with her work. It had an honesty that made her smile. She would give it to Lizzie Borthwick. No, even better, she would do a painting of Annie's wedding, and give that to her. I'll let go, she told herself. Do what Ted told me, let go. It will be an honest depiction of the big day, a memory. Lizzie could hang it on her kitchen wall and be reminded always of how happy they'd been.

On the morning of the wedding, Madeline visited Ted. She'd bought a red velvet shift dress, which she wore with black patent high heels, long pointed toes. Hair up, lips coated with pale brown frosty lipstick, eyes caked with shadow and mascara, she hugged herself – how gorgeous she looked.

She had never accepted his illness. Thought that her old Ted was in there, locked in a private hell, waiting to come out. Every time she visited, walking the long corridor to his room, she'd think: This will be the time. This time he'll know me. And things will get back to how they were. They'd find a new place to live. He'd be older, weaker, but they'd manage. They'd joke, laugh, swap stories. They'd get by.

Today she walked swiftly. Heels clicking, echoing. The place always smelled of Dettol, and boiled vegetables. Ted must hate this, she thought. But in the dark of her mind, she wondered if he even noticed. Today, though, today would be the day. He'd remember the red velvet dress he'd bought for her when she was little. She'd worn it to a party. Had loved it too much to take it off and he'd given up trying to persuade her. She'd worn it to bed. For years he'd teased her about it. Seeing her now would jolt that memory. Whatever cog it was in his brain that had become stuck would be loosened up. His mind would ease, and he'd be freed from the secret hellish place he'd slipped into. He'd be Ted again.

Frail now, he seemed shrunken in his armchair by the window. He smiled to see her. He loved having visitors, though he didn't know who any of them were. She told him she was going to a wedding. Her friend, Annie, was getting married.

'Last wedding I went to was my own,' said Ted. 'Jem. Lovely woman. She wore a white silk suit, white flowers in her hand. Lilies.'

Ah, thought Madeline. So there's nothing wrong with lilies after all. She was cheered by this.

'I had on my new suit,' Ted went on. 'Light grey. The style of the day. I had a dark green silk shirt. Everyone said, "Don't wear that. Green's unlucky at weddings." Rubbish, I thought. Superstitious rubbish. Me and Jem loved each other so much, didn't matter what colour I wore.'

Madeline smiled and told him she was looking forward to it. She hadn't been to a wedding before. She was wearing her red velvet dress. 'It's new,' she said.

'I had a daughter had a red dress.' Ted's face lit up, remembering.

Madeline smiled. She thought the dress had worked. It had triggered something. She watched his face. He stared at the dress. Frowning. More than a frown. Straining. He almost swayed, the effort he was making. He reached out, touched her hem. Moving the velvet. Enjoying the way it shifted under his fingers.

'When she was born she was covered in hair, black hair. It was a surprise to me,' said Ted, shaking his head. 'It was all gone, time I got her home. Little thing.'

Madeline smiled. She was the little thing. Here she was. Hello, Ted. Are you in there, Ted?

'Jem died, though,' he said. 'She was lovely. If she was here, she'd be through there in the kitchen right now making you the loveliest cup of coffee. And some of her walnut cake.' He pointed into the distance behind him.

He doesn't even know where he is, thought Madeline.

His face clouded. 'She killed my Jem, that girl. We'd tried for a baby. Didn't happen. And we didn't mind. I had her. She had me. That was it. We didn't need anybody else. Then out of the blue she came along. Just like that. And Jem died right after the birth. And I wasn't even with her. Alone, she was. I could have held her hand, told her I'd be coming after her. I could have died, too. Gone with her. But I had the little thing to look after. I tell you if that thing hadn't been born my Jem would be through there, in the kitchen, making you the loveliest cup of coffee and some of her walnut cake.'

Madeline sat. Her stomach tightened. Hand to her mouth. 'Oh God,' she said. 'I didn't know. I'm sorry. I'm so sorry.' She got up. Fled the room.

'No,' called Ted. 'Don't go. I want to tell you about my little girl.'

But Madeline was gone. Down the long drive, and away. She had killed Jem. She had ruined Ted's perfect life. All those years, she'd thought he loved her. And he'd been lonely for Jem. His lovely Jem.

It was a pain too deep for tears. Moving along streets, wretched. Her face twisted in sudden grief and self-hatred. She had done this. She didn't deserve to be alive. It should have been Jem who lived. All those years, she'd thought he loved her. And he had been aching for Jem. She'd thought she was everything to him. But no, she was nothing.

She walked back into town. Hugging her coat round her. She thought to miss the wedding. But then she didn't know what else to do. It was spring. But cold. Skies overcast. She shivered. But shivering was good. She didn't deserve to be warm. She sat on a bench. Staring. Hardly thinking. She was all emotion. Grief. Her eyes glazed with tears. Her mascara smudged. Ran in thick black streaks down her cheeks. At last, with half an hour before the ceremony started, she got up and walked slowly towards the church.

At the home, Ted had watched her go. The sight of the person in a red velvet dress running away from him alarmed him. He stood, shakily, stumbled after her. Shouting a name that came to him suddenly from the depth of his tired mind. 'Madeline. Madeline.'

He couldn't understand why she was hurtling away from him. He only wanted to tell her about his little girl, who'd had a red velvet dress. Like she had. He moved along the corridor after her, reaching out for her. His legs were weak. His heart beat heavily inside him. He didn't quite know what it was – this thumping. It made breathing difficult. The air seemed to stop in his chest, and there wasn't enough of it. This confused him. After all, there was plenty of air about.

'There's plenty of it about,' he said to a passing nurse. 'I don't know why I can't get some.'

He could feel it chill on his face as he neared the door. He tried to grab a fistful and shove it down his throat. It was this grabbing and thrusting action that caused him to lose his balance as he reached the front steps. He tumbled down them. And lay gasping on the gravel path, wondering what had happened. Heard the sound of people running towards him. Shouts for an ambulance.

'No,' he said to the nurse who reached him first. 'No, wait. That young lady, I have to tell her something.' He wheezed, fought for air. 'She must take the dress off before she goes to bed. Even though she loves it. It'll get all sweaty and crushed.' The nurse, kneeling beside him, looked round and told Matron that he was rambling.

A Wanton Woman in a
Red Velvet Dress

Madeline was late for the wedding. She slipped into the church, sat at the back. Head down, she tried to fix her eyes. Smudging her mascara even more. And that was how she appeared in the photographs. Standing slightly aside from the crowd, eyes blackened, looking stunned. Not that anyone else, apart from Annie, looked particularly happy. Her brothers were glaring at Willie, faces raddled with scorn. Lizzie looked ashen, in the throes of some dire emotional upheaval. Douglas staring wide-eyed into the distance, a look of horror on his face. My God, I'm actually paying for this. But Annie, in true bridal tradition, glowed. She had hooked her Willie, and she had horrified her mother in one triumphant stroke.

Willie looked glazed. But then, he was glazed. He'd settled for the hair of the dog as the best cure for the hangover he had after a riotous stag night. And had tried to soothe his aching head and turbulent stomach churnings with half a bottle of whisky and a couple of cans of McEwan's.

'That man reeks of alcohol,' Lizzie hissed to Douglas at the very second the camera flashed.

The reception was in a small hotel just outside the city limits. Madeline was driven there by Richard. Twenty years older than she was, tall, greying and expensively dressed. He worked in advertising and was a golfing friend of Annie's father. He drove an MG, fast. He and Madeline had been thrown together in the post-photograph swirl of people moving off the steps of the church towards their cars. Douglas supervised.

'Has everyone got transport?' he shouted.

Madeline and several other people shouted, 'No.'

Douglas took her, and an elderly maiden aunt of Willie's, under his wing. And waved at Richard. 'Can you give one of these lovely ladies a lift?'

Richard smiled, said it would be no problem. He looked at Madeline. Small and looking a little tear-stained. Weddings did that to women, he thought. He liked the way she dressed. And it seemed a better deal to drive this stranger to the reception than the elderly aunt, who had an interesting moustache and, at fifteen stone, might have a problem getting into and out of his car. So he took Madeline by the arm, asked her name and said he'd parked down the street.

As they whizzed through the greening landscape Madeline remarked that she was glad it was spring. That February was over, and done with. 'I hate February, don't you?'

It hadn't, till this moment, occurred to Richard to dislike one month more than another. But right then, thinking about it, he agreed.

'I mean,' said Madeline, enthusing about how awful February was, 'everything is grey. It rains. Not decent rain that cleans the streets. That you can stand out in, and hold up your face and get fabulously wet. And it makes you laugh. But thick rain, murky rain. That soaks you, and chills you to the bone. And makes you sad. February skies hang low. And the wind whips along streets, catches you on corners and wraps round you. It's cruel, February wind. I hate it.'

He looked at her. She was interesting. Her mascara was a mess. 'Have you been crying?'

'Yes. You know weddings. They do that to you. Don't you think?'

He told her no. He wasn't a wedding man. And if Douglas hadn't been such a good friend he wouldn't have come to this one. And asked, if weddings so moved her, was she thinking of having one of her own?

'Heavens, no,' said Madeline. 'I'm never going to get married. I don't understand it. You go through this ceremony. You vow eternal love. Then what? You go eat a huge meal. Go off on honeymoon. Then come home and time passes, then you start to look like Mrs

Turner, with big hips. Eating biscuits and chatting to the woman upstairs. And complaining.'

The only marriage Madeline had seen working over a number of years was the Turners'. It seemed safe, but boring. Archie went off to do shifts on the railway. Mrs Turner stayed home. She baked. She made the tea. She and Babs had long conversations about the neighbours, holidays and, Madeline distantly remembered, pastry. Then Archie came home. They ate. Cleaned up the dishes. Watched television. Madeline was sure there must be more to it than that. After all, Ted and Jem had had, according to the stories Ted had told her, a wonderful time. Madeline decided that if she ever married it would be to have a wonderful time. Like Ted and Jem.

Once, while knitting socks for Archie, Mrs Turner had addressed the subject of men. There were, according to Mrs Turner, men you married and men you didn't. And you knew the ones you didn't because they always wanted to do – you know what. The needles quickened. Mrs Turner gave Madeline a swift glance, and nodded. Madeline nodded back. Enthusiastically. She was eleven. She knew this was a fascinating chat they were having. But it would be more fascinating if she knew what they were talking about.

However, she drew up a picture in her mind of the men that would make suitable husbands. She imagined them to be like the ones photographed on the front of Mrs Turner's knitting patterns. Clean cut, short hair, smiling, handsome. Good chins. The sort of men who could do handy things about the house. Fix things. The unsuitable men would be the likes of John Lennon or Mick Jagger. This was a pity. Since they were the only men she wanted. Just thinking about John Lennon made her go funny inside. But, she supposed, Mrs Turner was right. She didn't think he'd suit any of the jumpers she knitted for Archie. And she was sure he wouldn't know how to mend a tap. And she just knew, absolutely knew, that whatever it was Mrs Turner was talking about – the thing men wanted to do – John Lennon did it. There was something about him.

'You've got a weird view of marriage,' Richard told her.

'Do I?'

He nodded. 'Who's Mrs Turner?'

'She looked after me when I was little. I don't want to be like that. Sitting by the fire, gossiping. Knitting. Wearing a girdle. Just waiting.'

'For what?'

'Your husband to come home, I suppose.' She sniffed. 'Anyway, if I did marry, it'd have to be man like Ted. And I don't think there is one.'

A tear was forming in the corner of her eye. She willed it not to fall. It didn't obey. Richard saw it. Thought, Oh God, no, please don't do that.

'That's what I did,' said Madeline. 'I waited for Ted. Every day he'd come home to me. I made the tea. Though only after I was big enough to be allowed into the house straight from school. And I didn't have to go to Mrs Turner's any more. And Ted would come home. And he'd play his Buddy Holly records. And we'd read his Elizabeth David books. And we'd go water the orchids. He was lovely. He was all I wanted. People said, "Poor little Madeline, she's got no friends." But I didn't need friends. I had Ted. In school I'd sit and think about him. About what he was doing now. Then he wasn't Ted any more. But I always thought he'd come back. Get well. But he didn't. And now he says he only loved Jem, and all he wanted was for Jem to have lived.'

Richard pulled into a lay-by. Took Madeline by the shoulders. Asked her who the hell was Ted. And Jem, come to that.

'My dad,' she wailed. 'And I miss him. I've been waiting for him for years. And now I know he's not going to get better. He'll never come back to me.' She threw herself into Richard's arms. Let the rebel tears roll. And felt the comfort of a stranger. It all flooded out. Living with the Turners. How awkward she felt. Lonely. And the constant longing for Ted to return to her.

Richard, despite hating weeping women, was a gent. He held her, ran his fingers through her hair and said soothing things: 'There, there.' And: 'Hush. It's OK.' In fact he surprised himself. Normally when women cried he removed himself from the scene. He always felt it was terribly unfair of women to cry. It broke the rules. In any battle he'd had with a woman, as soon as he saw tears, he knew they'd won. 'You're not going to cry, are you?' he'd shout. They'd nod. Howl. And he knew that was that. He'd lost.

But this was different. Well, he could hardly walk away. He was in the middle of nowhere. Only fields and mud for miles. Furthermore, it was his car. He wasn't going to leave it in the dubious hands of a deranged and wretched young woman. But mostly these tears were forgivable. The girl was mourning her father. These tears were manageable – he hadn't caused them. So he hugged. And patted. And touched the head buried somewhere between his armpit and his shoulder with his lips. And when he was not staring anxiously through the windscreen wondering when they could get going, they'd be late for the reception, felt, for the first time in years, like a decent chap.

When at last she surfaced, Madeline sniffed. Blinked. She'd been pressed against Richard's jacket for so long, she'd forgotten where she was. Her eyes couldn't focus. She rubbed at them with the backs of her hands. Apologising. She sat staring at her feet, cursing herself for being so foolish. He handed her a handkerchief. Pristine white, freshly ironed, neatly folded. She hesitated. Was not *au fait* with the etiquette of hankies. Did she scrub her damp and mascara-raddled eyes, blow into it. Then hand it back, blackened and filled with snot. She stared at it. And at him.

'Take it,' he insisted.

She accepted. Dabbed the eyes. And blew. Then blew again. Crumbled the hanky up, looked at it. Slowly handed it back. He waved it back. 'Keep it.'

She shoved it in her pocket, thanked him. She sat wallowing in her grief. Cursing herself for telling this man more than she felt he needed to know. 'I've never told anybody about Ted. I always say he's dead. It was easy that way. I didn't have to talk about him. People always ask questions about things you don't want to talk about. Why's that?'

Richard shrugged. 'I don't know.'

'It's about power,' she said. 'People see they're hurting you and can't resist having another little dig.'

He told her she was too young to be so cynical. Though he quite admired it.

'Ted got ill years ago. Dementia. He was taken into a home.' She turned and saw his damp, mascara-stained shoulder. 'I've made a mess of your jacket.'

'So I see,' he said. 'It'll clean.'

She rubbed it with the hanky. Apologising. Then looked up at him. Their faces close. He couldn't resist. He kissed her.

Madeline had been kissed before. But never like this. She liked it. And now knew that this had been what Mrs Turner had been trying to warn her about. The warnings were for nothing, though. Madeline ignored them. The pleasure was too much to resist.

This was the kiss of kisses. It didn't last long. It started as a sweet little peck of sympathy – there, there, little Madeline, cheer up. And at that, it was only because their faces were too close not to do something about the nearness. It was either that, or stare at the small open pores on their noses. Then it deepened into something more sensual. His lips folded on her. Wet. But not slobbery. His tongue slipped softly between her lips. Before, when boys had tried to push their tongues into her mouth, Madeline found it frightening, hard, choking. She'd done vodka, smoked a little dope. But sex was still to come. So far she'd been involved only in gropings in doorways near to the club she'd frequented in her days before Annie came into her life. They'd been thrilling, but she'd always stopped before things got too out of hand. This was lovely. She gave herself to this kiss. Kissed back.

As they pulled apart, as Madeline was touching Richard's cheek, faces still close, telling him what a good kisser he was, the Borthwicks' car whooshed past. She saw through the glass a row of familiar faces frozen in astonishment, staring at her. And, she could tell, they did not approve of what she was up to.

'Oh God,' she wailed, realising that all the other wedding guests would have passed, and seen her locked in Richard's arms. And would, no doubt, have thought the worst. Richard laughed. This might be fun, after all. He started the car. And drove slowly to the hotel.

It was an old Victorian building. Up-market. Slightly stuffy. It was a place for afternoon teas. Middle-aged ladies draped their fur coats over the backs of their chairs whilst they delicately selected scones or cream cakes from a towering cake stand, set centre table. And sipped tea poured from a heavy silver pot whilst they discussed other people's medical conditions. The carpets were faded tartan; huge windows looked out on to rolling lawns. The walls were hung with Highland scenes – stags on heathered hillsides, lochs glimmering under watery skies. In the hall a wide staircase swept up to the bedrooms; a huge stag's head loomed over the reception desk. Crossed swords were pinned on to the wall either side of the entrance to the dining room. The staff, wearing black and white uniforms, turned and watched with thinly veiled censure as Madeline and Richard walked in.

They were late. Madeline slipped to the loo to fix her face, swollen from crying. Lipstick kissed away. When at last she entered the reception, the room turned, as one, to stare. Those who hadn't caught an actual glimpse of the kiss, had been told about it. The story had swirled through the crowd, gaining momentum as it was passed on and as the gossipers helped themselves to the Borthwicks' tray of drinks. By now the kiss, in Madeline's mind, had diminished into a swift and only slightly passionate meeting of lips. She decided it had been more a sweet and moist display of sympathy than a full-blown snog. To the gossipers it had developed into a quickie in a lay-by. Madeline was nearly naked and Richard's bum had been viewed moving in swiftly snatched ecstasy through the steamed windows of his natty little car.

Madeline, aware that she was a fallen woman, a hussy, glowered back at the starers. Not looking at what she was picking up, she helped herself to a glass of whisky. Something she never drank. This was also seen as a wanton act. Women at such gatherings drank sherry or orange juice. Men took whisky. In one fast, fiery gulp she compounded her reputation as a loose woman.

Since it seemed that nobody – except Annie, who gave her annoying winks and thumbs-up, and mouthed 'Nice one' from across the room – was talking to her, Madeline sat with Richard during the meal. And amazed him, as she amazed everybody, with her appetite. She soundlessly ate her prawn cocktail, duck in orange sauce and raspberry pavlova. Head down, no time for pleasantries, conversation was not an issue when there was food in front of her. Eating for Madeline was a serious business. She knew she was getting looks, gathering more and more disapproval. But tomorrow she'd be back to Mrs Turner's shrivelled offerings. She would make the most of this. And regretted only that she hadn't the nerve to ask for second helpings.

Richard was quietly impressed. And wondered if Madeline pursued other, more carnal, pleasures with the same dedication.

After the meal and the speeches, everyone drifted into the bar. The afternoon dipped into an alcoholic haze. Annie dragged Madeline off to the loo to discuss the naughtiness in the lay-by.

'But you were kissing him,' she said, incandescent with the knowledge of kissing. The urgency of it. The need for lips. Madeline denied everything. 'You were seen,' protested Annie.

'It was nothing,' Madeline told her.

'It was never nothing. Nothing is nothing. That's what I have come to think.' Annie disappeared into a cubicle.

Madeline heard the rustling of bridal gown, and Annie's curses as she yanked at her underwear. 'Sodding things. These frocks aren't made for peeing in. Nobody thinks of that. Anyway, he fancies you. I can tell. He never takes his eyes off you.'

Madeline had nothing to say about that. Today her heart was heavy. Every now and then she'd visit the darkness within. And think about Ted. Was he sitting in his chair by the window, expounding to some stranger about *the thing – the little thing –* that had ruined his life, killed his precious Jem? Every time she indulged in this sorrow, tears would glaze her eyes. As they did now.

'Can't wait to get going,' said Annie from inside her cubicle. 'Get some serious consummating done.'

'You've got years to do that,' said Madeline.

'No,' said Annie. 'No. I have to do it soon. Then it's done. The marriage is set. He's mine. No getting out of it.'

Madeline was surprised Annie didn't see it. Willie didn't want to get out of it. It was plain to anybody who saw them together that Willie adored Annie a deal more than Annie adored him.

Just after seven in the evening the disco started. And the throngs of friends that the Borthwicks had not been prepared to feed – Willie's rugby crowd – arrived. The sweat and stomp started. Madeline got lost in it. Only music in her head. Shimmying. Waving her arms. 'Ah . . . haaa . . .' Sweet, 'Blockbuster', thumping out. A song she normally didn't particularly like. But this was movement to blast away the blues. She hardly noticed who she was dancing with. It was Richard, who was making moves, forming juicy plans for later in the evening, and was too drunk to notice that Madeline was not really paying him much attention. Tonight, in her head, she was dancing alone. Chasing memories.

The ruckus had being going on for some time before it filtered past her rhythmic strut. Shouts, screams, laughter nearing hysterics. Shrieks. Thundering feet. She stopped dancing. Moved towards the noise. As did everyone else.

Willie and Annie had gone upstairs, to the room they'd booked, to change into their going-away outfits. They had been followed by a group of drunken friends, who had removed the swords from the wall before taking over the bathroom, clambering half naked into the bath. Singing songs Annie would prefer her mother not to hear. They had then decided to hunt the bridesmaids. And were now charging in their underpants, carnations sellotaped to their nipples, in sets of piggy backs through the reception. Not that the bridesmaids were objecting. Their squeals and hoots rang through the hotel. Diners from the regular dining room emerged to watch. Everyone was watching, urging them on. Except for Lizzie Borthwick, who was sitting on one of the polished leather sofas, fanning herself with a menu, stating loudly that this was not the sort of thing she'd imagined for her only daughter's wedding, and demanding to be taken home.

Annie and Willie were conspicuously absent. And had seized the moment, at Annie's insistence, to consummate their marriage. The half-dozen or so of Willie's mates who were not chasing the bridesmaids, sitting in the bar, knowing what was going on upstairs, were thumping beer mugs in a thrusting rhythm, urging him on.

'Where's my Annie?' Lizzie shouted.

'Humping her Willie,' she was told by an underpanted man she'd never seen in her life before. She sank, in a hopeless swoon, back on to the sofa.

At this moment Annie and Willie appeared. Annie in a navy silk suit, looking glowing and undeniably orgasmic. She gave Madeline the thumbs-up. The job's done. He's mine.

'We're off,' she shouted. 'Honeymoon time.'

She had, in her hands, a lustrous bridal bouquet, dripping carnations and roses. From halfway down the stairs she prepared to throw it. Single women clustered round, ready to catch. They'd be next. Madeline found herself propelled to the front of the throng. Annie eyed her. Aimed. And threw. Madeline saw the flowers skimming towards her. Clasped her hands behind her back. And tried to retreat. Saying, 'No. No. I don't want them. Not me.' As the flowers hit her, she stepped swiftly back. Shoving against the grabbing crowd. She felt them trip and fall behind her. Felt herself lose her balance, spread her arms, then felt them squirm and squeal beneath her as she collapsed on top of them. Perfect bouquet on top of her. No apologies. All she could shout was, 'I didn't catch them. I refuse to catch them. I'm never going to get married.' It was a perfect rounding off to her reputation as a loose and wanton woman.

Striking Out

Annie, seeing the seething mass of friendly bodies, launched herself into them. Shouting that she didn't want to leave the party. Willie let her know that if she didn't come away with him right now, he'd divorce her. He didn't mean it. He just thought he should assert himself in front of his friends. Lizzie marched to reception, insisted they brought her coat and told Douglas that if he didn't take her home immediately, she'd leave him. Richard snuck off to the phone and booked a room in a nearby small hotel. He thought he'd found the perfect woman – small, defiant, with a mass of black curly hair, in an interesting dress, who never, ever, it seemed, wanted to get married. He had plans for Madeline.

Had he known her actual age (he put her down at twenty-two) and her virginal state, he wouldn't have bothered. But her youngness attracted him. There was something glitteringly positive about her youth. As if young was the only thing to be. The world was hers to do with as she pleased. He remembered feeling like that. He didn't feel jaded, these days. Just a deal more cynical than when he was the age he imagined Madeline to be. He doubted other people's motives. He wanted some of Madeline's vibrant self-assurance. In some vague, unexamined way, he hoped her youth, freshness might be infectious.

He was surprised by her willingness to spend the night with him. He'd thought he might have to use some gentle persuasion. 'Great,' she said. Nodding enthusiastically. Why, she thought, should Annie have all the fun? Plus she didn't want to go back to the Turners' tonight. She didn't want to be alone tonight in their little spare room. Didn't want to think tonight. And she deemed it time she lost her virginity.

That took him by surprise. He sat on the side of the bed, complaining that she hadn't told him.

'I worried you mightn't want to do it, if you knew,' she said.

'You were right. I wouldn't have.'

She sighed, lay back. 'This is a lovely room.' She'd done it. At last. She felt beatifically adult. And a little bit sore. 'It's got a kettle. We could have a cup of tea. And a telly. We could watch the late film. Or, we could do it again. I need to get the hang of it.'

Richard had forgotten how energetic people under twenty could be after sex, after midnight. Right now, he was contemplating sleep. When he'd discovered he was her first he'd asked her age. 'Oh my God,' he'd moaned. 'I'll be called a baby snatcher.'

'I'll have a bath,' said Madeline now.

He heard the rush of water in the *en suite*. Her delight at the selection of shampoo and bath foam. Then the night enfolded him. His eyes shut. He slept.

In the morning he was ready, and willing, to indulge Madeline's new enthusiasm. With the sounds of hotel morning shifting in the rooms and corridors around them, Madeline, at last discovered the pleasures of the skin. His lips on hers. His tongue. And she moving with him. So this was why Annie was so fervent. This was what it was all about.

He drove her back to town. She didn't want him to see where she lived. Or rather, she didn't want Mrs Turner to see him. Besides, she wanted to walk, to think. To mull over her new persona as a woman. A woman of the world. At last.

She walked slowly through leafy suburban streets. Blackbirds calling. Cherry trees heavy with bloom. She thought the world beautiful. When she reached the house, at midday, she could tell by the silence, the heaviness in the atmosphere, that something was wrong. And when Mrs Turner did not stand in the centre of the hall, arms folded, demanding to know where she'd been all night, Madeline knew something was very wrong.

'Come into the kitchen. Sit yourself down,' said Mrs Turner softly. 'I've got something to tell you.'

Madeline followed Mrs Turner into the kitchen. Sat at the table.

'It's Ted,' said Mrs Turner.

And hearing that, the first time Mrs Turner had called him anything other than Mr Green, or that man, Madeline knew tragedy had struck once more.

'He's gone and died,' said Mrs Turner. 'Last night.'

'When?' Madeline wanted to know. 'When exactly?'

'Just after midnight,' Mrs Turner told her.

'Oh my God.'

He'd had a bad fall, following a heart attack, Mrs Turner told her. 'He never fully regained consciousness. Where have you been? We've been trying to get in touch all last night. We phoned the hotel where the reception was. But what a noise. There was a ruckus going on. Then later nobody could find you.'

Madeline was flooded with guilt. She couldn't tell Mrs Turner what she'd been up to. And through the mists of growing sorrow, she realised that her name would have been called throughout the hotel. Her absence would have been noted. Richard's too. She was a public disgrace.

'I left the reception early. I stayed the night with a friend. I missed the last bus home.' She felt her blood draining from her. Cursed herself. Her wantonness. She was a fool. Whilst she'd been pleasuring herself, Ted had been dying. Maybe he'd called out her name. She hated herself. Vowed that she would never do that again. You just let go, once, enjoyed yourself, in the dark of a strange and exciting room, and something awful happened. That was the way of things. She'd never do that again. She vowed never to have sex again.

It was a vow she never could keep. But for a few weeks, she tried.

'What will I do?' she didn't so much ask as wail.

'First things first. A wee cup of tea. Then we'll talk about it.' Mrs Turner knew what to do. She swung into action. Arranged the funeral. Loved every moment of it. She liked a good death. And this was a fine one.

'He's at peace,' she told Madeline. 'It's for the best. Poor soul.'

Madeline never knew if Mrs Turner meant her or Ted. But she agreed anyway.

After Ted was buried, Madeline had some money left in her

tragedy fund. It was time to strike out on her own. Mrs Turner fussed and worried. 'She's too young.'

Archie sucked in his breath. 'She is that. But if she wants to go, let her.'

Madeline found a small flat in an old building not far from Tollcross.

Mrs Turner came with her to look it over. 'It gets the sun in the morning,' she said. It was all she could find to say that was positive. The place horrified her. She despaired of the neighbourhood. 'Buildings,' she told Archie. 'And not a plant in sight. How could she leave a nice street like this, with the cherry trees and green lawns and pansies growing? There's only lino and we've got fitted carpets. And a fridge. And there's stairs. They'll need scrubbing. Wee Madeline scrubbing a stair – I can't see it. I don't understand it. It's like losing one of your own. You should never become attached to folk. They go and break your heart.'

But Archie said Madeline needed to find herself. And besides, the door was always open. She could come back. And what Mrs Turner needed was a cup of tea. He'd put the kettle on, and they'd get on with their lives.

Mrs Turner fished a hanky from up her sleeve. Dabbed her eyes. 'I've seen that one through everything. She was such a wee thing. All that black hair. And she was crying her eyes out. So I went to the door and I walked straight to her, even though I'd never crossed the threshold before. It was homing instinct. I have a way with babies. And I picked her up. "She just needs a wee cuddle," I said. Oh, she was lovely when she was little. A lovely wee thing. But that's what they go and do to you. They grow up.'

And Archie said, 'Well, let her.' And went to put the kettle on.

The Masterpiece

Madeline's flat had two rooms – a living room, with a tiny cubicle kitchen hidden behind a multicoloured beaded curtain, and a bedroom with a large wooden bed, a wardrobe, darkly varnished, and a draught that hummed and whistled under the door, through the gap at the top of the window that would not properly close. Off the hall there was a tiny toilet with a sink and no bath. Mrs Turner had noted that. But as she could remember her own bathless childhood when, on Sunday nights, an old tin tub was filled with boiling water in front of the fire, and they took it in turns to use it, didn't think that too much of a drawback. Madeline could wash at the sink. 'All over, like,' she advised. 'With a cloth.'

It was the dark outer hall and stairway that bothered her. 'You'll have to take your turn doing the stair,' she instructed Madeline.

'I'll do nothing of the sort,' said Madeline, shocked. 'I'm never cleaning a stair.'

'There'll be ructions if you don't,' said Mrs T.

'Let there be ructions, then,' said Madeline.

She stayed up all night painting her living room, listening to the radio. And discovered, as Ted had discovered the joys of Buddy Holly years before, Bob Dylan. The nasal whine, scraping harmonica, searing lyrics. She was hooked. Sang along. It was easy. Easy as speaking. '. . . like a rolling stone . . .' It gave her a natural sneer. Which suited her mood. She was too young to know she should allow herself to grieve. She rebelled against her wells of sadness. Sneered and snapped. Fell into silent rages.

Meantime, decorating her flat, she discovered skips. Raking in skips after dark. The art of the skip – where to find the best ones, when to visit them. Skip philosophy. The things people threw away became treasures. A small blue jug, a family photograph – taken sometime in the thirties, a large aproned woman standing at a doorway with half a dozen skinny children sitting at her feet. Madeline had no idea who they were, but took a shine to them. Put them on her mantelpiece. And gave them all names.

In the weeks following the wedding, Richard had tried many times to contact Madeline. He phoned her at work, but she refused to speak to him. He tried the Borthwicks. Got Lizzie, who told him she had no idea where Madeline lived. A lie, but she was reassessing the girl. Madeline, it appeared, was not the innocent she'd thought. She'd worried that Annie might be leading her astray. But now she was wondering if it was not the other way round.

Richard waited outside the shop in the evenings, hoping she'd come out. But she never did. She always spotted him and slipped out the back door. This man had lured her into pleasure when Ted was dying. And though she longed to, she wouldn't see him again. She didn't deserve to see him again. She knew what would happen. And she wanted none of it. She would never again lose herself to the joys of flesh on flesh. She'd be chaste. For Ted.

Years later, considering this, wondering what her life would have been like if she'd allowed it to take a different turn, follow another path, she thought herself foolish. And yet, looking back, Madeline often longed to be again the person she was in the months after Ted died. She would want to get back that clarity of thinking. The simplistic purity of her decisions. When Madeline was approaching eighteen there were no grey areas in her philosophy. There was right. And there was wrong. She would do this. She wouldn't do that. It seemed simple, then.

Unwilling, unable, to spend evenings alone with the memories of Ted, and the guilt she felt for not being with him when he finally slipped from the world, she started to work on a canvas. It was time to repay Lizzie's kindness of months ago. Madeline decided to put the wedding in oils. She did not realise that this was one event in Lizzie's life that she wanted to leave behind. She'd had such dreams for Annie, for her wedding. She'd always imagined a beautiful affair, adrift with blooms, gentle music, a smiling demure bride. The drunken rampage had almost broken her heart.

Madeline got hold of one of the photographs of the wedding party on the church steps. And started to work. She wanted this to be honest. She wanted it to say everything the swift cheesy smiles in the photograph hid. How everyone really felt. To do Ted's bidding – let go. This would be real. This would say it all. It never occurred to her that perhaps Annie's family didn't want the world to see how they felt. Feelings, Lizzie considered, were things you kept to yourself. She released her feelings at the kitchen sink, washing dishes, peeling potatoes, when she muttered under her breath. A habit she didn't know she had.

By the time Annie returned from her honeymoon, tanned and radiant, Madeline had her painting underway. The background was greys, watery. Pale blues, browns. The group on the steps was multicoloured, vibrant. Seething with thoughts, doubts, dismay. She cast huge shadows up the wall. Caught expressions. Annie looked eager, randy, aglow with mischief. Lizzie's lips were tight. She was rigid with shock. Douglas was scowling sideways at Willie, repressing the meance he longed to threaten him with. Hurt my daughter at your peril, sunshine. Annie's brothers were eyeing the bridemaids, who were stifling giggles. One stood legs crossed, pained with the need to pee. Her eyes glazed with drink. The rest of the group were exchanging, my-God-the-girl's-a-fool glances. Eyebrows raised. Madeline put herself alone, to one side, a splash of red. Her expression, grim and sullen. A lost little rebel who'd forgotten her cause. But it was Willie who glowed. He, more than the bride, looked triumphant, radiant. Willie was too happy to smile. He had a huge, gentle arm round his Annie and, oblivious of the camera and the hostile glares, was gazing at her. His face soppy with restrained tears.

It was while painting a small landscape Madeline discovered a little letting go. She'd been doing a patchwork of fields. And been mildly bored by the ordinariness of it. The lack of surprise. She'd painted a field purple. Then another dark blue. It looked interesting. She'd thought, this is fine. I can do this. I can do whatever I want. I am in control. And though she put her work aside and rarely looked at it, it was the beginnings of her freedom in oil. Letting go.

To the horror of Mrs Harkness, who lived below, Madeline worked through the night. And she was not quiet. She did not silently wrestle with thoughts, shapes, colours. She cried out. She stamped her foot. When, in the middle of some intricate shading, concentrating, some uninvited memory flashed through her mind, she exorcised it with a howl. 'Piss off.'

She chased off her guilt about Ted's death with noise. The radio hummed.

Nightly, Mrs Harkness would lie in bed. Curlers tight, pulling cruelly at her scalp. A pain she near as dammit enjoyed. She glared at the ceiling, cursing her new neighbour. 'This is a disgrace. Decent people need their sleep.'

When, six weeks after starting it, her canvas was finished, Madeline took it to the Borthwicks. This excited her. She imagined their joy at receiving it. They'd raise their arms in delight. She felt she'd caught the true spirit of the wedding. Captured the moments between the camera clicks. Small slices of actuality. She called it *Between the Shots*.

She wrapped it in a sheet, and treated herself to a taxi across town. Arrived at the Borthwicks' just after eight in the evening. They'd be finishing their evening meal. Annie and Willie would be there.

Annie had told Madeline she was nervous. 'Funny,' she said. 'It's home. I've been back since I married. To see Mum and Dad. But I've never been there with Willie. It's almost creepy. What will we talk about? I mean, we've been doing it. And they'll know.'

'I think they always knew,' said Madeline.

Annie needn't have worried. Lizzie welcomed her and Willie with open arms. Her married daughter complete with husband. Now they could be friends. They had mutual things to discuss. By the time Madeline arrived, Lizzie was mellow with preprandial sherry and several glasses of Valpolicella. She was in a good mood. The sight of the painting that was being lugged into the hall filled her with anticipation, joy. Things had worked out. Annie was safely wed. And now here was Madeline coming up trumps with the painting she had, so many months ago, helped finance. Life was sweet.

She wanted to rip open the sheet immediately. But Douglas said, 'No.' This was an occasion. They had to do this properly. They carried the canvas into the living room. Propped it centre room on a chair. And decided to have a proper unveiling ceremony.

They all trooped through, high on expectation. Douglas said they ought to open a bottle, 'Something a wee bit special.' With aplomb he opened the sideboard and brought out some vintage port. 'Been saving this. Over twenty years old.' Declaring that this stuff was the business, he opened it. Carefully easing out the cork. Pouring it gently. 'Got to keep the sediment at the bottom.'

When everyone had a glass, Douglas proposed a toast. 'To generations of Borthwicks and Melvilles. And to art.'

They drank. Lizzie, since it was her painting, unveiled the master-piece. Silence. A leaden loss of sound. The massed Borthwicks stared. Mouths open. Too shocked even to think of words to congratulate Madeline. However insincerely.

In what was one of the most horrifying moments in their lives, the Borthwicks saw themselves as others saw them. It wasn't a pleasant experience.

Lizzie, rigid, frosty, sherry-raddled. Douglas, grim, threatening – a tad overbearing. The Borthwick brothers, spoiled, moneyed, oozing lust for the bridesmaids. Annie, greedy, horny, filled with triumph at the consternation she was causing. Willie looked like the gentle, slightly drunken, love-soaked bear he was. He smiled. 'It's grand,' he said.

'It's called *Between the Shots*. I wanted to get the moment the camera missed,' Madeline explained. Nervously.

Willie drained his glass. 'That's just what it was like. You've caught the moment, Madeline. You're a genius.'

Madeline smiled weakly. The Borthwicks were still in shock.

Finally Lizzie sniffed. 'Well,' she said, smoothing her skirt. 'I think we could all do with some nibbles to go with this lovely port.' She turned, headed for the kitchen.

She hadn't reached the door when Douglas surfaced from his awe. He laughed. It started as a small giggle. Moved on to a chortle. And ended up hysterics. He had to sit down. He could hardly breathe. This hurt. Tears rolled down his cheeks. He held his sides. All the doubts he'd had about Annie and Willie were there. Released at last. His mirth was infectious. Annie's brothers, Annie and Willie joined in. They howled. Oh my God, that's exactly what it was like. Wasn't it awful? What a hoot.

Douglas reached over, took Madeline's hand. 'Oh, Madeline. You've got us all right. There we are, The Bewildered Borthwicks. Well done.'

This wasn't the reaction Madeline expected. She didn't know if she should join in the laughter, or cry. She felt like crying. This painting was everything to her. She'd given it all of her. Now, she was the bewildered one.

Annie put her arm round her. 'Don't mind us. We love it. We really do.' She turned to Lizzie, who was standing at the door, frozen. She'd forgotten about the nibbles. She weakly returned Annie's smile. She hated the painting. But her daughter was wonderful.

Half an hour before Madeline's arrival, Annie had announced that Lizzie was to be a grandmother. The wedding absurdity, the choice of husband forgiven. A baby was on the way. Annie was redeemed.

Madeline finished her drink and left. She felt crushed. For weeks after, she couldn't paint. But the humiliation passed. One evening she took out her sketchbook, and started on a new masterpiece.

Lizzie never spoke to her again. Next day she demanded the painting be removed from the house.

Douglas took it to work. Hung it in his surgery. For a while he looked at it often, smiling. It gave him pleasure. But in time he stopped. He forgot about it. It became part of his surroundings, too familiar to matter. The only attention it got was from the cleaner who dusted it twice a week. Over twenty years it was just there. A thing nobody bothered about. Till Hamilton Foster's hernia.

Douglas had retired. When he left his surgery, he did not take the painting with him. By now it was part of the internal landscape. So familiar nobody noticed it. During his examination, as Rodger

Franklin, Douglas's successor, probed the lump and surrounding area, Hamilton stared at Madeline's painting. He seemed hardly to register that he needed fairly urgent surgery; his eyes were fixed on the painting.

On being told the surgeon could fit him in the following Tuesday Hamilton said, 'It's an original. Very early. I never knew it existed.'

Rodger turned, looked at the painting. Said nothing.

'I've always suspected there were works out there nobody knew about. But this, what a find. It has its flaws. I'd go as far as suggesting it was before she went north. But it's there, that quirkiness, her honesty and, of course, as always, there she is, a tiny self-deprecating self-portrait. Her mark. It's primitive. Her early stuff was. But you can see the gift.' Without asking if he might, he walked behind Rodger's desk and stroked the work. 'How lucky you are.' He glanced round the room. 'If you don't mind my asking, what does your insurance company say about you having it here? So many people must come and go. Your patients.'

Rodger shrugged. 'Nothing. It isn't insured. It's been here for years. It was here before me. Is it worth something?'

He knew nothing about art. Didn't read reviews or watch anything vaguely arty on television.

'Good heavens, man!' Hamilton exclaimed. 'What you've got hanging there is an original Madeline Green. It's worth thousands. Thousands and thousands.'

Milky Days

Madeline withdrew from her world. She moved slowly. Said little. Her mind hollowed. She was lonely. The grief she'd denied herself in the weeks after Ted died welled up within her. And would not go away. At work, she stood staring from the window she was working on, watching people pass. Often she saw Ted, and thought to rush out after him. Then, she'd remember. Ted was dead. It couldn't be him. Once, in a flash of delight at seeing him, forgetting he'd gone, she'd banged on the glass, and waved. A stranger turned. Looked at her. Decided she was making a fool of him and walked on, shaking his head in disgust. Young people today.

Annie was caught up in her own life. A woman now, Mrs Melville, a ring on her finger. A baby growing inside her. The thrill of the new. She cleaned the flat. Bought flowers for the kitchen. Ordered a brass nameplate for the front door, William and Annie Melville. This thrill, this excitement lasted for two months after the honeymoon.

Thinking Willie a man of means, she had spent her entire pay packet on a velvet chaise longue for her new living room. Two days later she'd asked Willie for money so that she could go to the supermarket. He had none.

'But,' she said, 'you had money the other day.'

'Spent it.' He smiled.

'You had lots.'

'Spent it.' Bigger smile. Not a trace of contrition. He'd had money. He'd spent it. That's what you did with money.

In the month that followed, Annie learned that Willie was a squanderer. He squandered everything, cared for nothing – possessions, work – nothing, except Annie and, in time, his children.

Before they married, when Willie took Annie out, he always turned up with a gift for her. Perfume, flowers, a book of poems, a ring, a bracelet. If he took her out for a meal, he lavished her with wine, liqueurs. Spent every penny he had, then cadged food and beer from workmates and friends till he laid his hands on the next fistful of notes. Which he spent.

When she was seven months pregnant, Annie stopped working. Now she had no regular pay packet of her own, she reluctantly dipped into her savings. She also started to raid Willie's pockets every night when he came home. His money was always spread about his jacket and trousers in a series of somewhat grubby crumpled notes. He never noticed if some of it went missing. And if he had, it wouldn't have bothered him. 'So I lost fifty quid. Some lucky bugger out there's had a great find. Good luck to him. Or her.' Leaning towards Annie: 'You can only hope it's been picked up by some old lady who's a bit short. Or maybe some homeless kid. He can buy a pie and a pint tonight.'

Annie sighed. Shook her head. The fifty quid was in her purse. Where, she considered, it ought to be. She knew she would have to return to work as soon as possible. A baby on the way, she had responsibilities now. Besides, if disaster struck – and the way Willie carried on, she was sure one day it would – she had no intention of going home to Mum. She would have a secret safety fund.

Meantime, Madeline had slipped from her life. Annie noticed Madeline's withdrawal – she didn't phone, didn't drop by – but put it down to some sort of jealousy. She, of course, did not know of Ted's death. She thought Madeline's father died years ago. Madeline had told her so. She was too wrapped up in her marriage, her discovery of Willie the wastrel, and her pregnancy, to see Madeline's point of view. That she was embarrassed, humiliated. That the Borthwicks had been a tad tactless when Madeline's painting was revealed to them didn't cross her mind. After all, they'd said they liked it. Wasn't that enough? In fact, Annie had liked the painting so much she'd asked for it, since it was plain Lizzie didn't want it. Lizzie hated it. But Douglas refused. No, this was his. It was perfect. The real Borthwicks revealed. He would have it. Not ever having worked on something for weeks hoping it would give pleasure, Annie didn't know that the hysterical laughter which had greeted Madeline's painting could be demeaning. Madeline had felt shamed, cheapened, degraded. And couldn't bring herself to get in touch lest the laughter started up again. So, Annie misinterpreted the silence as jealousy. She couldn't quite define what sort of jealousy this might be, since Madeline made it obvious she didn't want a husband. Or children, Annie thought. 'Maybe, she secretly wants a husband,' Annie told her unborn child. Since there was nobody else in whom she could confide.

She certainly couldn't tell her mother about Willie's failings. That triumphant 'Told you so' would be too much to bear. And the good thing about conversing with someone who was yet to emerge into the world was that she or he didn't answer back. 'Hah,' she scoffed. 'If only Madeline knew. Marriage isn't what it's cut out to be. It's not romantic at all.' She snorted at this. 'Well, it doesn't seem to be for me.' She thought a bit more. 'Though it is for Willie.'

He was a dreamer, an idealist. Affectionate, almost overbearingly so. He'd return home from work, caked with mud and dried concrete, calling her name, spreading his arms when she came to him. He'd enfold her, hold her. Kiss the top of her head. 'My wife.' He was in love.

In love with Annie and his unborn child. Who was to be called Marcus if a boy, Sarah if not. The infant already possessed a rocking horse, a train set and a teddy bear. All carried triumphantly home by Willie. Nights, Willie would stroke Annie's swelling belly and weep with joy. His child.

It seemed to Annie that everyone for miles around knew Willie was to be a father. People she'd never seen in her life before, emerging from the lunchtime clamour in pubs, would ask after Marcus or Sarah, and wish her luck. Sometimes they would even press money into her hand and tell her to buy something lovely for the baby.

Annie would tell the little one inside that Willie was having a fabulous pregnancy – no nausea, no waddling about, no heartburn, no peeing every five minutes. It was fine for him. 'Marriage is great for Willie. It's being Mrs Willie that's the bummer. If only he wasn't so likeable.'

The thrill of being wed had faded. Now Annie considered herself a woman of the world who knew a thing or two about marriage, pregnancy, shaky finances and men you liked too much to leave. Willie was tender, affable, friendly. He exuded warmth. She was terribly fond of him. She wanted to mother him – and this surprised, and slightly upset her. She didn't think she was the mothering type. But she knew she didn't love him. Sitting alone at home, lonely, with her child shifting, kicking inside, she realised she knew nothing about love.

It was a boy. Marcus. Willie was ecstatic. He held his son, huge unashamed tears rolling down his cheeks. He thanked the doctor and nurses over and over. Annie, pale, tired, sweat-damped hair sticking to her scalp, pleaded for someone to bring her a cup of tea. Plainly Willie wasn't up to the task.

The child came home. Willie woke him to cuddle him, left him bawling with Annie. Willie complained about Annie's breast-feeding. He wanted to feed his son. And if not that, he wouldn't mind a wee suck himself. 'I mean,' he explained, 'I was breastfed myself. You can tell by my fine jaw. But I was too young to really enjoy it. I think I'd really appreciate it now.' Annie told him to fuck off.

Willie brought home a Victorian cot, a set of mobiles to hang over the cot, an antique replica of Pooh Bear, a tiny child's chair, a dark blue velvet outfit that could only be dry-cleaned. 'Dry-cleaning for a baby!' Annie wailed. 'You're insane.'

'My son,' said Willie, 'only gets the best.'

Willie appeared in the living room one evening with a complete set of Lego. The baby was eight weeks old. Annie could think of nothing to say.

'He'll need it when he gets up a bit,' said Willie. 'And I can work on it now. So I can help him when the time comes, when he grows into it.' So for a few evenings Willie did not go out to the pub – to wet the baby's head, like – he stayed in to play with his Lego. Annie watched. And sighed.

When the infant was ten weeks old, Willie suggested he might like a dog. And Annie hit him. It wasn't a hard blow. It wasn't even a carefully considered whack. It was a reaction. When Willie sulked, and near as dammit cried, Annie held his head to her breast. Gently massaged the reddening cheek. Saying, 'Sorry. But, Willie, dear, you go too far.'

Willie sniffed and said she smelled all milky.

Annie said she felt all milky. And as she did, it seeped into her brain, a slow spreading realisation, that she did not have one baby. She had two. And she better get her old job back as soon as was reasonable. Because they needed a responsible adult in this house. And it looked like it was going to have to be her.

When Marcus was crawling and, as she put it, just becoming interesting, she went to Mr Speirs, her old boss, and begged to get her job back. He took her on, but at a smaller salary, and a step down the pecking order. She was angered by this. But accepted, vowing to rise to her old status and beyond.

She started the next Monday. And now saw Madeline daily. They nodded. Smiled. Sometimes they met on the shop floor, or in the lift and exchanged small pleasantries.

'How're you? Enjoying married life?'

'Yes,' Annie said, 'And you? Still painting?'

Madeline nodded. 'Yep. Can't seem to stop. It's an affliction, I think.'

'Never that,' said Annie. 'You've got a gift.'

And Madeline thought: Then why did you all laugh? Remembering that laughter still stung.

After a couple of weeks of polite exchanges, Annie sat with Madeline in the canteen.

'I'm still the same old Annie. Why don't you come by for a chat one night. We could have a bite to eat. Talk about old times. I'll show you my baby, Marcus. He's lovely. Crawling all over the place. Into everything.'

Madeline smiled, said that would be nice. She'd do that. But made no firm date. Annie wanted to shake her, tell her to snap out of this doldrum. We're mates, she wanted to say. But didn't. Instead she said, 'Well, come anytime. I'm always at home these nights. Willie is always out.'

Madeline was jolted from her depression on a late spring evening. She was walking home. A rhythmic step. No thoughts of worth in her head. Just the blackness that had settled after Ted's death, and lingered on for a couple of years. She moved through the pavement crowds, staring ahead. Did not notice the thickening darkness. Or the dampening chill. The storm, when it hit her, was sudden. Sheeting rain crashed on to the concrete below her, smashed in ricocheting stinging drops off car roofs. Soaking her, and the scattering throng.

Madeline started to run. It did not cross her mind not to. Wet through already, she could not get any wetter. No matter, she ran. And when the sudden downpour stopped as abruptly as it had started, she still ran. Listening to her breath. Harsh with effort. Stinging the back of her throat. She flowed. Newly acquired red Kickers pounding the ground. And as she moved, the air chill against her pinking cheeks, a new elation warmed through her. For the first time in months she smiled. Really smiled. This was great. Running, getting thoroughly soaked.

She flew along new streets, turned corners. Stopped. And before she changed her mind, while her mood was still high, she headed for Annie's house. Stood breathless, gasping on her doorstep. Rang the bell.

When Annie opened the door Madeline wheezed, 'Hello. I was just passing. Thought I'd drop in. Like you said.'

Annie said, 'My God, you're soaked.' Hustled Madeline into her kitchen. Fetched a towel. Made her a cup of hot chocolate. And thought, dammit, here I am mothering someone else now. If it didn't give her a certain satisfactory glow inside, she was sure she would curse this mothering business to hell. Here was a quality (was it a quality?) she hadn't, until recently, known she had. She was examining this. Thinking about it.

They sat at Annie's kitchen table, smiling. They'd missed one another. Annie wanted to hear Madeline's news. What was going on in the world of pubs and clubs. And with all the crowd she no longer saw. Recently, alone in the flat at night, Willie at the pub, baby sleeping, nobody to talk to, she'd been hungering for those fleeting judgemental glimpses into other people's lives. She thought that

hearing about human absurdities committed by fellow beings trip-
ping, stumbling through life – as she was – always made her feel
better about herself. In what seemed now very distant, naughtier
times, the very juiciness of these absurdities had given her ideas.
Ooh, I never thought of doing that. Must give it a go. She stared into
her cup. All that was behind her now.

Now maturity and responsibility engulfed her. Things that amused
her a couple of years ago, before she was wed, amused her no longer.
Willie's farting, for instance. Willie took pride in his farting. He said
often that he could fart for Britain. And indeed expounded that such
an event ought to be included in the Olympics. 'It is the art of the
common man.' This was a five-pint opinion. Four and he wasn't
quite in the mood. Six and he was up for a demonstration. His eyes
would light up, a sudden shaft of glee would fleet across his face.
He'd raise one finger, calling for silence. Then he'd stand on one leg,
the other bent behind him, finger still raised, pointing at the heavens.
And fart. This, he called his classical fart. Assuming the Greek god
position, he would tell his audience. His preference, though, was for
the musical fart. When he would release, noisily, gases at key
moments during Rachmaninov's Second Piano Concerto. Not that
Rachmaninov was ever played in the pub. This was his dinner party
fart which Annie hated with a passion.

What was it about going through a ceremony, wearing a long
frock, that suddenly made this performance seem embarrassing, and
plain tiresome? Annie didn't know. But since getting married, it was.
'Willie!' she'd scold. 'Stop that.'

Willie would look huffed and hurt and tell her she should be
proud to have a man with such superb buttock control. But Annie
wasn't. Thing was, all the married women in their crowd agreed with
her. The unmarried thought it funny.

Now she leaned towards Madeline. 'Tell me everything,' she said.
'I want all the gossip. Who's sleeping with who. What's going on.'

And even though Madeline had been in a certain self-enforced
seclusion, she still knew enough about the old pub crowd to bend
her friend's ear. Come eight o'clock, when Willie appeared, they
were still sitting, still talking. Though they'd abandoned the hot

chocolate and moved on to wine. When Madeline left after ten, they arranged to meet again. She'd come round on Sunday. They'd walk with the baby. They'd chat.

'I need it,' Annie said. 'Babies are lovely, but they're a bit short on the conversation side of things. Weekends can be a bit lonely.'

It became their routine. Sundays. They'd walk. Chat. Confess. Pour out their doubts, fears, absurdities, embarrassing moments, drink and laugh. Mostly, they'd laugh.

'You should find someone and settle down,' Annie told Madeline.

'Why?' Madeline wanted to know.

'Because you just should. It would do you good.' It wasn't that Annie really wanted Madeline to settle down. She was of a mind that what she did everyone else should do. Not so they would be the same. She needed reassuring that she'd done the right thing. And if Madeline were to marry, have a child, somehow that would make her own present state more acceptable. 'You should find someone to love,' she said.

'I don't know about that,' said Madeline. 'Love's tricky. Do you love Willie?'

Annie poured another glass of wine. Drank. Thought about this. 'I suppose I do. It's different now. He's so lovable. But it's not wild and passionate like I thought it would be.'

Madeline nodded. 'See. Like I said. Love's tricky. You never know what it's going to do to you. Where you'll end up.' She put her glass to her cheek, sang a snatch of Billie Holiday. 'Fine and Mellow'. Sighed. 'I don't trust love.'

Annie said that was hardly surprising since Madeline hardly seemed to trust anything.

'It's the only way to be,' Madeline said thoughtfully. 'It's the way forward. Survival. You don't get hurt. No disappointments. No pain. You don't spend your nights with the duvet over your head, crying.'

'Pah,' said Annie. 'No joy. No leaping about, heart filled with wonder.' She leaned towards Madeline, pointing. 'One day it'll come to you – love, pain, heartache and wonder. And then you'll know the sweetness of tears under the duvet. Absolutely.' She leaned back, smug and sure of herself. It was wonderful to be wise.

Charlie Govan and Mr No-Topping

Madeline would, from time to time, take stock of her life. This was mostly a matter of lists. How Many Men have I Slept with? Which was a different list from How Many Lovers have I had? Sleeping with a man did not necessarily make him a lover. To qualify as a lover, Madeline thought, a man had to linger in her life, her bed, for longer than a month. A fortnight made him a boyfriend, of sorts. Some relationships seemed to splinter when you touched them. She could see someone for a couple of weeks and one day they'd talk a real talk beyond the exploratory things. And he'd say something, 'I don't think women should drink pints,' for example. And Madeline would think, what? Why ever not? What's it to you what anyone drinks? And she'd look at him and think, who are you? What are you thinking in there, in your head? That would be that. She'd stopped, looked at the relationship, touched it. And it had fallen apart.

That man – the man who didn't think women should drink pints – had become, in her memory, not one-night stand, boyfriend or lover. He'd been a ship that passed in the night. But he had a place in her list of people she'd slept with. Beside, by the time she was twenty-three, another fifteen men. Of these Charlie Govan was her favourite. If she'd written the list down, his name would be in italics – *Charlie Govan*. Or it would have an exclamation mark after it – Charlie Govan!

She'd met him in a café. One of the first in the city that had tables outside on the pavement, and that served alcohol as well as espresso, cappuccino and latte. Madeline always ordered latte. She thought it had mystique. Until she entered the Café Indigo she'd never heard of it. She'd started going there after work. The food was cheap and filling. The place was warm and noisy. Entering it, a woman alone, was easier that going into a pub. In time her face became familiar. She was on first-name terms with the staff. She got to know the other familiar faces. Wanda, Imogen, Paul, Justine, Ray and Charlie Govan. Charlie was the only one whose last name she knew. To Mrs Harkness's horror, they'd visit Madeline at strange hours, shouting as they climbed the stairs, bottles clanking in carrier bags. They'd sit in her flat smoking, expounding, playing music. Downstairs, Mrs Harkness would sweat and heave in fury. Decent folk needed a decent sleep. That girl was a menace and a pain and a hussy, and her stairs were filthy.

All of Madeline's new friends, like Madeline, said they did something other than how they were earning a living. They were painters, writers, actors who waited tables, delivered post, served in shops. Charlie, to Madeline's delight, delivered pizzas.

Four nights a week, he drove around town in a vividly red van, 'Pete's Pizzas' emblazoned on the side. Madeline went with him. This was heaven. Hurtling through darkened streets, cocooned in warmth, enveloped in the deep aromas of fresh baked yeasty dough, and garlic. The new love of her life at her side. Madeline thought this so wonderful, she wished she'd thought to become a pizza person rather than a window dresser. It took Annie several hours and a bottle of Chianti to persuade her not to change career.

Charlie taught Madeline a lot. An actor who'd had small parts in several soaps and television series, he found delivering pizzas the perfect job. It left him free in the afternoon to go to auditions. For Madeline, her relationship with Charlie was bliss: it was about sex and food. There were free pizzas, and Charlie was always willing. He was Madeline's first real lover. He showed her that sex needn't be urgent. There was more to it than instant gratification. 'We've got all night, girl.' And what they did in her little flat with the fraying curtains drawn and the door locked was nobody's business but their own.

'You've got a constant little smirk on your face these days,' Annie said. 'What've you been up to?'

'Not telling,' said Madeline. 'But it was fun.'

She loved Charlie. Everything about him. The way he dressed. The way he walked, smelled, spoke. She sighed for him when they were not together. Doodled his name on her sketch pad. *Charlie Govan. Charlie and Madeline. Madeline Govan.* She told Ted about him when she visited his grave on Saturday afternoons. 'I've got a boyfriend.' She felt smug about that. Walked through the streets smugly hugging this knowledge. I've got a boyfriend. I've got a boyfriend.

She loved delivering pizzas. More than the drive about the city at night, she loved the small peeks at other people's lives. A door would open and Madeline would see a hallway, and imagine a lifestyle. There were tips, which Charlie sometimes shared. And sometimes squandered on gifts for Madeline – books, perfume, flowers and, more importantly, to her at least, food. He'd bring goodies – pastries, salami, cheese, takeaway meals. Oh yes, Madeline loved Charlie. And always, when out on their deliveries, they'd stop in a quiet backstreet and turn to each other. Passion on the front seats, with the gear stick jamming hard into her backside, and Otis Redding on the tape deck.

It was through Charlie that Madeline met Hamilton Foster. A bitter night, Madeline was wearing her railway coat. A large, far too large for Madeline – when she wore it, it trailed along the pavement – thick nap affair. Leather trim round the cuffs, and thick tweed herringbone lining. Its big, black buttons were embossed with the official British Rail logo. She'd found it in a junk shop, and paid £5 for it. Years ago, in its glory days it had been an official British Rail coat, designed to keep out the foul chill that swept along winter railway platforms.

Wearing it, Madeline felt snug, buttoned into her own little microclimate, whilst the world beyond the nap and herringbone lining froze. She didn't care how she looked in it, warmth was everything. But she gave it a bit of class by sticking a black silk rose in the lapel buttonhole.

Charlie had two deliveries in Great King Street. He took one, Madeline the other. It was for Hamilton Foster, a regular customer who always ordered his pizzas without topping. Charlie and

Madeline were snobbish about pizza toppings. They considered those who ordered olives and anchovies to be a better class of pizza-eater than those who ordered gammon and pineapple. The mushroom orderers came somewhere about the middle, slightly below the clam and bacon. They both had to admit, though, that despite being the lowest of the low pizza-wise, the pineapples tended to tip better than the olives. Hamilton Foster was in a pizza class of his own. Soaring high above the rest, he liked to add his own topping – anchovies and buffalo mozzarella from Valvona and Crolla. His tips varied according to how much change he had. And, since he was principally a plastic man, not given to dealing in actual money, this was never much. Madeline was keen to see this exotic A-list pizza-eater who had become a legend in the gossipy, greasy and garlicky underworld of takeaway delivery.

'Pizza for Mr Foster,' she said when he opened the door. A sliver of light, and beyond – something sumptuous. The hallway of hallways. Dark ochre walls, black woodwork. A palm in a huge Chinese vase. She ducked from side to side, peering round him, forgetting to hand over the flat, greasy box that was heating her palm. He reached over, took it, a small waft of cologne.

He smelled expensive. He walked, with the pizza box, down the hall, barefoot, back straight, telling her to hold on, be back in a sec. He was wearing jeans and a crew-neck sweater, sleeves shoved up. Madeline hovered, but only briefly. It was not envy that drew her into the flat; she had no desire to see how the other half lived. It was curiosity. When the door was opened wide, the full view was revealed. One wall of the long passage that led to the interior was hung, top to bottom, the full fifteen feet length, with pictures. Madeline stood back, surveying them. There were prints, photographs and paintings, all sizes, all in black frames. A lot to take in. Madeline strolled along perusing, leaning forward, peering. She did not hear Hamilton return. She was, by the time he re-entered the hallway, crouched down in the corner furthest from the front room, staring in amazement at a small painting.

'You like that?' Hamilton asked.

'I did it,' she said. 'Me. It's one of mine.'

It was from what she thought of as her food period. When she'd moved into her flat and had lived on Pot Noodles. Since she couldn't cook, she'd put a lot of food on canvas. This was a plate of stew, scattered with parsley. It was on a table with a white cloth, against a blue background. Alone on the plate, with the stew, was a single Brussels sprout.

'I always liked that sprout,' she said, bending close to it, appreciating it. As if she hadn't been the one that actually created it. 'Took ages. Deep olive at the bottom, then lighter green, then at the top left some white tempera, just a touch. To give it that glisten. It's a bloody good sprout, that.'

He leaned down. Looked at it. 'Yes, pretty damn good sprout. In fact, as sprouts go, it's a fantastic sprout.'

Madeline looked at him, frowned. 'Are you taking the piss? How did you get this picture, anyway?'

'A woman brought it to me at my gallery. And, no, I'm not taking the piss. It's a lovely sprout, good enough to eat, and as I hate the things that's saying a lot.'

'What woman?' Madeline was keen to know. She'd given this painting to one of Annie's brothers. He, like Annie, had been keen to own the wedding painting. But Douglas had refused. So he'd phoned Madeline at work and asked if she had anything else.

It had been the beginning of her food period. Which had been followed by her quirky period. This had been last year. She had been attending art classes at night school for the past three years. Last year the end-of-term show had been reviewed She'd got a small mention in *Scotland on Sunday* (they'd called her work quirky), and sold several paintings.

The stew finished, she done a beetroot sandwich. This was hard. Her passion for them was done, spent. And she could not recapture their joy. That moment when, years ago, she'd be sitting at the yellow Formica table in the Turners' kitchen, legs encased in their sensible grey socks, swinging because they did not reach the floor, and a beetroot sandwich on a pink plate, garnished on the side with a smattering of cheese and onion crisps, would be placed in front of her. She'd lift it to her mouth, two hands, for it was a cumbersome thing, the Turner beetroot sandwich. Eyes shut, she'd bite dead centre, though Mrs T told her often the ladylike thing was to start at the side. But she'd be too hungry for manners. Back then a sandwich like this was a joy, a wonderful thing. It hit the spot. It never would again, not now. Madeline had left them behind with other childhood things – her skipping rope, sherbet, tinned spaghetti. They now tasted dreadful. Sad that. She'd paid tribute to the delicacy by immortalising it on canvas. She'd painted the anticipation of a Mrs Turner special. The lady herself, huge, busty, coating the marge on to a slice of white bread – the loaf prepacked, open on the kitchen unit beside her along with the packet of Stork and the jar of beetroot. Sun dappling in. The hydrangea in bloom in the garden beyond. Madeline sitting at the table, glass of milk in front of her, looking across, waiting. She was all hair, dimples, freckles and smiles. The kitchen, apart from the small flurry of activity of sandwich-making, was immaculate. Anyone looking at it would know that all the food prepared here was routine. Nothing fancy, just quick no-fuss nutrition.

Other paintings in her food period included the Borthwicks eating a takeaway round the television. Silently eating and watching in unison. A bottle of wine on the coffee table beside the wrappings that Lizzie looked anxious to tidy up. Madeline's favourite was her painting of Ted's moussaka. Ted in large striped apron, sipping from a glass of red, standing by the open oven, a tea towel in the hand that wasn't holding his glass. He was smiling in appreciation of the treat he was about to deliver. One of his ladies was sitting on the table, legs crossed. Next to the salad. She was smoking, drinking, showing a lot of thigh. Her hair hung across her face. She wasn't looking at Ted, she was eyeing him. Lascivious. She was plainly not here for the food. The kitchen was in turmoil, though there was verve, joy to the mess of peelings and dirty dishes. The excesses of the amateur cook. The moussaka, in a brown earthenware dish, was golden, tempting. Yet not really part of what was going on. It had a bit part in the kitchen scene. Madeline was looking round the door, un-observed and observing.

There was a painting of a waiter flambéing crêpes in a restaurant. A great whoosh of flames, awed diners and a small audience on the street watching through the window in the rain. Madeline was in the gathering without. Looking hungry.

Madeline had given Annie's brother the stew painting. She'd gone off it. It reminded her of the Borthwicks, of that first night at their table when she'd put her head down and eaten, silently stuffing herself whilst the family watching in a mix of horror and fascination. And just after their ribald reception of her depiction of Annie's wedding, she'd gone off the Borthwicks, too.

Standing in Hamilton Foster's hallway, Madeline guessed how he'd got the painting. Lizzie. She probably hadn't wanted it in the house and had brought it to Hamilton to see if it was worth anything. In fact, Lizzie had thought the painting an insult. A statement in oils about her cooking. 'A plate of stew,' she'd scoffed. 'Who'd paint such a thing? With a sprout?'

'Stew,' Madeline said. 'Not bad. I wouldn't do that now. I went through a food thing. Mostly food in preparation and the mood around it. The Dutch went in for that. You'd think it'd be the French. How much did you pay for it?'

'Hundred and fifty, I think.' He shrugged, apologising for his cheapness. He usually forked out a lot more, especially for the work he hung on his own wall.

But Madeline was delighted. 'That much.'

He mistook her glee for sarcasm. And apologised, telling her he'd paid more than that for the other one, leading her out of the hall and into the living room. Here, not dominating the room, but certainly with more prominence than the plate of stew, was one of her nudes.

'Oh, one of my quirkies,' she said.

It was from her night class. A nude. But she'd tired of doing the required pose and had sketched the model during his break when he, a man past fifty and plump, was standing, completely comfortable with his nudity in the midst of forty students, smoking a small cigar, staring out of the window, slowly scratching his sagging, hairy paunch. Later, at home, she'd turned that sketch into a painting. It amused her.

'Quirky,' said Hamilton. 'But I like it. It tickles me every time I look at it.'

105

'Yeah,' said Madeline. 'I liked him. Most models put something on when we've done drawing them. But he used to wander about like that. Quite the thing. With his little willy dangling there. And nobody thought anything about it.' Somewhere in the middle of saying this, Madeline got embarrassed. She thought she was sounding quirky.

He noticed, offered her a cup of coffee. Which she accepted.

His kitchen, and Madeline was interested in kitchens, was a wonder. White. Walls, units, worktops and floor. The worktops lit blue from beneath the upper units and on them was a stainless-steel juice extractor and a Pavoni espresso machine, and the Pete's pizza box. It seemed offensive. Hamilton made her an espresso in a tiny dark red cup, slowly lowering the handle of the machine. He hadn't asked if she wanted sugar. He thought he didn't need to, and heaped in two spoonfuls of tiny brown crystals. Madeline downed it in one, then unashamedly dipped her finger into the cup, retrieving the sweetness at the bottom.

'The best bit,' she said. She wanted another cup, but thought that would be pushing her luck. So she said she'd better go, someone was waiting for her.

'Is this what you do?' Hamilton asked. 'Deliver pizzas?'

'Just helping a friend,' she said. 'I'm a window dresser.'

'But you paint?'

'Yes. That's what I do. I dress windows to make a living.'

He handed her his card. A gallery in Dundas Street. Told her to bring him some stuff to look at. He was around most of the time.

She returned triumphantly to Charlie, who'd been waiting for over an hour in the van.

'Where the hell have you been? I was just coming to look for you.'

'I've been chatting up Mr No-Topping. He's got a gallery. He wants me to take some of my work round to him.' Madeline said. She overflowed joy. 'Isn't it great? Fantastic.'

'Maybe,' said Charlie. 'But we won't have time for a snog.'

No time now to park somewhere dark, and snuggle up. And more. The pleasure of getting the van steamy when the world was chilly and raw. What, he thought, was the point of bringing her along if they couldn't sneak half an hour to do that? Bloody Mr No-Topping.

'Sorry,' said Madeline. 'I got caught up.'

'Oi know that,' he said.

'You sound Irish.'

He said he was working on his Irish accent. It wasn't as easy as he'd originally thought. He had to get it right.

Not wanting to appear overeager, Madeline waited a fortnight before taking her portfolio to Hamilton Foster. She took paintings from her food period, some she'd done at her art class and a few of Mrs Harkness downstairs. He took Ted cooking moussaka, the beetroot sandwich and one of Mrs Harkness scrubbing the stairs, viewed from behind – red elbows sticking out, bony bum, fading dark red walls and highlighted cleaning stuff by her side. His deal was she'd cover the framing costs and he'd take a hefty percentage of any sales.

'That's not very nice,' said Madeline. 'I do all the work and you get a whack of the money.'

'It's business. It costs to run a gallery. You get my name. And you sell, which you are not doing now.'

She grumblingly agreed with this but added it still wasn't very nice. It didn't take long, however, before he sold all three. This filled Madeline with glee, and broke her heart.

'They were mine. Who bought them? What are they like? What sort of rooms do they have?'

'Madeline, take the money and forget the paintings,' said Hamilton.

'You don't understand. That moussaka one. That was Ted. Do you think the people who bought it will understand? Will they appreciate that it's Ted? He was lovely.'

'Move on,' Hamilton told her. 'Work.'

Madeline took her cheque. But didn't work. That evening, Charlie took her in his arms, kissed her and told her he too had good news. He'd landed a part in a film as an Irish immigrant in New York. Shooting would start next week.

'I've got lines,' he said. 'In a movie. It's incredible. "Over here, Mick." And, "It isn't tea I'm after." ' The Irish accent.

Madeline swooned joy. This was amazing. 'Success for us both. At the same time. Oooh, New York.'

'I know,' he agreed. 'New York. Like, wow.'

She had a full two minutes imagining herself in New York. They'd find a place. Probably not Manhattan. But she could work anywhere. No matter how small. The things they could do. 'New York,' she said.

'I'm staying with a mate,' he said. 'But I'll probably find a place over there when I get a work permit.'

I, he said *I*. In the headiness of the moment, she'd presumed it would be *we*. Looking back over their brief conversation, she wondered how she could have got that impression. He never even hinted at asking her to come along.

'It was never an issue,' Madeline cried on Annie's shoulder. The triumph of her sales forgotten. 'I loved him.' And she loved him more now that she couldn't have him. 'It's not fair.'

'Why is it not fair?' said Annie, opening a bottle of Chablis. She'd looked at her wine rack, weighed up the situation. A drink both to celebrate the cheque in Madeline's pocket, and to offer sympathy for being abandoned. Chablis, she thought. Though there was no reason for this, other than that she quite liked the word. 'If you'd been invited to New York would you have asked him to go with you?'

She shrugged. Wasn't prepared to answer this. 'I'll miss delivering pizzas,' was all she could say. 'That was lovely.' The loss of Charlie and the nights in the pizza van clouded her sense of success. She never did realise what a coup it was to sell three paintings in a short time. And Hamilton Foster, thinking she must surely know how successful she'd been, never mentioned it.

'He maybe thought it was the right time to part,' said Annie. 'Maybe he sensed you were both on the verge of new things. Maybe he felt things weren't settled enough in New York for him to invite you along. I don't know.'

But she did know. Madeline never quite gave herself to people. She hung back. Then again, nobody she met was ever quite as good as Ted. Madeline adored him. He was, she assured Annie, perfect. Annie doubted this. Nobody was perfect. She figured if he hadn't died when Madeline was so young, Madeline would have grown to see his flaws. Maybe she'd also have learned that relationships were two-way things. Furthermore, her relationships, apart from the one with Annie, were all based on the same thing. The secret, unspoken condition – since all Madeline's friends did something other than how they earned a living – that they cared more about what they did than about each other.

Sometimes Madeline would sit dreaming, planning, painting in her head for hours and forget to speak to whoever she was with. She'd turn up for dates hours late. Then be surprised, insulted, when the man she was to have met had left. She never left when a date kept her waiting. But that was only because she could happily stand on a street corner or sit in a bar for hours, staring, looking at the people around her. In fact, she often got so engrossed in this she'd be startled when the date arrived and jolted her from her reverie.

'The trouble with Madeline,' Annie told Willie, 'is that she gives the impression she doesn't need anyone. She's self-contained. I mean, sometimes I think they could drop the nuclear bomb and she wouldn't notice. She'd come out in the morning and say, "Where is every-body?"'

Willie had pulled her down on to the sofa beside him. Kissed her. Wetly. 'Can't say that about us, eh? We need each other. Fancy nipping through to the bedroom before Marcus wakes?'

Madeline sighed. Wiped a tear with her sleeve. Then since it was in the vicinity, used it on her nose at the same time. 'Now I'll love him for ages. That's always the way when you get dumped. You slag him off whilst secretly loving him.'

'I know,' said Annie, pouring Madeline more wine. But not refilling her own glass. She was two months pregnant.

'No you don't,' said Madeline. 'When did you last get dumped?'

'It's been a while.'

'I'm giving up sex,' said Madeline. 'That's it. I'll be celibate and work. I'll produce work of purity and beauty.'

Annie nodded. 'You do that.' She was always sorry when Madeline vowed celibacy (so far she'd done it three times). Annie lived a secret wanton life through Madeline, for Madeline was doing all the things she'd planned to do but missed because she'd married Willie.

'Didn't you get dumped in the years before Willie?'

Annie shook her head. 'Not really. A couple of teenage crushes. But I got over them. There's only been Willie.'

'What do you mean, only Willie? Have you only . . .?'

Annie nodded. 'Yes. Only Willie. I haven't slept with anyone else.'

'Not ever?'

'Not ever.'

'Goodness,' said Madeline. Quite shocked. Wasn't it strange how things turned out. A few years ago Annie had been her mentor and her idol. She'd wanted to be like Annie. Or at least how she'd imagined Annie to be. Now Annie was the quiet one, working hard, looking after her family. And she, Madeline, was the one who had lovers. Who drank too much, too often. Who stayed up late talking to friends from her art class and the Café Indigo. 'I never guessed,' she said. 'I always thought you were a bit of a goer.'

'Who says I'm not?' said Annie. 'Even if it is only with one person.'

Madeline looked contrite. 'Sorry.' Then: 'Bugger Charlie Govan.'

For eighteen months Madeline forsook love and sex. And cursed Charlie Govan. After that, she forsook only love. She had a series of one-night stands and one or two boyfriends. But no lovers, as she defined them, men who lasted for more than a month. All that was behind her. She took her paintings to Hamilton Foster, sold quite a few. But never enough to give up the day job. She still dressed windows.

Annie, meantime, produced another son. Took three months' maternity leave. And, not long after her return to work, was promoted to head buyer. Four years after that, she gave birth to Flo. On her return to work she applied for the job as undermanager of the store and was passed over. 'Bugger them all,' she said to Madeline. 'I'll skip that and make manager when Speirs retires. See if I don't.'

Madeline, holding baby Flo in her arms, gingerly, because she wasn't sure of babies, said, 'By that time I'll have made it as an artist. You'll have to phone me to tell me. I won't be dressing windows any more.'

Love

By the time Stuart McKinnon met her, Madeline was already well known. Not exactly famous, more heard of in certain circles. She was still attached to Hamilton Foster's gallery in Dundas Street. She sold (with some reluctance, for she hated parting with her work) five or six canvases a year. Not enough to live on. Well, not for the prices she got. She still dressed windows.

Her paintings were still considered quirky. This annoyed her. Some people even said sweet. This infuriated her. 'Sweet. How dare they say I'm sweet? If anyone says that again I'll nut them.' She couldn't imagine what people meant. As far as she was concerned she put down on paper or canvas what she thought, what she saw. It didn't seem quirky to her. It seemed normal. She'd stamp along the street thinking about this. Quirky. Quirky. What the hell do they mean by that? She tried. Tried with every fibre of her to paint what she felt to be true, and it always came out the same. Quirky. She'd stop and, oblivious of who was about to hear her, she'd shout, 'I am not quirky.' She was oblivious, also, of the quirkiness of this.

They met, Stuart and Madeline, at one of Willie Melville's parties. It was a lurid affair; Willie's parties always were. Lit by enough candles to make the fire department nervous. Awash with vodka and red wine. Noisy, you could hear the bass thump three streets away. Willie only had parties when he was broke and boozeless. He knew that in the post-party debris there was always a lot of alcohol. You always ended a party with more wine, beer, vodka and whisky than you started it with.

Stuart came with Abbot, who wasn't quite a mate but was more than an acquaintance. Stuart had no real friends, until Madeline. He liked Abbot because of his amazing capacity for trivia. Abbot could talk for hours about a line in a song, a man he'd been stuck behind in a traffic jam, the superiority of one lager over another, who had been the most charismatic member of the A-Team. 'I'm a Murdock man, myself. Who did you like?' Stuart shrugged. He'd had a lonely childhood, no proper access to television. He knew nothing of *The A-Team*. But promised himself he'd find out.

Abbot, John Abbot, but always called by his last name, was quite small, dark curly hair and thick Buddy Holly specs. He'd been the school heartthrob. But since leaving and going to university, his sex appeal had waned. Women thought him cuddly. Which wasn't the image he was after.

'I've peaked,' he complained to Stuart. 'I've fucking peaked. What sort of effing life is it when you fucking peak at fucking sixteen?'

Stuart shrugged again. He had no idea. But thought it would be nice to peak sometime. Preferably when he was old enough to appreciate it. Or at least recognise it when it happened.

'I had my first shag at fourteen,' Abbot told Stuart. 'When did you first do it?'

'Hmm,' said Stuart, working out what would be an acceptable age to confess to Abbot. 'Eighteen,' he said.

Abbot nodded. 'Good age. Not too old as to appear a bit backward. Which could be embarrassing. Not too young as to appear forward. I like it.'

Stuart smiled, relieved. Actually it had been twenty-one, with a woman he hadn't known very well, or liked very much. It had been fine for him. But, he knew now, it hadn't been fine for her. He cringed at the thought. And cringed at what Abbot might say if he knew the truth. But there it was. He never was much good with women. All the flirting. The small talk. The eye contact. On dates he worried about whether he should kiss the woman he was with or not. And when. And then there was bed. And if he slept with her and didn't want to see her again? Was he using her? And after sex, should he go home? He usually wanted to; he preferred to sleep in his own bed. And if she was in his bed, he wished he could ask her to go, but never liked to say. He liked his bed to himself, when the pleasuring was over and slumbers began. He shouldn't, he decided, read so many women's magazines. But the girls at work bought them, and he never could resist having a peek. They only upset him. He had come to the party only because he knew Madeline was going. He didn't like parties. And said he didn't like people. This wasn't wholly true. He found it hard to communicate. He was a loner.

He moved through the crowd, clutching a bottle of Burgundy in one hand. A bottle of Smirnoff in the other. It was fancy dress. But Stuart had welshed on that. When someone asked him what he was dressed up as, he smiled and told them he was thinly disguised as an ordinary person. People were drunk enough to think that very clever. But these were clever people. One woman was tricked out as a crab, complete with dark red shell. Another had come dressed in a fishing net, and not much fishing net at that.

As he shoved towards the table, which was heaving with drink, Stuart heard snatches of conversations. Two men comparing the cost of their jumpers. A woman discussing a Russian film that nobody had seen, which left her free to rant. Creatively, she drunkenly thought. A woman dressed in black grabbed his arm and said she *just loved Sartre* and was deeply into minimalism. Stuart nodded, and said so was he. Another woman, with glossy red nails, dyed, immaculately groomed hair, was talking about the enlightenment she'd experienced in Thailand. He glanced into the kitchen and saw a woman sitting above the throng, peeing in the sink. He thought she'd wake in five years' time, sit bolt upright, remember this. And die with embarrassment.

But there, at last, was Madeline. He'd seen her around for months. Desperately wanted to get to know her. He knew all about her. Her work. Where she lived. He had thrown coins into the up-turned velvet hat she kept by her when she did her pavement art at the foot of The Mound.

They had someone in common – Willie Melville. Stuart gleaned information about Madeline whenever, wherever he could. Annie, Madeline's best friend, was Willie's wife. Though Annie wasn't at the party. She was in Milan, buying the new season's clothes for the store. Marcus, Douglas and Flo were with their grandmother.

Annie adored her job, and the money it brought in. Barely took time off. At home, she said that she hated leaving her children. But, secretly, she rather enjoyed the moment she walked out of the door, and left all the feeding, changing and sorting out of tantrums to Willie.

All this suited Willie nicely. He took over the home. He said the conversation of a two-year-old was just about his standard. And the mess was appealing. He said it had a juvenile charm. As Annie was now earning, he didn't have to. Which was fortunate – his building business ended in ruin. He'd taken up antiques. He bought and sold. Things, dressers, tables, armoires appeared in his flat. Stayed for a week or two, then disappeared.

Willie passed his days playing with his children, dropping the boys off at school, picking them up again at half-past three, taking them to child-friendly pubs to do business that was constantly interrupted by him saying, 'Don't do that.' Or, 'Leave that alone.' Or, 'I'll take you to the loo in a minute.' He drank. He smoked a little dope. He wandered the streets saying hello to the many people he knew. He was a happy man. Though he worried about what he'd do when his children finally left home and his days would be his own again, and he would have to account for himself in a mature and grown-up fashion. But, he comforted himself, that was a long time away.

The party hummed and seethed. Stuart put his booze on the table at the end of the room. Madeline was there, talking to a couple of women about her life, and plans for the future.

'I think,' one woman was saying, 'that ambition is sexy. I love it. I just can't relate to people who aren't ambitious.'

Stuart winced. He had no burning desire to do anything. It wasn't that success wasn't on his agenda. He was just putting it off. He'd get round to it – one day.

The other woman asked Madeline if she was ambitious.

Madeline nodded. 'Oh, yes. Of course, I am. But as my ambition has developed, it's not a matter of the indefinite article any more. It's a definite thing now. I no longer want to be a successful artist. I just want to do good work. *The* good work. Something that I'll look at and say, "I did that. Me." And I'll be proud of it. In here.' She rapped the area somewhere between her chest and stomach. 'With all of me.'

The two women nodded heartily. Drinking this in. Madeline moved off.

Stuart poured himself a drink and stood to one side, feeling a little spare.

'My ambition has matured,' he heard one of the two women who'd been talking to Madeline say to a new woman. 'It's not a matter of the indefinite article . . .'

In time he would find this often happened with Madeline. People took her words, passed them off as their own. Madeline overheard the little bit of party plagiarising, turned and shrugged.

She started talking heatedly to Willie Melville. He had, over an extremely boozy lunch, and in a moment of angst about where his life was going, persuaded a small, independent publisher to commission him to write a book. *A Hundred Things to Do with Whisky*. It was part of a series of pocket-size books – *A Hundred Places to Go on a Rainy Day*, *A Hundred Birthday Cakes*, *A Hundred Ways to Say Hello*. But now he was regretting the whole thing. The publisher was pressing for delivery of his typescript. And Willie had got, with difficulty, because the only thing he knew to do with whisky was drink it, to twenty-three, and stuck. Madeline was saying, 'I know what you can do with whisky. Whisky art.' And she stuck her finger into Willie's glass, drew on the mirror with it. Making patterns. Willie said, 'Wow.' And joined her. 'Whisky art. I'll put that in. Twenty-four.'

In those days, at that party, Madeline had been a different creature. It was 1986. She was thirty. Small. Rounder. Not fat. Just a gentle plumpness. Her hair was long, a tumbling mass of dark uncontrollable curls. In fact, from where Stuart stood looking at her, there seemed to be more hair than person. Her lips were full. She looked sulky. Her face, when she wasn't doing anything in particular with it, smiling, frowning – both of which she did a lot – fell into a natural pout. He didn't know why, but it made him smile. Always did.

He was the same age as Madeline, thirty. Two years ago he had finished university. After years of moving from course to course, he'd finally settled on film and media studies. He had vague notions of becoming a director, though knew he'd never do it. But it was a good notion, and he was a man of many notions. For the moment, he had a pleasantly undemanding job in the marketing department of an international bank.

He was relatively well off, rich enough, anyway, to pursue his many notions without ever having to fulfil any of them. Though in the company of impoverished students he'd kept this to himself, and pretended to be impoverished himself. His student life started when he was eighteen. And for a while he had thought of himself as a professional learner. He liked this notion a lot.

He'd started with theology, hated it, moved on through English and philosophy before switching to art college. Two years doing graphics and design (badly) before taking up media studies and film. This he liked. And was thinking he'd, at last, found something he'd stick with. Later, during Madeline's many absences he'd take to making pots. Shaping things, touching them gave him a pleasure he'd never known before. And he found, to his surprise, something he could do. Was even good at.

His father died two years before he met Madeline, leaving him a largish house on the west coast of Scotland. It was set on a cliff near a village called Gideon in Argyll, looked as if it might at any moment plunge into the sea. Marglass House, vast, draughty, not so much imposing as forbidding. A grey Victorian multiturreted Gothic nonsense of a building that seemed on the outside to have more rooms than it actually did inside. It was a building of many long corridors. Draughts that swept along them gathered speed, turned into small interior gales. Stuart grew up knowing cold. He never could acclimatise himself to heat.

'Someone actually designed that?' Madeline asked when she first saw it. 'Someone actually drew it on sheets of paper? Then someone else paid for it to be built? They brought stones and bricks and slates all the way up that windy drive, miles and miles, to put this together?'

He nodded. He'd never thought of it like that. It was Marglass House. His home. But now she'd mentioned it, it did seem absurd.

'Who?' Madeline demanded to know.

He shrugged. Hadn't any idea who designed the house. Hadn't before this moment thought to wonder. He supposed the architect had seen what he'd done and disappeared for ever, not wanting anyone to know. A monstrosity like Marglass House could ruin careers.

He never wholly liked the place. Didn't dislike it. It was there. It was his. He couldn't bring himself to sell it. His father wouldn't have approved. He may have been dead, but he wasn't gone. Stuart could feel his presence every time he went home. Silent, looming. Disapproval, though it came from the grave, was too much for an affable person like Stuart to bear.

Stuart's father had been tall, lean, a precise dismissive man who thought his son a good-for-nothing, and said so often. He was ex-army, and a Lothario of great renown. He liked blondes, small and thin. And seemed to have no trouble finding them. He kept them in Edinburgh. Far from his wife, Maria. Though she knew about them anyway.

She never complained about her husband's extramarital activities. They kept him at a distance, freeing her for her tapestry, which she sewed slowly, lovingly, in the cavernous sitting room of Marglass House, a pleasant room at the time. A selection of sofas, several huge plants, a log fire burning constantly in a hearth that stretched the length of the far wall.

The room was divided into sections where Maria followed her various pursuits. One twenty-foot bit where she kept her writing desk. Another by the fire where she read, magazines mostly, *Vogue*, *Tatler*. And where she did *The Times* crossword in the evenings, because the paper wasn't delivered till four in the afternoon. By the window was the area where she embroidered. The windows were all huge and looked out on to what ought to have been rolling lawns, but were a stretch of unkempt greenery, overrun with dandelions and daisies. Swarming with rabbits. Very happy rabbits. Stuart never thought to have it mowed and weeded. He liked it that way.

Later, by the time Stuart and Madeline moved in, the room had changed. The sofas were bursting, spewing horsehair on to the faded rugs. They had been joined by a couple of deck chairs, jolly striped affairs, green and red. Their bikes, both black, upright, and extremely elderly, they kept propped against the far wall.

The rest of the house was, when Madeline first saw it, mainly empty rooms. A huge dining hall, complete with huge mahogany table, once magnificently polished, now dulled, neglected. A library with several thousand books. Bedrooms, some still with beds. The kitchen was huge. Its cast-iron range still intact, but never used. All the food was prepared on an old Belling four-ringed cooker. Most of the copper kettles, fish kettles, and pots had been sold off. The entrance hall was charming in a decaying, rustic sort of fashion. It smelled musty. To the left was the drawing room, to the right the long staircase leading down to the kitchen, and straight ahead a huge staircase leading to the two other floors. On the wall two stags' heads, and below them one small slight table that seemed weary from the weight of a great brass pot containing an aspidistra and an old Bakelite phone that rarely rang. The days of big house parties, the laughter of guests, were long gone.

Stuart had his mother's looks. Tall, like she was, fair hair. He kept it short, swept back. Long hair, he complained, got in the way. You had to keep brushing it from your eyes. Though a single long lock fell over his face. It made him look rakish. He had his mother's high brow, slightly hooded eyes and aquiline nose. Lips, quite thin, though not tight enough for him to look mean. In a rare compliment his father had said he looked 'almost handsome'. His looks, Stuart's father told him, suited a man, were dreadful on a woman. A brief fierce look across at his wife. Who sat quietly moving a needle threaded gold in and out of a tapestry of a Victorian garden. She smiled to herself. She died four weeks later. Stuart was twelve.

'Your looks will improve as you age,' his father told him after the funeral. 'Your mother never was a beauty.' This was why he'd married her. That, and her money. He figured that nobody else would want a woman who looked arch and intelligent rather than stunningly beautiful. He'd been a shallow man. But he'd been right about Stuart's looks. As he got older, Stuart appeared more and more distinguished. When he met Madeline he was well on the way.

The party got wilder. The music throbbed in Stuart's head. It was at the sort of volume that should have made conversation impossible. But didn't. Madeline had left Willie and was standing with a couple of friends, expounding. From far across the room, Stuart could tell she was expounding about something that was close to her heart. He didn't know what.

She glanced at him. Knew that he was watching her. Expounded harder. Showing off. They did the noticing thing. Short, heated looks. Her knowing he was noticing her. Him knowing she was noticing him noticing her. Reacting to his interested glance. He crossed the room, held out his hand, asked her to dance.

It was September, still warm. He wore his pale linen suit. He had never, in all his university years, dressed like a student. He preferred suits. Still did. Moleskin in winter. Linen in summer. And for the months in between, a pale grey pinstripe. He lightened the formality of this with a gaudy floral shirt, open at the neck, or a T-shirt with 'Biro' on the front, that he'd got free with a set of pens. It was pale blue. And he was extremely fond of it. For work, however, he wore a shirt and tie. Never, however, a white shirt. He preferred pink or navy or dark red.

Madeline, in her usual 501s, a bright red silk shirt open with a black skimpy top, and strappy heeled sandals, toenails painted brown, took the outstretched hand, moved with Stuart through the small throng to a space in the middle of the floor, and danced. A slow shifting of feet in a dim and crowded room. Chuck Berry on the hi-fi, 'No Particular Place to Go'.

Willie was passionate about Chuck Berry. Though from the depth of the room some people, all a lot younger than he was, were complaining about that, wanting something more now. Stuart took Madeline to him, and did a little shuffle with her, scarcely speaking.

It was the only time they danced. At least, the only time they danced with their feet on the ground. Later they often jived in bed, lying side by side, staring up at the cracked and dusty ceiling over eight feet above them. Listening to a selection of Stuart's father's old vinyl LPs which were stacked eight deep on the rosewood radiogram that they had carried up from the drawing room. Elvis

Presley, Buddy Holly (Madeline's favourite), Sarah Vaughan and Harry Belafonte.

They also often did a choreographed routine on their bikes in the library, over forty feet long, wheeling round, skimming, inches from each other before racing round the room, backing up, or sailing round and round, pedalling in rhyme. They smiled, but didn't laugh. They took their cycle-dance routine very seriously. And, though it was only a daydream, another of his notions, Stuart even talked about taking the bike-dance to the stage. Touring the world with it. They cycle-danced to Strauss waltzes. And, sometimes, frenetically, to 'La Bamba'.

Before the song finished, Stuart led Madeline to the side of the room, filled a paper cup from a litre bottle of red wine, handed it to her. Filled one for himself.

'What were you expounding about?' he asked. 'Over there.' Pointing to the spot where, only minutes before, Madeline had been waving her arms and talking heatedly.

'Life,' she told him. At thirty she had only a small fear of mockery. Life was what a person expounded about. The world was hers for the changing. And change it she would, she was sure of that. 'Art,' she added. 'Monet. He's crap, don't you think?' For a brief, and horrible moment, she was reminded of the people at Ted's Sunday afternoon gatherings. But dismissed this. After all, she was right, and they'd all been wrong.

He shook his head. 'No. I like him.'

'How could you? My God, I can't believe you like him.'

Their first argument. There would be many more.

'All that romanticism. It makes you sick. That's not what art's about. It should be real . . .' At this point she floundered. Not only because she had no real opinion on what art should be about. She did what she did. And thought others should do the same. Often she'd look at other people's work, Picasso perhaps, Magritte perhaps, or the paintings of people in the same art class as she was, and wish passionately she'd thought of doing that. She always thought other people better than she was. And never ever appreciated her own abilities. Then there was the fact that she was telling Stuart a lie. She hadn't been expounding about art at all. She'd been talking about sandwiches. The fact that: 1. A really good one was hard to find; 2. Pre-packed ones were impossible to open; 3. She'd discovered a place where she'd bought a steak sandwich which was excellent. Steak, warm bread and a trace of mustard, onions on the side. She didn't want to confess to this conversation at this early, and perhaps crucial, point in what might be an interesting encounter.

Stuart smiled. He wondered why he had never felt like this. In fact, he couldn't recall ever being heated, passionate about anything.

Madeline watched him smile. It unnerved her.

Stuart offered her a cigarette. She refused. Didn't smoke. In time, though, she would get through two packs a day.

'I think,' he said. Slowly. 'That art is about everything. It is about joy and sorrow, moments encapsulated. It is to entertain and to shock and to amuse and to make people cry. It is an opening of light and shape and colour. Though there's something about the word. Whenever I hear it, art, I want to run away. It's too much for me.'

Madeline was impressed. She wished she'd said that. Except for the running away bit – she didn't know what to make of it. Though, yes, there was something in it. It was as if the word had got bigger than the thing it stood for. She liked his honesty in admitting this.

'Do you paint?' she asked.

He shook his head again. 'Film. I like the movement. And the music. A whole story unfolding before your eyes whilst you sit in the dark, just watching. Not thinking. Thinking comes afterwards when you go back into the light, into the world. I like the camera tricks.'

She liked that too.

'Though, right now, I work in a bank. Marketing.'

She didn't know about that. She didn't approve of banks. Then again, she didn't really use one. Except to put her pay cheque in. Then take it out again.

But, even though he worked in a bank, she decided she quite liked him. Though he smoked. His suit was cool. He had nice hands. It was enough to sway her into accepting when he suggested they leave this party place and go for some Italian food. What the hell, she could split when she'd eaten. She was more than hungry. She was starving. Today, she'd had only a carton of yoghourt and part of a slightly blackening banana. Food appealed to her. It always did.

He took her hand, led her from the room, waving goodbye to Abbot, who was in deep conversation with the Thailand woman, but took time to give Stuart the thumbs-up sign.

They went to a restaurant, more up-market than Madeline was used to. He ordered her a margarita as they waited for their meal. She drank it too quickly and asked for another. He watched her knock it back and told her he thought her cherubic.

'Fuck that.'

'Well,' he corrected himself. 'Sort of savage and cherubic at the same time.'

She said that that was OK. Well, sort of OK. If he cut the cherubic bit.

'What's your name, anyway?' she asked.

He told her. Stuart McKinnon.

'I'm Madeline Green,' she told him.

'I know,' he said.

'You like your women cherubic, then? That's a bit patriarchal of you.'

'No, I don't like them cherubic. I just said I find you a bit cherubic. Your looks.'

'How do you like your women, then?'

'Mostly unclothed,' he said. Amusing himself. He found such questions unanswerable. What the hell, he just liked women.

'Sexist shite,' she said.

He burst out laughing.

Their food arrived. She gave it her all. Squeezing lemon juice over her smoked salmon, licking the juice off her fingers, then wiping them on her jeans. Then stuffed as much as she could into her mouth, pointed to her pouched cheeks. 'Good.' After that, she ate chicken Milanese with potatoes, salad and roast peppers followed by sticky toffee pudding – two helpings with cream – then espresso with a glass of Drambuie. Stuffed, she sat back, patted her stomach. 'God, I needed that.' He shoved his food around on his plate, amazed at her capacity. Her enthusiasm. Most of the women he took to dinner ate little and always refused pudding. Though he suspected they were all secret chocolate eaters.

'When did you last have a proper meal?' he asked.

'Ages ago. Can't remember. I have to buy books and art materials. Pay the rent. Food's bottom of the list.'

'Do you come from an artistic family?' he wanted to know.

'My dad was a dental mechanic. But he did watercolours. And loved music. I never knew my mum. She died when I was born.' She returned to her coffee. Conversation about her past plainly over.

They walked back to her flat. Madeline walked everywhere. Top speed, little hurtling steps. Sometimes he strode ahead and walked backwards, looking at her. Listening to her. She talked constantly, using a fair bit of arm movement. He liked watching her in action.

He accepted when she invited him in. She'd recently painted her living room red. She had started it one evening. Worked through the night. Got exhausted at about six in the morning and given up. One wall was half finished. She couldn't face completing the job. 'Stuff this', she had written in huge letters over the uncovered area.

He looked at it, grinned. He knew exactly how she'd felt. That moment when waning enthusiasm finally collapsed, and she no longer cared what her wall looked like. What endeared her to him, the thing he was to come to love about her, was that she expressed it. Let it show. To hell with you, wall. I'm through with you.

He stood looking about him. This flat, where she had lived for years now, was full of her. Her things. Her books. Shoes, left where they had landed when she kicked them off, plants burgeoning from old clay pots. By the window an old easel, cast-iron stand, and beside that a table covered with inks, gouache, and acrylics. The colours spilled and oozed from tubes, squeezed and abandoned. A glass jar bristling with brushes. Rags, splattered with blotches of paint. Multicoloured. There were cups, each with the cold, sludgy dregs of coffee in the bottom. Candles, half melted, dripping with runs of blobbing wax, along the mantelpiece. Congregated there, between the candles, some stones – black, dark blue – and a lump of quartz. There was a picture. A family at a back door, taken years ago, sometime in the thirties.

'Who are they?' he asked.

'Jem, Aunty Jean, and the kids, Norman, Billy, Django and Jim. And that's little Fanny in the pram.'

'Your family?'

'Nah.' She shook her head. 'I've no idea who they are. I found the picture in a skip and stuck it on my mantelpiece. I took a shine to them.'

This surprised her. Normally, when asked, she pretended they were part of a huge extended family she did not have. But longed for none the less. It was a legacy from the Borthwicks. She saw the sibling rivalries, the pettiness, small jealousies. But saw, also, the closeness. The warmth. The safety.

She had spent a deal of time wrestling with why Annie misbehaved the way she did with her mother and father. All those years ago, before she married Willie, Annie had run up debts her father had paid off. She'd come home late, worried them sick. She'd spent hours on the telephone, hogged the bathroom, sulked, taken tantrums. Why, Madeline wondered, did Annie do that? At last, Madeline realised, Annie did it because it was safe. They wouldn't stop loving her, being there for her. She did it simply because she could. Madeline envied her that.

She offered Stuart a glass of wine. 'I sold a painting last month. Got a cheque. I have wine, and glasses.' She still hated parting with her work. But what could she do? She was running out of room. But she worried about them. Her babies with new families.

'How do I know what the people are like?' she had complained to Stuart on their way back to her flat. 'What sort of walls do they have, for example? Suppose it's all flowery? Or painted some hideous colour? What if my paintings are surrounded by cheap prints from Habitat? In a Habitat house with Habitat furniture?'

'I like Habitat,' he said mildly. Life in draughty Marglass House had given him a taste for Habitat's clean lines, its modernness.

She shot him a scathing look.

'I shouldn't have sold them,' she sighed now.

'Isn't that the plan?' he asked. 'Do paintings. Sell them. Make money to do more paintings.'

She had to agree with that. 'And Hamilton Foster at the gallery takes one when he's got hanging space. Though he has to put up artists that bring in money. Which I don't. And he takes a whack of everything he sells. Still, it's something. A chance to get shown. And some folks don't even get that.'

Her living room was littered with drawings and sketchbooks. Her paintings, mostly of grey canyon streets, or old women waiting at bus stops, or friends (mostly naked friends), lay everywhere. Stuart noticed a heap of crumpled sheets of sketchpad papers in the corner. She saw him looking at them.

'Crap stuff.'

He longed to smooth them open and look. But knew she wouldn't like it.

There was only one chair. An armchair covered with an Indian throw by the fire. He didn't like to sit down. Leave her standing.

'Burned the other chairs,' she said, indicating the armchair. 'It was cold.'

'You burned your chairs?'

'Yeah,' nodding. Looking chagrined. She was ashamed of that. 'And some of the other furniture. There was a horrible wardrobe in the bedroom. I was cold. There's no damn heating in this flat. It isn't worth the rent. Look at it. It's hardly a palace.'

He agreed with that. But felt it had probably been more palatial when she moved in. When it had furniture.

She caught his disapproving look. 'I know. It was a dreadful thing to do. It sort of grew. When I first moved in I was a junior window dresser. Peanuts, I earned. Winter came. I was freezing. Couldn't afford coal. So I sawed up a wooden chair. It was broken anyway. Then I did another. And another. Then, I don't know, I sort of seemed to have burned the wardrobe, bit by bit. It sort of happened.'

He noticed a rusty saw in the corner, and a pile of sawdust.

'I'm really tired,' she said. 'I have to lie down.'

Did this mean he could lie down with her? 'I should go then,' he said. Though he'd rather lie down.

'Stay if you want,' she said.

She went through to the flat's other room, across the hall. Stuart, not knowing what else to do, followed. She stripped off, and leaving on her bra and knickers, which were blue gingham – pleasingly innocent, Stuart thought – flopped into her bed.

'If you want coffee, the kitchen's through there. You'll have to wash a cup,' she said.

'No,' he said. 'I don't want coffee.' He stood. Didn't know what to do.

She curled into a ball, pulled the duvet over her head. Lay. Then, sensing his stillness. Popped her head out. 'Coming?'

He nodded.

'Shove the light off, then.'

Madeline's bed was a busy place. She didn't like to sleep alone. Sex wasn't necessarily part of her under-the-duvet deal. She liked the company and the warmth. Friends who stayed long into the night, talking, drinking, usually ended on the mattress with her. For Madeline it meant she could chat in comfort. Chatting lying down in the small hours was more amicable than chatting sitting on the floor.

He undressed slowly. Lay his clothes in a tidy pile at the end of the mattress. He put the light off, groped his way back to where she was and fell in beside her. He kept his underpants on. She pressed herself against him. 'Warm me.' He put his arm round her. Rubbed her, put his lips to her head.

'How old are you?' she asked.

'Thirty.'

'Me too. Depressing, isn't it. If you haven't made it by the time you're thirty, you'll never make it.'

'Made what?'

'It,' she said, irritated. 'You know. It. I haven't. Now I never will.'

'Right,' he said. Till this moment, making it hadn't been any sort of personal issue. He had everything he wanted. Except Madeline. And he would have her. He knew that now. He was about to tell her that he had no intention of making it. But Madeline was sleeping. He said nothing. Anything he might have said, even to himself, would have been drowned by her snores. Too much alcohol.

She lay sprawled over him. His arm, round her, grew chill as the night deepened. Then in the dawn, he watched her sleeping face. At last, shortly after seven o'clock, he rose, dressed and turned once more to look at her. He slipped from her flat, felt the fresh chill of city morning on his face, unleaden air. The sound of a blackbird in a tree nearby, laying out his claim on the day ahead.

Stuart walked home. He did not leave a note, no goodbye. He would see her again. He would not let her go. He thought her captivating. Entrancing. He had never met anyone like her.

Marglass House

After Stuart's mother died, his father disappeared to Edinburgh, leaving Stuart in the care of Muriel and Donald. In their early seventies now, at the time they'd been in their fifties, with no experience of children, and left Stuart to his own devices.

His own devices mainly involved not going to school. Mornings he'd set off on his bike, waving goodbye to Muriel, standing at the front door. Once round the corner, he'd dump his bike and satchel in the rhododendron bushes, and go fishing. The result of this was that his grasp of spelling, grammar and maths was poor. He'd only scraped into university. And into theology, at that, which was, at the time, unpopular. When he wasn't fishing, Stuart walked. He learned the flight paths of the birds that haunted the woods. Knew where to find a wren's nest, tiny and, inside, soft and fabulously warm. He lay flat on the cliffs watching otters play, sliding down the rock face and into the sea. He knew where to find a badgers' sett. Where fox cubs frolicked. He collected butterflies, then let them go, following their wavering flight to freedom. When he thought about all this, and compared his young life to that of people he met at university, Stuart decided that, despite his father, he'd had a perfect childhood. Neglected, but lovingly, patiently, by Muriel and Donald.

Muriel had come to Marglass House when she was fourteen, straight from school. She'd been a downstairs maid, helping the cook, scrubbing pots, peeling vegetables and cleaning the fireplaces. Donald was one of the gardeners. They'd had to ask Stuart's grandfather for permission to marry. They'd been in their late teens at the time. Both of them virgins.

During Marglass House's long decline all the other servants had left. Muriel and Donald moved into the west wing. Four rooms which were, like the other fifteen rooms, high-ceilinged, large and dusty. Muriel longed for somewhere small and cosy. 'Just a wee place to call our own,' she said to Donald. 'Where we wouldn't have to wear two cardies and a jumper to keep the chill from our old bones.'

Donald would protest that his bones were as young as they ever were. But, secretly, he agreed with her. He had his eye on the cottage by the river, that had, in the days long gone when Marglass had one, been the home of the gamekeeper. Once Marglass had boasted several maids, a cook, two gardeners as well as the gamekeeper. Now there was only Muriel and Donald. This suited them both well. The peace and freedom of not having colleagues, or a resident master, left them free to do as they liked. And mostly what they liked to do was nothing.

Occasionally Muriel, thin in a pale pink nylon overall, hair – once auburn, now grey, never cut since she was thirty-five – tied in a tight bun, would shuffle across the drawing room, pushing before her a small, howlingly noisy vacuum cleaner that had been bought not long after the war ended and had never been replaced. Sometimes she was seen carrying a duster, fussily wiping the odd vase or dragging it across the mantelpiece. She cooked porridge most mornings. And did something with chips every evening.

If Stuart was home she'd place a huge tray on the dining-room table, under a silver salver. He would find a lukewarm plate of haddock cooked in milk with a few boiled potatoes, or a dried lamb chop, soggy mashed potatoes and a scattering of peas. He never complained. He would eat whatever he was given, washed down liberally with wine from his father's vast and well-stocked cellar.

Muriel and Donald were a moral couple. They had, however, over the years devised their own set of morals. They had bent the rules of their employment to suit them, to give them what they considered their dues.

Not being given a pension, they decided that they ought to see themselves into comfortable old age. Over the years they had sold off quite a bit of the furniture and silver from Marglass House and used the proceeds to renovate the desired cottage by the river. Workmen had come, and those who had not received cash in hand, got paid by helping themselves from the Big House. Muriel sold some of Stuart's mother's clothes, her silks, her mink coats. The odd Chippendale chair here, crystal glasses there, bone-handled cutlery, serving platters, pewter mugs, copper kettles all paid for the dream home.

Turning a blind eye to the doings of poachers went towards its upkeep. Pheasants, rabbits, ducks were handed in, limp and lifeless. Muriel took them to the butcher in the local village and in exchange got lamb chops, steaks, sausages, anything that went nicely with chips. The local electrician, in exchange for a magnificent old horn gramophone, wired the cottage up to the mains that supplied Marglass House. Muriel and Donald thought free electricity their due. They did not touch the wine cellar. They were both teetotal. Though Muriel was more teetotal than Donald.

When Muriel and Donald moved, at last, into the cottage, their old sheepdog, McCann, stayed behind. He was a square and lumpen beast, like a solid loaf of bread with a leg at each corner. He lay daily on the steps by the front door, snoozing. Snarling white froth at anybody who ventured too close.

In addition to the money they made from selling off goods pilfered from Marglass House, Donald made quite a bit on the side from supplying the Inverask Castle Hotel with vegetables grown in the walled garden. He also shot deer and sold it to the local butcher. He was not a man to be bothered with the hunt. Stalking could be chilly business. So he stunned them with a searchlight. When the animal was caught, dazzled, one neat shot saw it off. The butcher did the rest, collected the carcass, cut it into joints. And sold it on. Mostly to Germany.

As they put all their money, including their small weekly wage, into the bank, and had been doing so for years, they were pretty well off. They never displayed their wealth, never spoke about it. But from time to time, they'd look at their bank book, and say, 'One day.'

A few years ago, the local bank manager had invited them in his office for a chat.

'You should make your money work for you. Money makes more money.'

'Does it?' Donald was interested in this.

'Oh yes. I could invest it for you. You could buy shares. Speculate. Buy when the price is low. Sell when it goes up.'

But Muriel didn't trust shares. 'I'm not doing that. It's gambling. I'll have nothing to do with that.'

'Well,' said their bank manager, 'what about property? You could buy a house. If you don't want to live in it, you could rent it out. It would be making money for you while it appreciates.'

Donald thought about this. He knew if he bought a house locally, people would want to know where he got the money. Nobody knew of their nest egg.

'It doesn't have to be around here,' said their bank manager, reading Donald's mind. He'd a shrewd idea where the money came from. But that wasn't his business. 'It could be anywhere in the country. It could be in another country.'

'Another country?' asked Muriel.

'Yes,' said the bank manager. 'There's a lot happening in Spain, for example. New buildings going up all over the place. You could buy one, rent it out. In fact, if you let your house in Spain you'd have a year-round clientele. People go over for Christmas as well as summer holidays.'

He showed them brochures of houses in Spain. And the pair were entranced. The sea, the white walls, the light, wonderful giant flowers in huge pots.

'My, that's lovely,' said Muriel. 'And you mean we could afford that? It's like some film star's house. It's got a balcony.'

The bank manager told them they could easily buy one of the flats. He told them it would be an ideal place to go to should they ever think of retiring.

'Retiring? Not me,' said Donald. 'Not yet. I've got life in me yet. I'll not be retiring for years. But a wee place in Spain would be fine. I could think of it when I'm tending my veg.'

So they bought a flat. Three rooms and a sea view. But they couldn't bear to rent it out. 'I'm not having strangers in my house,' said Muriel. 'Not when I haven't been there myself.'

Winter, when the wind whipped round their cottage and the snow lay three feet deep at their door, they'd take out the photos of their flat, and dream.

'One day,' Donald would say.

And Muriel would nod, agreeing. 'One day.'

Of course, Stuart noticed the gradual emptying of his home, and the splendid refurbishment of the cottage by the river. But he said nothing about it. He had a soft spot for the ageing couple. Their wiles amused him. Besides, he found this random dispersal of his worldly goods cathartic. They were his father's things, and he never liked his father. That the old man might be whirling in his grave when his precious china, silver, jewellery, stuff turned up in villagers' china cabinets, or on their mantelpieces, or in the local antique shops, pleased Stuart enormously. Then again, Muriel and Donald's cheeky villainy had boosted the place's little economy. Antique dealers turned up, browsing shops. They used Gideon's pub and hotel. And the stuff, now rehomed, was loved, polished, given pride of place.

Stuart counted his blessings. The cottage by the river was worth a bob or two. When Muriel and Donald passed on to their next cosy cottage in the sky, the lovely little place down here would still be his. He could move into it.

Mornings, he would look down from his bedroom window on the first floor, watching old Donald move slowly through the gardens he'd once tended. He'd bend down, nip a dead flower head here, remove a dried leaf there. Pull the twine that hung permanently from the pocket of his dungarees, snip off a length, lovingly tie up a dangling sweet pea. He wore the same dungarees week in week out. He had two pairs, one pair on, the other swinging on the washing line outside the cottage by the river. Winter and summer he wore a thick shirt, fraying at the collar, and a green quilted gilet. For good, trips to the pub, where he would down the occasional whisky – 'Only, mind you, to keep damp out. I'm teetotal, you know' – he'd wear a tweed jacket over the gilet.

Stuart would smile as the old man walked what once had been a thriving walled garden. His heart would fill with something. He didn't know what. Only in the evening, when the old man did his last wander through the roses, lupins and azalea bushes of his past, and

Stuart was mellow with the pickings of the cellars, Beaune, Margaux, Chablis, would he admit to what that something was. Love.

So he came home most weekends, ate the revolting food, drank the exquisite wines and cycled up and down the long corridors. Sometimes, bottle of 1961 Château Lafite-Rothschild in hand, swigging as he pedalled. The wheels ticked softly, tyres hummed pleasantly on the once-polished floorboards, McCann, the sheep-dog's, paws clicked against the wood he was padding over as he followed Stuart, his hero.

Feeling overwhelmingly mellow, Stuart would stop by the window. He'd look at the multicoloured flecks of dust dancing in the streams of sunlight that struggled through the grubby, storm-battered windows. He'd gaze down at the jungle of untamed rhododendrons, nettles, foxgloves and daisies that was his driveway and rolling lawns, and at the distant hills, and at the sea. He'd raise the bottle to it all: 'Cheers.' He'd drink heartily. Life was good. And when Madeline was his, it would be even better. He looked forward to the day. Never doubted for a moment she wouldn't come to him, live with him. Here in Marglass House. They were made for each other. He knew that.

Skip Poetry, Skip Philosophy

Two o'clock on Sunday afternoon, the day after he'd met Madeline, Stuart went to see her again. He'd had his usual lunchtime drink with Abbot and Willie Melville. Feeling three pints mellow had walked to Madeline's flat.

He had a pleasant life. He cycled to work, weather permitting. He'd lock the bike against the railings in the square beside the bank. Buy a newspaper from the shop round the corner, then tucking it under his arm, stroll to the office saying quiet good mornings to the people who had become nodding acquaintances. A pint at lunchtime. Then again in the evening, a couple of pints to set himself up for a meal. He'd a different restaurant for every night of the week. Then home to the flat he rented in Royal Circus. One flight up, a view over the gardens. A living room with two matching canvas-covered sofas. A bedroom with a king-size bed. A new oak-clad kitchen with dimmer lights and breakfast bar. Stuart read. He sat in his flat, feet up on the coffee table, listening to Miles Davis and Dizzy Gillespie.

Madeline, according Mrs Harkness from the flat below, was swimming. He walked through the quiet September sunshine to the baths. Bought a spectator's ticket and sat upstairs in the gallery, watching her.

She swam well. Wore a black sports swimsuit, goggles. She moved through the water, head up, deep breath, then head down, ploughing forward. She was impatient with slower swimmers in front of her. Sometimes ducked under, a couple of hard kicks and she was ahead of them . . . then on. Even from where he was, far above her, Stuart could see that Madeline had an affinity with water. It made her euphoric.

It scared him. He never swam. Even the sounds of swimming baths – that sodden echo – gave him tremors in the stomach. It took him back. Years ago, eight years old. In embarrassing towelling trunks that sagged worryingly when wet, skinny-legged, damp covered with goosebumps, standing with his father. Six-pack tummy, bronzed, hair slicked back, he'd just done a masterful crawl from the shallow end, pushing aside lesser bathers, and heaved himself out on to the tiled floor. 'Swim, boy,' he'd said. 'Nothing to it.' Then he'd thrown his son into ten feet of darkening water under the diving board.

Stuart could still remember the panic. Gulping, flailing. Heavily chlorinated liquid in his eyes, nipping up his nostrils, gurgling in his ears. He swallowed gallons. Was too engulfed, and scared to scream. He sank. His hair flowing round him. He drifted through the murk. Mouthing pleas for rescue. Then he gave up. He was going to die. He remembered, he stopped feeling fear. It was almost pleasant. His father's arm round him was unwelcome. He was yanked to the surface. Laid out on the shivering tiles. Air pumped into him, water out. The first searing breath he took hurt. Water spewed on to the floor. His father, kneeling over him, pressing on his lungs. Two hands, one over the other. Stuart squealed, pain, rage.

'For God's sake, boy, swim,' his father boomed. 'It's easy.'

He had taken Stuart down the pool to shallower water. Thrown him in again. This time, Stuart could, by keeping on his toes, stretching, gasping, arms moving the swirling wavelets away from him, keep his head above water whilst making a pretence of actually swimming. Years later, a friend's mother had gently held him by the chin as he splashed and heaved, and finally managed a few feeble breast strokes. It was as far as he got. He never trusted water.

Madeline had no fear. When she'd done twenty lengths, she pulled herself out. Stood, dripping, staring down at the shimmer. Then plunged in again. Another couple of lengths. Then out. Even from where he was, far above her, Stuart could see she was loathe to leave. But she turned. Hooked her thumbs over the hem of her swimming costume, yanked it over her bum, and disappeared into the showers.

He waited for her. Was standing leaning against the wall outside the changing rooms when she emerged. He worried that she might not want to see him. But no, she smiled. He took her for some hot chocolate and a Danish. Watched in astonishment a second time as she ate. The intensity, the silence. The enthusiastic chewing. He liked this woman.

They walked home. Again Madeline moving at a pace, surging forward. Cars skimming past them. Sounds of songs. Fleeting in the early autumn air.

She taught him the art of the skip. Peering into each one they passed. Spring was the prime skip time. But, this was the eighties. A time of greed, trading up, investing in property. A time of change. Throwing out the newly old. A time of skips. Buildings being renovated. So, even though it was late in the year, there were findings. Discarded things from unknown people's discarded lives.

'Skips,' she told him, 'are modern art. Tangible poetry. Places of sorrow and joy.'

The best skips, she told him, were in the posh areas. She boasted her loot. A whole kitchen — sold to a second-hand dealer for a hundred pounds. Radios, chairs, tables, a cruet set, cutlery — all lugged back to her flat, sold, burned and, occasionally, kept. Though she told him, she wasn't one for keeping things. Possessions only held you down. You got attached to them. 'I don't want to get attached to anything.'

She regularly took the things — a plant, some books, a couple of framed prints, plates — she worried she might get attached to and placed them at the front door of her building. A large notice beside them: 'Help yourself.' Mostly people passed and looked at the little treasure-trove with suspicion. There was no such thing as something for nothing. But Madeline's downstairs neighbour, Mrs Harkness, usually picked through the spoils and took anything she considered to be vaguely valuable to the second-hand shop nearby. She spent the money in the pub. Or, sometimes, backed a horse she fancied.

Madeline knew this. And sometimes spotted one of her ex-possessions in the shop window. Believing nobody should own anything, she'd steal the object back. And discreetly place it in the window of another second-hand shop. She had the notion she was redistributing her goods.

'I was hoping,' Stuart said quietly, 'you might get attached to me.'

She looked at him. Accused, 'You're rich.'

'How do you know that?'

'I asked Willie Melville about you.'

'You did?' Well, that was something. She was interested.

'You're rich. You've got a big house somewhere that you go to all the time. Never invite anybody. You don't care about work. In fact, Willie thinks you don't care about anything. You've got everything already. You know nothing of struggle. Trying. You've got it made.' It was a tirade. A small one. But enough to startle Stuart.

'Well,' he said, 'that's me told.' He put his arm round her, in a chummy way. 'You won't want to get to know a rich bastard like me, then.'

'That's right. I don't.' She was sure about that. But did nothing about removing the arm. So he kept it there.

'So you wouldn't want to go out with me tonight?'

'No, I wouldn't. Where to?'

'A meal. I could feed you. You could let a rich bastard buy you some food. Think of it as nurturing your art. I could be your patron.'

She smiled at him. 'I've already had a patron. It didn't work out. But if it's food you're offering – OK, then.'

He felt her press against him. Pulled her in, close. Felt her stir. An excitement.

'Look.' She pointed across the road. 'A new skip.'

On tiptoes, she peered in. 'Look. Wood.' She made to leap into it. Turned. 'You do it.'

He didn't want to. He was thinking about his suit. The mess he was being asked to leap into. But sensed he was being tested. This was a crucial moment in his new relationship. It would not blossom as he hoped it would if he did not leap. And leap with bravado. He could be a hero. He leaped.

The skip was half full. Not as cavernous as it would have been if it was empty. Still, he felt, momentarily lonely. A niggling fear. What if someone came along, didn't notice him in there and dumped some rubble on top of him? He lunged about looking at things. Picking them up with two slightly tremulous fingers, before throwing them away again.

'What is it you're after?' he called.

She leaned over the side, feet off the ground, legs dangling. Directing him to and fro from corner to corner, picking up this, examining that. He tossed out several sizeable lumps of worm-holed wood, which would, Madeline insisted, make good burning. Everything else was dust and bricks. He was climbing out when she spotted the gleam of something ceramic. 'That. That. Over there.' She pointed jiggling, too excited to specify what she wanted.

He picked up a broken toaster. 'This?' It was rusted. A small shower of browned crumbs tumbled from it as he held it upside down. It was a dated thing. Pride, once, of someone's kitchen. He wondered what had happened in its life that it had become so neglected. Where it had lain before it had finally been relegated to skipdom. If its owners had gone up in the world, deemed themselves worthy of a new, shinier toaster. 'Poor old thing,' he said. 'Years ago, someone took it from its box and put it on a kitchen unit. Made toast in the mornings. Butter, marmalade. Maybe it was a wedding present. Maybe they came to it after making love to have hot toast, before going back to bed. To love some more. Poor old thing.'

'You see.' Madeline was triumphant. 'The poetry of the skip. I want that ornament thing.'

It lay in the corner. Half-buried under some garden refuse. He yanked it out. It was a small china tiger. Sitting. A bullish, slightly vacant, bewildered expression. He handed it to her. 'Look at you,' she said to it. 'You're lovely. Who would want to throw you out?'

Stuart clambered back into the street, landed beside Madeline as she opened her bag, unravelled her damp swimming costume from her towel, and wrapped the tiger in it. He carried her wood back to her flat, as she enthused about the find.

'I will paint this. I'll put it on the windowsill. Crumbling buildings behind it. I'll paint its dignity. It's a skip survivor in a loser's world. I'll do that.' She nodded, knowing this to be a grand idea. And she'd make a fine job of it.

Irritated that she might be deeper than him, that she had seen some meaning in this cheap and, he thought, a little nasty, ornament that he hadn't, he wanted to say it was an effing trinket, probably bought for a couple of pounds in a Hong Kong market. A piece of rather mediocre ceramic. Rather a dull thing. Nothing much to it. But he held his tongue.

Home, she unwrapped the tiger and put it on her windowsill. 'Excellent,' she said. Then turned to him, put her arms round him. Squeezed into him. Kissing him. Unbuttoning his shirt. 'Sex first, then we'll eat. Because if we eat first, then we'll maybe drink too. And then it'll be drunk sex. Which is fine. But for the first time, it's best to know each other, what we're like. First time's best sober. Don't you think?'

He thought: Fine by me.

She loved as passionately as she ate. Curled her legs round him. And like everything else in her life. When it was over. She wanted more.

Undying Chumship

Since Charlie Govan, it was Madeline's intention never to have a regular man in her life. Occasional flings were what suited her most. Her friends, the people from the Café Indigo and the art class, and Annie asked, 'Don't you want a bloke? A regular man? A relationship?'

Secretly, Madeline thought she might. But she denied it – to herself more than anybody else. 'No,' she'd say. 'He'd only make demands of me. Tie me down. In no time I'd be caught up worrying about him. Who he was with. If he was being faithful. Then it'd be all the settling-down stuff. You know, finding a place together. Buying stuff for the place together. I don't know. It just isn't me.' What she didn't say was, 'He might get horribly ill on me. Die on me. Or bugger off to New York.' It wasn't a relationship she didn't want – it was pain.

But there was something comforting about Stuart. His constantness. 'He's always in the same mood,' she told Annie. 'He's never nasty. Me, now, I'm nasty all the time.'

Annie agreed with both these statements.

'I mean,' said Madeline, 'look at me. I don't dress up. Swimming buggers up my hair. I only think about me. Christ, I wouldn't take up with me. I'm the last person in the world I'd want to hang out with.'

'I know,' Annie nodded enthusiastically. 'One thing about you, though,' she said pouring more wine into both their glasses – they were in Annie's kitchen; Annie rarely visited Madeline, she found it depressing – 'you take insults well.'

'I know the truth about me,' Madeline agreed.

In years to come, Madeline was to say that Stuart wormed his way into her life. Into her heart. 'He was just there. So constantly reassuringly there.'

Stuart visited Madeline often in the early days. And when she was in a mood, or working, she'd hide from him. She wouldn't answer his knock. She'd stay in her bedroom, lying on the mattress, duvet over her head till he went away. Then she'd watch him disappear down the street. Never turning back. And she'd feel dreadful, about herself. What she'd just done.

'She's up there,' Mrs Harkness from downstairs would tell him. 'I heard her only a minute ago. Jumping around. Playing that music of hers.'

Madeline was into reggae at the time. Played Toots and the Maytals full blast. Singing along to 'Pressure Drop'.

But Stuart would only shrug. 'I don't mind. I'll catch her tomorrow.' He'd put a note through her letterbox. Or sometimes a flower. A winter pansy he'd stolen from a window box on his way to visit.

'Don't know why you bother,' Mrs Harkness would say.

But Stuart bothered. It had become a thing with him.

'How are you getting on with Madeline?' Abbot would ask.

'Great,' Stuart would say. And sometimes it was. When she opened the door to him.

'You're on a losing wicket with that one.' Mrs Harkness was taking an interest in this affair. But then she took an interest in everybody's affairs. She thought of it as her business, almost her job.

'No I'm not,' answered Stuart. 'Never fear for the only child, failure never occurs to them.' He thought this true. Failure never crossed his mind. Neither, of course, did success. He just plodded on.

Mrs Harkness said, 'That'll be right.' And shut her door on him.

Madeline felt Stuart was beginning to wear her down. She found she missed him when she hadn't seen him for several days. And wondered why this was.

'I must be getting used to him,' she told Annie.

Annie sighed and said that it was the human condition to get used to anything. Including warts and ingrowing toenails.

'Do you think I could be falling in love?' Madeline asked. 'Only if I am, I don't want it. I don't know what I make of love. It only leads to tears.'

Annie sighed once more and said that most things did. Including warts and ingrowing toenails.

'See,' said Madeline. 'That's what I mean. I remember when you and Willie got together. You were the ones to know. The faces about town. Now you hardly leave the house together. You were always feeling each other up in public.'

'Now we don't have to feel each other up in public. We can feel each other up in private.'

Madeline leaned forward. 'Ah, but you don't.'

Annie said nothing. It was true. Ah, but they didn't.

'Well, that's love for you. You shag away like rabbits. Then you have children. And you're too tired. Or when you fancy it, there's a little person wedged and sound asleep between you.'

'That's love?' asked Madeline.

'Yeah. Part of it.' Annie shrugged. It didn't sound like love to her either, now she thought about it. 'Oh, come on, Madeline,' defensive now, 'you must have been in love sometime.'

Madeline had. Often. It came on her like a rash, sweaty and fevered. Then disappeared as swiftly as it had struck. She couldn't count the number of times it had happened. She might have placed it along with other things with which she'd been omitten during the years – chickenpox, measles, mumps, a verruca from the swimming pool. But knew this wasn't true. She knew from the way she'd felt about Charlie, love was sweeter than any of these things. And more painful. But sex with love was always better than sex without it. Her ruling on love was that as long as it didn't go beyond sex, it was fine.

Yet, she wondered. She would look at couples walking hand in hand along the street and she'd be filled with curiosity about what they said to one another when the passionate exchanges were over. The swapping of lifestyle stories. Revelations about their childhoods, past loves, lost loves, heartaches, little triumphs, big triumphs. What was there to say when they'd told each other everything? She once saw an old couple, well into their seventies walking hand in hand and stood staring at them. Had they been together all their lives? And did they ever run out of things to say? And did they still make love? And was it good? Did it get better? Or did they know each other's every move? She longed to go up and ask, but knew her intrusion, the intensity of it, the intimacy, would not be welcome. So she continued to stare till the couple, sensing her presence in their quiet little moment together, turned to look at her. Caught gaping, she walked away, embarrassed. Still, she wondered. What did all this relationship stuff mean? She didn't know.

October came whirling in with a fury that year. Winds swept down the narrow crumbling street where Madeline lived, hurtling dust and dirt and litter before it. It rained. Madeline unearthed her railway coat from the bottom of her cupboard. Told Stuart how she had found it in a junk shop during one of her shoplifting-shopdropping expeditions that were part of her skip philosophy. Discarded things belonged to everyman. Nobody had a right to make money from them.

'But,' protested Stuart, 'you sell stuff from skips.'

'Ah, but,' said Madeline, 'that's to get money for food.' In pursuit of food anyone could be forgiven anything, short of murder or rape.

'I think your shoplifting-shopdropping exploits are just mischief,' Stuart told her.

'Well done, McKinnon,' she admitted. 'I do believe you have me there.' She even had the decency to redden, slightly, at the accusation.

Madeline selected junk shops or downmarket antique shops that were either side by side, or across from one another. She'd steal goods from one, deposit them in the other. Sometimes, she'd then take something from the other, put it in the first shop. Sometimes, she would take the mischief further by removing the object – an old brass microscope – from shop one, putting it in shop two. Then, she'd return to shop one and ask if they had such a thing as an old brass microscope. Delighted, they would tell her they had. And then, unable to find it, would apologise. At which point, Madeline would look in glee across at the rival shop and declare that there was one in the window. The assistant might then look with deep suspicion at the shop window opposite. But so far there had been no confrontations. Madeline was disappointed at this.

By mid-October Madeline had painted the tiger four times. And four times ripped up her efforts. Burned them. She'd spread her open palms before the spurting flames, saying that paintings were of more use as fuel than as things to look at. 'I just can't get it. It just looks like a china tiger. A cheap, old china tiger. I feel there's more to it. When I touch it, it feels old, really old. I want it to look like a skip survivor. I want it to look noble.'

Stuart didn't know what to say. All the paintings looked fine to him. He stole one, had it framed and hid it from her. He thought in years to come, when she saw it anew, she might change her mind.

'It doesn't look noble,' he said. 'It looks slightly mad.'

'But I want it to look noble.'

'Well, that's why you're having problems. You're giving it something it hasn't got – nobility. Actually,' he picked it up, turned it over, examined it, 'I think it's Japanese.'

'Is it?'

'I don't really know. All I know is, it isn't noble. It looks a little manic. Bewildered. Actually . . .' He stopped. He was about to tell Madeline it looked like her.

She took it, held it from her. 'It looks how I feel,' she said.

By now, Madeline had stopped hiding from Stuart. They were seeing each other most days. He would finish work, cycle down to her place. And, if she was out (she often was) would sit on the stairs waiting for her to come home. She was usually glad to see him. It meant company. Abbot, however, made Stuart doubt himself.

'Sheepdog,' he said.

'What do you mean by that?' asked Stuart.

'You're drooling over that woman. Hanging about her. She's got you here.' He crushed his thumb into the bar they were sitting at.

Stuart thought this might be true. Next day he went straight home. Stayed in. Drank too much wine. Fell asleep in the chair in front of the telly. Mouth open, snoring, legs splayed. He woke at two in the morning, hung over and shivering because the heating had gone off. He opened his eyes, saw in front of him a large woman in a thong, tassels hanging from her nipples, sitting atop of a small man lying on a rumpled bed. The door of the pea-green-coloured room they were frolicking in burst open. An unshaven man in a black suit heaved in, waving a gun that he used to smack the woman across the jaw. Stuart stared at all this blearily. He thought it must be the worst film he'd ever seen. He had to watch it. It was fascinatingly awful. He went to bed at quarter to four. Slept in. Stumbled into work at quarter past ten, unshaven and wearing the shirt he'd slept in.

'You prat,' said Abbot. 'When that happens you phone in sick. Say you've got flu.'

'I never thought of that,' said Stuart, feeling foolish. It seemed so obvious now Abbot mentioned it. If he'd done that not only would he have had a whole day in bed watching daytime TV, but nobody at work would have seen the state he was in. He cursed his stupidity. Then went to find Madeline.

'You didn't come yesterday,' she told him.

'Nah. Things to do.'

'What?'

The question was so sharp, so swift, so direct, it took him unawares.

'Um . . . can't remember.'

She put her hands on her hips. Looked like some terrifying matriarch. 'What do you mean, you can't remember? It was only yesterday, of course you remember. I hung around here waiting for you.'

'Nobody asked you to.'

'You always come.' They were starting to shout.

'Well, yesterday I didn't. I was doing something.'

'What?'

His brain abandoned him. He couldn't think of an excuse. This grilling was making him feel weak. 'I was watching television. I got drunk. Then I fell asleep. Then I woke and watched a crap film.'

'Instead of coming to see me?'

'Well, Abbot said I was acting like a sheepdog. Hanging around you. Under your thumb.'

'Under my thumb? Under my thumb?' She ran at him. Shoved him back towards the door. He reeled. Stumbled. She shoved again. 'Get out.' He fell into the hall. Another shove. She opened the door, pushed him on to the landing. 'Get out from under my thumb. I don't want you there.' She slammed the door.

He stood looking at it. 'No,' he said. 'I didn't mean that. What I meant was . . .'

But Madeline wasn't listening. She'd gone back to her bare little bedroom, lay on the bed. And cried. This was what love did to you. It hurt. It made you angry. You wanted to own and be owned. And, she decided, she wasn't up for it.

Stuart spent two miserable days. He listened to Billie Holiday. He was wretched. He cursed Abbot. He drank. He was late for work. Couldn't work. Stood in the pub with Abbot, looking morose.

'Christ,' said Abbot. 'The state of you. You shouldn't let a woman do that to you.'

'Fuck do you know?' snapped Stuart.

Abbot thought about this. 'Not a lot,' he confessed. 'But, if I felt like you feel, I'd do something. Go see her. Take her flowers.'

Stuart's brain, after two thick and muddled days, returned to him. 'Not flowers,' he said. 'Not for Madeline.'

An hour later he was on his knees shouting through her letterbox. 'Open the door. I know you're in there.'

'No. Go away.'

'I've got food,' he called. 'I've got a takeaway. Prawns in black bean sauce, fried rice, chicken and cashew nuts, some duck thing, prawn crackers, extra noodles.'

He could hear her on the other side of the door. She was tempted.

'I got crispy roll things, and two bottles of Australian Riesling.'

She let him in.

'I'd just like,' he said, mouth filled with duck thing, 'to define our relationship. I'm not your sheepdog. Am I your boyfriend, or what?'

'You're not my boyfriend,' she told him. Denying, to herself, that she might be falling for him.

'What then?' He had thought he was.

'You can be my mate, a chum. A chum with sex. Best thing ever.'

He agreed to that. 'I've never had a chum.'

'Never? Not even at school? A best friend? Someone you told your secrets to? Who was the one you stood next in line? Who watched *The Six Million Dollar Man* with you? Played with? Ran bionically across the garden?' Madeline left her plate by the bed where they were eating, did a demonstration bionic run across the room.

Stuart smiled and shook his head. 'No.'

'Goodness. Well, you can be my best friend.' She held out her hand.

'OK,' he said. 'It's a deal.' They shook on it. He made to kiss her.

She backed off. 'No. Kissing's too much fun for a best friend vow. We need a handshake.'

This was serious. 'Best friends. For ever,' she vowed.

It was a bitter night. The fire crackled. Stuart wondered what she was burning. They listened to Lou Reed. Every now and then, sitting side by side on the floor, they stopped eating, and snogged. Madeline loved kissing. She warmed into him. Pulling him closer.

'Tell me everything's going to be all right.'

'Everything's going to be all right. What have you got to worry about?'

'Everything. I worry. What if I can't paint? What if I'm no good?'

'You're good. You're great.'

'Tell me again.' Moving against him. Kissing his neck. His cheek. His lobes. On her way to his mouth.

'You are wonderful. You are fabulous.'

This was Madeline of the night. In the daylight she was all bustle, busy movements, thrusting forward with her plans, her life. In the dark she lay next to Stuart, pressed against him. Not clinging. She never clung. But, he felt, drawing from him. His calm.

'Aren't you ambitious?' she asked in bed one night.

'No,' he said. Voices in the dark.

'I am.'

'I know,' he said. Fearfully, because he worried he was not part of her plans for the future. 'Ambition scares me. I have a little prayer. Please keep me safe from the savagery of ambition and the bigotry of innocence.'

'Ambition isn't savage,' said Madeline. 'It's healthy.'

'Other people's can be. It is foolish to get tangled in other people's dreams.' He knew he'd get tangled in Madeline's. Nothing he could do about it. That was the deal.

'Innocence is sweet. How can you say it's bigoted?' Madeline asked.

'You get those innocent people who come from comfortable homes. They aren't driven. They've known little pain. No strife. They meet someone who is, who has. Who is no longer, or has never been, beautiful. Who uses driven words. Fuck. Cunt. And the innocent one looks appalled. How dare you shock me? I'm innocent.'

'You think that's bigotry? To be shocked at swearing?'

'To be shocked at driven attitudes is a kind of cosy bigotry.'

'Well, if you admire driven people you mustn't be as unambitious as you claim. You must want something. What do you want?'

'Just to be.'

'Happy?'

'Probably,' he admitted. 'But not really that. Just to be. To wake every morning. Clean, and with all my dust washed away.' He wanted that. No worries. No problems. No painful memories – his father.

The simplicity of his longings touched her. Filled her with shame – slight shame – at her own dreams of success, critical praise. Praise? Dammit, she wanted adulation.

She sighed, had satisfied her need for kisses. Turned from him, and slept.

The day after Stuart and Madeline had declared undying chumship, Madeline met Hamilton Foster on her way to work. She was wearing her railway coat, which always amused him.

'What's a nice girl like you doing out this time of a morning?' he asked. His gallery never opened before ten. He was rarely out this time of a morning himself.

'Going to work to make a buck,' she told him.

'You should be painting. That's the only work you should be doing.'

'Doesn't pay.'

'Money,' he scoffed. 'That shouldn't bother you. You're young. You have your art.'

'I have my rent. I like to eat,' she told him.

'Indeed,' he agreed, remembering the most recent painting of hers that he'd sold. It was a restaurant in Leith. Viewed from the outside. It was steamy, busy. Sepias, blacks. People leaning over tables.

Looking at it, you could almost hear the thick babble of conversation, smell the food. Men in dark suits. A woman waiting tables, in a waiter's outfit. Black suit, white starched shirt, long pristine white apron. She was glowering out. Which made the place look all the more élite, desirable. Of course, it wasn't really. Only to a small and scruffy artist with too much hair, in a damp railway coat and hunger growling in her stomach. She'd called it *From the Outside*.

'Working on anything at the moment?' he asked.

She was. The tiger. 'Yes,' she told him.

'A tiger? Really? How intriguing. Can I see it?'

'It isn't ready.'

'When is anything ever ready? Bring it round. I want to see everything you do. You're going to be a star someday.'

'Am I? I don't think so.'

'Well, you wouldn't.' He started on his way. Turned. 'Love your coat, by the way.'

Madeline clumped towards the shop. She didn't want to show him the tiger painting. It was boring. In fact, she no longer knew why she'd felt such an urgency to paint the tiger in the first place. Except she felt it was special. She was fascinated by it. The oldness of it. Running her fingers over it, she'd wonder where it had come from, who had made it, the times it had known, things it had seen. Why it had been discarded. It was a fascinating object tossed away because it no longer fitted in. A sign of the times. All that, but somehow when she tried to paint it, all that appeared on canvas was an china tiger. Seated and slightly insane.

Tiger, Tiger

Madeline became crazed. She worked. She tore up her work. Worked some more. Stayed up nights. Fretting. Stuart would wake, shaken from sleep by a movement, a sound from the room across the hall. Pencil scraping over sketch pad. The atmosphere was thick, Madeline's angst. 'I'll never do it. I can't do it. I'm no good.'

He'd sit by the fire, watching her work. Her face moved with each thing she drew. Minute to minute, emotions reflected from canvas to her face. She ran her fingers through her hair, muttered to herself. She put on some music. A Bessie Smith tape.

He thought she was lost to him. Felt spare. A gooseberry at a one-woman party. 'Am I disturbing you?' he asked. 'Would you get on better if I wasn't here?'

'What?' She looked round. Suddenly remembering he was there.

'I'll go,' he said. Backing from the room. 'I feel in the way. See you tomorrow.'

'Yeah, right,' she said without looking at him.

''Bye, then,' he said.

'Yeah, right,' she said again. Did not even turn.

He left.

All his life Stuart had wanted a friend. A real friend. He knew many people. Drank with chums. But had nobody he could call at any time of the day or night. Nobody to confide in. Share private jokes with. There was Abbot with his trivia, who was a mate. But Abbot had his own life. And friends. Stuart was one in many. Not a real mate. There was Willie Melville. But Willie's life was full of Annie and drink and children and lack of money. People were for laughing with, or for borrowing from. Willie had no sense of friendship. Willie didn't need a friend, he had himself.

151

Willie thought Willie the grandest person alive. Stuart found it wearing.

Stuart had seen many friendships, envied them. Now, at last, he had Madeline. She'd take his hand when walking along the street, would suddenly, apropos of nothing, kiss him, hug him. She put her head next to his, whisper little things. Silly things that made him laugh. They shared secret jokes. She was all he wanted. Sometimes when he saw her from afar, he would smile. He couldn't help it. There she was. A little hurtling person in a floppy velvet hat and huge railway coat that was shredded and ragged and grubby round the hem because it was two inches longer than she was, and scraped the pavement. She was his joy.

Now, he felt left out. Abandoned. He was jealous of her paintings. Home, he sat in his bath, drinking – straight from the bottle – a twelve-year-old Côtes du Rhône, and considered this. He was a logical person. He figured, if Madeline wanted fame, then he wanted fame for Madeline. He resolved to dedicate himself to this, as Madeline did.

He would cosset her, love her, buy her art materials, clothes, food. He would keep her warm. Safe. If anyone hurt her, they hurt him. He would fight for her. 'After all, look how I fought for Billy Robertson. I wouldn't let them get rid of him. And,' stepping from the bath, carefully lest he slip and spill the wine, 'Madeline has one great advantage over Billy Robertson. She's real.'

When Stuart was a boy he had a friend, Billy Robertson. Billy was taller than he was, dark hair, didn't have to wear sturdy shoes that his feet would grow in perfect shape. Billy wore trainers. Billy wore jeans. Billy played football. Billy knew everything about everything. Nobody could argue with Stuart about this, because Stuart was the only person who saw him.

Billy, the invisible boy, was for many years Stuart's best friend. At first, he'd been a secret pal. Nobody knew about him. But as time passed and Billy became more and more real, it seemed unfair to Stuart that at meal times Billy went unfed.

'What about Billy?' he asked his mother. 'Doesn't he get any steak?'

'Who is Billy?'

'He's my friend. He's sitting next to me. Why can't he have supper, too?'

His mother looked. Saw nothing. Nobody. But complied. The boy had a secret friend. How sweet. She fetched another plate. And filled it with a slice of her own steak and some potatoes. Apologised to the empty space. 'So sorry, Billy. I didn't see you there.' What fun. His father thought so, too. For a time Billy Robertson even became the son he wished he had – a tall, strapping lad, army-bound. He and Stuart and Billy played cricket on the lawn. Billy was a fine cricketer. Days, Stuart and Billy played. They tracked wild animals together. Rode the range. They hunted buffalo. Billy went to school, and, at last, Stuart had someone to chat to on the bus. But it all went on too long.

It broke Stuart's mother's heart when she discovered that all the children in Stuart's class at school had been invited to a party – except Stuart. He lived too far away. 'It's all right,' Stuart said. 'Billy's going. He'll tell me all about it.' No hint of tears from Stuart. But his mother went to her room and shed a few for her lonely son.

The time came when Stuart's mother refused to put out an extra plate for the invisible boy. 'There is no Billy.' She was finding it a strain talking to an empty space. And a strain reprimanding Billy for any mischief Stuart got up to. 'Billy did it,' Stuart would say, wide-eyed, innocent. His mother would repeat, 'There is no Billy.'

After almost two years of Billy, and Billy's needs and demands, Stuart's mother took him to the doctor. 'We have an imaginary friend,' she said. 'I fear my son is slipping into his own little world.'

The doctor told her it was a phase many children went through. Not to worry. It would pass in a month or so.

'This has been going on for over two years,' she told him.

'Ah,' said the doctor. He turned to Stuart. 'Well, my boy. It's time to grow up. You must face up to things. No blaming the invisible friend. Be a man.'

Stuart nodded, sitting neatly on the doctor's ancient leather Chesterfield, Billy at his side. On the way home, Stuart, sitting in the back of the Land Rover, said, 'Well, what do you think of that, Billy?'

'Not a lot,' said Billy in the voice Stuart used for him. Slightly deeper than his own. 'It's tough when people say you're not here. I don't like being ignored.'

His mother pulled over to the side. Put her head on the steering wheel. And sighed.

Stuart sneaked food from his plate and after meals took it upstairs to Billy, who, by now, was living in the wardrobe. His parents would overhear him and Billy having long conversations at night, after Stuart's bedtime. They feared for him. His father decided the boy was loopy, beyond help. His mother knew loneliness when she saw it.

In time, Billy slipped from Stuart's life. Almost. At moments of despair, crisis, disappointment and humiliation, he was always there. To offer words of comfort. When Stuart was the only boy not to get picked for one of the school's three football teams, Billy was there. 'Never mind, Stuart.' In his usual deep voice. 'It's their loss. We know what a great midfielder you are.' Stuart nodded in agreement.

But slowly, slowly Billy faded away. One day, when he was sixteen, Stuart remembered him. He thought how silly he'd been to have such a long-term invisible friend. How sad he'd been. And he also thought he missed Billy. Billy was everything he wished he was.

Still, now he had a real friend. His love. Madeline. He had a notion that he would save her. From what he did not know. He wanted to do something brave, gallant, something showy. He wanted to take her to him, shelter her from the storm that seemed to be her life. He thought of her as an exquisite thing, a fabulous bird, like the goldfinches he'd seen moving busily through the sycamores and rowans that lined the drive to Marglass House. He wanted to spread crumbs before her.

This passion, this obsession of his was taking its toll. Feeding her, staying up late, watching her, making her coffee, bringing her drinks. She seemed energised, empowered, driven. He was exhausted. He was late for work daily. He crept in, trying not to look guiltily furtive.

But his laxness had been noticed. He was getting looks, hostile disapproving looks, from people in senior positions.

One day, climbing the long dimly lit stairway to her flat, he could hear her music. James Brown, howling full blast. He knocked at her door. No answer. No wonder with that din going on. He went in, uninvited. Just above the music he could hear a thump. Thump. Thump. Slow thump. He found her kneeling on the floor banging her head against the wall. Tears streaming down her face. She was sobbing uncontrollably. Scarcely able to breathe.

'What the hell are you doing?' Dragging her back. A huge bruise already swelling. Blood trickling down her face.

'It's my brain. It's not working. There's nothing in it. It's empty. I can't think. I can't do this.'

'You will. For Christ's sake. Stop beating yourself up.' Curling behind her, legs wrapped round her.

She fought. Wriggling. Writhing. Biting his gripping hands. Twisting to punch him. 'Let go.'

But he had her in a half-nelson. 'You'll give yourself brain damage. You idiot. Then the thing really won't work. You'll end up in a home, sitting in a corner, talking to yourself.'

She cried, struggled, beat her heels on the floor. He gripped tighter. Keeping her close to him, till the craziness stilled. 'Sssh, Madeline. Sssh.'

She stilled. Stiffened. 'Don't say that.' She hissed the words. 'Don't say I'll end up in a home talking to myself.' She twisted round to face him. Suddenly sane. 'Not ever.' She rose. Smoothed her jumper. Sniffed. Tantrum over, returned to her board. 'I've got emotional constipation,' she said. 'I can't think.'

'You're trying too hard,' he told her. 'I can't understand why you want to paint that thing. It looks like someone won it at a fairground. Except for its expression, which looks—'

'Like me,' said Madeline. 'I know. You don't have to tell me.'

'I just don't know why you're knocking yourself out painting something that's already there, when you're so good at doing things that aren't,' said Stuart.

'What do you mean?'

'I mean,' he shrugged. What the hell did he know about art? 'The stuff that's in your head is so much more interesting. Christ.' He crossed the room, picked up the ornament. 'It's a cheap china tiger. Who the hell wants a picture of that?' He went up to Madeline, tapped the aching head. 'We want pictures of what's in there. Relax. Be Madeline. That's what we want.'

He left her looking surprised, went to the kitchen, made her tea, sweet and hot, for ragged nerves. But she was calm when he brought it to her. He laid it on the table next to her. And went to the shops, bought a packet of frozen peas to place on the damaged forehead. By the time he got back with them, Madeline was engrossed. Lost in her world. She flapped her hand at him. 'Leave me alone.' So he drank her tea himself. Then lay back, breathing deeply, icy peas on his own head. Intense emotions always brought on headaches.

After weeks of tears, cries of despair, rage, tantrums and, towards the end, outbursts of joy, Madeline was done. She had three new works to show. Tiger paintings, from what she would call her tiger period. A time when she'd taken Stuart's advice. She'd relaxed, was Madeline. And a time when she'd seen her own belligerent, bemused and slightly glum expression on the face of what she thought was a cheap china ornament that looked, to Stuart, anyway, like it might have been won at a fairground.

Tiger in the Window was the tiger sitting in the window of the shop where she worked. Everything grey, even the street beggar sitting cross-legged on a blanket on the pavement, except the tiger, which filled the window. Stared out. An iridescent figure. But with that expression Madeline so empathised with, slightly aggressive, slightly glum, slightly vacant. Passers-by were paying it no attention.

The Life of Tiger was a tiger prowling the night streets. That soft padding step. Head lowered. Dark pavements, littered with crisp bags, beer cans. But the beast still had that expression. It seemed to say, 'What the hell am I doing here?'

Tiger Trip was an open-topped bus full of tigers, all with the same expression, driving through the city, looking at the people they passed. Who are they? What are they doing, scurrying about?

The quirkiness of it all amused Hamilton Foster.

'Don't you dare say it's quirky,' said Madeline.

'OK,' he said, 'I won't.' He thought he would just think it.

Still, he knew talent when he saw it. Madeline had a gift. She just didn't know what to do with it. Her thoughts were bubbling, tumbling in her head. She had something to say, if only she knew what. When she had come to herself, smoothed out the torrents in her mind, he would be there. Meantime, he knew that the people who visited his gallery would make up stories about the tiger and find meanings in the paintings that Madeline hadn't thought of. This sort of work got people talking. And the people who visited his gallery loved to talk.

He listened, joining in with her enthusiasm as Madeline frothed, waved her arms, explained. 'See,' she said. And, 'You know.' And, 'What I am saying.'

And he said, 'Absolutely.' And, 'They're wonderful. Wonderful. A joy. You're a breath of fresh air.'

Madeline grinned. Praise was all she wanted. Hamilton stroked his balding head, put his manicured hands in the pockets of his Austin Reed suit and gave her what she was after. He gushed.

'You have such a gift,' he told her. 'A real talent.' He leaned his genial face near to hers. 'I will love watching it develop.'

She stilled. Beaming. Soaking up the words. Waiting for more.

'That's it,' he told her. 'No more. Till next time.'

'There'll be a next time?'

'Absolutely,' he said. 'Get out of here. Get on with more work.'

Madeline left. But at the door, she turned. Hamilton was standing staring at the pictures, scratching his head. My God, he was thinking, that tiger looks exactly how I feel. A bit vacant, a bit belligerent, a bit glum. And, yes, he leaned forward, peering, thinking, and what? Yes, that was it, self-mocking.

Madeline watched him and mistook the head scratching and staring for criticism. He didn't like her work. He'd been lying to her. Flattering her.

Hamilton hung the pictures in the corner, leaving the main hanging area for his regular, better-selling artists. He thought he might sell two of them. *Tiger in the Window*, and *The Life of Tiger*. The other one he

thought would reprint nicely on a postcard. If he could persuade
Madeline to agree to it, he could put it on his Christmas cards. But
every time he passed the Tiger paintings, he smiled. She had the
skill. Her technique was developing nicely. She just hadn't found
herself yet. It was as if she was holding herself in. Wouldn't let go.
He reckoned she was afraid of all the stuff she had inside. Whatever
the hell it was. He didn't know. But whenever it did all come tumbling
out, and she put it down on canvas, he'd be there. There was money
in that one. He was sure of that.

Madeline came out of the gallery. Stuart was waiting for her. 'He
doesn't like them.'

'What?' said Stuart. 'I don't believe you. What did he say?'

'He said they were wonderful. A joy. He said I was a breath of
fresh air. I had such a gift.' She spoke in a monotone. Stared down at
her fingers, linking them, unlinking them. She was on the point of
tears.

Stuart was confused. 'You're wonderful. You have a gift. Sounds
good to me. What's the problem?'

'As I was leaving, I turned and saw him looking at my work. I *saw*
him.'

'And?' asked Stuart. 'So? He looked at them. Like what else is he
going to do? Eat them? Madeline, lots of people are going to look at
them.'

'I saw his face. He thinking what a load of crap. He lied to me.'

Stuart sighed. They walked back to Madeline's flat in silence.
He'd had enough. He'd thought now she was finished, he would
have her to himself. Work done, she'd be his again. By the time they
got to Madeline's building, Stuart's fury peaked. It tumbled out.

The sound of raised voices brought Mrs Harkness to her window.
She watched as Madeline and Stuart argued.

'Pack it in, Madeline,' said Stuart. 'He loves the stuff you did.
Loves it.'

'You don't understand,' said Madeline. 'You didn't see. I saw his
secret face. I know what he's really thinking. He only says he loves it
so's when I do something good, really good, I'll take it to him.'

'Crap,' said Stuart.

'Nobody'll want it. They'll all laugh at me. And they won't want me.'

'Bollocks,' shouted Stuart. 'He wants you.'

'You stupid shite,' said Madeline. 'You don't understand anything. I can do something good one day. It's in here.' She beat her chest. 'And here.' She thumped her forehead. 'I just can't get at it. Shit. Shit. Shit.' Banging her head with her fist.

Stuart grabbed her wrists. 'Stop it.'

She fought him. Started beating him. Their voices ringing out in the afternoon chill.

He gripped the flailing fists. Held them down. Pulled her to him. 'Stop it,' he said in her ear. He kissed her neck.

Madeline wrenched herself from him. 'You don't understand,' she said again. Half crying, half shouting. Little throbbing voice. 'I gave it everything. And everything is not enough.' She beat him, because she had to beat something, someone. And he was there. And beating him was safe. He would not go away.

To ward off the rain of blows, feeble though they were, he slipped his hands inside the railway coat. Shoved her against the railings. Kissing her. Pushing into her. 'C'mon, Madeline. Leave it. Forget about the paintings. They're done. Move on.'

'It's all in here,' she said. A stray strand of hair slipped into her mouth. She chewed it. 'Everything. Poems and prayers. Shapes and songs. Beautiful things. Rage. Things I feel. But it doesn't come out right. None of it.' She looked at him, could hardly see him for the blur of tears. 'It won't come out. None of it.'

All he could do was tell her to stop it. Hold her. Scenes alarmed him. He fled from them. If not physically, then in his head. He could count the number of arguments he'd had in his life on the fingers of one hand. He'd frustrated the women he'd known. They always felt they were arguing alone. He'd never join in. It wasn't the same with Madeline. She pulled him into her moods.

'It's crap,' she cursed herself. 'It's all crap.'

All the time, he was stroking her hair. Rocking her. Like she was a baby. This surprised him, he didn't know he could do things like this. Feeling her respond he felt somehow worthy. Useful. Like he was doing some good. She had stopped sobbing. She was giving in to him. Responding. Kissing him. Tongue in his mouth. Unbuttoning his shirt. Moaning. Sex always took her mind off her things. Sex and food.

Mrs Harkness, at the window, smoked, watching. One arm folded under her tits. The other, her cigarette arm, propped on it. Look at them. What were they like? Couldn't wait to get indoors. Fighting one minute. At it like rabbits the next. Then they'd be doing it upstairs. The noise of it. Yelling. Then there'd be the music. And the jumping around. And the sawing. At first the sawing puzzled her; what on earth was the little madam up to? But slowly it clicked when the sawing was followed by raking in the grate. A fire being lit. Knowing from the close watch she kept on Madeline that no coal or wood had been brought into the flat, Mrs Harkness realised that it must be the furniture getting broken up and burned. I'll have you for that, she thought. One day. You see if I don't.

He was all right, she thought. Bit posh, bit uppity. But that Madeline was trouble. Mrs Harkness loathed Madeline. It was a chemical thing. A bilious brew of envy and wretchedness. Madeline's seemingly carefree life, her own miserable one. This hatred had come swirling through her the first time she'd clapped eyes on her. It was just there, bubbling in the unreachable murk of her mind. She hated the way Madeline looked, how she dressed, how she moved, how she galloped up the stairs two at a time. She hated the way Madeline spoke, quiet voice, 'Morning, Mrs Harkness.' 'Nice day, Mrs Harkness.' She'd imitate Madeline behind her back, bobbing her head from side to side as she spoke. 'Lovely morning, Mrs Harkness.'

'Who does she think she is?' Mrs Harkness would say out loud to herself. 'Pretending to be an artist. She's a bloody window-dresser, that's all.' She'd bustle through her flat, taking out her venom on the curtains, furiously straightening them. She'd empty an ashtray into the fire, wipe it with her apron, and replace it, face rigid with wrath. 'Artist? Artist? Artists don't live round here. They live in Paris or London. We don't have artists here. Janette across the road works at the bookie's. That's the sort of people we have here. Decent, ordinary, down-to-earth, no-nonsense folk.'

Everything about Madeline, Mrs Harkness despised. 'Bloody little hippie,' she seethed. 'And hippies are past it. Even I know that. Then there's the stairs. She's too bloody full of herself to even clean the stairs.'

The stairs were an issue. Had been since the day Madeline moved in. On her first day there, Mrs Harkness had waited till she heard Madeline coming down the front hall, and had burst out. She hadn't said, 'Hello,' or, 'Hope you'll be happy here.' She had told Madeline who she was. 'You'll be the new one. I'm Mrs Harkness, downstairs.' Noting, with horror, Madeline's youth. Young people, she knew, were never ones to clean stairs. She thought to mention them now. Get things off on the proper footing. Let this one know what was expected of her from the very start. 'You'll be doing the stairs. Next week'll be your turn.'

Madeline said, 'Stairs?'

'Yes. Stairs,' insisted Mrs Harkness. 'We take turns. One week you. Next me. That's the way of it.'

'What do we clean them with?' Madeline asked.

'Good hot water, a scrubbing brush, soap. And bleach if they're bad.'

'Bleach?'

'Bleach.' Mrs Harkness was firm on the matter of bleach.

That week she scrubbed. On hands and knees, elbows out, fierce face close to the stone she was cleaning. Next week, Madeline's turn. Mrs Harkness waited. Madeline did not comply with the stair rules. The following week, Mrs Harkness scrubbed again. The week after, when Madeline showed no sign of doing her duty, Mrs Harkness left a bucket, scrubbing brush, bar of household soap and bleach at her door. Madeline placed them all back at Mrs Harkness's door. Mrs Harkness returned them to Madeline's door with a note, brief and to the point: 'Clean the stairs.' Madeline put them back at Mrs Harkness's door with her reply note: 'I have no intention of cleaning the stairs.'

This exchange of brief notes and the depositing of the bucket at doors went on for some weeks. Mrs Harkness scrubbed furiously. She was so angry, the stairs gleamed. At last, she decided the only way to sort this out was confrontation. She watched for Madeline coming home. And pounced.

'The stairs,' she cried. Coming straight to the point.

'What about them?' shrugged Madeline.

'You're needing to clean them. It's your turn. I've been doing them for you.'

'Nobody asked you to,' Madeline pointed out. It was past six. Raining. She was soaked. And broke. Her money wouldn't stretch to a bus fare and food. She'd chosen food. Had a small tin of beans she was looking forward to eating, on toast, with a cup of tea.

'I'm not living with filthy stairs. That's not my way.'

'So clean them,' said Madeline. 'I'm not going to. They don't bother me.' She stumped off. Up the stairs. Into her flat.

The confrontation was discussed with other residents of the building. Madeline was decreed a filthy little madam. Mrs Harkness vowed never to clean Madeline's half of the stairs again. She did the first five, leading up to Madeline's landing. Left the rest. The woman from the flat above did the first five leading down to Madeline's landing. Left the rest. Each flight had five bleached and sparkling stairs, and five grubby neglected ones. This infuriated both Mrs Harkness and the woman from the flat above. Madeline didn't notice. Every time she passed up and down the hall, Mrs Harkness would hear her and mutter, 'Filthy little madam.'

Stuart and Madeline went upstairs. Stripped in a frenzy. Made love on the rumpled mattress. Madeline clinging to him. Pumping out her frustration. She lay in a sweat afterwards, foot sticking out from underneath her duvet, cooling off. The room was too cold to expose any more of her body. She lay looking up at the sky outside, at the gathering dark. She watched a whirl of starlings grouping, ready to roost. A small group sped over the rooftops, disappeared. Then returned, swept another small flock into its ranks. Disappeared. Came rushing back, chorusing, calling, enfolded another small flurry. Then off again. More and more birds joined the gang till there seemed to be thousands of them, hurtling, fretting in that small space just beyond her window. She envied them.

'Seems like the life,' she said. 'Lots of gossipy chums to snuggle into in the dark.' She was calm now, frustration spent.

Stuart had soaked it all up. And was sleeping it off. She turned to watch him. Ran her finger down his face. Nice face, she thought. She played with his lips. Leaned over, blew on his ear. Kissed it. Wished he would wake and chat to her. She licked his neck to get the taste of him. She liked tasting people.

For a long time Annie, when Madeline kissed her, tasted of babies. Madeline wondered if rich people tasted better than poor ones. She supposed they did. Better feeding. Like pigs fed with apricots and acorns were bound to taste better than those kept in battery farms and fed – what? She didn't know, but was sure it was rubbish. The porky equivalent of Pot Noodle.

Stuart tasted gentle.

'What do you mean by that?' Annie had asked when Madeline told her.

'Gentle,' Madeline said. 'You know. Gentle.' She could think of no way to explain it.

'I have no idea what you mean,' Annie told her.

'I know people who taste gentle.' Marcus came to Madeline's rescue. 'Granny tastes gentle.'

Annie turned to look at him. Surprised to find such sensitivity in a boy who had, only five minutes ago, been stopped from shaving the cat.

'And melons taste gentle,' continued Marcus. 'Crisps don't. They taste nippy and wrinkly. They taste old.'

'Yes,' agreed Madeline. 'And ice cream tastes soothing. Like fresh sheets.'

Annie felt excluded as Marcus and Madeline exchanged tastes.

Madeline's relationship with children interested Annie. If children came to her, Madeline was fine. If they didn't, she was edgy with them. Marcus never had any problem coming forward. But Flo, her daughter, was reserved, a shy little one who weighed up adults from a distance. She'd never taken to Madeline.

Looking at Madeline now, sparring with Marcus, Annie realised what it was bothered Flo. Madeline was a rival. She was a child still herself; she hadn't rounded off into proper adulthood. There was something infantile about her craving for attention and approval. Marcus, in his little childish way, sensed that, didn't mind it. Dealing with that sort of rivalry was part of his life; he thrived on it.

'Hmm. So how does Madeline taste?' Annie asked Marcus.

He climbed on Madeline's knee and licked her neck. The most succulent bit of human beings for tasting purposes. 'She tastes young,' he said. 'Young like a raspberry which looks all hairy and knobbly but tastes nice when you eat it.'

'Well, thanks for that,' said Madeline, not knowing whether or not she should be offended.

But Annie thought he had a point. She thought that tasting people might be a fine way of discovering their personalities. But doing it, especially to strangers, might get her into trouble.

When Stuart didn't wake, just irritably brushed away her lickings and strokings, Madeline got up, ran shivering to shove on the railway coat. And, in the kitchen, hopped from foot to foot waiting for the kettle to boil. 'Hurry up.' She took her coffee back to bed. And sat drinking it, waiting for Stuart to return to the living. When at last he did, she was there, in the dark, waiting for him to love her again.

They cooked omelettes, squeezing past each other in the cupboard kitchen, enjoying the closeness, deliberately brushing hips and groins, thinking of passions to come, later. He whisked the eggs, she chopped an onion, grated some hardened sweaty cheese. They ate in bed, keeping warm. Drank vodka Stuart had bought to celebrate. Listened to John Lee Hooker, full blast – 'Dimples'. Madeline, soothed by sex and booze, danced round the room, arms raised. When the sweat of movement, happiness, triumph and booze hit her she slid out of the railway coat and threw it into the corner. Mrs Harkness, in the room below, thumped the ceiling with a broom handle, and Madeline jumped on the floor, answering. At last she came to lie beside Stuart. They did a lying-down jig. They were too legless to boogie standing up.

Downstairs Mrs Harkness raged. Dammit, she was awake. The little minx had woken her for what must be the thousandth time since she moved in. Mrs Harkness knew that once awake, it would be hours before she slept again. She glared at the ceiling.

'Girl,' she said, 'you have got to go.'

Rapture

In the night Madeline would move close to Stuart, demanding he put his arms round her. Hold her. 'Say something nice to me.'

'I think your bum's getting bigger.'

'That's not very nice.'

'It's the middle of the night.'

'I know. Say something nice so's I can sleep.'

'You've got lovely skin. It's like silk.' Stroking her.

'More than that.'

'Christ, Madeline.'

'What about my work? My paintings?'

'Your paintings are fine. I like them.'

'Like? Fine? They're just fine. Is that all?'

'No. They're wonderful. Fantastic. I love them. Please go to sleep.'

She'd turn, punch the pillow. Heave the duvet round her. And finally sleep. But sleeping for Madeline was almost as traumatic as being awake. She dreamed. Every night visions flew before her. Mornings she would rise, rumpled and exhausted. During the day, the dreams hung about her. They did not leave till early evening. She'd stay up as late as possible, keeping herself awake with vodka and coffee. Till, three or four in the morning, she'd give in. Go to bed. And dream some more.

Stuart needed eight hours a night. More if he could get it. Madeline's habit of staying up into the small hours left him wrecked. At work he'd stare into the distance, aching to lie down. His limbs were heavy with exhaustion. He smoked, drank coffee. Struggled with his workload. Sometimes, in the evenings, he'd walk slowly through empty streets. Listening to blackbirds. He thought their call sweetened the air. He needed time alone, away from Madeline. Her doubts and fears. Sometimes, he felt she was sucking the life out of him. Though he loved her, he longed for the emptiness of Marglass House.

If Madeline had left her paintings at Hamilton Foster's gallery, the paintings hadn't left her.

They were in a bar, deciding where to go to eat.

'Thai?' asked Stuart. 'Italian? I think Italian.'

'I want to go back and get my paintings,' she said. Suddenly. 'Why?'

'I've just thought of a better way to do them. I want to fix them. There's bits here and there I could tickle up.'

'They're fine. Leave them. Forget about them. Move on.'

'No.'

The further she got from her paintings, the more she thought about them. Longed to have them back. She clutched Stuart's arm. 'What if nobody likes them? What if people laugh at them? What if the word about them goes round and people come to laugh?'

'It won't. They won't. Forget it.'

He had thought she'd finish her work and come back to him. But she was reliving each brush stroke, each mixing of every colour.

'They're crap,' she said. 'I hate them.'

He sighed, told her they weren't. 'Come back to my place,' he invited. 'I'll cook for you. We'll get drunk and you can relax.'

She thought about this. She rarely visited him. Stuart thought it had something to do with his money. He wondered sometimes if she was jealous of his wealthy background. Her scathing comments were too scathing.

Looking at an antique rocking horse in a shop window, 'Bet you had one like that,' she said. Before he could say that he hadn't, she said, 'Bet you had half a dozen. Your mummy would just pick up the phone and order them for you. A stable of rocking horses, please.' In a mock pukka voice.

She looked at him. Knew she was being awful, but couldn't help it. The mood, the despair, was bigger than she was. 'Can I have a bath?' she asked. Baths were important to Madeline. Not having one of her own, she cultivated people who had. Of all her bath contacts,

Stuart was the best. His flat had an old roll-top, brass taps, claw feet.

'There's lots of hot water and some lavender foam. For relaxing.' He could tell she was tempted. 'I'll bring you a vodka and tonic. Ice and lemon.'

She was weakening.

'I'll cook for you. You'll lie back, eyes shut, breathing in the steam and heat. And you'll hear me in the kitchen rattling pots and crockery. Then you'll smell the thick scents of cooking.' He leaned towards her, drawing her in. Luring her to his den. 'You'll hear the sizzle of onions then the smack of steak hitting the pan. Fillet in olive oil. The aroma flooding the flat. Food.' He said it again. 'Food.' She never could resist food. 'Then we'll sit in the warmth and drink wine. And you'll feel better. A bath and food fixes most things.'

'What things do I need fixing?' she asked.

'Your worry. Nerves.'

She leaned back in her seat. Weighing up her options. Go back to her place. Sit on the floor. Eat a Pot Noodle and a packet of crisps. Coat on, because she had nothing to burn. Or go to his place. A hot bath. Hot food. Wine. 'OK,' she said.

She walked in front of him as always. She never could bear his slow stroll. She ducked through the Friday evening crowds. Walking faster and faster. Till she was running. Coat flying behind her. It wasn't a joyous sprint. It was a race against her fear, her worry. The chill air caught, raw, in her throat. Her left side ached. Stuart jogged along behind, feeling ridiculous. Eventually he stopped, let her go. Stood, hands in pockets watching her till she disappeared. He felt tired. Infected by her nerves. He went into the nearest pub, drank a slow pint, smoked a couple of cigarettes, recovering, before strolling down the hill to his flat.

She was sitting on the pavement at the end of his street. Shivering, head on her knees.

'Where the hell have you been?'

'Coming after you.'

'You took your time.'

'Yeah,' he said. Walking past her, along the street and up to his door.

She followed. Then walked inside after him. Flopped on the sofa. Immediately got up again. Peered into the bathroom with its roll-top bath, brass fittings. She stroked the Regency stripe wallpaper. And inspected the paintings. Misty glens, stags, a faded, badly executed watercolour of Marglass House she hadn't noticed before. 'This is where you live?'

He nodded.

'It's nice in a hideous sort of way. Decaying opulence.'

'That's me,' he agreed.

'Good. You're sort of on your way down.'

'And you are on your way up?'

'That's the long-term plan.'

'And the short-term?'

'A bath. I'll leave you to cook.'

He heard the bath running. Smelled the lavish amount of foam she poured in. Sat counting the moods she'd run through in the couple of hours since they'd met. From foul-tempered with nerves, to insecure, to absurd when she ran down the hill. He sank into a chair, slumped across the table. Madeline was exhausting. He didn't know how she lived with herself, coped with her shifting emotions. He felt he had two basic frames of mind, happy and sad. And a normal day was spend somewhere between them both. Neither completely one nor the other. A normal day for Madeline was a flood of moods, feelings, reactions and she knew nothing of keeping them back. Everything showed. Bottled up? She didn't know the meaning. He didn't know why this didn't drain her, as it did him. He supposed she got rid of her tensions, anger, nerves. Let them loose. He soaked them all up. And it shattered him. He felt dull inside. Then again, Madeline, with her complex whoosh of emotions, made him feel rather ordinary. All he wanted from life was peace of mind, a bit of happiness and a chum. She wanted so much more.

He got up. Made Madeline the promised drink. Took it to her. Stood for a few minutes watching her lie, head back, eyes shut, soaking. Water always soothed her. Water and food and warmth. Primal things. He sighed. Went back to the kitchen, and started to cook. Peppered steak in Madeira sauce. It was his recipe. He did it to impress women.

Half an hour later, Madeline, wrapped in his towelling robe, came through to watch.

'You must have had a lovely childhood,' she said. 'Big house. Money. Everything you wanted.'

'It was a bit lonely,' he told her. He had told her this often, but she didn't seem to believe it.

'But you had so much.'

'I always felt my father was disappointed in me. I never was the laddish boy he wanted. And my mother spent her days embroidering, writing letters, visiting her friends. She didn't have much time for me.'

'That's so sad,' she said. 'I had a lovely childhood.'

Turned over the steaks. Moved the onions about in the pan.

'My dad used to tell me stories. He'd sit me on his knee and he had all these wonderful tales. About a secret wood. And Mrs Turner from three doors down made beetroot sandwiches.'

'What?'

'Yeah, I know. Sounds awful. But I was little. White bread, beetroot. There was a texture about them. And they were a good colour. I made one once, a few years ago. It actually tasted awful. I'll just have to leave them back in my childhood. They belong there.'

Stuart fetched a bottle of Madeira. Poured some into his pan. Watched the mixture spark and froth. Madeline was impressed. She was meant to be. He poured some brandy into the thick jammy mixture in his pan. Lit it. Flame spurted towards the ceiling.

'Cool,' said Madeline.

He turned to her, grinning. This was what he wanted, praise. He wanted her to let go and love him. And to take the love he had on offer for her. Though sometimes, her lust for life, her longing for more – always more – made him wonder if he could love her enough. If anyone could love her enough. She seemed insatiable.

He put her steak on a plate, covered it in sauce. Put salad on the table, and a loaf of crusty bread. Filled a glass of wine. She drained it. He filled it up again. And then she ate. Silent as always, wiping her plate with the bread till it shone. He thought her a pleasure to feed. She looked at him. She was shining. She reminded him of a little girl. Look, I've finished it all. Can I have some pudding? He fetched her a slice of supermarket cheesecake. She smiled at it. Then ate. Silent again. She ran her fingers round the plate, scooping up the pools of sweetness, licking them clean.

They took coffee and brandy through to the living room. Madeline was fed and warm and mellow. She opened up about her young life. The beginnings of her. The small terraced house where she was brought up. Ted and his orchids. And his ssshh plants.

She helped herself to more brandy. 'Lovely stuff. Is it old?' Lovely. Tonight, replete and curled up before a fire, everything was lovely.

He told her that what she was drinking was older than she was.

She swirled it in her glass. 'When I was growing up, going to school, learning to swim, riding my bike up and down the street, this brandy was lying in a cask, maturing, ripening, waiting for this moment for me to come to it and drink. All those years. Lovely years.' She sniffed it. Letting its soft fumes warm her nostrils. 'Lovely. Even though it was just the two of us, we had a good time at Christmas. Did you?'

He shook his head. Christmas they were often snowed in. His father bought him shares. His mother, books. Always the same. They ate goose that his father bagged; it was always peppered with shot. He remembered eating it with caution, lest a tiny lead pellet stuck in his throat or cracked a molar. It was prepared, with her usual disinterest, by Muriel, who hated cooking. Soggy sprouts and charred roast potatoes. 'Though,' he told her, 'she did a mean pudding. She made Christmas pudding in September, soaked it weekly in brandy. She never drank herself, and had no idea of quantities when it came to alcohol. So when she soaked a pudding, she soaked a pudding. It was extremely alcoholic. Good. It certainly made you forget the goose.' He nodded.

'We had turkey,' Madeline told him. 'And on Christmas Eve my dad would read that poem. " 'Twas the night before Christmas, when all through the house, Not a creature was stirring, not even a mouse."

And we'd go all still and listen. We'd go outside, see if we could spot Santa storming across the sky.'

It touched Stuart that she would revel in such simple memories. His other friends, Abbot, for example, told very similar stories with derision. Recalling how bored he'd been.

But Madeline was entranced by it all. It seemed to Stuart that she relished her past as much as she anticipated her future. She ate, she drank, she reminisced, she made love with breathtaking gusto. In bed she drained him. Moving against him with passion, clutching him, nails into his back, his bum, reaching into him for instant gratification – instant, intense gratification. And sometimes he soared with her, and sometimes he lay back afterwards, knackered. Yet, he loved her. And, right now, listening to this little memory, he envied her.

He felt it showing on his face. And no matter how hard he tried to smile, look interested, entranced, as she was, he couldn't stop the way his lips tightened, the creases round his eyes. Visions of himself, all those years ago, standing alone in his bedroom at Marglass House, holding his Christmas games compendium, and nobody to play it with. Parties on the television, people laughing. His father drinking brandy in the drawing room, his mother in the lounge writing letters, mouthing, with a slight whisper, the words she was putting on her lavender-scented paper. Shutting him out even more than she had done already. Making the silence more awful. He always hated Christmas. It was not a good time for lonely children.

Madeline came to him. Sat on his knee. Stroked his cheeks. 'I didn't mean to make you sad. I didn't mean to gloat. It wasn't that wonderful.'

'It sounds it,' he said.

She kissed him. 'Let's go to bed. I'll make it up to you. You can punish me for being so callous.'

'I don't want to punish you. Never that.' Touching her. Her hair. Fingers through its tangled mass.

They lay in bed. Curled together under the giant eiderdown. And when they loved it was as near perfect as it could get. She lay under him, breathed his name. Hand on his head. Kissing him. Swooning.

Her lips were soft, wet. And when she'd come she put them to his ear and told him she loved him. They lay in mutual sweat. And outside the night turned chill. Dark. Edinburgh shivered. Stuart thought he was as near to rapture as he'd ever be. Love. A shot at happiness and a friend. A real friend, at last. He didn't want to sleep. He wanted to stay awake. To keep these moments close for ever. But he did. A long deep sleep.

It was past ten when he woke. And Madeline was gone.

Stuart's Notions

Stuart went round to Madeline's flat. But she wasn't there.

'No sign of her,' said Mrs Harkness. 'You usually hear her,' she went on. 'She's a noisy bugger. The music. The jumping around. Dancing, I think. Sawing wood? Could she be sawing wood?' she probed. She had to be sure.

Stuart nodded. 'Yeah,' he told her idly. 'Her furniture. She likes to keep warm.'

Ah-ha, thought Mrs Harkness. Got you now, little madam.

Stuart got the impression Mrs Harkness did not like Madeline very much. Then again, he thought maybe Mrs Harkness didn't like anybody very much.

On the way to find Annie Melville to ask if she knew where Madeline was, Stuart decided that life had not been very kind to Mrs Harkness.

He was walking at his usual slow pace. He wished he'd taken more time with his socks. He had on a green one and a yellow one. The green one was fine. The yellow, three days worn, was crispy, hard on the sole of his foot. Too sweat-encrusted to keep out the chill. His left foot was cold and sore. It irritated him.

He and Abbot had a sock theory. It wasn't worth washing them. Not when they could buy packs of six cheaply at car boot sales. Abbot bought only black, and threw them out after he'd worn them once. Put fresh on everyday. Stuart couldn't bring himself to part with them. And never could resist packs that had a selection of colours. He had two drawers full of them, in a wide range of shades, and smelling of feet. Old feet, he thought. He discovered that socks left lying for a fortnight or so lost their crispiness and became wearable again. And had, as well as the socks in the drawer, several piles lying in his bedroom. The piles were dated, day old, week old and fortnight old. Today he'd shoved on the yellow sock he'd had on yesterday and, unable to find a partner for it, had selected a green from the fortnight pile. He was regretting not taking another from that pile. But at the time, that would have meant removing the yellow sock, and he couldn't be bothered.

Hands in pockets, stopping now and then to stare at things, people that interested him. An old lady carrying a string bag containing two onions and a leek. He wondered what she was going to cook. A white limo sleeking through the late December afternoon. Black windows. He wondered who was in there. A bronze sculpture of a lizard in a shop. He wondered who had done it. Decided he didn't like it. Longed for Madeline to be by his side so they could discuss together how much they loathed it. And to make up stories about the sculptor, and what a miserable life he must be having. He watched a man walk stoop-shouldered into a pub. His suit was worn shiny, long out of fashion. He had a clumsy walk. Stuart wondered if he'd always walked like that, or if, like Mrs Harkness, life hadn't always been kind to him. But then, he thought, perhaps Mrs Harkness hadn't been kind to life. Madeline would agree with that.

'You have to give to get,' Madeline often said.

Stuart nodded. He found these days that when Madeline wasn't with him, like now, he'd still have conversations with her. Imagining her answers to his thoughts and observations. He wondered where the hell she'd gone to. Then congratulated himself on a fine twenty minutes' musing. He thought he was born to stare and muse. Stuff working. He could happily while away his life standing on a street corner watching the world go by.

Annie, when he reached her flat, was sitting in the kitchen. A big room, huge old pine table with a collection of mismatching chairs round it. She was sitting at one end, the Sunday papers and a collection of empty coffee cups spread before her. Willie was out.

'Christ knows where he's gone,' Annie said.

Stuart looked around. He found the domesticity beguiling. Flo was wearing only a T-shirt. She'd already wet two sets of pants. 'A surfeit of Ribena,' Annie said. 'All her other pants are in the wash. I decided to give up. Let her roam free.'

Stuart could hear the roar of a football match on the television in the living room. And howls of joy or derision from Marcus and Douglas, who were watching it. Curled in the old armchair beside the Aga, Teddy, the cat, slept.

Flo eyed him. A grubby torn blanket, clutched against her flaming cheeks.

'Teething,' said Annie. 'Teeth, who needs them?' She wasn't talking sense and knew it. But it had been a day. And she needed to speak. Not talk. Just say words that someone understood, out loud.

'Well, me,' said Stuart. 'I like having teeth. In fact one of my secret dreads is losing them. I don't want dentures.'

'You've got lovely teeth,' Annie told him. 'Coffee?'

He nodded.

Flo turned her attentions to the cat. Tried to lift him from the chair. He was too big for her to lug around. She had to put her arms round the animal's middle and heave. The cat struggled, and lost. Now hung upside-down looking resigned. 'Time for your bath, Teddy,' Flo told him.

Stuart looked alarmed.

'Don't worry,' said Annie. 'It won't happen. So what brings you here, anyway?' She heaped grounds into the cafetière. Poured in boiling water.

'Madeline,' said Stuart. 'Have you seen her?'

'Done a bunk, has she?' Annie put a steaming mug in front of him. 'She usually comes here on a Sunday.'

Stuart nodded. 'It's like she was there one minute. Gone the next. I mean, she was there when I fell asleep. Then when I woke . . . nothing. Nobody. Empty bed.'

'Empty bed. Sounds lovely,' said Annie. She looked round. 'Time is it?'

'Half-past two,' Stuart told her.

'Damn.'

The child abandoned the cat, climbed on to Stuart's knee. Waved a model car under his nose. Stuart said, 'Cool.' And started to run it up and down the table making car noises. 'Why damn?' he asked.

'Half-past two's too early for a drink. It has to be after five.'

'Not on a Sunday,' Stuart said. 'You can drink earlier on a Sunday. In fact it's not only allowed, it's considered civilised.'

'Excellent,' said Annie. 'Madeline will come back. She'll be striding about mumbling to herself. She does that.' Then, seeing his look, knowing what it meant: 'Don't worry, she's not with someone else.'

'How do you know that?'

'She's a one-bloke-at-a-time person. Always has been. Let her go. She'll be back. Also, she's nuts about you. She thinks you taste gentle.'

'What the hell does that mean?'

Annie shrugged.

'But what if she's in trouble?' he asked.

'Madeline? If she was in trouble you'd know all about it. She's a dumper. Never bottles anything up. She just goes off on her own now and then. Wouldn't you like to?'

He made a face. Didn't know, really. He supposed so. 'There's been times.' He thought of himself as a person who mused. But not in any mind-twisting, soul-searing depths. He mused to enjoy himself, it entertained him. It was his hobby.

Flo ran her toy car up Stuart's shirt. On to his face. Making wild revving noises whilst navigating his nose. Annie told her to stop it. Stuart told her he didn't mind.

Marcus came through. Opened the fringe, stared in, complaining there was nothing to eat.

'There's apples,' said Annie. 'And cheese.'

'That's not proper snack food,' said Marcus. He took a can of Coke and went back to his football.

'Marcus,' said Stuart. 'Who thought of that?'

'Willie,' said Annie. 'He got enthused about having a son. Couldn't decide on a name. He wanted to call him Marcus Horatio Zorro Borthwick Brando Melville. We had a bit of a bicker about that. Willie said that as a boy he'd loved to have been called Zorro and as a teenager he wished he'd had a name like Brando. He thought we were covering every angle and Marcus would be grateful.'

'He's got a point,' said Stuart. 'I can see the logic.'

Annie gave him a look. 'He's Marcus Borthwick Brando Melville. We compromised. But, in fact, I think Willie won.'

The only Marcus in Stuart's life so far had been his father's lawyer. A elegant man in bespoke suits, well into his sixties. Stuart had never thought of Marcus as being a child's name. But the first Marcus in his life must have been a child at some time. It was hard to imagine. Maybe this new Marcus would become soft-spoken and gentle like the other one. It was in his name. A bespoke name. A bespoke life. Perhaps if his father had called him Hector or Nelson rather than Stuart, he might have risen to his expectations. Done nobler things.

Stuart took the little car from Flo, ran it over the child's tummy and up round her neck, enthusing about the squeal of tyre over little ear and gear changes whilst screeching over the top of the head and back down towards the tummy. Flo laughed, a squeaky childish giggle. Stuart dropped his knee so that she slid towards the floor. Then caught her before she landed.

'Again,' said Flo.

Stuart obliged.

'You've got a friend,' said Annie. 'You'll never get rid of her now.'

Stuart lifted the child high. This was the sort of friend he wanted. One you could never get rid of. He looked over at the pine chest in the corner, overflowing toys. He wished he could go over to play with them. He was becoming aware that if he had children, it would be the only acceptable way he could have the childhood he'd missed.

'I could have one of them,' he told Annie. 'They're quite nice. I quite like them.'

'Oh, have one,' Annie offered grandly. 'Take two. Two for the price of one. There, it's the retail in me. I can't resist making a bargain offer.'

'No, really,' Stuart said. He had a sudden vision of himself as a dad. 'I could have one at Marglass House.' He saw himself and a milling crowd of his offspring playing chasing games across the weed-infested lawns. 'We could play hide-and-seek amongst the rho-dodendrons. They're huge. We could roll down the slopes towards the walled garden.' Leaning towards Annie, ablaze with this new idea: 'We could set up a huge model railway in the dining hall. Guessing games beside the roaring fire in the drawing room.' He leaned back, letting his mind spin. He'd read them stories, all the books he hadn't had – A. A. Milne, Roald Dahl. They could put a net across the grass, play badminton in the evenings with bats moving in and out of the trees behind them. They could track foxes, find where the badgers reared their young. Fish. Swim from the tiny shingled beach. Light fires, cook sausages in the embers. It would be wonderful. Stuart looked rapt.

'I love your vision,' said Annie. 'You think that's what it's like to bring up children?'

Stuart looked round the kitchen. The steriliser on the unit, a bottle of Milton beside it, a small row of bottles, a pack of nappies on the floor. Annie had, only moments before, rubbed some sort of gel stuff on the baby's gums. It all seemed complex and difficult. He didn't think he could do any of that. He was revolted at the thought of changing a nappy. Though he thought he might manage one that didn't have any shit in it.

He could hire a nanny. What with? Funds were running low. He had thought he was comfortable. But Marglass House was in a bad state of repair. It needed a new roof, some repointing, there was damp and dry rot. He had toyed with the notion of selling it. But wondered who would buy such a monstrosity. And what about Muriel and Donald and their dream cottage? He'd tossed all this about in his mind for three or four minutes before deciding it was too much to think about. It worried him to the point of hurting. He thought it best not to worry about it for the moment. Later, he thought. Head in the sand, he told himself, that's the best plan for now.

He leaned his head in his hand, watching Annie. She was his favourite person in the world. Madeline was his love, his passion. But there was comfort in Annie. She was easy company. He liked the way she moved, a fluidity of motion. Getting up from her chair, scooping up Flo on her way to the kitchen unit. Opening a drawer, taking out the teething gel, squeezing a blob on to her pinkie, rubbing the aching gums. Putting the child down again. All without interrupting her conversation. He thought it a dance.

Stuart liked women. He was content to be with them. He liked their chat. He enjoyed how they drank wine and tried to up one another with their absurdities. Awful things that had happened to them. He thought that men bragged. Woman also bragged, but they bragged about their nonsense. 'What, you went to work with your skirt tucked into your knickers? Nothing. I was at a presentation and sneezed, a stonker. It took me by such force I farted simultaneously.' And they would hoot, and howl and pour more wine and carry on confessing their silly moments. Taking comfort from one another. Thinking about it now, Stuart realised that was what he liked about women. Their comfort. The comfort of women. Gimme some of that, he thought.

'I know there's all sorts of messy stuff. Sleepless nights and that. Still, I'd like kids one day,' he told Annie.

'Who with?' asked Annie. 'Madeline?'

'Yeah, Madeline. I don't see it, though, do you?'

'I can't see Madeline having one baby. Far less half a dozen.'

'Oh no,' he shook his head. 'It's the one would be the problem. After that it'd be fine. She always wants more of everything.'

'Well,' said Annie, 'that's your family sorted. Now, if it's acceptable to drink before five on a Sunday, let's have a gin and tonic. That's Sundayish booze. And you can tell me about this Marglass House place. It sounds wonderful.'

'It isn't really. It's hideously ugly. And it's sort of falling down,' said Stuart. 'Well, not sort of, it *is* falling down. But it does have a faded charm. The lure of bygone days. Better times.'

He stayed with Annie till after seven. It was a comfortable kitchen. And Annie was always comfortable company. Stuart bathed Flo, and blissfully helped Douglas and Marcus with their homework. He was almost sad when Flo kissed his cheek good night. She smelled soapily sweet, little body hugging him, tiny lips against his stubble, and disappeared upstairs. But Annie was adamant. 'It's time for me,' she said.

'Yeah,' said Stuart. 'I want one of those.'

179

Annie reached over, touched his arm. 'You're a babe,' she told him.

He refused the offer of supper, anxious to get home. There might be a message from Madeline. There wasn't. He heated a pizza, drank too much wine. Listening for Madeline's footsteps outside. Sitting by the phone, willing it to ring. He went to bed after two. Slept fitfully till six, when he fell into a deep black slumber.

He woke at ten past nine. Stumbled about his bedroom in the gloom, groping for clothes. He picked up the shirt he'd worn the day before. Flo had spilled Ribena on it whilst he'd been giving her a drink. He looked around for another, panicking. Couldn't find one, so shoved on his favourite Biro T-shirt. He was half an hour late for the fifth time in a fortnight, and wearing a T-shirt instead of the desired shirt and tie. He wasn't popular. He was wearing the green sock from yesterday and a red one from the fortnight-old pile.

Outside the day was chill; the heating in the office was on full blast. At two in the afternoon the sun streamed in through the window. Stuart was hot, sweaty and exhausted. He rested his head on his arm, the buzz of office, phones ringing, voices, papers being shuffled, people moving around became hollow, distant. He woke an hour later. Looked round, chagrined. Had anybody noticed? Nobody was looking at him. He made a flamboyant show of clicking on his Biro, opening a file and scribbling some notes. 'Scribble, scribble blah blah. God, what a load of bollocks this job is,' he wrote. Then shut the file, turned to his screen and rattled his keyboard, typing a dirty joke Annie had told him. He faxed it to Abbot. He'd meant to stay late making up time. But, come five o'clock, was too tired. He went home. Bathed. Ate some toasted cheese and went to bed early.

The next evening, Madeline reappeared.

'I've been visiting Mrs Turner.'

'Beetroot sandwiches?' he asked.

She nodded. 'I didn't get one.'

'I was worried,' said Stuart.

'Oh, don't worry about me. I'm fine. I'm always fine.'

Stuart doubted that.

'We did a bit of gardening. You know, winter stuff. And I potted on some things in the greenhouse.'

'You could have got in touch.'

'I know. I'm sorry. I just go and see them sometimes.' She thought about this. 'Well, not very often. Not often enough, considering they took me in. In fact, I hardly ever go to see them.'

'So why now?'

'I just sort of found myself there. I started walking. And that was where I ended up. I didn't think about it. I just walked. And there I was. So I went and rang the bell.'

'What time was it?' asked Stuart.

'Half-past seven. In the morning.'

'Bet they were surprised to see you.'

This was a new thought to Madeline. What an odd time to drop in. 'Now you mention it,' she admitted.

She'd told Mrs Turner about Stuart.

'So you've got yourself a decent man, at last,' Mrs Turner approved. 'When do I get to meet him?'

'One day,' Madeline promised.

'I'd like to meet them,' Stuart said.

'One day,' Madeline promised.

Madeline had woken in the middle of the night. Lay beside Stuart, listening to him breath. She touched the back of his neck. Put her head on his shoulder, spooned into him, slight sweat, and thought, You're mine. It was as close to rapture as she'd ever got. She moved her cheek against him. Quietly hoping he'd wake, so she could tell him of this wave of warmth moving through her. He didn't. She sighed. Turned to look at the window. Thin streams of streetlights shafting across the ceiling. Slowly, slowly the rapture slipped away. And was replaced by worry.

She plagued herself with four-in-the-morning doubts and fears. Something could happen to Stuart. He might get knocked over cycling to work. Maybe he didn't love her as much as she now thought she loved him. Physical pain she could cope with. But emotional pain, no, couldn't take that. It sent people into a black and hollow abyss. Your eyes go blank, thought Madeline, and your cheeks ache from the constant grim expression. And the slightest thing – a stubbed toe, a sharp look from a colleague, a sip of scalding tea – could set you screaming. No more, no more, I can take no more.

'I'm not up for any of that,' she said.

This thought drove her from bed. She went to the kitchen where she could worry standing up, leaning against the sink. Drinking tea. Love made her vulnerable. She could give herself wholeheartedly, and he could reject her. Run off with someone else. She imagined that. The sadness. Sitting alone staring at the wall, unable to think, eat. Move. But the real bummer about being in love was that she was no longer in control of her feelings. Her moods, thoughts, were affected by Stuart's moods – though he only seemed to have three, affable, less affable and more affable – and thoughts.

'I don't know about Stuart,' she had said to Annie. 'He's always in a good mood. And, he doesn't seem to want much out of life. He lacks ambition. It's the eighties. Ambition's meant to be sexy.'

Annie had scoffed at this. 'It's up to you to motivate him. That's what women do, they motivate their blokes. Help them be all they can be.'

'You sound like an advert,' said Madeline. She looked across as Willie, who had hooked a chip into a fishing line and was hanging it from the ceiling that it dangled beside the chopping board. 'This,' he was expounding to Marcus, 'is the perfect chip. Note its size and shape. Small, but not too small, and not too fat. It is crisp on the outside, succulent within. We'll keep it here as a marker. A chip against which all future chips should be measured. This is the standard Melville chip. Nothing less will do.'

Marcus was agreeing.

Annie shrugged. 'Well, I try.'

Madeline sipped her tea, stared out at the dawn. Light slipped pale grey across the sky, the grey roofs shone. Buildings glinted. Madeline looked at the silent windows, curtains drawn. People in there sleeping. They'd be in bed, eyes shut, snoring maybe. Dreaming. And did any of them sleep like the Melvilles slept, with a child, or two, between them? Him, with one leg sticking out into the chill and dark, because the bed got too bleeding hot with all these folk in it.

She had a fleeting fantasy – Madeline the earth mother. Walking barefoot with a child on her hip. Another three or four trailing behind her. At first the fantasy was sunny. They were all smiling. But as she stared at the wall, sipped her tea, the sun went behind a cloud. The imaginary children started to cry. Complain they were tired. Wanted something to eat. 'Juice,' called one. 'I want juice, now.' Another screamed that little Stuart was pulling her hair. The child she was carrying on her hip was suddenly sick.

'Oh Christ,' Madeline shouted at her fantasies. 'Stop it. Stop it all of you. Now.'

How did Annie manage? Madeline wondered. She hardly finished a sentence these days. She'd be expounding about something, or telling Madeline about some new frock she'd bought, or how she fancied having her hair cut. And she'd have to stop to tell a child where the orange juice was, or she'd have to go sort out some tantrum or a small, but fierce, fight over what was on television. Evenings she was always picking one up and taking another somewhere. Or she'd be on the phone making arrangements with other mothers about picking children up and dropping other children off. Madeline knew she couldn't cope with all of that.

She remembered visiting one Sunday, finding Annie near to tears. Marcus was missing. Willie had driven Douglas to the hospital after he'd stuck a wooden bead up his nose.

'He whistles when he breathes,' Annie fretted. 'What if they can't get it out? And it moves up into his brain?'

Madeline was sure it wouldn't.

Flo was sitting in her high chair by the table. She was waving a half-eaten chip (a perfect Melville chip), her face covered with tomato ketchup. Annie had been trying to feed her soup. The child had resisted. Most of the soup was now on Annie. Marcus suddenly reappeared. He'd been playing football in the park, but hadn't said where he was going.

'You tell me when you are going out. Where you are off to. And when you'll be back.' Annie had seethed.

Marcus agreed glumly. And asked for some money for a bottle of Coke.

'That's all I am to you,' cried Annie. 'A cash machine. A dispenser of money.' She turned to Flo. 'And to her, all I am is the face behind the spoon.'

Madeline had shrunk into the armchair in the corner of the kitchen. Looking alarmed. Annie saw this. And apologised. 'Don't mind me. I'm just being a mother. It's hell.'

'Do you think,' asked Madeline, not thinking that this was not the moment to mention this, 'that this is it? Your life? I mean, what if it doesn't get any better than this? This is how it's going to be?'

Annie stopped. For a moment she thought of throwing Madeline out. 'Thank you for that,' she said. 'What a bloody awful thing to say. And what a bloody awful time to say it.'

In the kitchen now. Five in the morning. Drinking tea. Madeline could see she'd been a little tactless.

Too awake now to sleep, she decided against going back to bed. Especially since Stuart was sleeping too deeply to be roused into making her return to his side interesting. Thing to do, she thought, is take a walk. She dressed, pulled on her Docs, and set out. At first she had a mind to visit Annie. But at five in the morning, she didn't think she'd be welcome. She started along the street. Turned into another street and kept on. The air was cold and clear. Pure. She stuck out her tongue. Tasted the morning. Something she and Ted had done when they set out each day. Her to school. Him to work.

Madeline stopped walking, thought about this. Her and Ted walking along the street, tongues hanging out. No wonder the neighbours thought them weird.

She carried on. Reached the suburbs. Blackbirds calling. Sparrows chirruping, bickering. Hassle in the hedgerows, thought Madeline. By seven o'clock she was in the street where she was brought up. She stood outside the house she'd once shared with Ted. It had different curtains. Blue and green stripes. The garden had been dug up. Now it was covered with gravel, with a single, leafless winter tree in the middle. There was a collection of pots round the front door. She remembered how it had been all those years ago. Bursting, overflowing with plants: lupins, delphiniums, foxgloves, veronica and little pink flowers spreading, rambling among them. Madeline didn't like what the new people had done. She stared, scowling. And still.

She looked about. The street was empty. Silent. And a small wind, curled round her, flapping her coat. Dried winter leaves rattled. An abandoned sweet wrapper scraped the pavement. She suddenly felt odd. Spare. What was she doing here? Should anyone look out of their window they'd see a strange woman hanging about and suspect she was up to no good. They'd call the police. She was suddenly embarrassed. Exposed. Needed to get inside, out of view. She turned. Ran to the Turners' house. Up the path. And rang the bell.

Seven thirty. They weren't up. Madeline heard Mrs Turner say, 'Who could that be? This time in the morning?' Archie's voice from within: 'I'll get it.' Slippered feet scuffed the carpet on their slow journey up the hall.

'Madeline!' He was surprised to see her. 'Goodness' sake. Time of day.' He ushered her into the living room, switched on the electric fire, and disappeared to tell Mrs Turner who was here.

Madeline sat watching the fake flames. And the small whirly thing above the red bulb. Such comfort here. Amidst the many patterns. The wallpaper, pale lemon with green flowers climbing towards the ceiling. The carpet, blue with cream swirls. The curtains, green with dark ochre wavy lines. It was hideous. It was warm and safe, and, somehow, lovely. Mrs Turner's lounge. Exactly as it had been all those years ago when she was four years old, waiting for Ted to come home, and listening to Mrs Turner and Babs from upstairs talking about pastry. Except it seemed to have got smaller. From the room down the hall, sounds, whispers.

'It's Madeline.'

'Madeline? What's she doing here this time of day?'

People shifting slowly. The rustlings of clothes being stiffly heaved over sore bones. Small groans. Then Mrs Turner appeared.

'This is a surprise.'

Madeline nodded.

'Is something wrong? Has something happened?' Mrs Turner oozed concern.

Madeline shook her head. 'I was just passing. I thought I'd say hello.'

Mrs Turner let this roll round her mind a while. Sucked her teeth. Chewed an imaginary bit of something. Just passin', she thought, that'll be right. 'Well, that's lovely,' she said. 'And it's lovely to see you.'

She made Madeline breakfast. Eggs and bacon. Toast and tea.

Mrs Turner scowled Archie from the room. He gulped his tea, stood, and said it was a grand time to be getting on with things in the shed.

'Men and their sheds,' said Mrs Turner. 'I don't know, you have a house and you do it up lovely. And they go spend all their time in the shed.'

Madeline had seen the scowl. And knew Mrs Turner thought it time for a serious chat. Mrs Turner was a master scowler. A swift, fierce, no-nonsense glance sorted people out. She could scowl the butcher into giving her a good lean cut of meat. Scowl passengers on buses to give up their seats to her. Scowl, scowl, scowl. As a way of getting what she wanted, and she was a woman who always got what she wanted, scowling was far more effective than being nice.

'Well, now,' she said, 'what's all this about?'

'I was just passing,' said Madeline. 'I was looking at Ted's garden. I don't like what the new people have done with it. Ted had it so nice.'

This surprised Mrs Turner. Ted's garden had been a scandal. The whole neighbourhood tutted and sighed when it was mentioned. It let down the whole tone of the street. As, of course, did Ted. Plainly Madeline didn't know this.

'It had all those delphiniums and lupins. I can't imagine why they pulled them all out.'

Because they were dead, thought Mrs Turner. That lovely Mrs Green would have turned in her grave if she'd seen it. She planted them all. Went out nights with a torch to capture and kill the slugs. She kept it lovely. After she'd gone Mr Green hardly looked at it. Except that once, when the lupin got broke.

'It was just,' said Madeline, 'we had such a super day yesterday. Everything was wonderful. Then in the middle of the night I started to worry about stuff. So I got up. Then I knew I wouldn't go back to sleep. So I came out for a walk. And ended up here.' There, that explained everything.

Mrs Turner heard nothing after we. We? she thought. Who is we? A man. The girl's gone and got herself a man. She's getting married. She slapped the table. She knew it. There wasn't much got past her. 'Well,' she said, 'that's lovely. That's just lovely.'

Madeline looked round. 'You've painted the kitchen.'

'Five years past,' Mrs Turner told her.

'It's lovely,' said Madeline.

'Everything is lovely,' agreed Mrs Turner. 'So, has this young man of yours got a name?'

'Stuart,' Madeline told her, wondering how Mrs Turner knew she had a young man.

'And when do I get to meet him?' Mrs Turner wanted to know.

Madeline wasn't sure about this. She imagined Stuart sitting in this kitchen, drinking tea. Legs crossed. Odd socks showing. She imagined him enthusing affably about his sock theory. His sock piles. The fortnight-old ones that got the dirt aired out of them. She imagined Mrs Turner scowling his relatively harmless position on socks out of him. Him hanging his head, confessing it wasn't all that hygienic, now she mentioned it. Or, rather, scowled about it. She thought he might let slip about the burning of the furniture in her flat. And the scowling she'd get for that. They'd be scowled out of the house. Down the road. Fleeing shamefully. Never to return.

So she said, 'One day.'

'I went to see Annie,' Stuart told her, now. 'I played with her kids.' He put his hands behind his head, musing. 'I like kids. I wouldn't mind having a couple.'

Madeline looked at him. 'Kids?'

'Yeah,' he said. 'They're quite nice. I like them. Yeah. One or two of them would be nice.' He looked at her, caught her expression. 'One day.'

'One day,' she agreed.

That night she dreamed her long and dusty road dream. She was cycling along a winding road. The way ahead stretched before her. The road she'd travelled wound behind. She was passing through a tiny village. A woman came out of one of the houses. She was wearing a long coat. She took hold of the handlebars and led Madeline for miles. They didn't speak. They arrived at a house. People were gathered by a clipped yew hedge, beside which lay an abandoned baby on a white blanket. They pointed at Madeline. 'She's the one. She did it.'

Madeline protested she hadn't done it. But with sinking heart, she knew she had. That was her baby and she'd put it beside the hedge and forgotten about it. She dismounted her bike, and let the woman in the long coat get on. Then she led the way. They were passing a field, waving corn, shining green. Down the side of the field, a path. At the end of the path, a cottage. Chimney billowing smoke. A fire on. She knew that Stuart was in the cottage waiting for her.

She woke feeling calm, wondering who the woman in the dream was. Mrs Turner, she decided. And felt disappointed in herself for dreaming about her. And disappointed she hadn't gone down the path to the cottage where Stuart had a fire lit, waiting for her. And ashamed for going out cycling and completely forgetting about her baby. Then, she thought, it was something she might well do, since she definitely never ever wanted one.

What a Difference a Day Made

Once, when Annie was expecting Flo, Madeline had been sitting at the Melvilles' kitchen table, drinking tea and had remarked how she'd been thinking that she didn't know anybody normal.

'Well, thank you for that,' Annie said. 'I'm normal. Well, most of the time I'm normal.'

'Yes, you're pretty normal,' Madeline agreed.

'Well, in the middle of getting sued. It's good to know I'm not a freak.'

'Who decides?' Madeline asked. 'Who makes the normal rule? Is it an Act of Parliament? Do normal people have secret meetings and lay out lists of things people have to do to be considered normal?'

'You're not normal,' said Annie.

'People at work don't think I am, anyway. Just because of Ronald Reagan.'

Annie's cup stopped halfway to her lips. 'I don't think I want to know this. But tell me.'

'Oh, you know. I was working on a window and the blinds were up so people stopped to watch. I got fed up of it and put on a Ronald Reagan mask and stood staring back at them.'

'Right,' said Annie. 'Of course you did. I don't think you're going to make it to normal. What happened?'

'I got ticked off by Mr Speirs. But I said I wasn't sorry. And that I'd do it again. He just shrugged and said he wasn't surprised. He's normal. What do you mean, getting sued?'

'Willie,' said Annie. 'Over a set of French windows. He put them into a house when the owner was away. And it was the wrong room. The idiot put them into the man's bathroom instead of his kitchen. Do you believe it?'

'Of Willie, yes.'

They both nodded. 'Not normal.'

'Yeah,' said Madeline. 'I see normal people in the street. But I don't know any of them. How do you make friends with them? Go up to them and say, "You look normal, will you be my chum?" '

They both shook their heads. 'Not normal.'

'Willie's business has gone bust,' Annie said. 'He can't pay his bills. He won't answer the phone. And when he goes out he goes over the back wall into the neighbours' garden. Then over their wall into the street.'

Every time the phone rang in the Melville household, Willie would jump up and down, waving his arms, panicking. 'Don't answer that. Don't answer that.' He was convinced if it wasn't the man who was suing him, it would be one of his creditors. People were snapping at his heels. Looking for blood.

Several months before, a customer had asked him to install French windows in his house. He was going abroad for a few weeks, wanted the job finished when he came back. As he left, he'd indicated the room. 'The room off the hall,' he'd said. Waving his right arm. Willie had been examining the plans, not looking and had said, 'No problem. We'll get this done for you.'

The customer left. Willie went up the hall, turned left and into the bathroom. Oh, cool, he thought. What a great idea. The room was spacious. High ceiling. A large old-fashioned bath. Intricately patterned ceramic tiles. You could, he told Annie, have a bath with the windows open. Listen to the blackbirds in the garden. And it'd be like peeing in the open air. Which is the best kind of peeing.

He had, he claimed, made a fabulous job. He was so enthused. 'Craftsmanship,' he claimed. 'Pure and utter craftsmanship. But was it appreciated? Oh no. I mean, all I did was veer left instead of right. I'm a left-veering person.' He veered for Annie, demonstrating. 'See. I'm a leftish veerer. I vote left. I do everything left.'

Annie sat, stroking her pregnancy. Saying nothing.

'I don't know what the fuss is about anyway. The bloke says he has to pull the curtains every time he goes to the loo. Why are people so uptight? Everyone does it. It could be very pleasant taking a dump. Sitting there. Fresh air. Reading the paper. And think of the hygiene.'

Annie got up and walked from the room.

'What's the matter?' shouted Willie. 'What's wrong with everybody? You'd think the way people are behaving, that I'm not normal.'

'Willie is at odds with the world,' Annie said now. 'He thinks he's normal and everyone else is weird.'

'I wish I could think that,' said Madeline. 'People think I'm weird.'

'You are weird. You burn your furniture.'

'I just like to keep warm. But I know. That's wrong. I'm going to get my comeuppance for that. One day.'

Annie nodded. 'We all get our comeuppance. What goes around, comes around. One day.'

'Oh Christ,' said Madeline. Dreading the day.

It was, Madeline said later, creepy. On the day they woke and played 'What a Difference a Day Made', everything changed. Stuart went to work humming it. Happily. Madeline left his flat and walked, top speed, to her own, also humming it. She had the morning off, having worked on the Sunday afternoon.

'Twenty four. Little. Hours,' she sang. Pausing, soulfully, she imagined, after each word. The way Dinah Washington did. Breathing, panting, working up a sweat as she strode.

It had been a wonderful night. She's been for a swim. Forty blissful lengths, nothing in her mind. Only movement through the water. Back to Stuart's, more water – a bath. They'd cooked together. Stuart making pasta, whilst she did the salad. They'd eaten in front of the television, not saying much. Just odd scathing comments about the clothes the people in the programme they were watching were wearing. After that, bed. And love. And deep black dreamless sleep. And that made her evening perfect.

She knew something was wrong the moment she rounded the corner into her street. Nothing specific. Well, the landlord's Jaguar was parked by the front door, and it wasn't rent day. Mrs Harkness was standing, arms folded, by the door. Watching her approach, certain smugness spreading over her face as Madeline drew nearer.

But this morning, Madeline was aglow. She was in love. Aware only of her swelling heart, she did not see the signs. The self-satisfied shifts of Mrs Harkness's body, the slow spreading smirk on her lips. She did not hear the caustic ring in Mrs Harkness's tone as she greeted her: 'Good morning, Madeline.' It did not occur to her how strange it was that for the first time ever, Mrs Harkness acknowledged she had a name.

She was strutting. That same eager, gleeful, excited strut she had done when, years ago, she had gone to show off her red velvet dress to Ted. Head high whisking along the street, heart and heat throbbing exhilaration. She should have known. Hadn't Mrs Turner from three doors down always said, 'Don't get too full of yourself, young lady. You're only heading for a fall. It'll all end in tears'? A warning.

Norman Maclean, Madeline's landlord, was a small man, stocky. Hair that Madeline called crinkly, cropped short. He wore checked Viyella shirts and tweedy ties. Madeline hated them, but acknowledged they were expensive. His shoes shone. Madeline just knew he didn't do any polishing himself. He never, ever, had time for pleasantries. Especially not this morning.

'Where's my furniture?' Maclean wanted to know. He seemed reasonably affable.

Madeline looked round. She saw her flat through Norman Maclean's eyes. No furniture. A feature she rather liked. But looking round – a wall half painted. 'STUFF THIS' in huge scrawl over the abandoned area – she saw the untidiness. The scatterings of cups, newspapers, magazines, clothes. The splodges sprayed on the wall, where she'd whipped her brush through the air, drying it, for a rough effect of paint on canvas, emptying it that she could mix colours. Splatterings of reds, greens spread over the wall beside her easel. She could see how he might be irked. Fair enough, she thought.

'I'll clean it up,' she said. A bit too urgently.

He waved this remark aside. Shook his head. Smiled. 'The furniture. Where is it?'

'It's . . .' she said. 'I . . .' She knew now how absurd she'd been. It had seemed reasonable at the time. When the room was chill, damp and her breath hung in the air before her. And the tiny electric heater wouldn't work. Then, it had seemed like a fine quick-fix thing to do. Why not? she'd thought. It's crap furniture anyway. So she'd broken up a chair, and burned it. A fine heat it gave out, too.

It became a temptation, that furniture. It was bulky, clumsy. Cheap. She considered it better burned than cluttering the place. It was worth no other fate. But now, standing facing Norman Maclean, she thought perhaps she'd been a little hasty.

'Well?' he said. 'Where is it?'

'Burned,' she told him. Weakly. She felt like a naughty child. Wilting under Maclean's acid stare. Waiting retribution. And, as ever, the words of Mrs Turner from three doors down, echoed across the years. 'You never get away with nothing. What goes around, comes around. You reap what you sow.'

Norman Maclean looked pointedly at the mound of sawdust in the corner and at the saw lying beside it. 'That's what I thought. Have you plans to replace it?'

This was a new thought to Madeline. Actually, she hadn't. Lost for words, she shrugged. Blew out her cheeks. Made a spluttering noise. 'Sheeek. Um . . .'

'I didn't think so. But plainly I will have to be reimbursed for my losses.'

It seemed so reasonable. Madeline nodded. Agreeing.

'And obviously you are not really the sort of tenant I wish to encourage. I'll have to ask you to seek accommodation elsewhere. To speak plainly, because I'm a plain-speaking man. Get out, Miss Green. Now.'

Madeline nodded again. Thinking about it now, she wouldn't want a tenant like her either. She said she'd get her things.

Maclean shook his head. 'Sorry, no things. You can take your clothes. That's all.'

'I need my stuff,' said Madeline. 'My brushes. My paints.'

'No stuff,' Maclean repeated. 'Not till I get paid for my stuff.'

She felt a tremor inside. A chill. 'My paintings,' she protested.

'Yours?' Maclean smiled. 'They're not yours any more. Compensation for my losses. They might fetch a bob or two at auction. I'll keep them. Pay me and you can have them back.' Madeline saw that there was more to this than him being right, and her being wrong. He was enjoying this. Did taking her to task have to be such fun? Always after this encounter, Madeline would wonder what got into people. Were bullies born, or were they a product of their lives, their experiences? What turns had this man's time on earth taken that he got a kick out of shoving her around?

'You're enjoying this, aren't you?' said Madeline.

'Yes,' he admitted. 'And here's the best bit.' He handed her the bill. She opened the envelope. Looked at it and reeled. 'This is for thousands.' £6000. The items missing were neatly listed, priced and totalled. 'Your furniture wasn't worth this.'

'That was good stuff in here,' said Maclean.

'It never was,' Madeline protested. Looking at the list again, said, 'There was never a sofa worth eight hundred pounds in here. Or a pine dresser. Or an oak dining table.'

'Now, that's not very nice. I say there was. I say I put good money in this flat. And you destroyed it.'

Madeline stared at him. She couldn't prove Maclean's claims were untrue. Then again, he couldn't actually prove they were true. But she figured he had a lot more weight behind his lies than she had behind her facts. It was doubtful he'd paid more than £300 for the contents of the flat. They were more than second-hand. They'd knocked about a bit, these contents.

'There's things I want,' said Madeline. 'They're of no value.' Photographs of Ted. Some of his watercolours. His wedding ring. She made to go to the bedroom.

'Like I said,' Maclean repeated. He moved in front of her, blocking her way forward, easing her towards the door. Like a dance. A nasty dance. 'When I get my money.'

'But I want them. They mean something to me. My father's photo, his drawings.' She thought she might cry. Poured out her protest. 'It's all right for you, standing there looking spiffy and splendid in your shiny shoes. But you're leaving me with nothing.'

'Spiffy?' Maclean gloated. 'There's a word.'

'It just came to my lips. I don't think it's a word,' she said. Being discovered using dubious and silly words was the last straw. She sniffed. Swallowed. Knew that if she let go, if tears came, he'd smile more. She turned to go, and on the way out grabbed the small, ceramic tiger. 'I'll have this.' Of course, she didn't really want it. It was an act of defiance. A feeble show of strength. Nobody would push her around. She'd take the tiger. Have that, Maclean.

She clumped down the stairs. Numb, shocked. Passed Mrs Harkness, still standing, still smug at the front door. And at last Mrs Harkness could say the words she longed to speak out loud for years: 'Bye-bye, Madeline.'

Madeline stopped, glared. 'Bye-bye, Mrs Harkness. You seem pleased to see me go. It'll have been you reported me to the landlord.'

'I won't deny it. What do you expect? You never clean the stairs.'

'My God. The bloody stairs. Life's too short to scrub stairs.'

'If we all thought that, where would we be? There's standards, you know.'

'If your standards stop at a bleached step, God help you. Some of us want more than that. Don't forget what goes around, comes around. One day you'll get yours.'

'Oh,' Mrs Harkness quivered righteousness. 'I've had mine years ago. I just like to make sure everyone else gets theirs.'

Madeline gave her the Mrs Turner scowl. 'Vindictive old bag.'

'True. But I'm a vindictive old bag with a roof over my head. You are a filthy young slut without one.'

Madeline had to give her that. 'Fuck off and up yours,' was all she could say. She stamped off.

But Mrs Harkness was damned if Madeline was going to have the last word. 'We don't want the likes of you around here. Good riddance.'

This surprised Madeline. Despite having sawed up and burned her landlord's furniture, written 'Stuff this' on the wall, she regarded herself as a model citizen. But seeing the hatred suddenly apparent on Mrs Harkness's face she was shaken. 'Me?' she said. 'What's wrong with the likes of me?'

'As if you didn't know,' shrilled Mrs Harkness. 'The noise. Music all hours. Stamping on the floor. Comings and goings. All sorts of folk. Burning stuff that doesn't belong to you. I've been watching you. You're . . .' She shook with the effort of deciding exactly what Madeline was, pointing at her. 'Rubbish.' The word exploded from her mouth. And the effort of finding it, then getting it out seemed to exhaust her. She leaned back against the wall. Cheeks reddened, and patting her pounding heart.

'Goodness,' was all Madeline could think of to say. She turned and walked away, Mrs Harkness's outburst rattling through her bewildered brain. That she was rubbish bothered her more than the fact she'd just been evicted. 'I'm not rubbish,' she said out loud.

And from the depths of a dim doorway, a voice agreed with her. 'Of course you're not, darling.'

She peered into the gloom, saw a lumpen figure, lying beneath a pile of newspapers and a lifeless grey blanket. He was wearing a Balaclava and a thick army coat. When he smiled he revealed a set of gleaming gums.

She thanked him. Returned the smile.

'You shouldn't go around thinking you're rubbish,' he told her. The gums, the blanket belied the accent. Which was rounded and upmarket.

'I haven't until now. Someone just said I was.'

'Well,' he said, 'it's them that's rubbish. You wouldn't have a couple of quid for a cup of tea, would you?'

She gave him the contents of her pockets. Proof that she wasn't rubbish. Felt the glow of giving. And penniless now, as well as homeless, started the walk back to Stuart's flat.

He was there, sitting on the sofa, smoking, staring into the distance when she arrived.

'Been fired,' he said. 'Just like that. Well, not exactly just like that. I was warned a couple of times about my time-keeping. They said if I didn't mend my ways, start taking the job seriously, they'd have to let me go. I never thought they'd do it. Fired. Me. Who'd have thought it?'

Having recently caught a shocking glimpse of herself as an unworthy tenant and neighbour, Madeline was of a mind to see Stuart as his employer might see him. 'Me,' she said. 'I'd have thought it. Look at you.'

He was in his mid-season attire. A pinstripe suit, creased, a blue and green floral shirt, no tie, black chest hair curled over the open neck. His feet were encased in brown shoes that had seen better days, the laces of one had snapped and he'd replaced it with a lace from one of Madeline's Kickers, which was red. He'd got out of bed reluctantly at half-past nine, had a bath, and appeared in the office sometime after ten. He hadn't shaved. He hadn't actually shaved since Friday, and this being Monday, a fair shadow of stubble had gathered on his chin. He rubbed it. Considered himself. A moment of reckoning, when after a serious scrutiny, he was not impressed with himself. He greeted this revelation with the same resigned bafflement Madeline had, when only hours before, her messiness and disregard for other people's property had been pointed out to her. 'Right enough.' He looked at her, surprised. When did this happen to me?

Stupid question, he told himself. He knew when this had happened to him. His current state of dishevelment had been a slow-growing thing that had started when Madeline came into his life, and had worsened as his relationship deepened. It had reached its peak during the painting of the tiger pictures, when his involvement had driven him to distraction. Now, though, he felt he was improving. His sock rota had been abandoned and now he put on a fresh, if mismatching, pair every day. And even though today's shirt was creased, he now usually ironed the front at least, of whatever he wore under his jacket. And now that he was no longer staying up nights whilst she worked on her project, he was sleeping. Since the paintings were delivered he hadn't fallen asleep at work once. Today was the first time in a fortnight he'd been late. All in all, he thought his dismissal a bit unfair. He was mending his ways.

Madeline told him about her morning. The eviction. Mrs Harkness's hatred. The old man in the doorway. She showed him her bill. He said, 'Christ.' Then they both fell silent. Licking their wounds.

'It wouldn't be so bad,' said Stuart. 'But I agree with them.' He stood up, displaying himself. 'What sort of way is this to turn up at work?'

'So why did you do it?' asked Madeline.

'It wasn't planned. I seem to have slipped into sartorial disrepair. I was working on it. Trying to look presentable.'

'Yeah,' Madeline nodded. 'It was the same with the furniture. I slipped into it. It just happened a bit at a time. It was like a kid with a big box of sweets. Nobody'll notice if I take another one. Well,' she sighed. 'The world has come baying at our window. And it isn't very nice.'

Stuart disagreed. 'It's us that isn't nice. The world's fine.'

'It's fine for you not to be very nice. You're rich. You can afford it. But look at me. The bill I've got.' A vile thought. 'Do you think he'll pursue me for it?'

She indulged in this horror. Moments from movies she'd seen. Footsteps hollowing through the night, coming after her. Getting faster and faster. 'I haven't got that kind of money,' she said. To herself. To her ghosts.

'Don't look at me,' said Stuart. 'I don't either. If I had I'd give you it.'

'I thought you were rich.' Madeline looked round. There were signs of affluence.

'There's Marglass House. But that's not money. I don't have any actual cash. Pounds to throw about and squander. Christ, Madeline, look at how I'm dressed.'

'I thought that was just your style. An anti-fashion statement.'

'No, Madeline. I'm just a mess.'

'Me too,' she wailed. Broke down.

He came to her. Held her. Time to comfort her. No point in seeking sympathy for the mess he was. He had to touch her, stroke her. Tell her he loved the mess she was. Still, it was a lovely moment. To be captured together in this minute – two cockups, misfits bonded by their absurdness – was, for Stuart, pretty damn near perfect. They rocked, a clumsy sway. And he told her not to mind. And not to care about Maclean or Mrs Harkness. They were nothing. And she was the most gentle, beautiful and wonderful person he'd ever met. And he loved her.

'So, are you going to look for another job?' Madeline asked. When Stuart's magic few minutes ended.

Stuart shook his head. 'No. I'm going home.' Decision made. He strode across the room. Stopped at the door. Turned. Looked at Madeline. Who was standing where the clumsy comfort-sway ended, watching. Slightly surprised. 'Coming?' he said.

'OK,' said Madeline.

At the time, she'd thought it would only be for a few days whilst she recovered her peace of mind. It would be a holiday. 'I'm getting my head together,' she told Annie. But the days spread into weeks, the weeks to months. In the end, it was years before she went back.

Another One

It was eight o'clock, late spring. Madeline, clutching her tiger, a backpack strapped over her shoulders, moved in wonder through a new landscape. Everything that was familiar, comforting, to Stuart, came fresh to her. The hills, scattered with sheep, whose evening rantings blared through the silence. A curlew calling a shrill mewing cry. The movement of breeze through the rhododendron bushes that were flushed with blossom, reds and pinks. The peaty scents from the hills behind, salt and sea from the shore beyond. But mostly what she saw was sky. So much of it. Now it was reddening into night. Spreading streaks of colour against the paling blue.

Madeline looked up, and round. 'You've got a lot of sky here.'

Stuart nodded. 'Yeah. There's that.'

He was walking quickly, anxious to get home. And once they'd passed through the gates of Marglass House, his step quickened further. The gates, once tall, gleaming black, now were rusted, never closed, leaned into the weedy embankment either side. Two lions stood on pillars beside them; time and the weather had taken their toll. They were eroded, green with moss. One had an ear missing, the other no nose. Still, Madeline was impressed.

The drive wound and undulated. Grass pushed through the tarmac. Giant rhododendrons crowding into one another, narrowing the way ahead. From several points as they walked, Madeline and Stuart could see the chimneys of the house that was set in the flat ground before the cliff, shoving into the sky.

And when at last they rounded the last corner, and Marglass heaved in front of them, vast, grey, ominous, shouldering the sky, Madeline gasped. She was astounded by its ugliness. A mouldering grey, turreted monstrosity with far too many windows. Especially at the top. The top floor seemed to be all windows.

'That's your house?' Thus far, in her life, houses had been two- or three-roomed affairs with a neat patch of garden front and back. Except for the Borthwicks', which had been bigger, with a bigger neat patch separating it from other houses.

This, though, this was a monstrosity. No tidy garden, a huge pitch of a lawn, rabbit-infested, daisied and fertile with thistles. Flowerbeds lush with weeds. Sticky willy, dock leaves, nettles gone amok. Thrusting through shrubs, waving from the sides, out the top. Roses gone feral through neglect. As the year drifted into summer, odd flowers, survivors, would appear shining in the undergrowth. Lupins, foxgloves, marigolds. But right now the place was verdant with happy weeds in weed heaven.

Still, the building amazed, horrified Madeline. 'Someone designed this?' she protested.

Stuart agreed that indeed someone must have.

'You'd think they'd have had the decency to cover the front with ivy so's we wouldn't see so much of it. How could they get so many turrets on a building without it falling down? And the gargoyles. I know they're not meant to be pretty. But if I went about with a face like that, I'd get arrested. Who gave the go-ahead for it?' she asked.

'My great-great-grandfather Stuart,' said Stuart.

'So he's not around to explain himself?' said Madeline.

'Unfortunately not,' said Stuart.

In fact, Madeline was to become fond of the long-deceased great-great-grandfather. As she was to come to love Marglass House. It was a place of absurdities. Internal follies. Small staircases, leading nowhere. Run up the steps, round the corner. Blank wall. On the north wall facing the sea was a row of sixteen round windows, portholes. Madeline loved looking through them. For beyond them was nothing but ocean, moving, shifting under the lights and shades of morning, afternoon and evening.

Stretching from top floor down to the happy weeds on the exterior east wall of the building was a huge, grey spiralling fire escape. The windows all glinted dully in the evening sun. Madeline remembered going on an outing to a stately home with Mrs Turner and Archie. Mrs Turner had given the place the scowl. 'I couldn't be doing with a house this size. You'd be all day with the Hoover. And how would you get round them windows?'

'You wouldn't do it,' Archie scoffed. 'If you had a house this big, you'd have servants. They'd do it for you.'

'Not in my house they wouldn't. I'd have none of that. Nobody comes in to clean my house. If you want a job done properly, do it yourself.' She scowled at all the imaginary inept people who might do a shoddy job of the carpets and windows. 'Oh no, I'm not having that.'

If Mrs Turner would have given the outside of Marglass House the full scowl, its interior would have driven her into a fury. It was all nooks and crannies. It was beyond idiosyncratic. It was absurd. Large rooms. High ceilings, elaborate, and dust-encrusted cornices. Long, long unvacuumed corridors.

These corridors all had huge indentations, ornate alcoves large enough to hide a couple of busy, sweaty illicit lovers. Great-great-grandfather Stuart had used them all, often, when occupying himself with maidservants, or lady visitors who'd taken his fancy.

Great-great grandfather Stuart had been a man of many passions, plants, bodily hygiene and swimming being high on the list. Winter and summer, he daily swam the curdling sea at the base of the cliff where his monstrous house stood.

And, on the top floor, he grew plants he'd brought from his travels in Japan, China and South America. Giant palms, withering at the roots, scraped the sloping glass roof. Bamboos sprouted from enormous pots. Amongst the dying flowers were survivors, shoving upwards, bullying their colourful way to the roof. Madeline saw it and gasped. She thought of Ted's tiny greenhouse and his beloved cosseted orchids, and knew he would have seen this and wept. It smelled green, of warmth, earth, damp and neglect. High above her, nesting sparrows and chaffinches, who'd squeezed in through a broken pane, and thought they'd discovered heaven, squealed and chattered.

If anything made Madeline forgive Great-great-grandfather Stuart his hideous taste in architecture, this top-floor conservatory did. And so did his obsession with personal hygiene. He bathed three times a day. Once when he rose, once after his swim, and once again before dinner. He had notions about bathrooms. And Madeline loved these notions. Marglass House boasted seven bathrooms. Each one was unique. Some had huge potted palms. Some had showers that sprayed the body top to toe from tiny valves set in a large ceramic cubicle at the foot of the bath. Some were tiled. Some marbled. But Madeline's favourite, the one she used, was next to Great-great-grandfather Stuart's bedroom. Across a black and white marble floor, up six wide, sweeping steps, on a plinth was a huge, magnificent wide bath. It was set below the window, that bathers could sponge, and splash, lie back and soak whilst staring out to sea.

The plumbing, however, was not for the faint-hearted. Turning on a tap sent whines wailing down the corridors. Flushing a loo took courage. Pull one of the giant brass chains that hung from the overhead cisterns, and all hell broke loose. The house trembled. A deluge – from where? Madeline worried – she'd look tentatively up, imagining a cold water tank the size of a small galvanised bungalow resting on rusting brackets directly above her – whooshed into the lavatory. Swirled, stormed, then started, with the contents it had gathered, on what seemed like a noisy, swift, white-water journey through pipes that travelled the length and breadth of the house, tumbling, gurgling through every room, sweeping, gathering momentum as it went. Then gushed out into the septic tank at the bottom of weed heaven. For weeks, until she became accustomed to this, Madeline dreaded the calls of nature. Saw some small joy in the silence of constipation. Was horrified to think that everything her digestive system threw out rocketed in a terrible cacophony round the house, and was probably scooting through the kitchen when she descended the stairs, and re-entered it.

As they climbed the crumbling steps leading to the front door, which was always open, the dog, McCann, came stiff-legged to greet them. His welcome, once a bounding leap, was hindered by his arthritis, and the enthusiastic movement of his joyful tail made walking impossible.

Madeline reached down to pat him. His upper lip curled, revealing a set of yellowing teeth. A warning rumbled in his throat whilst the tail still wagged furiously. It seemed to Madeline he was saying 'Great to see you' at one end, and 'Bugger off' at the other. She swiftly withdrew the hand. Leaning down, she'd caught a whiff of his breath. It lined her nostrils, lingering. It was rank, foul. Decaying meat, rotting innards. She reeled. 'My God, that dog doesn't have to growl to keep people at bay. He just has to breathe on them.'

For the next three years, until he died, McCann never missed a chance to let Madeline know she was unwelcome in his world. His head lifted, lip curled, throat rumbled every time he saw her. Stuart stopped apologising for him, and said he was just too old to accept someone new in his life. But Madeline knew better. To McCann, she was a threat. She had stolen his love. The moment he'd sniffed her outstretched hand, he'd known he'd have to share Stuart with her. Instinct told him not to attack. If he'd sunk his teeth into that soft palm, as he longed to do, it would have been the end of him. Still, he'd not shift into second place without a fight. So he snarled, he growled, raised his hackles. It was war. In time, Madeline would come to admire the curmudgeonly old beast's tenacity. 'You have to hand it to him,' she said. 'He sticks by his guns. He should have gone into politics. He's wasted as a dog.'

A fire licked up the chimney of the lounge. Madeline looked round and marvelled. The home she'd shared with Ted could fit into this room. Evening light filtered through the windows, and occasional gusts of wind buffeted wood smoke down the chimney and sent small clouds out across the room. Madeline smiled, nodded. She liked this place. Inside at least.

Muriel appeared. Her shuffling approach, feet dragging along the corridor, slight wheezing breath, could be heard long before she finally arrived. 'Knew you'd be coming. Lamb's doin' under the grill.'

Stuart knew it had been there for a long, long, slow time. It would be dried and lifeless. It would require a deal of chewing.

'And who's this?' Muriel appraised Madeline. The full head-to-toe disapproving look that took in the small backpack, hair, shoes and the ceramic tiger. Another one, she thought.

Stuart introduced her.

'Well,' said Muriel, 'I expect you'll be wanting your tea, too.'

Madeline nodded, weakly. Yes, she would. Muriel shuffled off. Her echoing feet dragging down the stairs and along the seemingly endless corridor to the kitchen.

'Perhaps I should go help,' Madeline offered.

Stuart looked horrified. 'Don't do that. Nobody goes into the kitchen when she's cooking. She goes all frosty, and the food suffers. And to tell the truth, it's bad enough without that.'

Madeline shrugged. Flopped into a chair by the fire. 'Did you phone? How did she know you'd be coming?'

Stuart nodded at McCann. 'He always knows. He gets all restless and barks when I'm coming.'

'How does he know? Does he catch a whiff of your scent on the wind?'

Stuart shook his head. 'He starts up long before I can be seen, heard or even smelled. He'll have been watching out for me for hours. He just knows.'

Madeline looked at the dog. He was gloating. She was sure of it. She looked up at the ceiling way above her, round the room. It was cavernous. Made her feel small, even smaller than she was. Maybe that was why the upper classes were the way they were – they had to strut to live up to their surroundings. And their loud voices were nothing to do with the arrogance of privilege, they just had to shout to make themselves heard in their huge rooms.

In the warmth, the comfort of the ancient armchair, moulded into shape by generations of bums, Madeline shut her eyes. Drifted into a snooze. By the time, almost an hour later, Muriel came to say dinner was served, the snooze had deepened into sleep. She woke, shards of her day that had fragmented through her brief dreams still with her. For a moment, she could not think where she was. Muriel's time-worn face loomed down on her, and Madeline couldn't think who she was.

And Muriel thought, I was right. Another one.

She led Stuart and Madeline from the lounge, across the hall, down, down a long, echoing corridor to the dining room. The pace was painful. Madeline had never, in her life, walked so slowly. Three sets of footsteps rebounding. Or two sets of footsteps, and one shuffle.

The dining table was set according to Muriel's standards – one plate, silver cutlery and a crystal glass, either end, a lit candelabra, a bottle of claret and a gravy boat in the middle. The meal, lamb chops grilled dry and lifeless, mashed potatoes and peas, was cold, but not yet congealed. Muriel had carried it, at her painful pace, from the kitchen, laid it out, shuffled to the lounge to fetch Madeline and Stuart, then shuffled with them back to the dining room.

Muriel waited till they were both seated, told them to eat up. Watched Madeline's enthusiastic approach to food, any food, and thought: Definitely. Another one.

She left the gaping chill of Marglass House, crossed the tangled lawn, down to the path that led along by the river to her cottage, clean and warm, clematis clinging to the south wall, a garden where roses and lavender jostled for space.

Inside, Donald was sitting by the fire. 'He's back then?' he said. He sighed. Now, he'd have to get up early to take his veg to the Inverask Castle Hotel. The walled garden, unlike the rest of the grounds, was immaculate. Donald's pride. In it he nurtured strawberries, raspberries, gooseberries, peas, broad beans, cabbage, broccoli, potatoes, beetroot and other vegetables, all in perfect, weed-free rows. Since, except for potatoes, neither he or Muriel ate vegetables, and since only Stuart came to the house and at that only at weekends, there was a huge surplus. In fact, walled garden produce was all surplus. Unknown to Stuart, Donald not only sold it to the local hotel, but kept the profit.

Like Madeline's burning of her furniture, it had happened slowly. 'It more evolved than happened,' he said. After the death of Stuart's mother, and the disappearance of his father to Edinburgh, the house had emptied. There were no more guests. Nobody to enjoy the fruits of Donald's labour. The veg had been grown, then composted. Waste, waste, thought Donald. Once he'd been in the bar of the Inverask and had overheard the cook complain about the state of the onions.

'I do a good onion,' he'd said mildly.

Chef had asked to see them, and had next morning visited Marglass. From then on Donald supplied onions. That grew slowly into supplying broccoli. Then broad beans and peas. Eventually the hotel sent a van every morning to pick up fresh veg. As he hadn't had a raise in wages for fifteen years, Donald thought the money he got his due, for his hard work. It never crossed Stuart's mind to wonder what happened to the vegetables and fruit grown in his own grounds. The walled garden was there; it had always been there. Part of the landscape of his youth. He never gave it a second thought.

'I'll have to get the hotel to send their van early before he gets up,' said Donald.

'Yes,' agreed Muriel. 'And get it to come here to our door. Not the big house. He's got another one with him.' Madeline. An afterthought.

'Another what?'

'Another orphan, a stray, a runaway. One of them that's always coming here. City folks who've had enough, or done something's made them ashamed, so they hotfoot it to a place like this, 'cos it's as far from everything as they can get without toppling into the sea. And they spend their time here saying how peaceful it is and how friendly people are and how they love it. Till the quiet drives them daft, and they have to go back to where they came from. One of them. That's what's with him. A woman. Only she's wee. She's weeer than me.'

That's wee, Donald thought. 'And what else about her besides being wee?'

'A lot of hair. Pale. Big coat. That's how I know she's another one. Except she's got a ceramic tiger with her.'

'Oh?'

'Yes. Japanese, I'd say. I took a look as I was leaving and they were in the dining room. Seated tiger. Seventeenth century, late. Kakiemon, maybe. Worth a bit. Though she thinks it's a cheap import from Hong Kong.'

Donald whistled. They both took a keen interest in antiques since pilfering so much from Marglass House. They'd bought books, and never missed the *Antiques Roadshow*. Now they considered themselves experts. Which they probably were.

Back at Marglass House, Madeline moved her plate up the table, so she was sitting next to Stuart. 'That's no way to eat. Miles apart. It isn't cosy.'

Until he met Madeline, Stuart had no idea of coziness. But now, with her help, he was getting the hang of it. Quite liked it. 'We always ate that way. My mother down where you were. My father up here. Me in the middle.'

'You must have had to shout to make yourselves heard.'

'We didn't speak. Mealtimes were for eating.'

'That's not very nice. Just eating and not chatting.' She looked at the chops, lying dried, congealed on her plate. 'Especially since the food's so awful. You'd need a bit of conversation to take your mind off it.'

Stuart agreed. And since the food was inedible, did she want to take a walk? They'd bring the wine with them.

They went across round the side of the house, down the steps to the walled garden, which was, to Madeline's surprise, busy and flourishing. Herbs, rows of seedling vegetables, greening through the raked and tended ground. Donald grew thyme, oregano, fennel, marjoram and mint, as well as fresh vegetables and soft fruit. These also were sold to the Inverask Castle Hotel.

Drinking their wine, hands linked, Madeline and Stuart walked along the path to the sea. A tiny bay. No easy way into the water, Madeline noted. She'd have to brave the rocks, slippy with seaweed, and covered with limpets that would be cruel to her naked feet. Still, she'd do it. She'd swim.

'Well, here we are,' she said.

Stuart nodded. 'Yes, here we are.'

In the morning they walked to the village to buy clothes for Madeline. She was cheered. Had eaten, since there was nothing Muriel could do to ruin muesli. Except disapprove of it.

The village was a sparkling place. Whitewashed houses facing the sea. A small harbour where fishermen brought in prawns, lobsters and scallops. A small café that only opened in summer, a tiny art gallery and pottery, a baker's, a fruit shop, a butcher's, and Murchie's, a large, neglected building overlooking the harbour, that sold everything from condoms to week-old copies of the *Washington Post*.

There was no rhythm or reason to the display of goods in Murchie's. Things were placed where Murchie happened to be when they were delivered. A pile of tartan rugs beside a case of vodka at the front door. Nothing was unpacked. Boxes of washing powder lay on the floor beside boxes of tinned beans and toilet rolls and chocolate bars and liquid plant fertiliser. The condoms were behind the counter in a vivid blue neon display that, despite herself, Madeline found herself staring at.

The shop seemed to stretch back forever. Long lines of shelves, packed with whatever Murchie had in his hand when he passed and spotted an empty space. Tins of Pedigree Chum next to books on birdwatching. Tide timetables next to toilet rolls. A box of screw-drivers alongside a squint and dusty pile of Belgian chocolates. Murchie claimed to know where everything in the jumbled emporium was. But locals doubted this. When asked for anything, he would wave his hand in a sweep that took in the entire shop, and say, 'Definitely, I've got that. It's back there.' Which was daunting. Because 'back there' took in a lot of territory.

211

The ceiling sagged, worryingly. Dipped in a long low swell towards the floor. Murchie, when moving about in the area of the sag, moved his head to one side, to avoid it. This wasn't necessary, considering his height. But the closeness of what was meant to be ten feet overhead made the head tilt a reaction. Everybody, including Madeline, did it.

The most worrying thing about the ceiling, apart from the fear that it might crash down any minute, was how close it was to the large lump of unwrapped butter Murchie sold. It had a sign in front of it, 'Fresh Farm Butter. Morning Made.' Murchie deemed this fine, not a lie, since he did not specify any particular morning. He just implied that it was this morning. Locals knew this, and avoided the stuff. But tourists, and there were many, were entranced. 'Oooh, fresh butter. You never get that round where we live.' And they'd buy some. Murchie would smile and obligingly lay his cigarette on the counter, lit end facing out. He'd shove back the woolly hat he wore winter and summer and set to with a wooden paddle in each hand patting and shaping the sliced-off wedge into shape. Then he'd wrap it in greaseproof paper, weigh it, price it, and flamboyantly knock off a few pence. 'That's one pound fifty's worth, there. But to you, a pound.' This because if the buyers thought they'd got it cheap, they'd be less likely to return it when they discovered how sour it was. Besides, his scales were off balance, so it was probably a pound's worth anyway.

Apart from the condoms, the only order in the shop was in the wine. It was lined up on the shelves behind the counter, reached from floor to ceiling. When asked for a bottle from the upper shelves, Murchie would fetch his pole. An ancient thing, with a steel grip at the end. With this he would grab the desired bottle by the neck and bring it safely to earth. People in the know, who enjoyed seeing the pole in action, always asked for something beyond Murchie's reach, and as he was only five foot three, the choice was great.

Murchie was a poet and drinker. More drinker than poet. He had the looks of a labourer – old denims, hands that had seen softer days. He always wore a thick ex-army jersey with patches at the shoulders and elbows, and the skull-nipping woollen hat. But he knew his drink. And would eulogise about the grape: 'A grand choice, if I may say so, a muscular wine, a hint of blackcurrants and not too much tannin.' And the malt: 'Ah, now this is a fine bottle. Not too sweet, but there's a lingering sense of toffee and mints, maybe a little flush of jasmine tea. A wee drop of water will release the flavours, and you'll get a little taste of pear drops.' Visitors could never tell if he was making fool of them. But they bought whatever bottle he was talking about anyway.

In fact, he wasn't. He just liked to talk. And talk enthusiastically. Especially about drink. But only when he wasn't drinking. Talking about drink when you were drinking seemed, to him, excessive. When he was doing that he liked to talk about women, and books. He never spoke about his poetry. That would be letting people into something he held precious. That would be polluting his secret place.

His poems were long and winding things about the sea and legends and mystic women. They all started with And, or, Or. He liked that. It gave the notion that the poem started in the distance, and there were visions dancing in his head that he had not put down on paper. Very few had been published, but as far as James Murchie was concerned, that wasn't the point. The joy was in the writing, the fishing for words. If nobody wanted to read them, that was their problem.

Madeline selected two pairs of jeans, three sweatshirts, all black with the name of an American university on the front, several pairs of thick socks, red, four pairs of navy knickers that were built for comfort rather than allure, and a pair of walking boots, olive. Watching Murchie pack them up, she, once again, gazed at the selection of condoms. And at the bags of home-made tablet in front of the till. He followed the look.

'If you're after one, you'll not be needing the other,' he said.

'What?' asked Madeline.

'Well, if it's condoms you're needing, you'll not be needing the comfort of tablet. Women getting the other, as it were, don't need the one.'

'Sorry,' said Madeline.

'If you're getting plenty sex. You don't need tablet.'

Madeline supposed this was true.

'This,' said Murchie, lifting a bag, 'is the finest tablet you'll find anywhere in the world. Mrs Bartlett makes it. Never gives out the recipe. But it's grand stuff. Are you a connoisseur of tablet?'

Madeline shook her head.

'Tablet is the whisky of the sweetie world. Soft and addictive. Some say it's like fudge. But this isn't true. The nearest you could say is it's hyper-fudge. So sweet it draws your cheeks together. It looks like it's bad for you. But then, all truly tempting things do.' He was in his element. Talking. 'It's made from condensed milk, butter, sugar, and then more sugar. Take a bit, and your eyes pop open, the sweetness of it. And right off you need another bit, just to check your tastebuds didn't fool you. Was it really that sweet? Then you need another bit. And another. Soon as not, it's done. And you feel a bit queasy. The sweetness does that. But you'll be back for another bag. That's the addiction of it. We do good sweeties and drink here. Are you after some? Or,' indicating the condoms, 'is it the other you're needing?'

'Oh, no, no,' waving her hands in protest. 'It's just there's such a selection. I couldn't help looking at it.'

'Ah well,' he told her. 'There isn't a lot to do round here. Which means we do a lot of what we *do* do. And some folk are very good at it.'

He sounded to Madeline as if he were talking about golf handicaps, or the impassioned growing of prized vegetables. And when she picked up her parcel, walked to the door, looked back, he nodded to her. Affirming what he'd said. He knew she was thinking about it. 'Best to young Stuart,' he added.

Outside, it was starting to rain. A soft, drenching drizzle. Stuart was standing on the small wooden pier watching the water. Madeline held her parcel over her head, staving off the downpour.

It didn't bother Stuart. 'You get used to it,' he told her. 'I quite like it. It's life-affirming. Makes everything green.' Then, noticing her expression, 'I see you met Murchie.'

'He knew I was with you. How did he know that?'

He shrugged. 'Somebody would have seen us. I expect.'

'His shop's so messy. You have to search for things. I like it. You find things you didn't go in for and take a shine to.'

Stuart nodded. 'That's the way of it.'

'It's exciting. A whole new concept in retail. *You never know what you'll come across* – it could be big. And, he talks. On and on about tablet.'

'Well,' said Stuart, 'that's just him. Think yourself lucky you weren't buying drink. Then he really talks. I like his shop. It's been there for generations. I could spend hours in there, rummaging. He's probably got things that have been there so long they're antiques. Worth more now than when his grandfather bought them in.'

Madeline looked at him. He was different. He looked different. His face. The way he held himself. If he'd been older she'd have said he'd sagged. He looked looser, easier, constantly on the verge of yawning. She couldn't say this had happened suddenly. That was too sharp a word. He'd slipped into it without her noticing. A downward slide into laxness. He was becoming so mellow, it was irritating. He didn't even seem to notice the rain. It was sweeping in from the sea, softly soaking.

'Let's take the van home,' he said. He even seemed to be speaking slowly.

She noticed this before the van suggestion percolated into her brain. 'What van?'

He pointed to a small van, filthy, yellow, parked across the road. 'Ali's van.'

Looking up and down the street. Nobody about. 'Where's Ali? Have you asked him if you could take his van?'

Stuart shook his head. 'It's OK. He doesn't mind.'

'But what if he needs it?'

Stuart climbed into the van. Started the engine. 'Coming?'

'No. I'm not being party to theft.' She strode away from him, and the van, heading home.

Stuart followed, tooting. 'Get in, you silly bitch.'

She was torn between taking part in what appeared to her to be robbery and causing a disturbance. All this tooting and shouting was embarrassing. Her polite suburban upbringing won. Better be a thief than a street-shouter and rioter. She climbed in beside Stuart. Sat stiffly, staring ahead, as he drove the length of Main Street. 'I hate this. It's wrong.'

'It's OK. Really. Everybody does it. He leaves the key in the ignition.'

'It could get stolen.'

'That's the idea. He hates this van.'

Madeline said, 'But . . .' And gave up. But why didn't Ali sell his van if he hated it? But why did everyone speak so slowly? She thought she'd never understand this place, relax here. The tranquillity was unsettling. No, it was more than that. It was downright irritating.

As they reached the end of the village an old lady stood up from working in her garden. She loomed suddenly from the depths of a bed of roses, stood watching them pass. A mop of white hair ruffled by the wind, a fraying denim jacket, a trowel dangling from her soil-encrusted hand. She gently hoisted it into the air, hailing Stuart as he passed.

'There,' he said. 'Freda will tell Ali about the van.'

'Does she know Ali?' asked Madeline.

'Everybody knows Ali,' said Stuart. 'Besides, if she doesn't tell him she'll tell someone who will.'

Madeline said she'd never get the hang of this place. She turned, watched Freda slowly, slowly lower herself back to the ground.

Freda, mid-crouch, sensing the gaze, looked back at Madeline. Caught the bewildered look. And thought: Muriel was right. Another one.

Freda, too, was another one. Though from a different era. She'd arrived in Gideon years ago when hitching round Europe, and never left. She'd been with a friend, Lucy, and they both were recovering from broken hearts. In her time here, Freda had seen many comings and goings. She supposed remote places across the world were all the same. They had an allure for escapees. People shifting from one life to another, running away from something – a broken heart, the law, the rat race. Usually these people found some solace in the peace here. But in that solace they also found that what they were running from was in their heads, and, therefore, inescapable. They went back to wherever they'd come from.

A few stayed. The Watsons, who lived at Little Tofts, had come with their two children looking for a way of life. Self-sufficiency.

They grew all their own food, brewed their own beer and had even dabbled in making their own toothpaste. But that last had been given up. The paste they produced was so foul they had stopped brushing their teeth. Still they'd stayed, prospered – a little – and produced three more children.

George Richards had abandoned a successful life in banking to live in the wilds and write. He'd done a few whodunnits – unpublished – before turning to historical romances. Which he did with some success. Winnie and Hugh Livingston, an insurance broker and car salesman, had come with a dream of a seafront café and opened The Lobsterpot. Though the dream had lost its initial gleam, they stayed. The café only opened for four months a year, and it shut at five o'clock when tourists were looking about for somewhere to eat. Winnie and Hugh spent as little time as possible working, preferring to sail their little boat or walk in the hills. They were, Freda had to admit, extremely happy.

She yanked a dandelion from the ground, shook earth from the roots and tossed the weed into a plastic bucket. And set about some ground elder. 'Of course, these people are the exceptions.'

Most people came to Gideon and found the pace upsetting. They could not cope with the lack of facilities. There was no bank, no library, no dentist (which had proved unfortunate for the Watsons during their trials with producing their own toothpaste), no cinema, no video shop, 'In fact,' said Freda, 'no nothing, when you think about it.' She puffed – this weed was a fiend, deep-rooted. 'Muriel's really talking about the oddballs, though.'

The oddballs, strays, waifs who turned up, stayed a week or two, a month or two and sometimes a year or two, then disappeared. 'That model woman.'

Alexandra Hodges, a model from London, who'd come seeking, as she put it, a new fulfilment. She'd been exquisitely beautiful. Was seen daily walking the shore, always in a different outfit. She'd lavished money on her cottage. A spiral staircase from the living room to the open-plan converted loft. A red Aga. Furniture imported from France and Italy. Everything in natural shades.

'Lovely,' said Freda.

Then Alexandra had fled. 'Stir crazy,' she'd said. 'Cabin fever.' The silence disturbed her. Her friends had stopped phoning. 'Everyone's forgotten about me.'

There had been the pop group who'd bought a house at the end of the village and spent evenings on the beach. They'd build a fire and sit smoking spliffs, staring out at the deep. Once they'd had a party and cleaned Murchie's out of beer and cigarettes.

'I liked them,' Murchie always said.

'Kenny,' said Freda, digging at the ground elder, 'who thought he'd found a place where he could cultivate marijuana without being discovered. Nine months and a five hundred pound fine. Poor soul, he was harmless. I liked him.'

But then she would. He'd been free with his crop. And Freda liked the odd relaxing puff. And now, she thought, here's another one. With Stuart. Interesting. She decided she'd get to know her. It was always good to have someone new to chat to.

Verbal Waving

Freda Thorne had come to Gideon forty-seven years ago. She was from Pittsburgh. And had just finished an art degree, specialising in pottery. And had broken up with her fiancé. Nursing a sore heart, she, and her friend Lucy had ended up in the village only because that was where the lorry they'd hitched a lift in had stopped.

All those years ago, they'd jumped down from the lorry and looked round. Seen the sparkle – the sea, the whitewashed houses. Freda thought herself lucky. She'd stumbled upon some kind of heaven. Lucy found it unnerving, weird. The silence astounded them both. The raucous taunts of a gull wheeling above them was offensive.

'God, it's quiet,' said Lucy. 'I mean, it's really quiet.'

Freda agreed. 'Quiet.'

'Why is it so quiet?' Lucy wondered.

'I guess,' Freda ventured, 'there's no need to make any noise.'

They asked the lorry driver where they could get something to eat. He'd shrugged, and told them that since it was teatime, nothing would be open.

'Isn't there a hotel?'

'Aye,' nodded the lorry driver, who had come to collect crabs. Boxes and boxes that he would drive overnight to London. 'But it's their teatime, too. So they'll be closed while they're having their tea.'

'But . . .' protested Freda, though she could see some sense in this. 'Shouldn't they be serving tea?'

'Who to? Everybody's home having their tea.'

'There's us,' said Lucy, who thought this ridiculous.

'But they didn't know you were coming. You didn't even know yourselves that you were coming.'

They couldn't argue with this. They shared a tin of corned beef they bought at Murchie's. Served by the now Murchie's father, who also made them a mug of tea. Lucy said that they had to get out of this place as soon as possible. Freda wasn't so sure.

'Give it a go,' she said.

They camped on the beach. And went to the Inverask Castle Hotel for a drink. Silence as they entered the bar. Forty-seven years ago women did not go into the Castle bar without a man by their side. Forty-seven years ago women never went to the Castle bar at all. On the rare occasions they drank, they sat in the lounge. Jim, the barman and owner of the hotel, directed them there. Freda, ordering her second glass of malt, confessed that this five pounds was pretty damn near the last of her money. But they sipped slowly, chatting with Jim. Before the evening was out, Jim had offered Freda a job behind the bar. Which she accepted.

Two days later, Lucy, unable to bear the silence and slowness of Gideon, left on a bus for Glasgow. Freda stayed, moved into the hotel. Her accent, for a while, was a source of income for Jim. People came to hear it. The only time they heard vowels twanged this way was in the movies. They'd ask Freda to say favourite lines from favourite films. She always obliged. Back home, she was ordinary. Here she was a star.

A year later she married Jim. And for twenty-five years they ran the Castle together. Different times, people came for a fortnight's holiday. The same people year in, year out. In the absence of any serious law enforcement brought about by the absence of any crime, the bar stayed open as long as there was someone willing to buy a drink. Freda made friends. Nights, she would stand on the long lawns with their nine-hole putting green, smell the sea and the thick scent of roses drifting through the dark, look up at the sky and think what a stroke of fabulous luck it had been that she'd hitched a ride on that lorry. If she hadn't, she'd never have known this place existed.

A year after Jim died, she sold the hotel to George and Betty Jackson, and turned to her first love – pottery. She opened the Campion Potter's Shop, selling her own creations, mostly large pots glazed dark red, and plates covered with flowers – green helebores, blue geraniums, thrift and campion – postcards, usually the work of local photographers, jewellery and odd trinkets. She made a living, of sorts. Didn't open regular hours. Instead left a notice on the door telling any potential customers to ring her doorbell – 'the house with blue shutters at the end of the street' – and she'd let them have a look round.

She worked at her pots most afternoons, evenings she had a drink at the Castle. The mornings were her gardening time. There was always something to do. And always somebody passing to talk to.

Muriel walked by everyday, unless it was raining. They'd chat. Conversations started with the weather. Moved on to the changes in the village. The new people who'd come to live there for a year, rarely longer than that, looking for a new life. A change of pace, room to breathe. It always seemed to Freda that they'd stand breathing and breathing. Till breathing wasn't enough. They decided there had to be more to life than breathing. Then they'd leave, saying the slowness got them down. And they missed restaurants, galleries, cinemas, life, they'd say.

'I really do think,' Freda said to Muriel, 'that these folks don't just move out of Gideon, they run for the horizon, screaming, waving their hands above their heads.'

Muriel agreed. 'They come here to find space and a bit time. Then when they get it they don't know what to do with it.'

They'd talk about what was in the news. Or at least what was news in the local paper. About what the young ones did these days. And how they did things they wouldn't have dreamed of when they were young. Then they'd sigh. 'Damn it,' Freda would say. 'I wish I'd thought of doing some of that stuff. They seem to have such a good time.'

Muriel would agree, nodding her head. Though, she didn't agree really. She didn't want to argue. They might fall out, and she'd miss the chat.

Then they'd talk about marriage. 'I miss Jim,' Freda would say. 'Though, I have to admit, since he died I have been able to finish my sentences. He'd always chip in and say what I was about to say just before I said it. Irritating habit.'

'Well, with me and Donald it's not a matter of what we say. Or what we don't say. We've reached a point of not having to say anything. We know what we're thinking. So we look and nod. But sometimes I think we ought to say something for the sake of it. To break the silence, like.'

Freda nodded. 'I see Stuart is back.'

'Yes,' said Muriel, 'and there's a girl with him. Little thing, too much hair. Scowly face when she's thinking nobody's looking at her. But quiet-spoken. He's quite taken with her. But she's one of them that comes only because they've got something they want to leave behind.'

'Another one,' said Freda.

And Muriel nodded. 'I have no idea what they think they'll find here. There's only seagulls and Murchie's, and the Castle for a drink.'

Freda nodded. Though she didn't agree with this. These conversations weren't about making points, they were about mutual agreement. You never argued. You nodded and thought inside how wrong the other person was. Still, she knew there was more to life in Gideon than seagulls, Murchie's and the Castle for a drink. There were night classes in the town hall – languages, art, history. There was the bridge club, the Women's Institute, Wednesday evening talks in the church hall. This year they had included Buildings before Architecture, Wild Flowers of the Area, Alpine Gardening, Marine Biology, and Mrs Bigelow had given her annual talk on Rock Climbing, this time round it had been in the Andes. Oh yes, there was a lot to do. If you fancied doing them, which Freda didn't.

She liked the Castle. She was a regular. She loved the moment of entering when heads would turn, and other regulars would shout, 'Freda.' And George Jackson would put a glass of her favourite malt on the bar before she'd even reached it.

Freda loved the warmth. The faces. Old, used faces. And the banter, the teasing. Best of all that moment when laughter took over the conversation and all these faces creased and cracked, and the sound of mirth moved through the room and she was part of it.

That was what it was all about. Freda knew that. The chat. The comfort of other people. Not being alone.

'Ah well,' said Freda, now. 'That's how it is with this place, you either get it, or you don't.'

'Well,' said Muriel, 'you've got it in a nutshell there.' And she moved on along the street.

Tomorrow she'd stop again. They'd chat again. Same place. Same time. More or less same conversation. As Freda often said, 'It's not what you say that matters, it's the saying of it. Letting other folks know you're in the world same as they are. It's verbal waving.'

Still, this Madeline person interested her. She looked arty. Furthermore, Stuart had brought her here. As far as she knew, and she knew just about everything that happened in Gideon, Stuart had come home often. But always alone.

She liked Stuart. He often dropped in to the Castle, and always bought her a malt. For a while, before he moved to Edinburgh, he'd come to her classes. He had the touch. She'd seen it immediately. But he wasn't interested. However, Freda believed in gifts. 'If a gift is with you,' she said to Murchie, telling him of Stuart's pots, 'it'll emerge. You'll come to it. Can't ignore it. It's like acne. It'll bubble up and burst out.'

Days of Heaven

Madeline's new surroundings took hold of her slowly. She felt she was uncurling. Letting go of something. Finding something. Yet found it hard to define what. At first she kept herself busy. She explored. Walked. She found books in the library, set up a reading list. She phoned Annie daily. And, daily, Annie asked when she was coming back.

'Soon,' Madeline would say. 'I'm thinking about it.' But she wasn't really. And after a month she phoned her boss to say she would not be returning to work. That was it, she thought. She'd committed herself to this place. Its slowness. Though it was coming to her that it wasn't really that Gideon was slow. More, there was no hurry. No need to hurry. Why hurry to do something that could easily be put off?

It seemed to Madeline that life in Gideon revolved round certain things. 1. The importance of being able to walk down Main Street, hands in pocket, smiling. 2. The banter. Which was linked to number one, since the sole purpose of sauntering down Main Street was to meet someone to banter with. 3. Enough money to buy a drink at the Castle. This was linked to number two. People didn't go to the Castle to drink to the point of drunkenness, though they often did. They went for the chat.

Gideon, Madeline decided, was founded and thrived on chat. Gossip. This gossip, often cutting, occasionally cruel, was rarely malicious. That kind of gossip rebounded, came back to you. 'A place this size is too small to talk nasty about others. They'll hear about it, and talk nasty about you. Keep your counsel,' Freda was to advise Madeline when they became friends.

'You what?' said Annie when Madeline phoned to tell her she'd quit her job.

'I told Mr Speirs I wasn't coming back. I'm staying here.'

'Why?'

'It's kind of relaxing,' said Madeline.

'What are you going to do?'

'Paint, swim.'

'Work, girl,' said Annie. 'How are you going to get by? Earn a crust?'

'Dunno,' said Madeline. 'I'll think of something.'

'I don't expect there will be much call for a window-dresser in a wee place like that,' said Annie.

'No. But there are other things I could do.'

'What?'

'I could start fishing for lobsters. I could work in one of the little shops. The fruit shop, the butcher's.' She could hear the doubt in Annie's silence, so changed the subject. 'How's everybody? The kids? Willie?'

'They're fine. And Willie is Willie. He was in court today.'

'Court? What's he done? Has he taken to a life of crime?'

'I wouldn't put it past him. But no, his French windows have finally caught up with him. He could have settled out of court. But not him. He's going fight it all the way, he says. What's worse, what's bringing me out in hives, is the fact he refused to have someone represent him. He has insisted on defending himself. He says he's seen enough of Perry Mason on the telly to know what to do.'

'How did it go?'

'Who knows? He hasn't come home. It's past eight and no sign of him,' Annie sighed.

'Where could he be?' asked Madeline, knowing this was a stupid question.

'Where do you think?' Annie sighed again.

Willie was in the pub. He no longer knew which pub. The case against him was not going as he'd thought it would. He thought he was losing. Which seemed strange to him. What was so terrible about putting French windows in the bathroom instead of the kitchen? It was a simple misunderstanding, he thought. Not so simple to rectify. He no longer worked as a builder, and footing the bill for someone else to do it was well beyond his means. So, too, was the cost of a court case. But, until this morning, Willie had thought right was on his side. Now, it all seemed different. He was beginning to feel foolish.

He'd worn his suit. He only had one. His going-away outfit. He hadn't worn it since his wedding day. It no longer fitted. 'Annie,' he shouted. 'This suit's shrunk.'

'No, Willie,' Annie said – tired voice; she'd known this was coming. 'You've expanded.'

'I have nothing of the sort. Clothes shrink if you leave them too long in the wardrobe. It's a fact.'

Annie brought him his shirt, freshly ironed. This had been a matter of hot debate. Annie thought he should wear a white shirt. Willie thought this the colour of surrender and said he should wear red to show he was ready to do battle. Annie thought this brazen, and might be held against him. They settled for pale blue with a navy tie, which Annie had to knot. Willie was too nervous.

He'd been avoiding this day for two years. Every time a date was set for the case to come up in court, Willie would write with an excuse. He was ill. He would be away on business. He was due to have an operation he'd been waiting months for. He'd broken his leg. He would be in Tasmania. At this point his opponent's solicitor had written to say that if Willie was going to Tasmania, he would like to see his ticket, or the receipt for his ticket. Willie relented and wrote saying that as this case was so important, he'd delay his trip.

Things went badly from the start. He didn't file his papers properly and angered the judge. He imagined himself strutting in front of the witness box asking pertinent and piercing questions. He'd make his opponent seem a little absurd for not being specific about which room he wanted the windows put into. But this didn't happen.

'Of course,' his opponent, a Mr Wishaw, shouted, 'I wanted them put into the kitchen. There's a patio out there with a table and chairs. Isn't it bleedin' obvious?'

From the murmur that shifted round the room, it seemed it was.

When Willie took the stand he couldn't help but expound on the glories of having French windows in the bathroom.

'Did you not think it a little extraordinary that someone would want French windows in the bathroom?' Willie was asked.

'No,' he said. 'Seemed like a grand idea to me.' He went on to explain about taking the wrong turn at the end of the hall and being a naturally left-veering person. He'd demonstrated this.

'When you went into the kitchen and saw the patio area outside, complete with built-in barbecue and table and chairs, didn't it cross your mind that the windows should go there?'

'No. I was delighted that someone would be bold enough to do something interesting with their bathroom. I mean . . .'

At this point Willie had enthused, as he had to Annie, about the joys of peeing in the open air. And the joys of sitting on the loo, hearing the blackbirds outside as you read the *Sun*, with nature's breezes '. . . billowing round you. It's healthy. There's nothing grander than peeing in the open air, one of life's grand simple pleasures,' he'd said. At the time, saying this, Willie had been sure the court would absolutely agree. But as soon as the words were out, he knew they wouldn't.

The court thought this hilarious, and had to be brought to order. At this point the hearing was closed for the day, and Willie headed for the pub. He knew he'd got carried away. He knew he was about to lose. He knew this was going to cost a lot of money. He tried to tot it up. Remove French windows from bathroom, rebuild wall, redecorate bathroom. Put French windows into kitchen. Plus cost of court case. Plus cost of Mr Wishaw's solicitor. He didn't want to go home.

On the phone to Madeline, Annie fretted, 'I know why he hasn't made an appearance. He's lost. It'll mean not only do we have to fix the window situation, we'll have to cover costs. Oh my God.' She slumped into a chair.

Madeline wished she was there with Annie. 'It'll be fine. You'll see. He's probably celebrating his victory right now. He'll come charging home soon, waving a bottle of champagne.'

Annie said she very much doubted that. 'But thanks for trying, anyway. So what do you do away up there?'

'Walk,' said Madeline. 'Hang about with Stuart. I know, I'll have to get a job. Money. But right now, for the moment, it's fun. I swim.'

Madeline swam every morning. She'd walk the thick heathery path from Marglass House to the shore. The sea sucked and swirled round the rocks that were covered with broken limpet shells, hard on the feet. There was no easy way of entering the water. Madeline slid in off the rocks. Clambering out again was harder. She found a small shelf just under the surface; once standing on this, she could lever herself on to the rocks. But it was hard to avoid the splintered shells. Her legs were covered with cuts and scratches.

The swim was worth the pain. Once the first gasp of icy sea hit her chest, and she heaved her breath against it, she could move across the bay, head level with the horizon. Salt water nipping her nostrils and the back of her throat. Cool air on her face. The throaty call of summering terns. And, sometimes, when the world was calm, the sea glassy still, the only waves were the small disturbances she made on the surface. She felt an abandonment. Alone, moving through water. She could think. For a while, thinking, swimming, she didn't want to come on to dry land again.

Stuart hated her swimming. The sea, he told her, was unpredictable. Sudden squalls struck up. There were currents. She must not swim beyond the small bay. She must not go past the bell-shaped rock. There was a fierce undertow. She'd get sucked out. He'd lose her. He watched her through the tall windows of Marglass House. Binoculars jammed against his eyes, steaming against the chill of the room and the heat of his face. And worried.

Standing outside the walled garden, Donald watched, too. He thought her lovely. The smallness of her, head above the waves. Strong movements. Strange things stirred within him. He wished. Wished he'd done that when he'd been young enough, lithe enough. He wished Muriel had been with him. That simple pleasures had not occurred to him years ago made him slightly crazy within. He tutted. He'd wasted away his time saying yes to people he hadn't liked or respected. And he'd worried too much about money, his work and what other people thought of him. He thought it would be fine to be like that one swimming there. The way she did what she wanted. That was the way to be. All those years with Muriel, and he'd never seen her naked. And apart from the war, he'd never left this place. He didn't dare start listing the things he'd never done. He thought that list would go on and on. And on. It would never stop. Swum naked, he thought. Visited Paris. Eaten oysters. Kissed anyone other than Muriel. Held his own child in his arms. Big things. Little things. Ordered wine in a fancy restaurant – though Muriel would have none of that. He'd never told Muriel that he loved her. All he'd said, and at that, not nearly often enough, was that she was fine. Fine to know. Fine to be with. For heaven's sakes, he'd wonder, watching Madeline, what was wrong with him? Everyday now, watching television, reading the paper, talking to someone at the Castle, he'd come across something new he hadn't done. And the stirrings would be there. No matter what he did to curb them, they came. Bugger, he thought. And that was another thing, Muriel forbade him to swear. But swearing was fine. A good curse helped.

Early summer took hold. The world turned balmy. Tiny insects danced in the shadings under the bushes. Swallows skimmed through clear blues skies. From the depth of the bushes birds called and sang, declaring their presence and availability. Hormones surging in the undergrowth.

Hormones surged through Madeline, too. She found a new sexuality. Nightly she enfolded herself into Stuart. Holding him. Moving with him. It seemed the very night was thick with wanting. Outside, beyond the window, the sea surged and hit the rocks on the tiny bay.

Daytimes, she looked through every room in Marglass House. The bedrooms with their large carved wooden beds. Most with ornately floral chamber pots tucked discreetly below. Some rooms were empty and it was hard to know what they'd been used for. But the drawing room on the first floor still had a large leather chesterfield that had been too heavy to be pilfered, a dusty chaise longue and several small tables. The library, though empty of furniture, was full of books. Leather-bound volumes – Charlotte Brontë, George Eliot, Thomas Hardy, Dickens. Books on birds. Books on butterflies, flowers, pottery. Atlases. Books of health and wellbeing that advocated enemas and cold baths. Madeline would find something that interested her, sit on the floor for hours, engrossed.

Sometimes Stuart would notice her missing, go searching for her. And find her huddled at the foot of the shelves reading about dinosaurs, or Richard Burton's travels, or *Rhymes and Roundelays in Praise of Country Life*.

'Listen to this,' she said. ' "Hush'd the howl of wintry breezes wild; The purple hour of youthful spring has smiled." Isn't that wonderful?'

Stuart took the book. Laid it down. 'Let's have a purple hour.'

It was their ambition to make love in every room of the house. Though Muriel's daytime presence, turning up unexpectedly with her tiny vacuum, tin of Sparkle and feather duster, saying, 'Oh, I was about to do in here,' made this difficult. Still, they persevered. And had favourite places. 'To the library,' Madeline would whisper in Stuart's ear, and they'd race up the stairs. Elbowing one another aside to get there first.

They cycled the long corridors. The hum of tyre over wooden floors. It seemed almost indolent to Madeline, using a bike indoors. There was something naughty about it. Whizzing past windows. Mrs Turner would have scowled. Maybe that was why she loved it.

They walked the woods. Chatting, keeping close. Inventing names for one another.

Madeline, pointing to a tiny spring gurgling up not far from the stream that flowed through the grounds: 'I say, Burton old chap. I do believe I've found the source of the Nile.'

Stuart: 'By Jove, Speke. Well done. Been looking for that these past fifteen years or so.'

They reminisced. Madeline looking around her, remembering childhood games. 'This would be wonderful for cowboys and Indians. You could really get into it. Creeping through the undergrowth. Watching the great wagon trains rolling over the prairies. The Sioux called the white man Pull-a-Wagon, did you know that?'

'No. How did you know that?'

'Read it in one of the books in your library. Funny,' said Madeline, 'how when you're a child you can play these games. And believe.

You really are out there in the old West, and nothing can spoil your imaginings. Passing cars. Grown-ups going about their day. You can make your own world. You never get back to that.'

'No', sighed Stuart. Though his imaginings were always his own. Never shared.

'Did you watch *Champion the Wonder Horse*?' asked Madeline. 'I used to. On Mrs Turner's telly. Huge thing with a tiny black-and-white picture. You used to have to adjust the vertical hold and keep the aerial pointed at the window. But it was worth it. Champion was an amazing horse. Brown with a pale gold mane.'

'How did you know that if it was black-and-white?'

'You just knew. Don't meddle with my childhood fantasies. He was a wonder horse, he could do anything.'

'Could he knit?'

'Almost anything. Most things. God, you're a cynic.' She sang the theme tune. 'Frankie Laine.'

'We've got him in my father's record collection. Singing "Jealousy". Better than your rotten wonder horse.'

'Don't mock Champion.'

They played the records that night. Found others. Nat 'King' Cole. Ella Fitzgerald. Louie Prima. Sarah Vaughan. Julie London. Peggy Lee. Piled them eight deep on the old gramophone, lay by the fire, listening. Drinking from the Marglass cellar.

It was reached from a trapdoor in the kitchen. The first time Madeline saw it, she could hardly believe it. Down the old wooden stairs, that looked like they'd been taken from a ship. And there were walls and walls of bottles. Sherries, some whisky and wine, which was mostly French. Claret, Bordeaux, Chablis, Sancerre. The ranks of wine stretched, three deep, the length of the house from the kitchen to the dining room.

'It'll take us a while to get through this,' said Madeline.

'We can do it, Speke. We discovered the source of the Nile today. This is a trifling thing for us.' Placing a manly hand on her shoulder.

'Good man. Well spoken, Burton. Let's get to it right away.'

They took a bottle apiece. And settled to drink and dream. Logs crackling. Door open, the scents of summer drifting in through the door. Lilac that had survived the weeds, blossoming. Drunk and silly with booze, Madeline had climbed on her bike that they kept for convenience by the living-room door.

She cycled the corridor. Swigging. Stuart joined in as Madeline was returning to the living room. They met mid-corridor, clinked bottles. Turned and cycled and clinked once more. Then she moved into the library. Started to cycle in time to a Percy Faith record. 'A Summer Place'. He followed. And soon they were dancing. Round the room in time. Swishing past one another. They started shouting instructions, turning the waltz into a square dance. 'Left and down the middle, meet and CLINK.'

'No hands,' instructed Stuart. Whizzing down the room, arms wide. Bottle still tightly held.

'Not fair,' said Madeline. 'I can't ride with no hands.'

They'd given up then. Run to their bedroom on the top floor. Loved. And slept entwined.

Next day their adventures started again. Wandering, giggling, fantasising. Bike dancing after Muriel had gone home.

They had other games. Hide-and-seek in the woods. Rolling down the hill that spread down to the stream. Putting the length of the hall into a cup, using Stuart's granddad's old wooden golf clubs. And they worked on their room tally for lovemaking.

They loved so much, rolling, holding, moaning. Sometimes Madeline thought she'd die from it. They exhausted themselves. Setting out to walk to the village, turning after half a mile to come home and lie down. They were aching love. And knackered.

Muriel saw it all. Even the bike dances, one night when she came across to the house to pick up her *Woman's Realm* magazine that she'd left in the kitchen. They hadn't seen her as she stood for a few moments at the library door, watching. 'Children,' she'd said, under her breath. 'No good will come of it. It'll all end in tears. Passion always does.'

Madeline, however, thought she'd left all her tears behind her. Though through it all, the bliss, she nagged herself that she had to paint. She couldn't let that part of her go. And in a way she did paint.

She registered the things she saw, the light, the shapes, and in her head worked out how she'd put them on to canvas, or how she'd sketch them. And for that small while, that was enough.

For a few fleeting weeks she joined in. She just lived. She let go. She did not stand back and observe. All her life, thus far, she'd been looking on, watching. Thinking how she'd paint this or that. Herself in the pub, walking down the street with Stuart, in Annie's kitchen. She rarely did anything without, at some point, stepping back, emotionally, to have a look, to peruse it from the outside. It was years before she thought to paint herself and Stuart skimming round the library. Right now, she just laughed.

Thinking back on these few heady weeks before she found a job, and set up a studio in the conservatory on the top floor and started to paint again, she saw from the distance of time and reason that they would have had to end. But while they were there, these times, lilac-scented, wine-laden, filled with love. The softness of their bodies. The sea beyond the window. They were days of heaven.

A Narky Old Bag with
Hairs on her Chin

By the time Annie came to visit, Madeline had, according to her friend, turned feral.

'Look at you. What are you like?' Annie said.

Madeline was wearing a pair of denim dungarees she'd found under a pile of blankets at Murchie's. Little more. Canvas shoes. She was sitting, foot resting on opposite knee. Hands in pockets. Moving slightly in time to a song playing on the old wooden radio in the corner. Not really a radio, more a wireless. Mrs Turner would like it. Annie Lennox and Aretha Franklin were belting out 'Sisters are Doing It for Themselves'.

'When did you last shave your legs?'

Madeline looked down. Considered the expanse of black unlady-like sproutings spreading up her calf. 'It's been a while.'

Annie quivered disapproval. With tweezers, Immac, a razor and Willie's shaving foam she waged a private passionate war against any hair that dared to grow anywhere on her body other than her head. She looked in horror at the black sproutings round Madeline's ankles, spreading upwards. There was more. Madeline's hair had grown. She'd shoved it back from her face, held it in place with a long silk scarf. Purple. Annie hated purple. But it looked good on Madeline. Annie hated that. Then there was Madeline's face. It was different. Tanned, thinner, softer. As if she'd just relaxed all the muscles, let them fall their own natural pattern. There was something smiley about her. Which, to Annie, who was feeling distinctly unsmiley, was extremely irritating. Also, Madeline had lost weight. A person could hate her for that. All the swimming had made her wiry and trim.

'Actually,' said Annie, 'you look quite good.' She would have said terrific. But her eyes kept wandering to the hairy legs. And no, Madeline didn't make it to terrific. Not till she returned to the hairless fold and became again dedicated to the sacred act of daily depilation.

Madeline asked if Annie would like a cup of tea. And Annie said that she'd said yes the last time she'd been asked. And that was at least twenty minutes ago. She'd noticed that Madeline seemed to speak slowly. It was irritating. But then this place was irritating.

Annie had stopped at Murchie's on the way here, thinking to buy something to bring to Madeline and Stuart. As she entered the shop Murchie and the customer he was serving turned, stared. Silently. Noted slowly that she was not local. Resumed their conversation. Ignoring her. They were speaking about someone called George who had bought a new car and who was, according to Murchie, not short of a bob or two. The customer remarked that there was money in plumbing. They both nodded at that and agreed they were in the wrong business.

Annie coughed. They both turned again. Looked at her. She looked back. Smiled. They nodded, smiled, and resumed their discussion about George. Annie coughed. Said, 'Um . . .'

The discussion group turned again.

'Now,' said Murchie. 'Is there something you're wanting?'

'Wine,' said Annie.

Knowing Murchie, and how Murchie liked to talk about wine, the customer excused himself, left.

'Now,' said Murchie. 'Is it a white or a red you're after?'

'Both,' said Annie.

'And what are you having them with?'

'I don't know. It's a gift.'

'Who for?'

'Madeline and Stuart at Marglass House.' It surprised Annie that she answered this. She was thinking this odd little man ought to mind his own business.

'Right. Though with the cellars they have, they'll not be needing any wine. But I see what you mean, you can't turn up empty-handed. Madeline's a white wine person. But you're more red, aren't you?'

How did he know that? thought Annie. She told him, 'Yes.'

'Well, you'll not go far wrong with a Sancerre for Madeline. And I have this lovely Burgundy, velvet smooth. But robust. Blackcurrants and tangy with it. Full-bodied and gutsy. But then again if you're after light and fruity . . .'

Is he taking the piss? Annie wondered.

'The Sancerre and the Burgundy will be lovely,' she said.

As Murchie wrapped the bottles, Annie looked round, and up. The sagging ceiling made her nervous. What if it fell down? She wanted out of here. She noticed a bunch of colanders hanging from a beam. They were old-fashioned enough to be back in style. She thought to buy half a dozen and sell them at a profit. She bought one. And a copper pot that Murchie was selling for half the city price. And a couple of bags of tablet.

Murchie watched her climb back into the car. Noticed she was driving. Willie sat in the passenger seat, reading, with unrestrained interest, one of his children's books. She'll be a tablet woman, he thought. She'll not be getting much of the other from him. Madeline never buys it.

Annie followed Madeline down to the kitchen. Sat at the table whilst the kettle boiled. 'So,' she said. 'This is it. And you're staying.'

'Yes,' said Madeline.

'It's an ugly old house,' said Annie. 'Still, it could look great inside. It'd need a bit of money. Millions,' she reckoned. 'Millions,' she sighed. She hated thinking about large amounts of money these days. Not with the amount Willie now owed. He'd lost his battle in court.

Madeline looked up at the yellowing and cracked ceiling. 'Millions,' she agreed.

'Our flat is worth a bit now,' said Annie. 'House prices are zooming.' She knew exactly how much the flat was worth. They'd had to remortgage.

Madeline made a face. Property didn't interest her. She could remember sitting in Edinburgh bars and all around her people were talking feminism. Just before she left, she sat in the same bars, surrounded by what seemed to be the same people. Now they spoke house prices.

'Not that it matters. Willie'll never leave that flat. It's way too small. Not a problem you have. You're going to freeze come winter.' Then, spotting the china Madeline was using, 'Don't let Willie see these cups. He'll be off with them. In fact he's sizing up quite a lot of Stuart's stuff.'

Willie had become obsessed with money and how to get it. Large amounts of it. The mortgage and remortgage were crippling. Now the very mention of the words French windows made him shudder, and caused Annie to glare at him. It was odd how often these words came up. He hadn't noticed before. But there they were in magazines, on the radio, on television. In the pub, someone would say, 'Thinking of getting French windows put in.' And Willie would turn and say, with a deal of bitterness, 'Don't say those words in my presence.'

'Stuart wouldn't notice,' Madeline told Annie. 'I'll just have to wear a lot of jumpers.' She put a cup of tea on the table. 'In winter.'

Annie stared out of the window. Swallows were swooping, crying. The dying sun spread grey-gold light on the sea, and on the ivied pale pinky brown bricks of the walled garden. She had to hand it to Madeline. The girl had done something drastic.

Lately drastic appealed to her. Annie had visions. She lived by them. Though life rarely came up to them. It seemed to her that life interfered with what she wanted. Reality got in the way. Also, irritatingly, the other people involved in her vision refused to play. Or were too insensitive to her perfect dream to join in. She found herself saying, 'This isn't right. This isn't how it's meant to be.'

She had imagined family life. A Sunday supplement daydream. A big kitchen table, children gathered round, laughing. Happily eating, without complaint or mess, wholesome food. Sun coming in the windows. Glossy pot plants. There would be books, music, rugs on the floor. Sunday lunches where friends gathered, sipping wine, sharing food, talking fabulously. There would be an atmosphere of relaxed sophistication. Her house would smell of fresh coffee and lavender wax polish. Her children would be quietly cultured, might even take up piano lessons. She knew children like this existed. She'd seen them in the street. Walking pleasantly, carrying music cases. In her Sunday supplement vision, there was not an ancient blackened perfect Melville chip hanging by a length of fishing line from the ceiling.

Her home wasn't like that. The living room was littered with brightly coloured plastic toys. Her plants withered and died. Her kitchen table was covered with tabloids, left open at the racing page. Or comics. The smell that greeted her when she opened the front door was heated-up pizza and beans. Which, apart from chips, was all Willie could cook. The only friends that ever called, mostly because she felt she couldn't invite anyone home because of the mess, the noise, the squabbling, were pals of Willie's, come to take him off to the pub.

If she wanted drifts of fresh coffee, an atmosphere of affable sophistication, she'd have to create it. But all she felt these days was exhaustion. When she got home from work she needed to sit on the sofa and watch television. When she'd suggested piano lessons to Marcus, he'd sulked for a week before telling her he was considering moving in with his best friend, Jason, whose mother, fed him takeaway food and let him stay up till midnight every night. Sparkling conversation was impossible. If Willie wasn't out drinking, he was fast asleep in the chair opposite her. And if he wasn't zonked, she was.

She'd considered brightening her life with an affair. But realised the impossibility of meeting someone. Doubted she was still attractive enough to interest anybody. Especially since, not long ago, she'd discovered a single, black wiry hair sprouting on her chin. It would multiply. Hairs did that, like weeds. Who'd want a woman with hairs on her chin? Besides, she knew she was too constantly tired to indulge in any naughty and illicit carryings-on.

She was almost thirty-five. Had reached the what-about-me time of life. Lying in bed, three in the morning, desperate to sleep. And wide awake. Thinking: Is this it? My life? It's gone all grubby and noisy and full of plastic things. I don't think any more. Used to enjoy a good think. Now I can't even remember what I used to think about. And I'm always carrying things. I used to have all sorts of things that were luxuries. Now it's walking down the street with my arms free. That's lovely.

She thought she was turning into a nag. She was always telling people what to do. Pick your toys up, Marcus. Have a bath, Douglas. Will someone switch the television off? Willie, will you *please* cut down that chip hanging in the kitchen?

The whole family had protested at that. 'We like the chip.' They'd started banging on the table with their spoons: 'Save the chip. Save the chip.'

They'd all turn against her. She knew it. Bugger this, she thought. They'd all leave her because she was a battleaxe. She didn't used to be. But they'd done it to her. Not doing what she wanted. Not fitting in with her vision, her plans. She saw herself at forty. A lonely old draconian bag with a painted face like Mrs Findlay in cosmetics. Oh Christ, she moaned into the night. She'd seen the future. And it was hell. Lonely, hairy hell.

'Do you worry about the future, Willie?' she asked.

'Nah.'

'Well, do you worry about the present?'

'Nah. Why worry? What happens, happens.'

'I don't think that's true. You can shape your future. You can control your present. You just have to take charge.'

'Take charge of what?' He looked baffled.

'Your life.'

'Nah. I just like to flow along. Take things a day at a time. You used to be like that. What happened to you? Where's my old happy Annie? You've got all practical and efficient. I wish you'd bloody well stop making sense. It's upsetting.'

'Willie, we just get by. We have no savings. I barely earn enough to pay the mortgage and the car and feed everybody. Everything you earn you spend on the kids. Buying them stuff they play with for ten minutes then abandon. We don't have room for any more stuff. Doesn't any of this bother you?'

'Nah.'

She picked up the car keys and walked out of the house. And drove. Hit the motorway. Foot to floor. Windows down. Talking Heads blaring 'Once In A Lifetime'. She skimmed over tarmac, moving easily into the fast lane, overtaking.

She pulled over. Stopped in a parking bay. Sat, breathing, staring. Buried her head in her hands. And that was when she discovered the hair. She thought it might be the worse thing that had ever happened to her.

Now she ran her fingers over her chin, checking. And sighed.

'That's a lot of sighing you're doing,' said Madeline, now.

'Is it?' Annie was unaware of her huge and voluble exhalations. 'It's just life and the living of it. You know, that moment when you stop and look round and think: What the hell am I doing here?'

Madeline nodded.

'I feel like I'm living in a tunnel. Everything is going on round me. And I'm not part of it. I'm just going through the motions. I mean, my life would be fine if it weren't for the other people in it. They're getting in the way of my life with their lives.'

Madeline nodded again.

'It's just not fair,' said Annie. Sighed again. And wanting more than a sympathetic nod from Madeline, added. 'Also, Willie's having an affair.'

'No!' said Madeline. 'I don't believe you. Not Willie. He adores you.'

'He adores me. He adores the kids. He probably also adores this other woman. Willie's like that. He adores people. He adores anybody that isn't Willie.' She was aware she was on the verge of ranting. 'He just adores to adore someone. And he doesn't adore me so much now that I'm turning into a naggy old bag. But he did it to me. He doesn't do things I want him to do and I'm right. Take green. I'm right about that.'

'Green?' asked Madeline.

'The other day I came home, carrying piles of things as usual. Groceries. Proper groceries. Fresh food. A chicken. Vegetables. Salad stuff. And they were all sitting round eating food Willie had made. Sausages, beans and chips. I said, "Willie, can't you give them something healthy? Just once? Cabbage? A salad?" He said, "Cabbage's green. So's salad. That's not right. Proper food isn't green. Proper food is brown, or reddy colour. Green is no colour to eat."

And all the children agreed with him. And he's turning them against me. Because I'm turning into a nag. Nagging them to pick up their toys and eat green food. But I'm right. I know I'm right. I'm right about green and I'm right about everything else.'

'Of course you are,' agreed Madeline. 'But are you right about Willie having an affair? Maybe you're imagining things. You're a bit overwrought.'

Annie banged the table with her fist. 'I am not overwrought. I am right. He smells of her perfume. He disappears. And when I phone the pub he's not there. The phone rings and if I answer, whoever it is puts down the receiver. Also, he ironed his underpants. If a man like Willie irons his boxers, before he goes out at seven in the evening, saying he's going to the pub, there's only one explanation. An affair.'

Madeline could see this might be true.

'Our sex life isn't what it used to be. In fact, it's nonexistent,' said Annie. She sighed. 'We have to be quiet because of the children in that small flat. Besides, I'm tired all the time. And I've turned into such a nag. I mean, who'd want to shag a narky old bag with hairs on her chin, who tries to get you to eat broccoli?'

'I quite like broccoli,' said Madeline.

'You would,' said Annie. 'Look at you. You're bursting hormones, the sex you're getting. You're glowing. It's almost obscene.'

They looked at each other. And laughed.

'So what about you? How're you doing?'

'This is me. Living here. Big house. No money. Old couple looking over our shoulders. Disapproving,' Madeline told her. 'I've got to do something. Find a job. Start working again.'

'What will you work at?' said Annie.

'Painting. A job's not work. A job's what you do to get money. Painting's work. So Willie irons his underpants.' She didn't want to, but she smiled. 'If it weren't so sad, it'd be funny.'

Annie shook her head. 'If it weren't so funny, it'd be sad.'

The small rant seemed to settle Annie. Worries exposed, sorrows shared, she relaxed. She laughed when Willie thought Marglass House a grand place to have a music festival, and what thousands they'd all make. She cycled down the corridors to the loo. And, since

Muriel refused to cater for such a large amount of people, she helped Stuart cook the supper.

Seven people sitting round the table, eating pasta. Stuart watched. The children were pink-cheeked from playing outside. They leaned close to their plates, scooping penne into their mouths, chewed bread torn from the long loaves and looked round, grinning. Willie poured wine, told jokes which weren't dirty, just bluish. Annie nudged him and glanced at the children. 'Willie,' she said. 'Enough.'

Outside the world turned dark, they turned on the lights. Put logs on the fire, played old records and drank more wine whilst the children ran up and down the corridors. Stuart heard their cries and laughter. And thought, That's what I want. A house full of noise. Children. I want lots and lots of children. He smiled to Madeline. She would want that, too. He was sure of that.

Later, sleeping in the guest bedroom on the second floor, when her children were all a floor above near Stuart and Madeline, Annie deemed it private enough for love. For a couple of days she liked herself again. She was not a narky old bag. She let Willie adore her.

Muriel had absented herself. At one time the arrival of guests would have meant extra work, now she let them fend for themselves. 'I'm not cooking for all them people.' She did not want to see the copious amounts of booze they drank, nor hear the thrum of their music resounding from the lounge and kitchen. 'It's not right. None of it is right. Next thing you know, they'll be noticing how cold it is up there in the big house, and they'll be wanting to move in here. Just when we've got it the way we want it. Just when we are settled.'

'Stuart would never do that. He's too nice,' said Donald.

Muriel thought about this and nodded her head. 'Yes. That's true. Nice is an awful thing to be in this day and age. You'll get taken advantage of.'

'Let them be.'

So she did. Though she was not without opinions. 'The bairns are wild. The Willie person isn't another one. But one day he will be. He's got it written all over him. Soon he'll be running from something. Hearty, though. Likeable, I'll give him that. The Annie one's fine.

Got her head together. Marglass could do with the likes of her. She'd put it back to rights. I've got time for that Annie. Yes.' She nodded, agreeing with herself.

Pick a Bale o'Rhubarb

It was clear to Stuart and Madeline that they needed money. Stuart suggested to Donald that they grow produce to sell to the Castle Hotel, and to the Brown sisters who ran the fruit shop in the village.

Donald said, 'Grand idea. But these places already have a supplier.' Him.

Madeline called the Brown sisters' fruit shop the limpy shop. Both sisters were large, wore identical blue overalls and limped. They took pride in their business. The place sparkled. The fruit gleamed. Asked for a pound of apples or tomatoes, they'd hold each one aloft and examine it before popping it into a brown paper bag. They sold boiled sweets from jars lined in a perfect shiny row on a shelf high above the fruit. When a customer asked for a pound of black striped balls, or barley sugar, the queue would sigh in unison. It meant one sister would limp to the back shop, fetch the steps. Limp back with the steps. Slowly climb them. Lift down the jar. Weigh the sweets, pour them into a bag. Twirl the bag in the air. Take the money. Screw the top back on the jar. Climb the steps. Replace the jar. And limp again to the back shop with the steps. This usually took twenty minutes. Sometimes longer.

The Browns, as had the Castle Hotel, had been getting their root veg, cabbages, cauliflower and peas and soft fruit from Marglass House for years. Donald had been putting the money he got into his retirement fund, and had no intention of letting go of this source of income. When he told Stuart that he knew for a fact both these places already had a steady and reliable and extremely good supplier, Stuart looked at the rows of beetroot, broad beans, potatoes and other vegetables that flourished, green, in the walled garden. 'But,' he said, 'what are we going to do with all this?'

'Eat it,' said Donald. 'Good for you.'

'We'll never eat all this.' Stuart was sure of this.

'You'll be surprised what you get through in the course of the growing season.'

Stuart looked at him, puzzled. He had no recollection of ever eating a broad bean or beetroot whilst at Marglass House. He gazed round once more. Then at Donald. Realised that Donald had some vegetable scheme going. And let the matter go.

Neither Donald nor Muriel had ever been paid much for their work in the house or gardens. Sometimes, they hadn't been paid at all. His father had left Stuart in their care without asking if they minded. And certainly without paying them anything. Stuart supposed that people like Muriel and Donald, who were not treated with respect, found their own dignity. Fair play, he thought. People had to get by.

He stood breathing in the garden air. The smell of earth. Brown, he thought, it smells brown. The wind moved round him. A goldfinch settled in the branches of a rowan tree. He thought it a lovely thing. 'Funny,' he said to Donald. 'Goldfinches. Black and white tail. All that yellow, and red round the eyes. You'd never put on an outfit like that. But they can get away with it.'

'Aye,' said Donald. He thought Stuart needed something to occupy him. His brain was going soft.

'I'd like to garden,' said Stuart. 'I'd like to do this. It seems magic. Planting seeds. And stuff growing. Coming green and new out of the earth. I think I'll take it up. I can give you a hand.'

A hand was the last thing Donald wanted. Especially one from Stuart. He mumbled. 'Oh well . . .' He thought the rest of his sentence: . . . if you're sure, if you don't get under my feet. He'd fallen into the habit of not finishing his sentences. It was a Muriel thing. They knew one another so well, they could communicate without.

'I can do that. It'll be healthy. Out in the open air.' Stuart smiled to Donald. 'Man's work.'

Donald frowned. Bloody. Bloody. Bloody people, he thought. You get things going lovely. And they come along and interfere. 'I'm sure . . .' he told Stuart. You'll soon get tired of it, he thought.

Stuart was gazing round. There was a patch of rhubarb in the corner. 'Rhubarb,' he said. 'I'll nurture the ground and watch our rhubarb spring to life. Rhubarb is wonderful.' He lifted a handful of earth. Held it to his nose, breathed it in. This is mine. This is what I can do, he thought. 'Till the soil,' he said to Donald.

Donald, who was bent double, face to the earth, planting beetroot seeds, breathing slowly, nodded. 'Aye, something like that.' He was planning jobs for Stuart. Clearing the nettles at the back of the greenhouses. Bringing barrowloads of compost to the vegetable plot. He toyed with the idea of getting Stuart to weed the front gardens that hadn't been touched in fifteen years. That would keep him busy, and out of the way.

'This is me,' said Stuart. 'This is what I am. This place. This is what I can do.'

And Donald said, 'Aye. Right enough.' Then slowly, achingly, moving from bent double to upright, 'Rhubarb makes you go.'

'Go where?' asked Stuart, thinking Donald knew things about rhubarb that he didn't. Maybe it had magical properties. Perhaps he could try smoking it.

'To the toilet,' said Donald. 'Gives you diarrhoea.'

'Excellent,' said Stuart. Realising how stupid he sounded. 'We'll all have healthy bowels.'

And Donald, slowly, achingly, returning to his planting, moved his face back to the earth, and said, 'Aye.'

Stuart strolled back to the house. Found Madeline in the bath and sat on the edge. 'So,' he said, 'I'm going to help Donald in the gardens. I'll grow food for us for the winter. It'll be grand. I'll lift that bale, tote that thingummy. Work in de ol' rhubarb fields. What are you going to do?'

'About what?'

'Us. Our life. You. Your life. We can't just hang about here. Cycling up and down the corridors. Playing old records. We've been here a month. We've got to get ourselves together. Start acting responsibly. We need money.'

'What for?'

'Christ, Madeline. What do you think for?'

'Everything? And gin.'

He nodded.

'I thought you had money.'

He shook his head. 'There's a trust fund. It pays Muriel and Donald's wages, and that's not much. And the rest goes into the house.'

'This house?'

'It pays local taxes. And last year we got a new washer on one of the taps. That was it.'

'There's not a deal of cash there, then.'

'After the washer. Nothing.'

'Jesus, Stuart. You might've said. I thought you were rich. I'd never have run away with you if I'd known you were poor.'

'I'd never have asked you if I'd known you had such bad judgement.'

They made faces at one another. She slipped under the water. He thought a bath would be the thing for a gardener, and took off his clothes. Joined her. And that was as near as they ever got to discussing financial matters. Discussing anything.

Muriel was standing outside the door, clutching a bottle of bleach. This was Friday, and Friday, as everyone ought to know, was lavatory day.

'Who said you could come to my bath?' said Madeline. 'You should wait till you're invited.'

'Your baths are better than mine,' said Stuart. 'Hotter, deeper, foamier. How do you do it?'

'Just a natural gift, I suppose,' said Madeline. 'Don't put your foot there.'

'My foot likes it there. Everything and gin,' said Stuart.

'Everything and gin,' agreed Madeline.

'*Everything* and gin,' shouted Stuart.

'Everything and *gin*,' corrected Madeline.

'Gin,' Stuart cried. A jubilant yell.

'Agreed,' shouted Madeline. 'Stuff everything. We'll have gin.'

'Gin. Gin. Glorious gin,' sang Stuart. Splashing Madeline. Tossing the sponge in the air.

'Jump down, turn aroun', pick a bale o' rhubarb,' sang Madeline. 'Couldn't we come up with a scheme to make money? We could open the gardens to the public.'

Muriel, standing eavesdropping, almost dropped the bleach.

'These gardens?' said Stuart. 'I don't think so.'

'Let the people see the weeds,' cried Madeline. 'Let them roam through the nettles. Wonder at the thistles and dock leaves. Ogle the dandelions. And all the other things I don't know the name of.'

'I think they could do that in their own gardens,' suggested Stuart.

'No. They don't have weeds on the scale we have weeds. It'd make them glad to get home. Think of it, Visit the Country's First Unstately Home. Come see the decaying opulence, the empty rooms, the overgrown grounds of the fallen upper classes. We'd make a bomb.'

'Muriel could serve scones in the dining room,' Stuart enthused.

'She'll do nothing of the sort,' said Muriel to the door.

'Only if they're stale. And tea only if it's stewed and slightly cold. No, even better, plates of lumpen porridge.'

'Beetroot sandwiches,' Stuart shouted. A brainwave.

'Beetroot sandwiches. Yes,' said Madeline. 'Excellent.'

Standing at the door, Muriel raged. How dare they? She was damned if she would serve scones or beetroot sandwiches (what on earth were they, anyway?) to anybody. Stupid, impudent, indolent idlers. 'Hah,' she cried out loud. 'Cheek of yous.' She stumped down the hall, leaving the bleach at the door. They could scrub their own lavatory.

Inside, Madeline and Stuart stilled in the bath. Stopped splashing and wriggling in the warm and foam. Looked at each other.

'Do you think she heard?' asked Madeline.

'From the sounds of it, yes,' said Stuart. 'It was a joke,' he called feebly to the door. But, knowing the old lady was long gone, shrugged.

'What are they like?' Muriel said to Donald that night. 'First off, they shouldn't be in the bath that time of day. Baths are for morning before breakfast. Or night, before you go to bed. They shouldn't be in the bath at two in the afternoon. That's plain indolent. Then, they shouldn't be in the bath together. It's rude. It's unhygienic. Two folks' dirt in the same water. They're like a couple of kids playing, making silly suggestions at my expense.'

'He's going to help me in the garden,' moaned Donald.

'What?' cried Muriel. 'He can't do that. It's your garden. You grew it. He can't come along and meddle in it. Just 'cos he owns the house doesn't mean he can fiddle about in your gardens. I thought he was settled in town. I never thought he'd come and live here. It's not right. There they are the pair of them up there in the big house having baths, singing about gin and picking a bale of rhubarb. Making silly suggestions about opening Marglass to the public to show off the weeds. Who'd come and do that? Pair of cheeky beggars.'

The next day Madeline asked Murchie if he needed a hand sorting out his shop. She offered to pretty up his windows. She said if his windows were alluring they would attract more customers into his shop.

'There are no more customers,' he said. 'Everybody that wants anything comes here. And anybody that doesn't want anything comes here anyway because it's the only place to go. Apart from the pottery, but that's always shut.'

Madeline couldn't argue with this. 'I could sort things out,' she said. 'I could make displays. You would know where everything is.'

'It's not the Murchie style to have displays. Displays only get in the way. Also, they're bad for trade. If someone spots what they want in a display, they won't have to root around looking for it, and come across something they didn't come in for, but buy anyway because they suddenly remember they want it. Or because they think it might come in handy.'

Madeline thought he might be on to something. He could revolutionise modern marketing.

'Besides,' said Murchie, 'you're a woman. And sexist though it is, I couldn't be doing with a woman about the place. You'd put me off. I'd always be looking at you. And I like a crack. And you'd cramp my style. Being a woman, like.'

Madeline thought to argue with this, pointing out that there was nothing he could say that she hadn't already heard. But decided against it. She'd never change his mind.

'If it's work you're after, they're taking on up at the Castle. They always do, this time of year.'

She cycled up the long drive of the Inverask Castle Hotel, thinking, this is what Marglass House should look like. Clipped and daisyless grass. Tamed rhododendrons. Pristine flowerbeds. Roses glossing into leaf. She thought the very birds flitting about were more polite than the Marglass birds. A blackbird, hopping the lawn, seemed somehow better brought up than Marglass blackbirds, who burst yakking hysterically from the bushes, screaming panic. Feathered ruffians.

Inside the hotel was cool, airy. A wide reception area, thick blue carpet. It was chintzy. Swathed curtains. A large cream and green floral sofa. A huge palm in a ceramic pot. Through glass doors was the dining room, tables laid, white cloths, gleaming glasses. Front stage the hotel had a cosy sophistication. Back stage, as Madeline was to discover, was mayhem.

George Jackson, the owner, was working at the reception desk. He was tall, hearty. Prone to clapping his hands and shouting, 'Well done,' or, 'Jolly good.' Black hair, gelled into obedience, and a whiskied face that was used to smiling. To enhance the relaxed holiday mood of the Inverask Castle Hotel, where nothing is too much trouble, he wore white trousers, a striped shirt, open at the neck, and wide red braces. Madeline introduced herself, and said she was looking for a job. He told her they were looking for someone to work at the reception desk, and help out in the bar.

'I can do that,' Madeline told him.

He looked her up and down. She was wearing jeans, walking boots and a sweatshirt, and knew she should have dressed up. This was not an interview outfit.

'Do you have any experience?' George asked. Meaning had she worked as a receptionist before.

'Yes,' she told him. Meaning she had lots of experience. Though none of it had been as a receptionist.

He asked where she lived, though he knew already. Working in the bar, he knew all the gossip. Both factual and elaborated into fiction. In fact, he'd known she was coming. Ali, whose van she and Stuart regularly borrowed, had been at Murchie's and had driven to the hotel, arriving five minutes ahead of her.

'You'll have to be better turned out than that,' George told her.

'No problem,' said Madeline. Though it was. Jeans and dungarees were all the clothes she currently owned. She'd worry about that later.

In the absence of any other applicants (locals knew better than to work there), George said, 'Well, why not? We'll give you a try. You start Monday. Half-past eight.'

She cycled home feeling triumphant. That was easy. In fact it had been so easy, it was ominous. But, at that moment, all she felt was joy at her achievement. A job, money. Bills paid. Everything and gin.

Stuart had spent his first morning as undergardener. Was sitting in the lounge, on the only remaining armchair, legs splayed, arms dangling. His hands were encrusted with muck, a grubby sweat gleamed on his brow. Thorns had left thin, cruel bloody lines up his arms. 'Jesus, gardening is hell.'

'Is it? I thought it would be pleasant. You know, fun. Wandering about, pulling out odd weeds. Smelling the roses. Listening to the birds.'

'Yeah. So did I. But you spend your time bent double. And when you see a weed, then get down to pull it out, soon as your face is at ground level, you see another. Then another. Then if you turn and look along the ground, you see a whole stretch of brown earth, raddled with weeds, stretching to the horizon.'

'How do you know they're weeds? How can you tell a weed from a plant?'

'That's another thing. I don't know. I have to keep asking Donald. And he gets grumpy. Then there's all the nettles. Look at my arms.'

Madeline peered. Stuart's arms were covered with red blotches, swelling hotly, between the scratches.

'And there's trundling stuff in the wheelbarrow. Which means filling the wheelbarrow. Then emptying it. Then filling it again. It's knackering. And there's compost and mulches. Christ, I don't know what Donald's talking about.'

'What's a mulch?'

'Don't ask me. I don't know.'

'Sounds soggy,' said Madeline. 'Time for a gin and tonic. Working people need sustenance.'

'Absolutely. Like you said. Stuff everything. Let's have gin.'

Muriel, having decided that eavesdropping on her pair was now essential to her survival, stood, ear pressed to the door, shook her head in despair. What were they like? Infants. How did they get by when they knew nothin' from nothin'. She had worked all her days, wiping, polishing. Things she knew. Stains that vinegar would lift. Unblock a sink with washing soda crystals. A pinch of Epsom salts firms up the strawberry jam a treat. 'Just a whisper, mind you,' she said to nobody. She shuffled off to put pork chops under the grill. Soften brown sugar by putting a bit bread in the jar. Little bit rice in the salt shaker will stop clogging. Put damp tea leaves over ashes to stop the dust rising. Clean copper pots with lemon dipped in salt. 'I know these things,' she said. Feet scuffing along the stone floor. 'I've scrubbed these floors. On my hands and knees. Household soap and a brush and elbow grease. I've done these things. And they've done nothing. Sing and play and make jokes and drink gin, that's what they do.'

'It's not fair. It's plain not fair,' she said to Donald that night, as she served the microwaved chicken Kiev and chips. 'I've worked my fingers to the bone. I've scrubbed and polished and cooked and lifted and washed and ironed, and they've done nothing. And they know nothing. It seems to me there's them that has and them that hasn't. And them that gets and them that gives and gets nothing. And I'm one of them. And I'm sick of it.'

Donald nodded. 'That's true enough.'

'Look at this place. It's a palace. That's how I keep it. A palace. Up there, where they are – it's filthy.' That she was paid to clean it was, right now, not an issue.

Donald looked round at their brand new B & Q kitchen. Yellow

253

units, white tiles. A neatly pressed dishcloth hung over the handle on the cooker. The sun streamed through net on the polished windows. Two portions of strawberry Angel Delight were served and waiting in their ex-Marglass House crystal dishes. The floor, marbled lino, shone. There was a bowl of yellow peonies from their garden on the windowsill. The kettle gleamed. As did the ex-Marglass house Limoges teapot and all the crockery on the dresser behind him. 'A palace,' he agreed.

'Look at the age of me. And still working. That's not right. My time of life I should be taking it easy. I should be retired. Living a life of comfort and leisure. Listening to the radio.'

'True enough,' agreed Donald.

'Couple of apples among the potatoes stops them sprouting. That's another thing I know.'

Donald chewed his chicken and stared at her.

'I've gutted fish. Topped and tailed gooseberries. Spot of bicarb will clean the inside of a teapot.' She lifted her hands, spread them before Donald. 'Things these hands have done. Places they've been. Down their lavatories. Wiped their baths. Folded their underwear. Hung wee bit rue in the cupboard to keep the ants at bay. All these things. And where has it got me? Nowhere. And there's them up there in the big house, drinking gin, singing about rhubarb, knowing nothing, eating the lovely meal I've made.'

Donald rose, put down his knife and fork and said he thought he'd just go for a wee walk down to the Castle. It was a nice night, and he'd enjoy the air.

'Cabbage leaves'll bring up pewter,' said Muriel. 'Milk takes ink off the carpet. I know so many things my brain's bulging.'

In the dining room of Marglass House, Madeline and Stuart silently chewed and chewed their pork chops. Sighing.

'I used to like food,' said Madeline.

'We've got to do something about this,' Stuart said.

Too tired to do their nightly cycle dance in the library, they walked. Made love in the woods. Trees above them, light pouring cathedral-like through the leaves, long glittering shafts. And the musky smell of deer that had been grazing minutes before they arrived.

Madeline rolled in the bracken and grass and mourned that their freedom days were ending. 'I'll be a lackey and underling again. Still, I'll have money to send for art materials. Replace all the stuff Maclean took.'

Shattered Dreams and
Receptionist's Leg

Monday morning Madeline set off at eight o'clock. She was dressed in a white silk blouse and black skirt she had found in Stuart's mother's wardrobe. The blouse fitted, if she rolled up the sleeves, but she'd had to take up the hem of the skirt, which was long and pencil slim.

Muriel watched. Impressed. Reluctantly impressed. 'She's got a fine hand,' she told Donald. 'Neat wee stitches. If they're needing money, she could take in mending.'

Shoes had been a problem. The only footwear Madeline possessed was a pair of walking boots and two pairs of trainers. She'd phoned Annie and asked her to send her a pair. They'd arrived on Saturday morning. Black patent, absurdly high heels. Madeline loved them and, thinking she'd spend the day sitting behind the reception desk, answering the phone, signing in guests, thought them perfect.

She cycled off down the drive, skirt hitched halfway up her thighs. The shoes were in the wicker basket on the handlebars. As soon as she'd sent for art materials, she planned to take a sketch pad and pencils to work. She'd have plenty time to muse and wonder and draw. She thought.

Stuart waved her goodbye, shouting that whilst she was idling her day looking pretty behind a desk, he'd be doing manly things on the soil. 'Bring back baccy and beans and wondrous things,' he yelled to her disappearing bum. 'And look out for Apaches. They're massing in the hills.'

'OK, Pard,' shouted Madeline. 'Giddy-up, Silver.' Pedalling furiously.

Muriel and Donald, who were coming across from their cottage by the river, exchanged glances. 'Children,' they said.

'She'll learn soon enough,' gloated Donald, who knew a thing or two about the doings at the Inverask Castle Hotel.

Madeline cycled through the morning. Saw a heron flying low behind some trees. A deer bounding though a field of green unripened corn. Leaping high to see the way ahead over the waving sea of green. The air was soft, scented. A lark rose, singing. When she topped the hill, there was the sea. Shimmering. The village, painted houses glimmering. She sighed. This was nearly heaven. She zigzagged across the road, singing Van Morrison . . . 'Into The Mystic'. And was happy.

Madeline hadn't known how right she'd been when she'd said she'd be a lackey again. And how wrong were her fond imaginings of herself sitting behind a desk, answering the telephone occasionally, getting odd guests to sign the register whilst she busily pinged a small important bell, summoning some minion to come carry their cases to their rooms.

As soon as she arrived she was told to help serve breakfast. And found herself running to and from the dining room with plates of bacon and egg, pots of coffee, toast, croissants on Annie's absurd shoes. After that, she had to plunge her hands into scalding water, washing up twenty-five breakfast settings. Then she had to help set the tables for lunch. In between all this she ran to and from the reception desk, taking keys, getting the mail, answering the phone. In the afternoon, after helping to serve thirty-seven lunches, guests and passing tourists, more washing up. She served teas, washed up. And worked behind the bar. And, 'Be pleasant to our guests at all times,' George told her.

She'd thought there would be banter. Laughter. New faces. George Jackson, who smiled, clapped his hands, and was so hearty it was tiring, up front, fretted, bossed, nagged behind the scenes.

Betty, his wife, a large and terrifyingly strident woman, had the biggest bum Madeline had ever seen. It was so big, Madeline found it hard not to stare. Betty did all the cooking, sweated, cursed, said she hated frying eggs, frying anything, 'But that's how it is with holiday breakfasts. Muesli and prunes would do them all a lot more good.' A couple of times when a slice of bacon slipped off the plate to the floor, she scooped it up, put it back on the plate saying a few germs never harmed anyone.

When Mary, the undercook, bottle-washer, bed-changer, laundress, loo cleaner and wiper-up, saw the shocked look on Madeline's face, she said, 'Oh, you'll see a lot worse. That's nothing. You'll see a bit of life at the Inverask. If you don't see nothing else, you'll see that.'

At six in the evening, Madeline eased her feet into the fresh air, held them, one at a time, up into the breeze that was shifting across the small putting green. Dumped her shoes into the wicker basket and cycled stocking-footed back home. With every turn of the pedals, she groaned. 'Oh-oh-oh,' was all she could say. No singing now. She held on to the handlebars with one hand, placed the other on her aching thighs. Small support for overworked muscles. She leaned forward, urging the bike onwards. She thought she smelled of fat and frying and kitchens and booze. Her lovely silk blouse was sweat-drenched. She cared nothing for bounding deer, rising larks and glinting evening sunshine. She was sore. Dreams shattered. She'd never worked so hard in her life.

Stuart, when she got home, was lying on the bed draped in a towel. He'd finished his day's gardening, had a bath, lain down. And now thought moving impossible.

Donald had set him to work clearing out the flowerbeds at the front of Marglass House. The beds that had not been touched in fifteen years. The weeds were over six feet high. Thrusting through roses – long gone wild through neglect – rhododendrons, berberis, mahonia and all the other shrubs that had once flourished and glowed colour round the edges of the Marglass lawn. And it wasn't just happy weeds that were joyously bounding through the undergrowth that Stuart had to get rid of – each shrub was hung, garlanded, with long withered strands of weeds gone by. In eight gruelling mucky hours sweating under the sun, Stuart had managed to clear only three feet of flowerbed. And had for his efforts a mound of nettles, thistles, straggly grass, and mud almost as high as he was.

'And I've got to do it all again tomorrow,' he said.

'Why?' said Madeline. 'It's been like that for years. Why now?'

'I have a notion of returning Marglass to its former glory. Maybe then we could open the grounds. Sell produce to visitors. Make it pay.'

'Single-handedly?' said Madeline, easing herself down beside him.

'Looks like it. Donald isn't up to it. Or willing, come to that.' He turned to her. 'You smell sweaty.'

'Thanks for mentioning it.' She pulled at her blouse, stuck her head down inside it. Inhaled. 'I am sweaty. I smell awful. I smell like Mrs Turner's cooking. She used worrying amounts of lard.'

Normally Stuart was turned on by the smell of fresh sweat on a woman. He wasn't sure about this. But, still, he put his hand on her breast.

Madeline looked at it. Though didn't remove it. 'I've got receptionist's leg,' she said. 'It's all sore from standing on it when I answer the phone, whilst I hold the other one up behind me. Giving it a rest.'

'I've got gardener's leg. From standing in funny positions while I stretch over into the back of the flowerbeds, reaching weeds. I'm a wreck.' The hand stayed put.

Madeline put her hand over it. 'I don't think I can,' she said. 'I don't think I'm able. There's a bit of me willing. But it's on its own. The rest of me is saying to it, "Carry on. But we're not helping. We quit." I'll do it if you go on top.'

'I was hoping you'd go on top.'

'I couldn't. It's too far to climb.'

They lay. Staring up.

'Did you remember the baccy and beans?' asked Stuart.

'I brought us back a slice each of Inverask lemon cheesecake. A chef's special. Fresh tangy lemons on a bed of sumptuously rich creamy cheese with a crisp biscuit base.'

'I don't know about that.'

'Oh, it's all right,' Madeline reassured him. 'Betty didn't make it. They buy it in, in bulk. Frozen.'

'Oh, that's all right, then. Where is it?' Still not moving.

'In the basket of my bike. I hid it there, lest Muriel saw it and threw it out. Deeming it unfit food for Marglass residents, when she'd prepared rice pudding.'

'Rice pudding,' mused Stuart. His brain had joined the rest of his body. Stiff, still, tired.

'Rice pudding,' Madeline repeated, sleepily. 'Her rice pudding is truly dire. I don't know how she does it.' Madeline took Stuart's hand. They both remained staring at the ceiling.

'It's an art,' said Stuart. 'Takes years and years and years to master.'

They slept. Woke at eleven in the evening. Stiff and shivering. Stuart went downstairs to remove the uneaten food Muriel had left lying out for them in the dining room. Smoked haddock swimming, grey and lifeless, in milk, and rice pudding. He fetched the chef's special cheesecake from the basket on Madeline's bike. They ate it in bed, with Sancerre from the cellar. Then slept. Rose at seven thirty. Bones aching. Complaining.

'We'll never have sex again,' said Madeline. 'We'll never manage it.'

An hour later she cycled off down the drive. Stuart returned to his notion of single-handedly returning Marglass to its former glory. They did not shout or banter.

'Life,' said Stuart, 'has crept into our idyll with a vengeance.'

Two things soothed Madeline, painting and swimming. After two weeks running on absurd shoes at the Castle, she was fit enough to rise each morning in time to walk down to the sea before she left for work.

Swimming, water poured over her, and she moved effortlessly through it, eyes level with the horizon. Ahead of her a million ripplets, tiny waves stretched endlessly out, till they merged with sky. Or on perfect days, deep, still, glassy grey-blue. Daily, she'd rhythmically work her way across the bay in front of the house. She'd breathe the scent of air and water. Salt. She always swam alone. Though never felt alone. She was part of the landscape she loved. Still, she never could decide if it was better to stand watching the view, or to be out there, living it, breathing it, embroiled in it.

Meantime, some art materials had arrived at last. Energy restored, idyll interrupted, she painted on her days off and in the evenings when she got home.

There was the soft sound of sable on canvas. The mixing of colours, shapes. The slightly acrid tang of acrylics. The rattle of brush in jar as she exchanged one for another. It was a battle sometimes, and a triumph sometimes. A slog. And, when it was going well, a joy. That was what she sought. Those moments of pure concentration when she forgot who she was, where she was. It was like swimming underwater, soundless. Spontaneous. There was only movement. Then when she broke surface, there was the world that, for a few seconds anyway, she'd been lost to. The sun on her face. Sounds of gulls. Waves. The sparkle of light, the sudden dazzle of it.

So it was when painting was a joy. The phone would ring unheeded. Favourite tracks would drift from her radio into the room, unnoticed.

Now she was working at the Castle both these pursuits became precious. She set up a studio in the top-floor conservatory. In winter it would be cold. In summer it was too hot. But she feared comfort. It was tempting. A chair, and she might just sit, look at the view. A bed, and she knew she'd sleep.

She painted things around her. The walled garden. Donald sitting in a corner pouring tea from a tartan Thermos. Muriel standing in the dining room in her pink overall, holding a tiny feather duster. She painted Ali and his van. Him standing with his back to it, letting it know how much he loathed it. Murchie's shop. Murchie almost lost amidst the clutter. She painted Betty at work. Furiously frying eggs. Mary rushing into the hotel reception, hands raised in horror, as she'd done the day she'd discovered a used condom in the ashtray of one of the rooms she was cleaning. George had clapped his hands, 'Excellent. Jolly good. People are relaxing at the Inverask Castle Hotel. Madeline, go upstairs and remove the offending object. Plainly it is too much for Mary to do.'

The small ceramic tiger was on the table by the window, the view, the sea beyond. Sometimes she smiled at it. It was all she had of her old life. It seemed a million miles, a million years behind her. Distant times, lost people – Mrs Harkness, Mr Speirs, Mrs Findlay, the cosmetics lady, skip poetry, skip philosophy were all almost forgotten. Though, sometimes she worried that her old landlord would track her down and come to her new door, which was never locked, demanding money.

She painted the landscape, the view from the window. The overgrown flowerbeds. She painted the sea. None of it pleased her. She preferred doing people. She sketched Donald and Muriel coming up through the walled garden in the morning, which she thought more her thing. The smallness of the pair with a vast wildness, hills, forest around them.

Though in time she'd come to regard her first month at Marglass as precious, right now, when she was working, often spending ten hours a day at the Inverask Castle Hotel, she cursed the time she'd wasted. She had frittered precious time lying in bed in the morning, having midnight picnics under the blankets, playing dancing games on bikes with Stuart in the evenings.

Though, that had been fun. And how serious they'd been about getting their routines off pat. The soft hum of tyres on wood, the surge of Strauss waltzes and Ritchie Valens hollering 'La Bamba'. Whisking round the empty room, charging towards one another, meeting, linking arms and cycling round and round. Yelling instructions: 'Left, and down the middle. Then pit stop for gin.' Glistening sweat they'd stop, drink, and start up the drunken jig once more.

'What do you do up there?' asked Annie when Madeline phoned.

'Lots,' said Madeline. And told her.

A long silence. 'You're playing! You're behaving like a couple of children.'

'We're making up for lost time,' said Madeline. 'Having the childhoods we never had. Neither of us had someone to play with.'

'Like I said, playing. No good will come of it. You should be working. These are your getting ahead years. You'll regret your idleness.'

'You sound like Mrs Turner.'

'Christ, do I? I'm beginning to feel like Mrs Turner.'

'Narky old bag,' said Madeline.

'That's me. And I'll tell you. All this mucking around – no good will come of it. It'll all end in tears, my girl.'

'Piss off,' Madeline told her. Put the phone down. Got on her bike (which not unlike the one Ted had used when cycling across Edinburgh with Jem's flowers), whizzed up the hall to the dining room. 'On with the dance.'

Annie put down the phone. Narky old bag. Bugger that. 'Are you having an affair, Willie?'

He was putting on his jacket, having spent some time on it with an old clothes brush so matted with hairs, it put back more than it took off. 'Me?' Voice suddenly high. He near as damn it squeaked. 'What makes you say that?'

'You're wearing aftershave.'

'Am I?'

'Well, from the guff in here one of us is. And it isn't me.'

'Right,' nodding. 'Well, it must be me, then.'

'I think it must.'

'Right, well, I'll be off.' Making for the door.

'Willie,' Annie summoned him back. 'Tell me something. Why do people have affairs?'

'What? I don't know. They just do, I suppose.'

'There must be a reason. We fell in love. You more than me, I have to admit. I haven't cheated on you. Why are you having an affair? Why do people have affairs?'

'Curiosity,' said Willie. 'You want to know what other people are like.'

'In bed?'

'And generally. And excitement. People want to zap up their lives. And they want to know they're still fanciable. Still in the game. But that's curiosity again.'

'I think it's because they fear they're getting old.'

'Could be,' said Willie, backing out of the door.

'Willie, stay. Stay here with me.'

Willie heaved his shoulders, spread his arms. An apology. He continued to back out of the door.

'You're not old, Willie. And I'm very fond of you.'

He nodded and left.

Annie dropped her head on to the table, banged it with her fists.

'I'm very fond of you. Jesus, if Willie said that to me after over ten years of marriage, I'd punch him.'

Two days ago the phone rang. Annie picked it up. Silence. 'He's not here,' she said.

Silence.

'Don't you dare hang up,' Annie said.

Silence.

'I know you're having an affair with Willie.'

Silence.

'What are you like? Do you look a little like me? Are you a bimbo?'

A deep laugh. Sexy, mature. 'Yes, that's me. A bimbo.'

Annie was shocked. Five words, and she knew this was no bimbo. This woman was intelligent, sophisticated. And, knowing Willie, probably wealthy. 'Don't insult bimbos by pretending to be one,' she said. 'At least bimbos have the savvy not to pretend to be stupid. They let it come naturally. You sound like you're working at it.' She put down the phone. Sighed. She thought, though, that if anyone had made a fool of themselves, right now, it was her.

Soon, it would be Willie. This woman was too complicated for him. That voice was too rich for him. Too used to mocking. To her horror she wondered what she saw in him. 'Oh God,' she said. 'It'll all end in tears. And they won't be hers.'

Now, considering all this, and how she hadn't made a scene, hadn't given Willie an ultimatum – 'It's her or me, Willie' – she was surprised at herself. Not that she didn't care. She cared. Not that she wasn't hurt. But she was resigned to it. Had been expecting it for years. And now she was waiting for Willie's downfall. His pain. Soon, he'd come crying to her. And she knew she'd give him no sympathy. She'd tell him what a fool he was.

And this made her dislike herself even more. 'Narky old bag,' she told herself. 'And hard. Hard-faced bitch.' She stared ahead, at the fridge magnets and the children's drawings hanging behind them. A big sun. Flowers. A large woman with furrows on her forehead in a blue frock with her arms wide, her fingers spread, 'My Mum' scrawled along the bottom. 'That's me OK.'

And, suddenly, a revelation. 'I know why people have affairs. It's so they'll like themselves again.' She brightened at her little wisdom. 'That's it. That's definitely it. You fall in love because someone makes you like yourself. You glow. You float through life. I am loved. I am wonderful. Then you marry. Work, bring up kids. Get knackered. And it all gets tarnished. You turn into a narky old bag. You start to hate yourself. Then you meet someone who's interested in you. And you open up to them, and they like you. And you sleep with them. So you'll like yourself again. That's it. Easy.'

She moved through the flat, picking up abandoned things – shoes, a toy aeroplane, socks, a jumper. 'So why did Willie stop liking himself? I made him feel like a bumbling inadequate fool.' Arms full of toys and clothes, she sank on to the sofa. 'I make him feel an idiot.' She didn't like this thought. 'But then,' to comfort herself, 'he is an idiot.' Thinking of the French windows and the crippling effect they had on their finances. It would be years and years before the whole court débâcle was paid off. She decided a drink would ease her worries. On the way to the bottle she caught a glimpse of herself in the mirror. She was frowning. Walking shoulders hunched, in an almost cruelly self-defensive resolve. 'Oh fuck. What do I look like?' Right there, in the hall, she crumpled up. And cried.

Rejection

A year passed. Time, Madeline felt, was running through her fingers, like sand. She hadn't noticed it passing. 'A year,' she said to Freda. 'A year, just like that.' She snapped her fingers. 'Where did it go?'

'It's age,' said Freda. 'Years pass more quickly the older you get. If a year whizzed by for you at your age imagine how fast it went for me at my age. I just blink and it's gone.'

'I better get my act together, or I'll be standing here serving drinks when I'm forty. This job was only meant to be a stopgap while me and Stuart got on our feet. A year, God.'

'So get going, girl,' said Freda. 'Get on with your life.'

'It's hard,' said Madeline.

'What's so hard? You know what you want to do. Get doing it. How many paintings do you have in your studio at Marglass now?'

'Dunno. Six finished. One underway. And my sketches.'

'Well, get them out there. They're doing you no good hidden away.'

'I know. It's just . . .'

It was just she'd started to fear rejection. She remembered the way Hamilton Foster turned and looked at her tiger paintings. She was convinced he didn't like them. And living tucked away here in Gideon she felt out of the flow of things. She'd lost contact with all her old friends, except Annie. She was sure that by now Hamilton would have forgotten about her. Several times she'd picked up the phone, dialled his number, then was seized by shyness, and replaced the receiver. Once, she'd hung on and spoken to Peter Nuttall. Who was he? Hamilton's new partner, he explained. Who was she? Madeline Green, she explained. Where was Hamilton?

'Away at the moment. Can I help?'

Madeline told him that she'd been hung at the gallery and sold and she had some new work she wanted Hamilton to see.

'Well,' said Peter, 'bring it in. Let's have a look.'

But she hadn't taken her new paintings in. She felt she'd lost some of her edge. There was something about the snugness of this place, the smallness of her life, that made her feel like an outsider in the world she'd left. There was something about this little world she now inhabited, with its banter and friendliness and lack of any real competition, that made her feel safe, and made her feel, at the same time, hemmed in.

'I'll get round to it. When I'm ready. Soon,' she told Freda.

Stuart, meantime, was flourishing. He had transformed the area at the front of the house. He'd cleared the weeds from the flowerbeds, tamed the wild, rebel shrubs. He'd dug new areas to be planted. Begged cuttings, seeds and plants from gardens in the village.

'It's a wonder,' Donald said, grudgingly, to Muriel. 'He's done amazing things. It's messy, though. I like a tidy garden. Everything in its place.'

Stuart didn't want the old formal garden any more. He wanted a different, relaxed, tangled look. Now, without the cash to buy plants, he was begging and bartering stock from everyone he knew. Last week, he'd visited the Watsons. Seen their small self-sufficient smallholding. And seen, also, his future. He wanted to be like them.

The Watsons had come to the area seven years ago. They were following their dream. A life lived to the full with as little actual currency as possible.

'We don't need money,' said Christopher Waston. 'We barter. Exchange. We recycle.'

Stuart was impressed. This was skip philosophy lived to the full. Madeline would love it.

'We've got goats,' said Christopher.

Goats, thought Stuart. I could have goats. Make my own cheese. Hens, he thought. Eggs. Cheese omelettes. He saw it all.

He and Christopher were followed on the guided tour by Emily and Maeve, the youngest of the Watson tribe. Twins. They wore baggy misshapen dungarees and lumpen woolly jumpers. They'd recently been bought new wellingtons (the Watsons couldn't make everything) and as they couldn't decide which colour they wanted, they'd split them. A red and a blue apiece. Stuart loved this. This was his kind of dressing.

Over chamomile tea and home-made flapjacks in Marianne Watson's cluttered, busy kitchen, Christopher extolled the joys of the good life. Making his land work for him. Growing his own food. Wood-burning stoves in the living room and bedrooms. He got logs in exchange for Marianne's chutneys, jams, eggs, a day's work now and then at harvest times on the farm down the road and the odd loin of pork now he had pigs.

Pigs, thought Stuart. I could have pigs. Pigs and hens. Bacon and eggs.

Christopher told of his labours renovating his cottage. 'Got hold of some DIY manuals and got busy.'

I could do that, thought Stuart. I could renovate Marglass House. Plumbing. New floors. Fix the stairs. New windows.

'I wanted the best for my children,' said Christopher. 'Fresh air, organic food.'

Children, thought Stuart. I want them. He imagined a teaming brood of miniature Stuarts and Madelines. All mucking in, helping with the pigs and goats and hens.

'When I get my loom . . .' said Marianne.

Stuart didn't hear any more. A loom, he thought. Madeline would love a loom. Madeline in the evening, sitting at her loom whilst he carved toys for the kids. He was in raptures. He couldn't wait for her to come home from work so he could tell her about their new venture.

Since Madeline started at the hotel, her relationship with Stuart had changed. They no longer picnicked in bed. They'd abandoned their ambition to make love in every room of the house. They'd settled into a routine. Swift breakfast. Then they'd go their separate ways. In the evening, they spoke to one another about the day they'd had. Chaos at the hotel versus sweat and tears in the garden. But tonight Stuart was full of his new notion. The future he'd seen. The life he and Madeline would live.

'The Watsons have hens,' he enthused. 'We could have hens. Fresh eggs.'

'Good idea,' said Madeline. 'Why not?'

'And goats,' Stuart went on.

'Goats? Wouldn't they munch all your new plants?'

'I'd build a fence,' he waved aside her doubts. This was too exciting, 'when I'm building a sty for the pigs.'

'Pigs? Who is going to look after them?'

'Me. You can do the hens, and the goats look after themselves. And I'll have a poly tunnel, grow peppers and all sorts of things. Chilies, aubergines.'

'Where are we going to get money for a poly tunnel?' asked Madeline.

'Cheese,' said Stuart.

'Cheese?'

'From the goats. And courgettes.'

'What are you talking about? Courgettes?' Madeline was finding this hard to follow.

'I'll grow them and sell them. Get money for the poly tunnel and the stuff to renovate the house. Barter. Recycle. That's the way to go.' Stuart's mind was racing. He could see it all. He didn't want to go into detail. Not right now.

'Courgettes and cheese,' Madeline said. 'I'm not really with you here.'

'Self-sufficiency,' shouted Stuart. Why didn't she see it? 'Don't interrupt me. I'll get the range in the kitchen working. For the flapjacks and bread.'

'Sorry? Bread? I can't see Muriel making bread.'

'No, not Muriel. I'll tell her to stop coming in to cook for us. We'll make the bread, us.'

Muriel was in the hall, listening. Oh no, you'll not tell me not to come cook. I'll tell you I'm not coming. Cheek. After all the good food I've put down in front of you, she thought.

'We'll make our own. We can turn the onions and stuff into chutney and fruit into jams,' said Stuart.

'I'm not making chutney. I hate jam.'

'But the children will love your jam. And when you get your loom, you can—'

'Wait a minute. What?'

'Your loom,' said Stuart.

'No, forget the loom. I'm not having a loom. That's not an issue. It's the children bit. I don't want children.'

'But I do.'

'I just don't feel maternal,' Madeline said. 'It's just not there. When I look inside and think babies – nothing.' She raised her arms in the air. A demonstration of the intensity of the nothingness. 'I don't want them.'

'I want lots. Six.'

'What!'

'At least. I want to see them here, in this house. Running about. Abandoned trikes in the flowerbeds. A swing on the tree outside. I want to hand this place on.' Stuart couldn't understand why Madeline didn't see the importance of this. And he knew, he just *knew*, that if he could persuade Madeline to have just one child, she'd want more. She always wanted more. Sticky toffee pudding, sex, whatever. One was never enough.

'I don't want a baby,' she said.

Stuart protested the unfairness of this. 'But what about me? What about what I want?'

'I don't know. Don't ask me that. It isn't fair. You make me feel guilty. You have no right to do that. If you want a baby, go have one with someone else.'

'I don't want anyone else. I want you.'

'Well, if you want me, you can have me. And no baby. That's the deal. And while we're on the subject I'm not too keen on the hens and goats and pigs, either.'

'Madeline,' said Stuart, 'it's the way to go. To save this place . . .' But he'd lost her. He could see it. She wasn't listening. She was dreaming. She was seeing this moment from the outside. How they looked. How they were standing. How the fire flickered in the grate. She was painting it. Either that, or she was already, in her head, telling the whole absurd thing to Annie. What she'd say. What Annie

271

would say. How they'd laugh. He slumped. Dreams shattered.

Muriel, satisfied the fighting had stopped, came into the room and announced that food was on the table. 'Oh,' she said, 'and that's the last. I'll be leaving you to fend for yourselves from now on.'

Good, thought Madeline.

Excellent, thought Stuart. 'Oh, Muriel,' he said. 'That's so disappointing. Why?'

'It's time,' said Muriel. 'Time you got your own teas and suppers and breakfasts. That's what's best.' She left the room, and walked stiffly home. Wiping her tears on her apron.

'Well,' she said to Donald, 'he's made it clear he doesn't need me. I heard him only a minute ago telling that Madeline he was going to cook for himself. Make bread and flapjacks.'

'Flapjacks. I don't like the sound of that. He'll not be needing me soon. The way the garden's going.'

'He's going to grow courgettes,' said Muriel. 'And he's getting goats and a pig.'

'I'm not having the likes of that wandering about my garden. That's it. I'll tell him in the morning he can do the walled garden himself.'

'And hens and a poly tunnel,' said Muriel.

'What kind of stately home has the likes of that? The place is going to rack and ruin.' Donald shook his head sadly.

Madeline ignored her meal. She went to her studio, gathered her canvases and wrapped them, muttering, 'Jam, loom. Loom, for heaven's sake, a loom. Children. Oh, no. I'm a painter. Me. I paint.'

The next day she sent her package to Hamilton Foster.

A week later it came back. A polite note from Peter Nuttall: 'Sorry, Hamilton is away. We are not taking on any new work at the moment. I wish you success with another gallery. Yours . . .'

Peter had been with Hamilton for six months. He knew nothing of Hamilton's plans for Madeline. He'd forgotten about her phone call. He thought the paintings interesting, but not really his thing. He never mentioned them to Hamilton when he came back.

'So,' said Freda, sipping her evening malt. 'You got rejected. What of it? Who cares? It's only a letter. A bit of paper. Tear it up. All the greats got rejected. My God, if I had a pound for every time I've been rejected, I'd have . . .'

She'd have a pound. She'd only been rejected once, by her fiancé forty-eight years ago. That had been painful enough. She'd made sure, in all her relationships, that it never happened again. And, she'd never tried to sell her pots in anything other than her own shop. But that didn't stop her telling Madeline to dismiss the fool who didn't see her gift.

Madeline didn't see that. She saw only that someone didn't want her work. She felt humiliated. Embarrassed she'd sent her paintings to Hamilton. Embarrassed she'd caused his partner the embarrassment of having to return them. She imagined the derisory things that had been said about them. She doubted herself. Her ability to paint. And saw no way ahead. She was a failure. All that, and Stuart wanted babies. She knew she didn't. He wanted her to become an earth mother. He'd had a vision of her barefoot and pregnant. Feeding hens. Baking bread. Making jam. Working at a loom, for heaven's sake. She wondered how he'd got that idea of her. How he could have been so completely wrong about her.

Slipping Away

When Stuart thought about the night he'd told Madeline about his notion of self-sufficiency, the bread baking, the loom, the babies, he knew that was when he'd lost her. It wasn't a sudden dramatic break-up. It was a rift that grew slowly, slowly. They still walked the grounds together, ate together, laughed, got caught up talking till late into the night. They still made love. They avoided the subject of babies. But, as is the way of no-no things, babies kept cropping up. The first baby rabbits of spring appeared in the grounds.

'Oh, look,' said Madeline. 'Aren't they sweet? Little babies.'

And Stuart grunted, 'Yeah. Sweet.'

And there was a moment. A pause. A slight blip in the harmony. Babies. We don't mention them. Sorrow. Blame. A tiny silence as they wrestled with this. Him, with his need for children, his resentment of her absolute refusal to have them. And her with the remorse she felt for not giving him what he wanted, and the anger she felt at him making her feel so damn guilty. Meantime Stuart felt guilty about making Madeline guilty. Guilt and babies. Madeline and Stuart. Round and round. On and on.

It seemed there were babies everywhere. Babies in the newspapers. Babies on television. Baby rabbits. Lambs. Calves. Young deer, trotting by their mothers' sides in the woods. Marianne Watson was pregnant, blooming. Glowing. She and Christopher came to dinner. Stuart fussed over her, offered her the best chair, asked if she needed to put her feet up. Bought a bottle of elderberry cordial, because she wouldn't be drinking. He kept asking what it was like to, you know, have a little life in there. Did it move about? Was it kicking yet? And after they left, Stuart and Madeline argued.

'You made a fuss of her. Rubbing it in a bit, aren't you?'

275

'I don't know what you mean. I was just being polite. Making sure she was comfortable.'

And Madeline said, 'Pah.' And stamped from the room.

'Bloody babies,' she complained to Annie. 'They're ruining my life.'

'And that's without even having one,' said Annie. 'I like babies. I even like being pregnant. Well, some of the time.'

'Well, you have Stuart's baby, then,' said Madeline.

'I don't think so. Life's messy enough as it is.'

'Stuart wants to mess up our lives with hens, pigs. The full self-sufficiency kick. Baking bread, making jam, chutney. Children running in and out. A loom.'

'I don't know about the loom. But the rest of it sounds lovely. I quite fancy it.'

'You would,' said Madeline. And rang off.

Annie sat and dreamed. A big house, hens, fresh eggs. Pigs, she didn't know about that. Lots of children running in and out. It sounded, to her, like heaven.

Stuart worked in the garden. And set about renovating the house. Rolling lawns, rooms decorated, refurnished, filled with life, laughter. Though where the laughter would come from, he didn't know. Laughter meant people, and his circle of friends was small. If he examined this laughter thing, tried to hear it in his head, he knew it was high-pitched, infectious. The laughter of children. His children. People he could not discuss with Madeline. Still, he thought if the house was comfortable, homely (or as homely as Marglass could be) Madeline might, as he put it to Annie when she was visiting, 'come over all maternal.' So, he painted the kitchen, and cleaned out the old range, coaxing it back to life, after over a decade of inactivity. The kitchen warmed, smelled of burning wood. But that was as far as Stuart's renovations went. He knew the house needed rewiring, new rumblings were to be heard in the plumbing, creaks and rattles on the stairs and there was a worrying groan from the roof whenever the wind blew in hard from the sea. But all that happened slowly, and Madeline and Stuart became accustomed to them. They were part of their internal soundtrack. Stuart's thick DIY tome lay at the far end of the kitchen table, part of their internal landscape, gathering dust, neglected, unopened for weeks. Months.

And the months slipped into years. The road Madeline cycled morning and evening moved through seasons. Summer, the crops ripened, campion grew by the roadside. Autumn, the balmy air filled with blown seed, the first geese keened across the sky. Winter, she struggled and shivered through gales cruel enough, icy enough, to claw into her skin, bring tears to her eyes. And the snow came. Huge drifts that blocked the road to the village, and piled six feet high at the gates of Marglass House after the snowplough went by, cleaving a path and shoving it aside as it went. And she and Stuart, shut the big front door, only left the kitchen to fetch wood for the range, and to go to bed. Then spring, when, suddenly, it seemed, the woods were filled with snowdrops that she always welcomed, lest they took offence and didn't come back next year. 'Hello, youse.'

She felt her days were filled with minutiae. Minutiae of moments. Noticing the fleabane Stuart planted in the ancient bricks of the walled garden. Strings of pink-tinged daisies. Watching a goldfinch pull seeds from a teasel. A greedy bee, too loaded with pollen to fly, waddling, hopping top speed, across the lawn. A plate thick with spilled yoke and tomato chutney, plunge into scalding water, come up shiny. The scent of potted gardenias on the desk. Cases piled in the Inverask reception, people arriving, people going home. The petty squabbles and laughter of children out on the putting green. Picking thyme, marjoram, dill and chervil from the herb garden Stuart grew outside the kitchen door. The bar at the Inverask where she worked three evenings a week, filled with the crack – speculations, gossip, idle remarks that led to more, even idler remarks – and explosions of mirth. Smoke from the wood fire.

And minutiae of getting by. Keeping the kitchen range stoked with wood. Keeping a supply of wood in the store by the back door. Winters, it froze; ice and deep frost welded the logs together. Madeline sometimes took a blowtorch to it, fanning the fierce flame over the pile to loosen the logs. She'd bring them in to dry off in a stack beside the range. 'Dry wood,' she said to Stuart. 'The secret of life.' Having clean clothes ready for next day's work. Remembering to bring home necessities – washing powder, milk, coffee – from the village. The thick wool gloves she wore when cycling to and from work on chilly days, because her hands froze numb holding the handlebars.

'Do you realise,' she asked Stuart one morning before she left for work, 'that I have been here for five years? I thought I'd stay only a couple of weeks. But, five years. My God, where has the time gone? What have I done with it?'

'Lots of things,' said Stuart. 'You work at the hotel. You helped me in the gardens. You paint. Swim in the sea. What more do you want to do?'

As soon as the words were out, he regretted them. They would only lead to The Discussion. The discussion they both worked to avoid but were always having, because all discussions seemed to lead to The Discussion. And it was about longing, lost dreams and frustrated desires. His and hers.

'What do you want, Madeline?'

'I want . . .' And she'd fall silent. She wanted more than this. This house, this place, these people round her, whom she liked but who, except for Freda, knew, and wanted to know, nothing of the world Madeline yearned to get back to. She wanted recognition for her paintings.

'What do you want, Stuart?'

'You know what I want.' Children. To build a home. A place to be. Commitment.

'Look at me,' Madeline sighed now. 'If I don't watch out, I'll be forty. And I'll have nothing. What if something happened to you? Where would I go? What would I have? Forty, Stuart. And nothing. No money. No home.'

'This is home.'

'This is *your* home. It's where I live. The only thing I have is a room full of paintings nobody wants.'

'That's not true. You can't say that. You don't know nobody wants them. Nobody has seen them.'

This was true. But she didn't want to address this. This truth had no part in her worries. Worrying and gripping were what she wanted to do. She didn't seek solutions. They didn't help. They aggravated her angst. Made her realise that if something was to be done about her situation, she would have to do it. And that scared her.

She sighed. 'Forty. Bloody forty. It's a watershed moment.'

'I know,' said Stuart. 'So take your paintings to Hamilton. Let him see what you're doing.'

'I can't. He rejected me.'

'His partner said no to a few pictures ages ago. Hamilton didn't. He's probably wondering what happened to you. Let him see your work. He can only say no.'

She looked horrified by this. 'I'd only embarrass him.'

'These people are thick-skinned. They say no all the time, think nothing of it.'

'You have your garden. You have this house. I have nothing,' she said.

'Marry me. Then you'll own half of me.'

'Having half of you isn't what I want. I want something that is all of me. Mine. People my age have mortgages, careers, Filofaxes. They do things.'

Her life had become full of things she couldn't do. Films she couldn't see. Exhibitions she couldn't wander round. Books she had to send for, and never did. Bands she hadn't heard. She lived a secret life, through the review pages of the newspapers delivered to the hotel every morning. She gleaned information from the columns of newsprint, and knew everything about distant places – Edinburgh, Glasgow, London. Restaurants, galleries, shops, styles, clothes, people, and was racked with longing.

Stuart had only one longing. He wanted children so much, he'd started to imagine them. Sometimes he walked in the garden, holding an imaginary tiny hand in his. He'd look across the grass and wish children into life, running there, waving to him. He wanted a row of tiny wellies at the kitchen door. Mess and clutter. He wanted to read his children stories. Watch them play. He wanted to build a swing on the branch of the apple tree. He wanted to make them puddings, steamy and drowned with custard. Wipe dirty faces. Pin their pictures on the wall. To take them out on the sea in a little boat. It had become a hunger, this longing. He wanted to give his children all the happiness, all the attention and love he'd been denied. And he wanted Madeline to be happy. He wished she'd let him take her paintings to Hamilton. But she wouldn't. Her yearnings hurt him. He realised he wasn't enough for her. And all these unfulfilled needs led to The Discussion. Which they had, almost daily, and never reached any kind of resolve.

Madeline felt there was no point in telling Stuart things. He only put them into perspective. He only offered logic. Logic, she cursed inwardly. I don't want logic. I want a cuddle, a stroke. Told it doesn't matter. I'm lovely. And loved. I want to be kissed. Someone to kiss me better. Kiss my worries away. Kiss me nice. She privately had started to dislike herself. That she had so easily turned her back on what she wanted to do. She still painted. But in the last few years she'd been torn by fears. She feared not painting. And she feared painting. She feared she would paint and paint and nothing would come of it. She'd die, and all her work would end up festering, covered with mould in a corner. Or burned. She wanted to show her work. Yet feared what people might think of it. She feared criticism. She feared rejection. There were times she quite enjoyed working at the hotel. Yet feared the security, the respectability it brought. They made her dull. She feared that all these fears were making her quietly insane. And in a way, she also feared sanity. She thought it made her unimaginative. Mediocre.

She had sometimes tried to explain all her self-doubts and apprehensions to Stuart. And he had soothed them momentarily with explanations, encouragement. 'What does it matter if nobody sees your work? You do it to please you. It gives you pleasure.'

To him, it was logical. It was easy. And when he offered solutions, they seemed that way to her. But when he left her, and she was alone with her dreads, it all became that impossible knot of interwoven consternation. That was the trouble with men, she thought, they're all logic and no tears.

She worried. Mostly at night, in the dark when Stuart was sleeping. Sleeping was easy for him. He took off his clothes, lay down, punched his pillow, pulled the blankets round him, and that was it. Sleep.

'How do you do that?' Madeline asked. 'You bastard. I'm tired, aching with it. And still I lie awake, staring and worrying.'

'Just empty your mind. Let go. Sleep. It's easy.'

But it wasn't. She'd take off her clothes, lie down, punch her pillow, pull the blankets round her. And stay wide awake. 'It's a horizontal thing,' she decided. 'And a dark thing. Lying down in the dark, my worries surround me. Close in. Standing up in the daylight, they drift off. I can keep them at bay. Maybe I shouldn't go to bed. Maybe if I stayed up all night with the light on, I'd stop worrying. Then I'd sleep. Though, I have problems about doing that.'

Her problems were her dreams, that she remembered them. All of them. Other people would tell her they'd had a bad dream, or a funny dream, or a wonderful dream. She would ask what it was, and be told that they couldn't remember. Or that they had remembered it for a few minutes after they'd woken up, but it had gone.

Madeline remembered her dreams, everything about them. Colours. Faces she'd never met. Building she'd never entered in her waking life. Places she'd never visited. Things she'd never done. Flying. Though she hadn't had a flying dream since she was a child. They'd been lovely. And they'd been frightening. One, she'd had often, when people were chasing her, and all she had to do to get away was fly. But she couldn't remember how. She'd try and try and couldn't get off the ground. Then, she'd do it. When she'd given up. Relaxed. All she'd had to do was believe she could.

In her most recent dream, her easel had been outside the house, in the walled garden. She couldn't lift it to bring it indoors. Some tribesmen with painted faces has climbed over the wall, surrounded her, thumping their spears on the ground. 'Who are you?' they shouted. Louder and louder, till the words, rolled together, became a chant, 'Who are you?' She'd run inside, locked the door. But they had followed, stood outside, thumping their spears, chanting till the words became rhythmic, indecipherable. 'Whaaryou.' She did not tell Stuart about this. She thought it too obvious. It would only lead to The Discussion.

She did, however, tell Freda, who patted her hand and said it was time to do something, girl. Before something happened.

'What do you mean?' said Madeline.

'I mean, you better fix your life before your life fixes you. Take charge.'

Madeline stared at her, thinking about this. And Freda knocked on her forehead, saying she was glad she wasn't her. 'It must be hell in there.'

Most mornings, Madeline would sit up in bed and recount her sleeping adventures. Stuart would marvel. He felt his dreams were so mundane, he never liked to tell her about them. They paled beside hers. But she'd be too tired to notice his inadequacy. Hair askew, face ashen, every wrinkle, every blotch glowing in the cruel sunlight that streamed through the bedroom window. Bags under her eyes. Sometimes she had to lie down for a sleep to recover from the night's fatigue. Dreaming knackered her.

'Bloody bunch of old men in white suits and straw hats sitting round a table on a weedy patio singing "Row Row Row the Boat", waving wine glasses. And me, in an orange frock. I don't *have* an orange frock. I wouldn't have an orange frock. Not my colour. But me in an orange frock trying to tell them to keep it down, someone was dying in the room across the way. They all had big walrus moustaches. And they wouldn't listen to me. My voice went. I couldn't hardly speak. Hundreds of windows all round, people watching from them. All in black. I was the only colour.'

Stuart nodded.

Another morning. Looking even more harassed than usual. 'Dreamed my thumbs turned into woodpeckers. Tiny woodpeckers. Green and red. Couldn't open the tomato ketchup. They kept pecking and moving and fluttering and I couldn't stop them. I was so embarrassed. I tried to explain to folk. But they all just looked at me silently. And me with thumbs with a life of their own.' Madeline slumped. Lay frazzled and exhausted across the table. 'I hate this.'

Stuart nodded again. 'Paint it,' he said, sipping coffee lazily from his favourite black mug. 'I'd like to see it.'

It was so obvious, she wondered why she hadn't thought of it before. She stared at Stuart, jaw agape. 'You're right. I should paint them.'

She'd been so enthused, she wanted to start right away. But it was July. And there were guests to see to. The Inverask Castle Hotel was busy. Breakfasts to make. Beds to change. Suppers planned. Food bought in. Teas to serve. Passing people dropping in for a meal or a drink. Evenings, the bar was crowded.

Six in the morning. Time for a swim. Then she would drink coffee. Wave goodbye to Stuart and cycle off down the drive.

Marglass had changed. Stuart had cleared the flowerbeds, planted clematis and roses that entwined and sprawled up the walls. Salmon pinks, apricots, dark blue. He'd widened the borders, filled them with blue poppies, tall delphiniums, campanula, sprawling red potentilla, verbascum, her favourite since Stuart told her they were randy buggers.

'They're promiscuous,' he told her. 'Cross-pollinate like mad. You never know what colour they'll be. You plant a Helen Johnson with a Pink Domino and a yellow Gainsborough and goodness knows what you'll get the next year.'

Madeline didn't really know what he was talking about, but she loved the flowers for their lecherous ways and would call to them mornings as she passed: 'How're you doing, Helen Johnson? Good night last night with the Pink Domino?'

The walled garden was now filled with asparagus, garlic and celeriac, along with the vegetables Donald grew to sell to the Inverask. And Stuart had expanded his herb patch. He grew dill, flat parsley, chervil, savory, sorrel, fennel, rosemary and thyme. A selection of basils in the greenhouse. He cleared the tangled woods of brambles and nettles. Planted foxgloves, anemones and fritillaries – with speckled ochre and claret-red heads. He loved everything. Mornings, he emerged from the house, saw and marvelled. Not at what he'd done. But at the fabulousness of the flowers he grew. Their colours. 'Hello, my lovelies,' he'd call. And wave. He always thought, the way it moved in the wind, the garden was waving back to him. If it weren't for The Discussion, his longing for children, he'd be a happy man. Calm. Brown. He knew he was a lot wiser than when he'd arrived home all those years ago.

He knew the ways of plants. To split the astrantia major in October. How to take root cuttings of poppies. Which clematis to prune, and which to leave to their own devices. He'd experimented with his hellebores. Mixing the slate blues with the pinks and greens. Had a whole spring border of blues and deep salmon pinks.

He made something of a living. Selling whatever he could from a long table in the front of the house. Season to season his table was crammed with bedding plants, salvias, lupins – white and blue and yellow. Veronicas, chrysanthemums. His reputation spread. People came, bought his plants, vegetables and herbs. Marvelled at his flowerbeds. But to Muriel's relief he never opened the grounds to the public. Stuart thought he didn't have to. The money he made covered his gardening needs, bought new plants. He ate a lot of what he grew. Madeline's earnings paid their bills, bought the occasional treat. He got by. And getting by was all he thought to do.

Every morning in his tidy, gleaming kitchen, sipping tea from his perfect china, Donald would hear Stuart welcome his day, greet his plants. And he'd sigh. He didn't mind that Stuart had taken over the grounds. Ousted him. He'd long known the day would come when he'd no longer be able to tend the gardens. It had come four years ago, when he'd had a heart attack. He'd been told to take it easy. Now he slowly, puffing with effort, walked the gardens every day, looking in amazement at the transformation. Tutting at the plants he hadn't, till Stuart imported them, known existed. He didn't mind that Stuart had taken over his small sideline selling vegetables to the hotel. Stuart always saw him all right. Gave him part of the proceeds, which were considerably larger now. Stuart grew rocket, and what Donald scoffingly called 'weird trendy things' in the greenhouse – peppers, chillies, a selection of tomatoes. But Donald didn't mind that. 'Progress,' he said to Muriel. 'You'll never stop it. You just have to get out of the way of it. Or it'll knock you down.'

What Donald minded. Really minded. Was Stuart's apparent happiness.

'I was never happy,' he complained to Muriel. 'It just wasn't the thing to be happy in my day. It didn't cross your mind. Nobody said I could be happy. It was just get on with it. In fact, I'd go so far as to say it was considered a sin. If you were happy you were thought to be a wee bit simple.' He screwed his finger on the side of his temple, 'Thon way. Now there's him out there, whistling, talking to his flowers. I heard him telling them what was on the news. He's bloody enjoying himself. And I'll tell you the truth. It pisses me off.'

'Donald!' Muriel scolded. 'Language!'

'Well, it bloody does,' said Donald. Only slightly repentant.

'Ah,' said Muriel, who still went every morning to dust and clean. Though age had limited her dusting capabilities. She moved through the rooms with a duster picking things up, putting them down again. Keeping an eye on things. 'Just you wait. It'll all go wrong up there. Bound to. The three of them mixing and mingling. That Madeline one's so wrapped up in them weird paintings she doesn't see what's going on. That Annie one's moving in on young Stuart. They're together at the table, making plans, talking gardens, laughing even, heads close and that Madeline one never as much as notices. It'll all come to tears. You'll see. Wait. Everything comes to those who wait.'

Through the years, Annie had come to Marglass House often. Now she came every weekend. Fridays, filled with joy, she'd climb into her car and drive north. Leaving Willie to his mistress, and his drink. And the tears she was sure he was one day going to shed. Though, she admitted, this tear thing was taking its time. Willie seemed to be enjoying himself. Still, she was grateful for the mistress. She had taken Willie off her hands. Leaving Annie free to bring her children up as she'd planned. They ate vegetables. They worked at school. Well, sometimes.

Marcus, now in his teens, was planning to study law.

'I wanted so much for you,' Annie sorrowed to him one evening. 'I wanted you to learn to play the piano. Or the cello. I wanted you to go horse riding. To play chess. To be in the school swimming team and the rugby team. And the debating team. And to play tennis in the summer. And to maybe go rock climbing or sailing. You didn't have the childhood I planned. Your dad took over. All those pizzas. I'm sorry.'

He'd got up from his chair, put his arm round her. 'Well, lecherous old fart that he is, thank God for Dad. You make childhood sound very tiring.'

She'd laughed. 'I suppose I do.'

'Like it was me who'd be playing the cello after swimming and rugby and rock climbing at the weekends when I wasn't playing tennis or taking part in a chess championship. Did I ever get to lie about in your plans?'

She shook her head. 'I don't think I fitted that into your busy timetable.'

'And what were you doing?'

'Watching you,' she told him. 'I wasn't doing any of the cello playing or rugby or swimming. I was sitting somewhere comfortable, with a blanket over my knees, telling other spectators that you were my son.'

They looked at one another.

'You had a fine time in your dreams,' said Marcus.

'Yes,' agreed Annie. 'And it was a very tasteful blanket over my knees, too.'

It was Annie who had encouraged Stuart to do the gardens. She had helped. In time her enthusiasm matched his. As Willie slipped away from her, she soothed herself with plants and earth. She marvelled at things she'd put into the ground. How they grew. Rewarded her weeding and feeding with colour. She fondled the gentle petals on her aquilegia, the spurs that shot out behind its nodding head. Drew her fingers up the lupins. Squatted on the ground side by side with Stuart, heads together watching the first shoots of their blue aster seeds greening into life.

'It's so wonderful,' she said. 'You plant them, nurture them and they grow. And they don't leave home. They don't refuse to eat their greens. They never answer you back. They just flower.'

'Not like your kids,' said Stuart. 'But your kids are great.'

Evenings they'd sit at the kitchen table, plotting their garden year. They drew up designs. Visited market gardens. They sorrowed over clematis wilt, slug infestations, mildew. Shared small triumphs. A stubborn peony coaxed into flower. Hollyhocks self-seeding wherever they pleased. Verbascums promiscuously cross-pollinating.

It was Annie's idea that Stuart grow plants and herbs to sell. And Annie's idea that they grow asparagus, courgettes, rocket, basil and cherry tomatoes for the Inverask Castle Hotel. Annie had been the making, the saving of Stuart. They both knew that. But never mentioned it.

Muriel watched as Madeline furiously worked in her studio, ignoring the other two, lost in her private agonies. Painting her dreams. And Muriel watched as Annie and Stuart walked closely. Touched. Laughed, waiting for tulips to burst into flower. Watching the buds swell.

'Do you think that flowering is pleasurable for them?' asked Annie. 'Do they get a buzz?'

'All that sweaty budding, then, whoosh, out they come. An orgasm of colour. Come summer the flowerbeds will be moaning and swooning.'

They argued. Made up. Played on the lawn with Flo, soon to be a teenager, who always accompanied Annie. Marcus and Douglas were finding the city was too juicy a place to abandon on a Friday night.

So Annie soothed herself with flowers and the lushness of what she helped to grow. And the smell of wet earth and new-mown grass. And Stuart's company. Muriel soothed her anger at their intrusion on her routined life by watching, waiting for it all to end in tears. And, unaware of what was going on, Madeline soothed her agonies, frustrations and fears in the silence of her studio, only the sound of sable on canvas and her whisperings as she told herself what shades to place where, as she fervently, passionately painted her dreams. And she soothed herself by swimming, the coldness of water, the smell of salt, the cries of gulls. The paths of sunlight on the surface. And the ripplets that spread before her to the horizon.

A Fabulous Remark

Madeline cycled to the village. Tuesday evening, she was going to the committee meeting of the Gideon Arts Festival. Freda's idea. Not so much an idea, more a remark. A fabulous remark, she thought. Something she'd said out of the blue. It had surprised her as much as it had the others round the bar.

'There are so many artists and musicians round here, we should have a festival. Attract tourists. Sell our wares.' She looked round at the other faces. Saw them taking this in, weighing it up. Wondering about it. Looking pleased with herself. 'Good for me,' she complimented herself. 'I've had a wonderful idea.'

A small buzz sped through the room. Eyes lit up. Invisible tills chinked. Money. Murchie, who never missed an opportunity to read one of his poems out loud to people, who might or might not be interested in hearing them, said, 'That's a grand idea, Freda. In fact it's so grand it's a wonder nobody thought of it before. In fact, it's so grand it surprises me you came up with it, and not me.'

Freda acknowledged this with a small lift of her whisky glass in his direction. 'Why are you so small, Murchie?'

'Small but perfect. Actually, I'm not. I'm misshapen. I'm like a teapot. Firm, round, hot body and big spout. Do you want to see?'

Freda debated this a moment. She knew Murchie. If she said yes, he'd oblige. 'I'd rather imagine,' she told him. 'Imagining's so much more fun.'

'We need to form a committee,' said Murchie. He was fond of committees. And Gideon had many. They involved a swift meeting. Reading the minutes of the last meeting. Whipping through the agenda at a cracking pace. A bit of arguing and point-putting. An apprehensive mention of 'Any Other Business', this,

289

lest anybody had the effrontery to have any. Nobody ever dared. Then off to the Castle bar. Where the real meeting got underway. It seemed to Murchie that all committee meetings should actually be assembled in the bar in the first place. But that wasn't proper. The right way of things was church hall, swift meeting, pub and real meeting.

'I'm up for that,' said Ali the Van. He never sat on committees. But this was different. If this came off, it would mean a gig for his band, Steal the Van, which played stomping cajun music.

'Right,' said Murchie. 'That's me, Freda, Ali and we need another.'

Madeline's heart sank. She was in the wrong place at the wrong time. Standing at the bar handing Murchie his fourth pint of the evening.

'Madeline,' said Murchie. 'You'll do.'

'Will I?'

This was taken as an OK.

'That's it, then,' said Freda. 'First meeting of the Gideon Arts Festival Committee next Tuesday, seven thirty. The church hall.'

Madeline was swept along. Sucked into something she felt she hadn't really agreed to. And definitely did not want to do. Though she had enjoyed the committee meetings. They had slipped swiftly from dealing with matters in hand to gossip, banter and mild flirtation. Whilst Freda teased Murchie mercilessly, Madeline flirted with Ali. She was a bit ashamed of this. Not that she was betraying Stuart, because this was purely verbal, with a little naughty eye contact. Which she considered more of an ego massage than flirting. She had no intention on letting it go further. She was ashamed of her feelings about him. He was tall, dark-haired, handsome. He made a living from fishing for lobsters and prawns. His skin was bronzed. In fact, he was the perfect flirtee. Until he opened his mouth. He had the worst teeth Madeline had ever seen. Chipped, blackened, crooked. They seemed to grow at odd angles to his gums. His two front teeth were mismatched. One long and rotting, the other short and surprisingly white. Madeline wondered if he'd ever in his life visited a dentist. But never liked to ask. She supposed that Ali's teeth had reached such a state of decay, visiting a dentist would be daunting, and undoubtedly painful. He'd probably been putting it off all his life.

It was decided, owing to lack of funds, which meant no funds, to keep the festival local. They couldn't afford to pay anybody to come. They advertised in the local paper, inviting any artists to come along, display their wares. There would be music, poetry readings, exhibitions of art and photographs and anything else anybody thought befitting of such an occasion. People were asked to write, detailing their interests, to Murchie's shop.

In the weeks that followed letters flowed in. It surprised everyone. It seemed that Gideon and the surrounding countryside was full of painters, photographers, basket weavers, authors, poets, flower arrangers and all sorts of musicians.

Cycling home through the village, and up the long hill to Marglass, Madeline would look at all the houses. Lights on. And across the landscape, houses, dotted here and there, lit against the night. She'd wonder what was going on in all those rooms. Painting, poems, books being written, tapestry, basket-making. For years she'd assumed all the people in all those houses were watching television. Now she thought they were busy creating. Expressing. Aiming for higher things than she'd given them credit for.

Through winter evenings when the rain spat and draughts howled under the doors of the church hall, the four sat and talked art. Was basket-weaving art?

'Depends on the basket-weaving,' said Madeline.

'Depends on what's been woven with the weaving,' said Murchie.

Should Mrs Lamont from Seaview be allowed to perform her own compositions on the flute?

'How do we know? We haven't heard them,' said Freda.

'Do we want to hear them?' said Murchie.

A tight silence. When the wind crawling under the ill-fitting window frames made a disturbing bass wailing. Nobody wanted to hear the flute compositions. Nobody wanted to admit this.

They decided Murchie would read some of his poems. Freda would display her ceramics. Madeline would contribute several of her paintings (this was put forward by Freda, seconded by Ali and noted in the minutes by Murchie, on the one evening Madeline couldn't attend because of a bout of flu) and the whole thing would be rounded off with cajun music from Steal the Van. This pleased them.

'And what about the basket weavers, the flute players, the flower arrangers, the Box Brownie poppers, the authors of tomes about Mary, Queen of Scots, the singers of musical operettas, the dozens of poets, the painters of seascapes and landscapes and horses and cats at windows beside pots of geraniums, the basket makers, the embroiders, the string quartet and the eighty-five-year-old accordion player who says he can give a rousing rendition of "Jailhouse Rock"?' Murchie asked. 'Are we to deny them? Have we a right to deny them? Say no to them? You're not coming to the party.'

Nobody spoke. It was February now. They'd started their committee meetings weeks ago. So far nobody had been invited to take part in the festival. The room was thick with guilt. And very, very cold. A small oil heater burned feebly and made little impression on the chill. They sat round the table with their coats on. Collars up. Longing to get away and up the road to the Castle Hotel to sit by the log fire and drink something warming.

'Who are we to say what is art?' said Madeline.

'You're right,' said Freda. 'Let them all come. Invite everybody. We are artists, not judges.'

Murchie was enthused. 'That's right. Let artists place their pictures on any open space of wall they find. Let writers read where they find someone who'll listen. Let music gush from open doors.'

Freda sighed. Raised her eyebrows. 'All this, and he's sober as a stone.'

Murchie, next day, composed, on his computer, a letter to everybody that had shown an interest in the festival, inviting them to come along. Exhibit what they had to exhibit, sing what they had to sing, play what they had to play, read from whatever they had to read. He told people to reply if they were available in the last week of May. They'd sort out times, venues later.

He imagined a thriving scene. Music, dance, colour. He imagined the street filled with people inspired, enlightened by the goings-on. He imagined baskets filled with flowers. He imagined nights filled with song. And talk that went on past the dawn when a pale light would seep across the sky and send glinting shafts between the cracks of the curtains in the Castle bar.

A Kiss is More than Just a Kiss

It happened, they thought, by accident. But on thinking more knew it was no accident. It was an inevitability. It had been bound to happen one day. The surprising thing being that all the time they'd worked together, planned together – that harmony – it hadn't happened sooner.

It was April. And the sun shone. And there were a million things for two gardeners who were just good friends to do. They'd sprayed the roses. Heeled in two new ones. They'd prepared the seed beds, her raking, him pulling the back of his rake over the ground, flattening it. They stood breathing in the day. The wind came off the sea. Salt. Ozone. Shifted through the pines. The first goldfinch of the season, always a good moment, landed on the feeder by the lilac, which was in bud. Annie smiled at a ladybird crawling beside the aubretia – a cascade of purple in the rookery. 'We should throw some peat over the heather and we might get a second flush in September,' she said. Lit up, for she knew these things. And once, not that long ago, she hadn't.

Stuart nodded and said that he'd noticed the lupins were coming up again. 'Always good to see them. I like lupins. Madeline likes verbascum because I told her they were promiscuous. Serious cross-pollinating.'

Annie smiled at that. 'She would.' She rubbed her cheek. A long mud streak.

'Look at you,' said Stuart. 'Mucky pup.' He wiped his hand on the back of his jeans, then tried to remove the stain. Made it worse. 'Sorry.'

'So you should be.'

They were standing close. They'd stood this close before. But it hadn't been like this. She searched in her pockets for a hanky. And when she looked up, he was staring down at her. And he kissed her. It wasn't a passionate embrace. But it was more than a peck on the lips. He pulled away. Thought to apologise, but didn't. She dropped the handle of her rake. Put her arm round him, pulled him to her. And kissed him back. All the feelings she'd had for him for years – ever since he'd come to her kitchen looking for Madeline, and had played with her children and told her he'd like a few of his own – were put into that kiss.

'Have you got them binoculars you got from Boots?' Muriel asked Donald.

'They're in the writing bureau, along with the camera and my old dental plate and your mother's wedding ring.'

'Get them quick. I've got to see this.'

Donald fetched the binoculars.

Muriel glued them to her eyes. 'I knew it. I just knew it. They're mucking about. Stuart and that Annie one. Kissing in broad daylight where everybody can see them.'

'Especially if they've got binoculars,' said Donald. 'Give's them.' He rammed them to his face. 'You're right. They're at it. That's a kiss all right. No mistaking it. Oh look, now, they're going inside.'

'Let me see.' Muriel grabbed the binoculars. 'Well, we know where they're going.'

She looked at Donald. They both nodded meaningfully. They knew.

Stuart and Annie went to the kitchen to have a cup of tea and discuss the kiss. Which they both agreed was an impulse and neither had meant it to happen.

'But it did,' said Stuart, putting on the kettle. Feeling he had the right to open the discussion as he was the instigator of the meeting of the lips. 'And I enjoyed it.'

'Well, so did I,' said Annie. 'But that's hardly the point. I'm a married woman. And you are in a relationship. We shouldn't be kissing.'

'Absolutely. We shouldn't.' Stuart put a teabag in each of the mugs he'd set out on the table.

Silently, not looking at one another, they waited for the kettle to boil.

'I like this kitchen,' said Annie. 'I always wanted one like this. It has such potential.'

'Has it?' said Stuart.

'Yes, of course it has. Old flagstone floor, a lovely range, beams. It could look wonderful.'

He looked round. 'I suppose it could. It's always been like this. I don't see it any more.'

'No. You stop seeing things.'

Stuart said, 'Yes, you stop seeing things.'

The kettle boiled.

'You don't see this house any more,' said Annie. 'It's falling down round your ears. It needs a new roof. I don't think the stairs are safe. Someone's going to put a foot through them one day. Either that, or the banisters are going to collapse. You can smell the damp. There's bound to be dry rot.'

Stuart put a mug of tea on the table in front of Annie. Sat opposite her. 'Please. I don't want to talk about this.'

'What about Madeline? Can we talk about her? How unhappy she is. She's all caught up in some private battle.'

'I know,' said Stuart. 'She doesn't communicate any more. I don't want to talk about that either.'

'What do you want to talk about?'

'The garden.'

'What about us? The kiss?'

'Yes, I'll talk about that.'

She leaned back, waiting to hear what he had to say on the subject of the kiss.

He felt he was being dealt with. She dealt with so many things, people. Her work, her children. This came easily to her, this dealing with things business. Coping. Confronting. He hated all of it. 'Couldn't we just do it again? And not talk about? That would work for me.'

'It wouldn't work for me. I like to know what I'm doing.'

'Why?'

'What do you mean, why? I don't want to get hurt, that's why. And I'm not particularly keen on hurting other people either.'

'Neither am I. But, Annie, we're going to get hurt. And we're going to hurt other people. That's what life's about. Along with trying to get happy, and growing things and all the other stuff. But if we don't do things. Make love. Hurt. Get hurt. We'll end up like Muriel and Donald, spying on all those people who are ploughing into things, making mistakes, making fools of themselves. And being jealous. And making judgements.'

Annie looked at him. Sipped her tea. Considered this.

'You don't have a marriage. You have a convenient arrangement. You don't love Willie. He comes and goes, and you hardly see him. Don't you want more than that? How long are you going to ignore how unhappy you are?'

Annie didn't answer this. 'Do you still love Madeline?' she asked instead.

'Yes. And I love you, too. Is it possible to love two people?'

'Oh yes. It's just that the two people you love are not likely to like being one of the two. Both of them are going to want you to dump the other one.'

'I know,' he groaned. 'I just don't want to think about that now.'

'What do you want?'

'I want to kiss you again. I want to hold you. I want to take you upstairs – if they don't fall down as we climb them – and make love to you and hold you. And smell how you smell and, you know.'

'No, what?'

'Shag. When did you last have a good shag?'

'I'm not answering that.'

'Exactly,' he said. 'Knew it. It's been a while.'

Annie answered this by breathing as resentfully as she could. Now, here was something she didn't want to talk about.

'Annie, please.' He got up and came to her. Lifted her from her seat. Kissed her. 'Please.' And kissed her again.

Annie kissed him back. Let him lead her upstairs to bed. Because it had been so, so long.

Afterwards, she lay looking at the ceiling, listening to the day outside. The sea, the wind, pigeons in the woods. She felt calm, serene. A kind of peace that had evaded her for years. She relaxed. It was wonderful. It lasted for almost a minute.

'Spying? What do you mean, spying?'

'What?' said Stuart.

'You said Muriel and Donald were spying. In the kitchen, remember. Just before we came up here.'

'Oh yes. They were watching us through binoculars.'

'And you saw? And you didn't say?'

'No. I'm used to it. They've been spying for ages. Keeping an eye on things. They can't let go. Donald wanders round the garden, tutting and sighing. Muriel still cleans. Sort of. That was the first time they've used binoculars, though. I suppose that's the most interesting thing they've seen. The kiss. Apart from the magnolia. They both came to stare at that.'

'I'll bet it was. The kiss. Not the tree. What are we going to do?'

'Nothing. They won't do anything. They just watched.'

'Our kiss? I don't like that very much.'

'The kiss? Or them watching?'

'Them watching. It's creepy. Anyway, the kiss was more than a kiss. It was an expression of a long-repressed longing.'

He said he knew that. Pulled her to him. And they kissed again.

Muriel and Donald sat by the fire and talked about the kiss.

'It's not right them carrying on like that. The three of them up there. Him whistling and talking to his plants, telling them what's in the news. Then kissing the Annie one when the Madeline one's away working her fingers to the bone. Though, mind you, I always preferred the Annie one to the Madeline one. Still, it's wrong. Them enjoying themselves like that. They're near forty. They should know better. They should be settled down.'

'I know,' said Donald. 'It gets on my nerves the way Stuart enjoys himself. I'm going to tell Madeline. I always liked her best. She should know.'

'Oh, I know she should know. But we're not going to tell her. That

would be telling, and we don't do things like that. No, there's ways.'
Muriel nodded wisely.

'What ways?'

'We'll tell somebody who'll tell somebody who'll tell Madeline.
That way it won't have come from us.'

Donald nodded. 'I like that.'

Dreams and Knowing

The first dream Madeline painted was her aubergine dream. She'd dreamed it years before. Ted was sitting at a desk in his room in a white house and she had pole-vaulted out of the window.

After years of painting what was in front of her, what she'd seen, she found it hard to put her imaginings, her dreamings on to canvas. Which moment to depict? The moment of leaping? The moment before leaping, when it was obvious what she was about to do?

No, this was a dream, she would paint herself flying. Face awed, and more than slightly scared. The maid stood at the window in her black skirt and white shirt, hands to mouth, horror. Her father sat behind his desk absorbed in a ledger, columns and columns of figures, not noticing her derring-do. His room was aubergine, matched his shirt, which was open at the collar. Below her the forest canopy, thick, lush, green. The air below her was hazed with bloom, insects flitting and parrots squabbling, shrieking.

She wanted to show terror in the lushness. The joy and fear of the leaper over the forest. What have I done? Where will I land? And the total disinterest of the man lost to her, busy with his columns of figures.

It took her weeks, and obsessed her. She worked in the mornings after swimming, in the evenings after work. On her days off. She thought about it constantly. Every waking minute. At work, serving teas, washing the breakfast dishes, pulling pints in the bar, the painting was with her. She thought of that painting waiting for her in her studio, and longed to get back to it. It became a living thing. Part of her.

'You're not quite with us these days,' said Murchie one lunchtime as Madeline idly set his pint in front of the wrong person.

Madeline said, 'Sorry.' And looked at him blankly.

Murchie waved to her. He was a few feet away across the bar. She was lost in her personal distance. Miles and miles away.

'I was thinking,' she apologised when she returned to him.

'To be avoided,' said Murchie. 'It'll only bring you grief. I try not to do it.'

Madeline said she'd noticed, and returned to her thoughts.

At home Stuart was too engrossed in his garden to notice Madeline in the distance. And Madeline was too wrapped up in her new mission to put all her dreams on canvas to notice Stuart slipping away from her. She didn't think it at all worrying that he spent so much time with Annie. It didn't cross her mind as odd, suspicious even, how often Annie phoned.

'Hi, Madeline,' Annie would say. 'How're you doing?'

'I'm fine. How're you?'

'Fine.'

'And Flo? And Marcus and Douglas?' She never mentioned Willie.

'Fine. Everyone's fine. Um . . . is Stuart there?'

And Madeline would say, 'Yes, here he is.'

For Stuart would be hovering ready to take the receiver from her. It didn't occur to her as odd that he'd wait till she was on her way upstairs to her painting till he started to speak. She didn't notice how his voice changed when he spoke to Annie. The warmth. The longing. She thought nothing of the way he held the phone close, how he smiled when he heard her voice. And the soft way he said, 'Hi, Annie.'

Madeline had started to mutter. Paint when she wasn't in her studio. Paint all the time in her head. She'd make sudden, and sometimes quite scary, slashes at an imaginary canvas with an imaginary brush, wild midair movements. She'd enter the dining room, carrying a tray and say, to nobody really, 'I've got the parrot wrong.' And to a woman who was quietly buttering a scone, 'What green would you say a parrot was? Apple?'

'No, greengage,' said the woman.

And Madeline agreed. 'Yes. I've got it too green.' Walking out again, taking the tray with her, forgetting to serve tea to the couple in the corner who had brightened when they saw her coming and watched her go in dismay. Arms stretched out, snapping their fingers saying, 'Miss . . . over here.'

She started new conversations in the bar. 'If you were pole-vaulting, would you be to one side of the pole?'

Freda said she hadn't a clue. She hated sports. Never watched them.

But Murchie thought you'd be flying over the top of it. He could always be relied on for an opinion about anything from the price of prickly pears to the problems of bungee jumping. Not that he knew anything about either of them. He just liked to talk.

Madeline finished painting her pole-vaulting dream. Started immediately on the one she'd had after her morning visit to the Turners days before she'd come to Marglass House. A woman in a long coat coming to lead her bicycle down a long winding road.

She mumbled now about perspective and handlebars and the exact flap of tweed with wind and movement.

Stuart, lost in his garden and his affair, weeded, pricked out his seedling rocket, planted asparagus. Spring and he'd talk to his primulas. 'Hello, you lot. You look happy there. It's a grand life being a primula. Growing, soaking up the rain and being red. Such a lovely red. I wouldn't mind being you. I have done a terrible thing. I have fallen for my best friend's best friend. I love Annie. I hate me. The tabloids would call me a love rat. That's the trouble with us human beings. We complicate things. Break hearts. Better to be a primula. And keep yourself busy being red.'

Sometimes, when Annie was visiting, he'd watch her and Madeline. How they moved. Annie hanging out washing, pegs in her mouth, clipping a sheet to the line, as it flapped in the wind.

He watched them washing dishes together. Madeline soaking plates slowly, watching water seep over the sides, sailing them in foamy water, dreaming. Annie wiping briskly, thinking, planning. Saying, 'Hurry up, girl. You're slowing down the work line here.'

'Oh, piss off,' Madeline replied. 'You've got to dream when you're washing dishes. It's the rule. "Sail plates to distant shores. Where the golden apples grow . . ." something, something.' Stopping the dishwashing whilst she gazed out the window fishing in the depths of her mind for a distant poem, raising a finger, turning to Annie. ". . . And where in sunshine reaching out, Eastern cities, miles about, are with mosque and minaret among sandy gardens set." I used to love that poem. Off you go, plate, sail away.'

Annie smiled. A flush of affection. Followed by guilt and a heated look at Stuart. We've got to tell her.

Stuart got up, walked into the garden, considered his primulas. Remembered innocent days before he kissed Annie and cursed himself. And life. Why did it have to be this way? He toyed with the notion of a *ménage à trois*. He imagined himself selecting whose bed he would visit tonight. Then shuddered, imagining what Annie would say if she knew what he was thinking.

'Do you and Madeline still do it?' Annie asked once.

He shook his head. 'We used to. All the time. Couldn't keep our hands off each other. The plan was to do it in every room of the house.'

'Did you manage it?' Annie said, trying to sound like she didn't care.

Stuart, noticing that she was trying to look like she didn't care, told her no. Ah, but the fun they'd had when they were pursuing the notion. He smiled to himself. Then told Annie, 'No.' Again.

He reached down, held a budding primula, deep scarlet, in between his fingers. 'It's all right for you. All you have to do is grow and be red.'

Donald passed, stumping through the evening. 'Aye,' he grumped. 'Nice night.'

'Yes,' said Stuart. 'Lovely.'

Donald stumped on. Hardly looking at the garden. He thought it would be tolerable the way Stuart behaved, chatting to plants, calling hello to them if only they didn't flourish. If only it had all come to nothing.

'Bloody Stuart's talking to his flowers again,' he said to Muriel when he got in. 'Telling his primulas to be red. What else would they be? They are red. He doesn't need to tell them. They know what to do. And, I see that Annie's there. There's goings on in that house.'

'We'll see about that, though,' said Muriel.

This morning she'd taken the bus to the village. She'd walked slowly past Freda's garden.

'Grand day,' she called.

Freda appeared from behind a rhododendron bush. Hair tousled, hands encrusted with earth. 'It is that. We don't see much of you these days.'

'I'm not up to the walk any more. Getting on.'

'Aren't we all?' said Freda.

'Yes,' said Muriel. 'Time passes. Things change.'

'You can say that again,' said Freda. 'You'll be feeling the changes up at Marglass now that Stuart's taken over the garden.'

'Yes,' sighed Muriel. 'But it's time we had a rest. It's all a bit much for us now. And Stuart has Annie to help. She comes all the time. She and Stuart are always together in the garden. Heads together, discussing this and that whilst Madeline's away at work.'

'Oh?' said Freda.

'Oh, yes. There's doings up at Marglass, these days. Not that I'm saying anything. I'm not a one to gossip.'

'Doings?' said Freda.

'Doings,' said Muriel. 'And that's all I'm saying. But I see them. I see the two of them when that Madeline's away working her fingers to the bone.'

And Freda said, 'Oh my. Poor soul.'

Muriel said, 'Well, much as I'd like to stop and chat, I must get on and get my bits and bobs before the bus comes.' She walked on and could not help smiling. Freda would tell Murchie. Murchie would tell absolutely everybody. And somebody would tell Madeline. And that would be the three of them sorted out. That would be them and their goings-on put a stop to. And maybe the Madeline one would leave. Maybe they'd all leave. And she and Donald would get the place to themselves again. She sighed and thought she could fairly dance a jig at the mischief she'd done.

But Freda didn't tell Murchie. She didn't tell anyone. She decided she'd have a word with Stuart about this. She was fond of Madeline. And didn't want her hurt.

Madeline finished painting her long and winding road dream. Then did a small watercolour of herself as a child, sitting on the floor painting poppies whilst her father sat sideways on a chair, legs draped over the arm, smoking a spliff, staring, smiling out of the window. At the rain.

It took her to another time. A Wagon Wheel on a plate with blue flowers round the rim on the table ready for munching into when she'd eaten the egg Ted had boiled for her. Nat 'King' Cole singing on the radio 'Unforgettable'. And rain on the window, spattering, tricking down the pane. A wind blowing. Dipping the soldiers into the yoke so it swelled up round the toasted, buttery bread and spilled down the shell. And her telling Ted about it. How she liked her eggs runny. Him saying, 'Hmmm . . .' Rolling a cigarette, though he'd just finished one. The smell of bread browning under the grill, and herby smoke. Then, she'd told him how she couldn't wait to eat the Wagon Wheel. They were her favourites. And he smiled at her, though he seemed miles away and said, 'Uh-huh.' And she'd thought he was too tired to talk. She looked up. Ted was always saying, 'Hmmm . . .' Or, 'Uh-huh.' Or sometimes he'd laugh and sing and sweep her high to the ceiling. Then laugh some more. Laugh and laugh.

She remembered coming home late one night. Waking up, wrapped in a blanket, in the back of Ted's car. Some sparkly guitar music was playing. She looked out of the window.

'Where are we, Ted?'

'I don't know,' he said. 'I love this music. It's all round me. I can touch it. I'm driving along it. I don't know where the music ends and the road begins.'

They'd got home at five in the morning. And she'd been too tired to go to school next day. Mrs Turner had giving Ted a talking-to about the hours he was keeping, and about not taking Madeline with him when he went to wherever he went to nights. And after that his women friends had visited him. The laughter and smells – food, wine, smoke – that had drifted through to the strange bedrooms she'd slept in, drifted through to her own little room.

'My God,' she said. 'He was stoned. My whole childhood, Ted was stoned out of his brains.'

Outside the wind that had blustered round Marglass House all day hissed along the walls, rattled the windows.

Storms and Hugs

For years Annie had accepted that Willie was Willie. He was extravagant, generous and absurd.

'If only I didn't like him,' she said to Madeline.

'Do you think that liking is enough?' Madeline asked.

'It'll have to do,' Annie told her. 'It's all I've got.'

She knew she should leave him. For years she'd saved what she could. Though that wasn't much as she paid for everything. But at least she'd kept some money safe from Willie's squandering. She knew she should leave him, or make him leave her. Throw him out. But she found something addictive about him. She would miss him. He still made her laugh. He was buoyant, filled rooms as soon as he entered them. He livened dull parties. Something about him, the way he opened his arms, he seemed to embrace everyone there. He'd burst into spontaneous song. And set everyone singing with him.

She still loved the way he looked at her. That adoration. How to be adored, she thought, be the adorer. Everyone adores an adorer. She loved the way he touched her. Put his arm round her, a warmth. 'You're a good hugger,' she told him.

'I'm master of the hug,' he'd said.

And she said, 'He who lives by the hug, shall die by the hug.'

He thought that a fine way to go. He'd put his arm round her. Another hug. Called her his wife. 'Don't worry, old thing. I can hug my way out of anything.'

That had made her feel steady, reliable, middle-aged. It was the only thing she didn't like about him. She'd wondered if he made his other woman feel that way too. Or, did he still make her feel young, desirable, fragile? Precious, she thought, that's how he used to make me feel. Important.

He still brought her gifts. Things he'd spotted on his travels in the city. A painted wooden egg, a carved musical box that played a high-pitched tinkly 'Rule Britannia', an old tattered book of butterflies filled with intricate and wonderful illustrations, a cashmere sweater.

'Willie, where did you get the money for that?'

'I stole it.'

She'd laughed. Then wondered if it was true. And what did he steal? The money or the sweater? The sweater. Willie wouldn't steal money. That would be stealing. Taking a sweater would simply be acquiring something he'd taken a shine to. In Willie's book, that was all right. Still, she rarely wore the thing. She worried she might meet its owner.

What upset her was that she knew Willie would hug his other woman. Kiss her on the top of her head. Make her laugh. Bring her gifts. Then again, who was she to criticise Willie, now that she too was having an affair? She wondered if Willie felt as guilty as she did, then decided, no. Guilt, Willy? He doesn't know the meaning.

One thing she knew, she'd fallen in love with Stuart. Hopelessly, completely. She thought of him when she wasn't with him, wondering what he was doing. Found herself smiling softly into the distance, imagining him working in his garden. And, wasn't life a bitch? All those years of cursing that other woman, she thought, now I'm one. She knew it would all end. She knew a crunch would come. It had to.

'Crunches always come,' she'd said to Madeline. Who didn't know exactly what she was talking about. But she agreed anyway. Sometimes she got the feeling Annie was about to tell her something, but changed her mind. She decided it was Willie and his affair. And Annie didn't want to talk about it, really. She came to Marglass to forget.

Sitting in the kitchen, far from Willie, what she should do was clear to Annie. It seemed straightforward. 'Willie,' she should say, 'enough is enough. I want you to go.' A clean break. No ifs or buts. She should be firm. Cut him from her life and never let him back in. She could sell the flat, which was in her name now as she paid the mortgage and the remortgage. Give Willie half the profit. And she'd still have enough, with her savings, to put the deposit on somewhere new. A house big enough for her and Flo and the boys when they were home from university. Yes, in Madeline's kitchen, with a glass of wine in front of her, and Madeline's sympathy spilling over her, it was obvious.

At home with Willie, and Willie's laughter and hugs, surrounded by the things they'd gathered through the years, and the memories that lived in the house with her, her resolve slipped away. It all became complicated. There never seemed to be a moment when she could tell him to go. Or tell him she was leaving. So she got on with things, her job, her life, and told herself, One day.

When Mr Speirs, manager of the store where she worked as a buyer, retired, Annie applied for his job. She thought it was in the bag. She was highly qualified. She'd worked in retail for over twenty years, knew the shop and its customers. She had plans that would move it forward without, as she said in her interview, losing any of its existing client base. She'd said this crisply. With the assurance of someone who knew what they were talking about. Congratulated herself on making an impression. And when, as she was leaving, her interviewers had shaken her hand, patted her shoulder and told her how delighted they were with all her ideas, she'd thought; It's in the bag.

She'd celebrated that night with champagne. Had worked out what she'd do with the extra income. A new car. Clothes. She'd thought she could buy Flo a place of her own when she went to university. It would be an investment. After four years, she could sell it. At last, she thought, I am on the up. She'd let Willie make love to her.

She didn't get the job. It went to a man six years younger than she. They'd told Annie they thought her too concerned about people, too involved, too caring a person. 'We need someone who can be a little more detached,' they said. She gritted her teeth, told herself, Hey, what did you expect? They see a woman, and think mumsy. She cursed herself for indulging in high-flown plans. Counting her chickens. Stupid girl, she told herself. She should have said, 'Let's wait and see. Let's not get too excited.'

She was almost over it. Resigned to staying in her old job. Accepting a new boss. But when that new boss started using her plans, putting her ideas into action, she snapped. It had come on her suddenly. She had calmly watched as an area of her sales floor was turned into a small boutique specialising in new, young designers. She saw the old tearoom change from a place where old ladies were served by waitresses in black and white outfits, complete with little starched caps, carrying trays heavy with silver teapots, to a modern brasserie with salads, wine and espresso. The addition of new trendy ranges to the cosmetics department. The selection of olive oils and breads and specialist herbs in the deli. She thought she'd accepted it. She'd thought, Oh well. Bound to happen anyway.

But walking home one Thursday night carrying food for supper, she'd suddenly shouted, 'You old bastards. That was my job.' And once the anger was released, there was no stopping it. She stormed. She burst into the flat. Slammed the door. Kicked open the kitchen door, dumped her shopping on the table. Threw her keys at the wall. Started to unpack her carrier bags furiously. Banging olive oil, coffee, garlic on to the unit, cursing.

'Scumbags and arseholes.'

'What's up?' asked Willie.

'Everything's up,' said Annie. 'Fucking everything. That was my job. My ideas. Now that scumbag is using them. He's getting all the praise. All the money. And they're mine.'

Willie said, 'Never mind. There'll be other jobs.'

Annie said, 'There will not be other jobs. Not like that. I wanted that job. I've worked there for years. I've given it my all. I deserve that job.'

'I know you do. You deserve a lot more than that job. You deserve . . .' He was about to list the glistening things Annie deserved. But he saw her by the unit, spitting rage. And he thought, God, she's lovely.

'God, you're lovely,' he said. And he went to her. Folded his arms round her. A hug.

Annie was to say that was what did it. That hug. A hug too far.

'Get off me,' she yelled. Elbowing him away. 'A hug doesn't fix everything. I don't want a hug. I want that job.'

'But,' said Willie, not really realising exactly how angry she was, 'a hug is as good as it gets. A hug soothes everything. A hug and a drink and a cuddle. All you need in this world.'

'No it bloody isn't. A drink only takes your mind momentarily off your problems. And your hugs are worthless. You hug every-one. You don't care who you hug. Just so long as you hug. You,' she pointed at him, a savage accusing finger, 'are a promiscuous hugger.'

'Not true,' he cried, approaching her once again, arms out-stretched. 'I save my prize hugs for you.'

She shoved him away. 'Get out,' she said. 'Get out of this house. Go to her. Hug her. I don't want you here.' She was holding a bottle of balsamic vinegar.

Willie held his arm up, protecting himself, thinking she was going to throw it at him. He always said that was the moment he lost Annie. If she'd thrown it, as she was tempted to, everything would have been fine. She'd have got it out of her system. She'd have seen the mess and cried. And he'd have cleaned everything up, telling her not to mind. Maybe if he'd been lucky the bottle would have hit him, bruised him, in the eye would have been good, a bit of blood. Then Annie would have been shocked at what she'd done and come to him, apologising over and over, and he'd have hugged her.

But she didn't throw the bottle. She gripped it till her nails went white. And she told him to get out. 'I'm going up to Madeline's. I want you out of here when I get back. Move your things into that woman's house. Hug her.'

'Hug her,' said Willie in the pub. 'She said, "Hug her." And she made a lovely thing like a hug sound despicable.'

Annie made arrangements for Flo to stay with a friend, and drove to Marglass. She was too angry to notice the weather. The gales that buffeted her little Peugeot as she hurtled, mumbling furiously, west. But by the time she arrived and battled out of the car, fighting the wind to shut the door, struggled, blown and battered, up the steps, clutching her coat round her lest it get whipped from her back, and whisked away over the treetops, she realised that this was more than a gale. This was some kind of hurricane.

'What are you doing here?' asked Stuart. 'It's Thursday. You come tomorrow.'

'Well, thanks for that,' said Annie. 'Aren't you pleased to see me?'

He said of course he was. And kissed her.

'I threw Willie out of the house,' she told him.

He looked at her. Taking in all this meant. She'd ditched Willie. Now it was his turn to leave Madeline. Declare himself to her. He knew he should. Only this morning when he'd been in the village, Freda had cornered him outside Murchie's and given him a talking-to.

'Are you having an affair with Annie?'

Stuart had looked at his feet. He couldn't deny it. 'Who told you that?'

'Muriel. Who else? You are, aren't you? You're blushing. Stuart, how could you?'

'It just happened. I didn't mean it. I didn't plan it.'

'Well, you better start planning something. I don't want you hurting Madeline. I'm fond of her. This fooling around will only bring pain to one or all of you. And if Muriel told me, she'll tell someone else. Soon everyone will know. And someone will tell Madeline.'

And Stuart had slunk away like a scolded schoolboy.

He held Annie. A moment's comfort. He could breathe her in, and forget about everything else. The wind flew round the building, then seemed to sail, zoom up it, heaving under the eaves, billowing under them. Like a sail. The house groaned. Seemed to lift off the ground.

'Been doing that all day,' said Stuart. 'Scary.'

'Yes,' said Annie. 'Really scary.' She looked across at the kitchen table. A bottle of whisky, half-empty, and a glass. 'Have you been drinking?'

'All day. What else is there to do when this weather strikes? It's terrifying. Want one?'

'After the day I've had. Absolutely.' She drank. 'That's gorgeous. What is it?'

'Bowmore. Been in the cellar for years. I don't drink whisky much. Apart from today.'

'So I see,' said Annie, eyeing the bottle.

'I know,' said Stuart. 'It's so old. It slips over the throat like silk. You don't notice it. You don't even notice how drunk you're getting. God, I should go and see if Madeline is coming home through this. But I'm so drunk, I'd get blown over.'

The storms had come late that year. Usually they hit in March. When the sea would churn and curdle, charge to the shore, giant white-crested waves. And lift seaweed, rocks and sand from its bed, lash them on to Main Street, leave it all in a tangled layer over the tarmac, as it sucked away, gathering strength for its next lashing, seconds later. The wind would shiver through leafless trees, rattle windows and sweep expressions from frozen faces.

May, and there had been a blow on for days. Carpets of fallen pink blossoms thick on the ground. Flowers bending in the breeze. It rained. The weather replaced the Arts Festival as the main topic of conversation in the Castle bar. They did not talk about the recital of local musical talent, or Madeline's paintings, which were now hanging in the church hall. There was talk of great storms. Trees uprooted, blown five miles. Waves higher than the church spire. Murchie said it would die down soon. But Freda said that in her experience it would have to get worse before it got better. To which George Jackson said that it couldn't get much worse.

And Murchie agreed, 'This is worse.'

But Freda said, 'No. This isn't worse. Worse is a lot worse than this.'

And nobody said much about that.

Thursday night. Madeline left for Marglass House just after six. The journey to work had been exhilarating. With the wind behind her she'd whisked along. Arrived red-cheeked, breathless and high on speed and wind. The journey back was gruelling. Into the gale. She pedalled painfully, pushing slowly forward. Head down. Face squeezed with effort. She gasped and panted, the wind whipped her breath away. It started to rain. A few warning wet splatters before the deluge. It crashed into her. Relentless. She was soaked. Small rivers running down her back. The light on the bike cast a thin wavering shaft before her. It took over an hour to cover her first mile. Then she stopped cycling. Walked, pushing the bike before her. Leaning against it. Watching the road beneath her feet. For the weather was flying at her too fiercely to look ahead.

She arrived at Marglass, drenched, shivering and scared. The roar of wind, moan of moving trees had engulfed her. She stood, shaking, in the kitchen. Unable to speak. Stuart and Annie fussed. Annie removed Madeline's coat, said she'd run a bath and why the hell did Madeline come home in weather like this? She should have stayed at the hotel.

Stuart said, 'Whisky. Whisky. What we need is whisky.'

And the wind hit the building, hissed and whooshed round it. Howled under the window frames. Outside in the woods they heard a tree crack and crash to the ground.

Madeline bathed. Slipped gingerly into hot water and felt her numbed body come back to life.

Stuart brought her a glass of whisky. Sat on the side of the bath. Watching her drink. 'You, OK?'

She nodded. 'Bit shaken up. I've never known weather like this. It's hell out there. I didn't know you had whisky. I thought all you had was wine and sherry.'

'Been down in the cellar for years. Years and years. Long before I was born. It was kept for emergencies. But any time an emergency happened people were too fussed to remember about it.'

They sat in the kitchen, eating stew. Then, started on more whisky. And the storm raged, fumed round their walls. The house creaked. Tiles whipped off the roof and smashed on the ground. Every time this happened, they looked at one another in horror.

'Christ,' said Stuart, 'there's going to be some damage tonight.'

'I know it'd be best to go to bed and sleep through this,' said Annie. 'But I don't think I could.'

So they sat. And drank. And worried.

At two in the morning the wind was gusting at around ninety miles an hour. They felt it hit the building. Felt it shake. Felt it sucking upwards. And the huge creaking heave as it lifted the roof from Marglass House and swept it into the walled garden. They felt the whole house shudder and groan. A chill as the hurricane came inside, hurled through the corridors, swished under doors, bringing with it the centuries of dust that had been trapped under the roof. Dark, choking clouds of it. Mixed, thick, with spores, the gnashings of thousands of woodworm. The wind whirled into the upper bedrooms, swept up sheets, books, lamps, crashed them into the walls then whipped them through the gaping hole at the top of the house, spread them across the grounds. The rain lashed into the room, open to the elements, and soaked what the wind did not steal. The lights went out.

Madeline, Stuart and Annie ran outside and stared up into the seething black. Through the dark and rain, frenzied air whipping round them, slapping their hair across their faces, billowing out their clothes, and the great, thick clouds of dust, they could see the roofless building and the devastation about them. And the only thing any of them could think to say was, 'Jesus Christ.'

They went inside. Back to the kitchen. More whisky.

'Your insurance will cover it, surely,' said Annie.

And Stuart said, 'Insurance? What insurance? This place hasn't been insured for years. Can't afford it.' He looked at her. The full horror sinking in. 'It's all gone. The garden. The house. Everything. All my work. There's nothing left.'

Annie didn't think. She reacted. 'Oh, love,' she said. Almost sailing across the room, to hold him. To take his head in her arms, stroking, kissing his hair. 'Oh, love. It's all right. We'll think of something.'

This business of hugging, touching, was a Willie thing. Something she'd picked up from him. She did it all the time. To her children. And, at work, gave colleagues, caught in moments of self-doubt, a swift cuddle.

Madeline watched this. It was occurring to her that this holding and stroking and kissing was a little more than an act of friendly comfort. They seemed used to it. It looked like they'd this done before. She watched. And, through the confusion, the shock, some-thing about the embrace touched the quick of her. She thought it ought to be her comforting Stuart. She thought to mention this, but Annie looked up.

'Oh my God,' she said. 'The interview.' She remembered it. Just when she'd put it away, tucked it up and promised herself not to think about it. It had come breezing back to her. They'd said she was too involved. Too caring. They wanted someone detached. But at the end of the interview, they had all been so delighted with her, shaken her hand, patted her back. 'Oh my God,' she said, staring embarrassed, horrified into space. And clutching Stuart all the while. 'What a stupid arse. I hugged them. All these crusty old suits and middle-aged men. I fucking hugged and kissed them all. Mumsy or what? I blew it with hugs.'

Oh, the Sobering and
a Seriously Expensive Pee

The next morning was still. The sea glistened. Wood pigeons called in the woods. The very air sparkled. It was warm. Madeline, Stuart and Annie had spent the night in the kitchen, listening to the weather rage, waiting, in the candlelight, for there was no electricity, for the calm. Just after six they came blinking into the garden, hoping it wasn't as bad as it had seemed last night.

It was worse. It looked as if there was nothing left standing. Trees had been uprooted in the wood. The flowerbeds flattened, shrubs pulled from earth. The walled garden was under a mass of rubble. And dust. Piles of it. Blackening what only yesterday had been green. One of the walls had succumbed to the force of the gale and crumbled on to the herb patch. Though the scattered bricks were scarcely noticeable amidst the thick shattered debris, rotted, crumbling wood and tiles, the roof made when it landed. There was nothing left of Stuart's years of work. Nothing.

Marglass House towered over it all, its upper rooms exposed to the sunlight. It looked almost happy to be relieved of its roof. Well, ninety per cent of its roof. A few tenacious tiles still hung on. A sheet whipped from Madeline and Stuart's bed curled round a remaining joist and flapped. Waving.

The three walked slowly around looking, gasping. Swearing. For none of them was fit to string words together. 'Christ,' they said. 'Oh my God.' And, 'Blimey.' They swore. They looked at one another, faces frozen in horror, and swore some more.

Stuart picked up plants, held them in his fingers. Looking stunned. Madeline and Annie watched as he tenderly put them back in the ground, firming the earth round them. Telling them it would be all right.

They went inside. Walked through the corridors, footprints in the dust and grime, that coated the floors, cornices, lay like thick matting over everything. And when their inspection was over, sighing and moaning despair, they went to the kitchen and made tea on the range. And Stuart said, 'That's it. I'm finished. It's over.'

'No it's not,' said Annie. 'We can clear the walled garden. Start again.'

Stuart said, 'Get real. It'll cost thousands. Thousands and thousands and thousands. And I've got no insurance and fifty quid in the bank. I am fucked.' He raised his arms in the air, this was the enormity of his fuckedness. 'Well and truly, utterly and completely fucked.'

Madeline and Annie looked at each other, saying nothing. They both thought he was probably right.

'Well,' said Madeline, 'we could probably clear the garden. It'd take a bit of heaving wood and sawing it up. We could get a chainsaw. But the roof. That's the bugger. I mean, we'd have to go up there to fix it. I'm not doing that.'

Annie fixed her with a look. 'Shut up, Madeline.'

But Stuart laughed. 'You could wear your receptionist's outfit. And carry slates up on a tray.'

'Excellent idea,' said Madeline. 'Held above my head with one hand. And I hope you'll be wearing a kilt.'

'Naturally,' said Stuart. 'But now I think of it I'd prefer you to wear only black camiknickers.'

'I hope she gets to wear a builder's helmet with the knickers. And I think you should wear a thong,' Annie joined in.

'No. No,' Stuart enthused. 'Nude. We'll all do it nude. We'll set ourselves up as the Nude Roofing Company.'

They were all laughing.

'The All-Weather Nude Roofing Company.'

They laughed more. It was, of course, mild hysteria. They could either laugh or cry. For a few seconds it could have tipped either way. Now they chose laughter. Or, maybe, laughter chose them. But reeling from shock, amidst the filth and chaos, they laughed till tears ran down their faces.

It was unfortunate, really, that that was the moment Muriel and Donald happened to be coming down the stairs, bringing scones and tea to the refugees.

'They'll be needing a bite to eat before their long journey back to town,' Muriel told Donald.

Donald agreed. It was plain to them both that now Marglass House was roofless, nobody could live there. They had stood and silently looked at the upheaval.

'All this devastation when our house is untouched. Not even a primrose out of place.' That it was in a hollow and sheltered from the wind was not an issue.

'True,' said Donald.

'It's a judgement,' said Muriel. 'A judgement on those irresponsible and godless folks in the big house.'

'True,' said Donald.

'Well, it's not for us to judge. There's higher powers do that. We'll take them some scones.' Carefully descending the stairs, tutting at the layers of dust, they heard the laughter. The crazed release of shocked emotions. The three in the kitchen were in such a state of bewilderment and trauma that anybody saying anything to them would have sent them into hysterics. So, when Muriel entered and said, 'I've brought you all some scones,' they collapsed.

'Scones,' said Stuart. And he thumped the sink, bent double, and laughed till he thought he was going to choke.

Annie and Madeline, sitting at the table, buried their heads in their hands, shaking with mirth. Madeline had tears pouring down her cheeks. She could hardly see.

'I know,' said Annie, heaving some air into her lungs. 'We could tile the roof with Muriel's scones. The Nude Roofing Company, scones a speciality.'

The exhilaration hit new heights.

Stuart held his sides and told Annie to stop. 'Stop it. Stop it. The hilarity is going through the roof.'

'We haven't got a roof,' cried Madeline.

And the three screamed with laughter again.

Muriel turned and left. Taking her scones with her. 'I'm black affronted,' she said to Donald. 'The three of them laughing at a time like this. And at my scones. Tile the roof with my scones. Cheek and impudence. Never in my life . . .' She couldn't finish her sentence. Rage engulfed her. As fast as her ageing legs would carry her she stormed up the stairs. 'That's it. That is definitely it. Enough is enough. Scones! I wouldn't give any of them a scone if they paid me.'

Donald shuffled after her, 'I think they were in a state.'

'They're in a state all right.'

'I think it was shock,' said Donald. 'I've read about it.'

'Shock? Shock? I've give them shock. I never want to see any of them again.'

'How're you going to manage that?'

'Spain,' she said. 'I'm going to Spain. You can come if you want. But I'm going. How *dare* they laugh at my scones?'

'No, wait,' said Donald. 'You're being a wee bit hasty.'

'I have never been hasty in my life. And I'm not being hasty now. I've been thinking about this. I want to go where it's sunny.' She leaned against the front door of Marglass House, staring across what once was the lawn. 'I've only ever known here. I've hardly been away from here. Now here's gone. Blown away.'

'It is that,' said Donald. 'Never seen anything like it.'

'Now what?' said Muriel. 'When Stuart stops laughing, what's he going to do? He can't fix the roof, even with my scones. He's no money. He can't live in a house with no roof. You need a roof. We've got a roof. Maybe he'll want that. He owns it. And even if he moves away, we'll be left looking at this all the time. I'm not doing that.'

'No,' agreed Donald. 'No, me neither.' He took a scone, munched it slowly. 'What a mess.' Crumbs tumbled down his front. 'Bloody devastation.'

They started to walk back to their cottage.

'Sun,' said Muriel. 'Everyday on my old bones. A cup of tea on the balcony every morning. A place of our own. Come and go as we please. Nobody bothering us. I'm not having a wee home that I've never seen. I'm going.'

'You're right,' said Donald.

'I'm always right,' said Muriel.

And Donald agreed with that.

Madeline did not go to work that day. She stayed and helped clear up. She was not in the village for the opening of the Arts Festival. But then, not many people were there. Most people were doing what Madeline was doing, clearing up after the storm. She was not there when a white Jaguar crunched over the sand and seaweed that had been thrown on to Main Street.

Alex, sweeping the road, heaping the sea's debris into piles, shovelling it up, heaving it back on to the beach, stopped. Watched as a man in pale slacks and navy shirt got out, looked around. He saw sea and a street empty but for a street sweeper, who was standing, mid-brush, watching him.

Hamilton Foster had, yesterday, become the owner of a car he'd ordered weeks ago. It was white, shiny and expensive. Leather seats. This morning he'd put a Mozart tape into the deck and set out. 'Just going to try her out,' he said to Trish, his young assistant at his art gallery. 'Open her up. See what she can do. Be back in a couple of hours.'

But, like a child on a new bike, once he got going he didn't want to stop. He whizzed up the motorway, foot down. Heading north. Following signs that took his fancy. Roads that looked interesting. Every now and then, he thought: I should turn back. But driving this car was so lovely, soft seat, purring engine. He didn't want to stop. 'Oh, you beauty,' he cried as he soared along. 'I love you.'

He turned west. Hurtled over moors. Saw mountains. Deer stopped grazing to stare as he whizzed past. He was high. He clicked Mozart out of his deck. Put on some Irish reels. Stamped his foot in time. The swirl of it made him higher. Umchee-umchee-diddle-dah. This was thrilling. When he was fifty miles past Oban, he finally stopped. Stepped from his car. Spread his arms into the soft and beautiful day and said, 'Ah.' He was a happy man.

Four in the afternoon, time, he thought, for a little sustenance before his drive back. He was looking forward to that. He took in the view. And wondered, as he always wondered when he came to this part of the world, why he didn't live here. He supposed he was too much of a city person. But he liked to indulge this dream of a house in the wilds, a pure hermit life where he'd grow his own veg, and sit of evening listening to opera, having dined, splendidly he imagined, on his own produce. He also knew that someone who spent most of their dreaming time wondering what would be the perfect outfit for digging up potatoes – he saw himself in Armani jeans, Timberlands and a soft grey cashmere sweater – would never hack it in the world of fertilisers and mulches and whatever else self-sufficiency people stuck their fingers into. He didn't like to think.

He got back into his car, drove slowly, looking for somewhere to eat. And when he saw a sign that said the Inverask Castle Hotel Welcomes You, he thought: Well, that'll do me.

He drove down the road that sloped towards the sea. A view of perfect blue, shining beyond the treetops. Arrived at the small village of Gideon, where chalked on a blackboard were the words: Gideon Arts Festival. Come Along. Bring Your Art. He thought that marvellous. And decided to have a look before he ate.

Looking round, he thought the festival might be over. And they'd all had a fabulous time. Some kind of party, he thought. He hadn't heard the news. Knew nothing of the storm. The bunting that had been strung along the street had been torn down, and hung in limp but colourful streams from the lampposts. The flowers looked battered and forlorn. There was nobody but a street sweeper to be seen.

Still, he noticed an art exhibition in the church hall and couldn't resist. He went in. There was some acceptable pottery. Some interesting photography. A few watercolours he thought insipid. Then he saw Madeline's paintings. Eight of them. And some sketches. He stood before them. 'Madeline Green,' he said. 'I know you. I waited for you to come back to me some day with some work. But you disappeared from view. And here you are.'

He thought the paintings wonderful. Lively. Full of longing. Quirky, but Madeline was always that. They had colour. Passion.

They made him want to laugh. A woman flying from a window on to a lush soft tropical forest canopy, whilst a man sat at another window, deliberately, it seemed, paying no attention. In another a woman led a younger woman holding the handlebars of her bike, behind them a long, winding road and a baby lay in a field they were passing. They were not looking at it. And in another a woman tried to serve beer but couldn't because her thumbs had, judging by the surprise on her face, suddenly turned into two vivid, noisy, flapping woodpeckers, drumming on the glasses.

Surreal, he thought. There was something haunting, dreamlike about them. He would have them.

He went to the Inverask. Ate some sandwiches with Earl Grey. And as he was paying, asked if anyone knew Madeline Green. And where did she live?

Ten minutes later he walked through the door of Marglass House. He'd knocked, but nobody had heard. So he went in, shouting, 'Hello. Anybody there?' Stepping gingerly through the dust, he moved towards the voices coming from the room below. He now knew about the storm. The roof, or lack of roof at Marglass, was the talk of the Inverask Castle Hotel. The bar had been hot with speculation. What were Stuart and Madeline going to do? Where would they live? And what about that Annie, who was always there?

'D'you think she and Stuart are, you know?' said George behind the bar.

'Nah,' said Ali. 'Not when he's got Madeline.'

'Maybe it's Annie and Madeline are ... you know?' suggested Murchie.

This was greeted with a shower of groans and shaking of heads. Then the conversation turned to roofs. Mostly roofs Murchie had known in his long and fascinating life. 'Knew a bloke had to mow his roof,' he was saying as Hamilton left.

He was sorry to go. Mowing a roof sounded interesting.

He found Madeline sitting with Stuart and Annie in the kitchen. Apologised for walking in on them, but the door was open. 'I knocked,' he said. 'But I don't think you heard.' He saw Madeline, and smiled. And said her name, 'Madeline.'

She was frowning. Put her glass of whisky on the table, staring at him through her alcoholic haze. I know that man. Who is he?

'You don't remember me,' said Hamilton. 'But I remember you.' Then with a sweep of his arm indicating the havoc outside, and in, he said, 'You've had a night of it last night.'

'You can say that again,' said Stuart. He grinned. Affably drunk.

The three had started clearing up. But without electricity, the vacuum wouldn't work. They'd tried to sweep. But after sweeping for two hours or more, they felt they'd made little inroads on thick coatings of grime that lay along the corridors. They'd picked up tiles and rubble from the walled garden, cleared a bit. Then tired. Last night had been sleepless, and drunken. So they went indoors. Stuart had felt more whisky was needed, 'Just to cheer us,' he said. 'And it is lovely.'

'It's fantastic,' said Madeline. 'I'm not a whisky drinker. But I'm going to start.'

'I've been drunk since last night,' said Annie. 'I'm not even hung over. I feel all happy and smiley.'

So he'd fetched a bottle from the cellar. They drunk. And drunk some more. Stuart and Madeline recalled their golden years together. Their cycling jigs.

'I want to do that,' said Annie. 'Now I'm sick of being upwardly mobile. And have thrown off the fetters of careerism.'

They ran along the devastated corridors shouting, 'Let's jig. Let's jig and be damned.'

'To hell with the roof,' Stuart shouted, waving his whisky bottle.

They played a scratchy but frenetic recording of 'Tiger Rag' on the old horn gramophone. Whirled round the room, shouting instructions. 'Up the middle, link arms and jig.'

The movement, the speed of it, made Annie high. Her cheeks pinked with joy.

It was Madeline who had the sobering moment. 'D'you think we're all drunk? D'you think we should be doing something more positive about the roof? Get estimates and such like?'

'We're drunk and roofless,' said Stuart, pouring more whisky. 'And we don't care. Let's drink. And dance. For life is fabulous.'

Then they'd returned, exhausted to the kitchen. To drink some more. And that was when Hamilton Foster had come to them. Tapping gently on the door, putting his head into the room first, apologising for disturbing them.

'I know who you are,' Madeline cried, pointing at him. 'Hamilton Foster. You have that gallery I sent my paintings to. Your partner sent them back.'

'Did he? I didn't know,' he said. 'I must have been away. I've just been to the local hall and seen your new collection. And to put it in a nutshell, I want it. Are there any more?'

And then he spotted the whisky bottle. 'Is that what you're drinking? My God.'

'It is a bit old,' said Madeline, who knew even less about whisky than Stuart. 'But it's lovely.'

'I'll just bet it is,' said Hamilton. 'Do you mind? Can I have some? I don't mean to be forward. But I've never seen an 1890 Bowmore before.'

Stuart poured him a large glass. Handed it to him. 'Help yourself, mate. It's gorgeous. Slips over the throat. This is the fourth bottle.'

'Do you always just swig it back like this?' asked Hamilton.

'No. Never usually touch the stuff. My family saved it for emergencies and the roof coming off is the emergency to end all emergencies. So. Cheers.' He swigged mightily. 'Aaah!'

'Only,' said Hamilton, '1890 Bowmore. It's worth about twelve or thirteen thousand a bottle.'

Oh, the sobering. Twelve or thirteen thousand a bottle. Six words that stunned them. They stared at one another, too shocked to gasp.

Stuart, after a long, thick silence, said, 'What?'

'Twelve or thirteen thousand, definitely,' said Hamilton. And sipped. 'A little water, I think. But, oh my, it's quite, quite lovely.' He sniffed his glass. Swirled its contents. 'Oh, yes. I thank you for this.'

'But,' said Stuart, 'four bottles that's . . .' he was too drunk to count, stared vacantly ahead wrestling with figures, '. . . a lot.'

'Indeed,' agreed Hamilton.

'We could've fixed the roof. Well, almost.'

'It certainly would have contributed hugely to your

reconstructions,' Hamilton agreed once more. He sipped again. 'But it is a wonderful dram.'

'I'm a fool.' Stuart hid his face in his hands. 'A fool. An idiot. An ignoramus. A fucking prat.'

Hamilton didn't like to voice his agreement on this point.

'I've drunk it all,' moaned Stuart.

'That's what it's for, after all,' soothed Hamilton. 'Drinking.' He raised his glass to the stunned and sorry little ensemble. He was a whisky connoisseur. He gloated that he could tell his fellow whisky lovers that he'd tasted a 1890 Bowmore. More than that, he had a cracking tale to dine out on. He couldn't wait to get back, and tell it.

Madeline jiggled. Looked pained. Pressed her thighs together. 'Oh my God. I seriously need a pee. And I don't want to go. It'll cost too much. I'm just going to squish this lot down the loo. The most expensive pee in the world.'

Moving On

Hamilton picked up Madeline's paintings and laughed all the way home. It had been a most fruitful day – a new talent, whisky and a story to chortle over. And the car was a joy.

Donald and Muriel took out their passports from the writing bureau where for the past three years they'd lain beside Donald's old dental plate and the binoculars from Boots. Muriel started her what-to-take list. Donald fetched their suitcases from under the bed. They were thrilled. An adventure.

'And it's been a while since we had one of those,' said Muriel.

'I don't think we've ever had an adventure,' said Donald.

'Well, that's a sin. It's high time we did.'

It was to be a secret. They would send a postcard when they got there. They wanted nobody to know about the money they had. They feared somebody might take it away from them.

'After all,' Donald said, not without contrition, 'it's stolen.'

'Stolen!' said Muriel. 'My money's never stolen. I have never stolen anything in my life. That money's my due. My fair pay for the days I've put in working my fingers to the bone. It's what they at the big house owe me. I'm having it. Still, we'll not tell anybody we're going till we've gone.'

In Marglass House, Stuart, Madeline and Annie brought mattresses down into the kitchen. It was the only warm room. They finished the whisky.

'What else is there to do with it?' said Madeline.

The others agreed. But with sinking hearts. And now they knew the worth of it, they didn't quaff it heartily. They drank slowly, feeling foolish and getting more and more sober with every sip.

Next day, Annie went home. Wondering with every mile she

329

covered if Willie would be there when she got back. So much had happened since she'd told him to leave, she realised, that for the past couple of days she'd forgotten all about him. And more, she didn't want to go back to him. In fact, for the first time in the years she'd been coming to Marglass, she didn't want go back at all.

She gave herself a talking-to. She was a fool. Having an affair with her best friend's partner. She'd fallen in love with Stuart. Stupid, girl. She would have to sort this out. And in the sorting out she'd lose a lover, or she'd lose a friend. And most likely, she'd lose both. No Willie, no pals, no lover. Children off to university soon. She'd be alone.

When she got back, Willie was gone. He'd left a note. 'Would be staying with her. But she only wants me as a visitor to her bed. Am living in the back room of the pub.'

Oh Willie, she thought. Then she thought, Well, the back room of the pub will suit you fine. You're not coming back here. And I'm not coming to see you. You'll only make me laugh. And give me a hug. Then I'll forgive you. And the whole mess will go on and on.

She ran a bath. Sank into it, sighing. Stiff, and not nearly as hung over as she ought to be. She thought of Stuart and Madeline roughing it in Marglass House. No electricity. No hot water. And thought herself sweetly lucky.

Six days later, at five in the morning a slow taxi slipped down the drive of Marglass House and stopped outside the old cottage by the river with clematis sneaking up its walls and roses budding beside the picket fence. Donald and Muriel, who had been sitting by the window with their coats buttoned for the last half-hour, quietly and saying nothing to one another rose, lifted their cases that had been waiting in the hall since the night before. And went out into the day. The first blackbird was hopping on the trimmed lawn. Chaffinches bickering in the trees.

For the first time since they'd lived in the cottage, Donald locked the door. He put the key under the scrubbing brush, worn from many scourings and white from bleach and sun, where he knew Stuart would, eventually, find it.

This was the first time in their lives they'd ordered a taxi. It had caused a deal of heart-searching to pluck up the courage to pick up the phone and do it.

'Seventy-five pounds,' said Donald.

'How else are we going to get to the airport without being seen? Who is going to carry our bags?' said Muriel.

'Seventy-five pounds,' said Donald.

'We're not going to lug heavy cases down the drive. We're leaving in style. Heads held high.'

'Seventy-five pounds,' said Donald.

'I know,' said Muriel. 'But that's the way of things these days. Time was I didn't earn seventy-five pounds in a year. But there you go. If that's what a bit of dignity costs, it's money well spent.'

They climbed into the car, told the driver, 'Glasgow airport.' And settled back. Donald turned to give the old, and roofless, house one last long stare. Goodbye. But Muriel would not.

'I'll not look at it. I'll not remember it this way. I'll remember it from the old days. When it was full of folk. And the business of folk. Moving along the corridors. And the men went shooting stag in the autumn. Hare in winter. Remember that winter when they shot five hundred and piled them high like a wall beside the steps? Deer coming down in winter looking for food. Men scything the lawns Sunday afternoon. For there were no mowers then. Dinner parties when the table was laden and silver shining, candles lit and ladies in evening dresses. And gloves on. I'll not remember it with these two being silly, playing games. And having goings-on. I'll not remember it with its roof shattered round it. And young Stuart with no money to fix it. It breaks my heart.'

'We could give him the money to fix it. We could give him our money.'

'It doesn't break my heart that much,' said Muriel.

Ten minutes later, Freda, bringing in her milk, saw a taxi speeding along main street. She stared after it. She thought she saw Muriel and Donald in the back. Then shook her head. Muriel and Donald never went anywhere.

It took Stuart and Madeline a while to realise they hadn't seen the old couple. Stuart stood at the window in Marglass House, staring down at the cottage. It was strangely quiet. No smoke pluming from the chimney. Donald hadn't taken his grumpy evening stump round the grounds, ruined though they were. Muriel hadn't hung out any washing. Several times Stuart walked by, thinking to go in. Then, remembering, the incident of the scones. How they laughed. He didn't dare. He was ashamed. He wondered if they would understand, they hadn't been laughing at them. It had been shock. A release. He thought now they had all been hysterical.

'Have you seen Muriel or Donald?' he asked Madeline.

She shook her head.

'No sign of them for days,' he told her.

'I think we really insulted them,' said Madeline. 'Perhaps we should go and apologise. Try and explain.'

'Maybe they're ill. You're right, we should go see them.'

They walked down past the walled garden to the cottage. Over the past few days, they'd cleared most of the mess. Trundling it by the wheelbarrow-load up to the side of the house. Piling fallen tiles into heaps. It was cleared. But still devastated. Only the thyme had survived the slicing winds.

The cottage was still. Seven in the evening, and no lights on. Stuart knocked on the door. No reply. He knocked again. Louder. Nothing happened. He looked through the windows. And could see nobody. He tried the door. It was locked.

'They never lock the door,' he told Madeline.

They walked round to the back, still peering in the windows. Stuart saw only immaculately tidy rooms, no sign of Muriel or Donald.

'Maybe they've gone visiting somebody,' suggested Madeline.

'I've known them all my life. They've never gone visiting anybody. Ever. Not even somebody who lives nearby. Not even at New Year or Christmas. They don't know anybody.'

He went round to the front door. Banged on it with the side of his fist. Nothing. He looked under the doormat for the key. It wasn't there. He considered kicking the door open. 'Strange,' he said. 'Very strange.' He was sure they wouldn't leave without saying something. 'They wouldn't just go, surely,' he said.

'I don't know. We were pretty rude. I didn't mean to be. But thinking about it now, I'm a bit ashamed.'

'They'd leave a key,' said Stuart. He searched under the tub of tulips by the door. Under stones. And, finally, lifted the scrubbing brush. 'Found them,' he said, waving a small bunch of keys.

He opened the door and went in. Madeline behind him. The house was silent. Hot and airless. They looked round. Wandered the rooms. No sign of Muriel and Donald.

'It's like the *Marie Celeste*,' said Stuart.

'Maybe they've been abducted,' said Madeline.

And Stuart said that this was no time for jokes. This was serious.

'It's a lovely cottage,' said Madeline. 'Light, spacious. Great fireplace. Deco tiles.'

Stuart told her it used to be in Marglass House. He sat down. 'So did this sofa. And the writing desk. In fact, everything, right down to the spoons, used to be in Marglass House.'

'They stole the furniture?' said Madeline.

'They requisitioned it.' He shrugged. 'It was there. Nobody was using it. They took it all down here. Polished it, cleaned it. It's looking better than it did before they moved it. But, where are Muriel and Donald?'

'God, it's clean in here,' said Madeline.

Muriel had spent the last two days feverishly scrubbing, washing and ironing the curtains, wiping down the walls and woodwork, vacuuming the carpets. 'I'll not be leaving a dirty house,' she'd said.

Stuart nodded. 'It's such a mess up at the house. You forget about clean.'

Madeline sat on the sofa beside him. They stayed sitting there for almost half an hour, hardly saying anything.

'It's very pleasant here,' said Madeline. 'I could sleep. What if they come back and find us sitting on their sofa? That could be embarrassing.'

'Won't happen,' said Stuart. 'I think they've done a runner.'

'Gone away? For ever?' asked Madeline.

'Yeah. They've buggered off.'

'But why?'

'Why stay? The house was their life. She cleaned it, served in it. He did the gardens. Now it's over. The house is finished. They've gone.'

'Where to?'

He spread his palms, raised his eyes. 'I haven't a clue. But they've gone. And they are right. It's time to go.' He put his arm round her, pulled her to him, kissed the top of her head. 'It's over, my sweet. The days of heaven are no more.' The way he smiled, the way he spoke, affably, joking, nobody would think it broke his heart.

The next day he called an estate agent and put the house and grounds on the market. The cottage was not included in the sale. Despite owning it, and everything in it, Stuart didn't really think it was his to sell. The estate agent told him Marglass House in its present state, roofless, wouldn't fetch anything like its potential price. But it was in a lovely position. There might be some interest. But he was told not to keep his hopes up. And Stuart said, that it was all right. His hopes, these days, were never up. But he thought that saying the house needed some renovation was putting it mildly. 'In fact,' he said, 'that's putting it so mildly, it's pretty much a bare-faced lie.'

The estate agent asked if the house was listed. 'It ought to be,' he said.

Stuart shook his head. 'No. I know it ought to be, but my father made sure it wasn't. He didn't want to pay the upkeep.'

'Only if it had been, you'd get a grant for the roof.'

Stuart shook his head again. 'I could still get a grant. But I'd still have to come up with a portion of the cost. I've only got fifty quid. No, I'll have to sell it. If anybody will have it.' He sighed, 'I shouldn't have drunk the whisky.'

The estate agent gave him a sharp look, wondering what he meant. But didn't ask. He sensed regret and pain.

When the postcard from Muriel and Donald arrived, it was not a surprise. Muriel apologised for leaving so suddenly, so silently. For not saying goodbye properly. She and Donald, she said, had gone to live in their little flat in Spain. And my, it was sunny here. Her old bones felt better already.

At this point Muriel's Biro hovered over the small space reserved on the back of the card for writing a greeting. She wanted to say how much she cared for him. How she'd seen him grow into a man, and she was proud of him. But couldn't. Words of praise, words of love were hard for her. She rarely, if ever, spoke them. Writing them down was impossible.

So, she wrote that they'd think of him often. And wished him well for the future. And hoped things would turn out for him. 'Kindest regards, Muriel.' She'd wanted to write, 'All my love, Muriel'. But some deep shyness welled up in her. She imagined him reading it and laughing, or scoffing. Though she knew he wasn't the sort to scoff. 'PS,' she added, thinking of his doings with Annie and Madeline, 'You be good, now.'

Stuart smiled. Put the postcard, carefully, in between the pages of a book. He knew what she meant by 'You be good, now', and told her, in her absence, that he would.

Annie had her first serious argument with her daughter, Flo.

'How could you let my dad live in the back room of a pub?' Flo protested. 'That's cruel. You are heartless.'

'No, I'm not. I imagine Willie will love being so near to a constant supply of booze. He'll probably never have been happier in his life.'

'He'll be cold and lonely.'

'He's never been cold or lonely in his life,' said Annie.

'I hate you for not letting him come home.'

'He's been having an affair. For years he's been having an affair. Probably two or three affairs.'

'I know that. Everybody knows that. He's Dad. That's what he's like. He's got too much love in him.'

'And how do you suppose that makes me feel?'

Flo stopped to think about this. 'I didn't think you minded. I thought you accepted it. You've never said anything before. You're my mum. You always sort everything.'

'I do not sort everything. I feel hurt, betrayed by your father. Him out drinking, making love to other women. It makes me feel like the little drab person at home. Doing the washing up. I hate it.'

'But you're my mum. That's what you do.'

How her daughter perceived her came as a shock to Annie. 'I hold down a good job. I pay the mortgage. I pay for the electricity and the phone. Which, may I point out, you use far too much. I pay for everything – your clothes —'

She'd been on the point of listing the things she paid for, but Flo waved her hands in the air, protesting. 'I think you're cruel and nasty. My dad's lovely. He hugs me, he brings me presents. I love him and I think you're horrible.'

Annie sank, demoralised, on to the sofa. 'My God. I'm horrible,' she said. And the words worked their way into the depths of her, set waves of guilt shifting through her. Willie, alone and lonely in a cold back room. She imagined the wafts of stale beer and tobacco smoke. She imagined drifting laughter, and Willie, too sad, too lonely to join in. She imagined a small iron bedstead, hard and with a single blanket to keep him warm. A relentless chill draughting under the door. Stained floorboards. An upturned beer crate on which there was a small dim lamp, no shade. Poor Willie. At half-past eleven that night, she went to fetch him.

In fact the room was quite comfortable. A beige cord carpet. A double bed, duvet. No draughts. A chest of drawers on which was a brass lamp, complete with shade.

'Trust you to land on your feet, you bastard,' said Annie, feeling foolish. Giving in to her imaginings.

'Annie!' cried Willie, holding wide his arms. 'You've come for me. You're a grand old soul.'

'Bugger off. I'm not a grand old soul at all. And don't you hug me. Don't you dare hug me.'

'Annie,' Willie repeated, advancing.

'Get off me,' said Annie. 'You can come home. But you'll sleep on the sofa. You're not getting into my bed. Not ever again.'

Willie's advances being faster than Annie's backing off, he reached her. Enfolded, and hugged. 'I knew you'd come for me. Oh, Annie.'

Annie gave in to the hug. She never could resist. Rested against him. 'Willie, you're a fool. And you are definitely not getting into my bed.'

He held her at arm's length. Looked into her face and smiled quizzically. 'Not never?'

'Not never,' Annie told him. 'Now get your things.'

He followed her triumphantly through the bar. Thumbs-up to his drinking cronies. Who cheered. 'Going home,' he shouted. And pointing to Annie, 'She's a grand old soul.'

Annie turned, glared. She was feeling like Andy Capp's wife, and didn't like it. Didn't like it at all.

As he left, Willie tweaked the barmaid's bum and she squealed. Annie turned again. Willie looked innocent. If Annie had seen it'd be the back room of the pub for him, for ever.

The next day, Annie put the flat on the market. 'Like it or not,' she told Flo, 'I'm leaving him. You'll have to choose who you want to live with. Your lovely dad or your cruel heartless mum.'

'I'm coming with you,' said Flo. 'I mean, Dad's lovely. But I wouldn't want to live with him. Not without you there to keep him in line. But I'll visit him for tea.'

Annie didn't know what to make of this image of her as domestic martinet. So she sighed, reached over and clasped Flo's hand and said, 'Good.'

For a month she did not go to visit Madeline and Stuart. She spent the weekends tidying her house, keeping fresh coffee brewing, leaving glossy magazines lying casually on the coffee table, giving her home the illusion, she hoped, of a lived-in, happy place. Every time people came to view it, she put Willie out. She feared what he might say. 'I think there's damp behind that panelling.' The man was a liar, a flirt, he cheated on her, he gambled, he drank and he was smitten with bouts of misplaced honesty. So when Annie was showing prospective buyers round he was dispatched to the pub and told not to come home till Flo came and gave him the all-clear.

The business of creating the perfect, harmonious, desirable home ended when the flat was sold. Annie relaxed, breathed out, left dishes in the sink, towels unfolded in the bathroom and thought: It's over.

Two days later, when she came home from work, Madeline was sitting in her kitchen, drinking coffee with Willie.

'Madeline,' said Annie. 'What are you doing here?'

'Going to the opening of Hamilton's exhibition. My paintings. Want to come?'

'Do I? Of course I do. How long have you been in town?'

'Got here yesterday. I'm staying with Hamilton. Stuart couldn't come. He's got the flu.'

'You've been shopping,' Annie looked Madeline up and down. Velvet jeans, roll-neck sleeveless sweater. High-heeled boots.

'Yes,' said Madeline. 'I love it. Haven't shopped in years. Now I'm going to shop and shop and shop.'

'And what about Marglass? Any buyers yet?'

Madeline looked away. Didn't answer. She didn't want to think about that. Not right now.

The gallery was crowded. People moving, mingling. People in dark suits, denims, silk. Looking sophisticated. Checking other people. Drinking wine. Standing long before paintings. Soft music played. Madeline hung back. Kept close to Annie. She did not go near her own work, lingered in front of other pictures, by other people. She did not want to overhear any comments about what she had on show. Something painful might be said.

Annie stared at the dream paintings. Saw them anew. Back at Marglass they'd seemed strange. Almost absurd. Neglected things, propped against the wall. But here, viewed from across the shiny maple flooring, framed, lit and hanging, each one alone on a vast space of white wall, they looked dazzling, colourful, wild. There was a buzz round them. She saw Madeline in new eyes. Her imagination, her passion. Her longing.

'My God, Madeline,' she said. 'You.'

'Me what?' said Madeline.

'You did these paintings. You're brilliant. I didn't know.'

'What do you mean, you didn't know? You've seen everything before.'

'Yeah, but it looks different here. I never really *saw* them. I mean look, they're amazing.' Annie knew she'd been too wrapped up with

Stuart, too enthralled with this new secret love, too busy keeping it a secret to notice what Madeline was doing. How good it was. She wondered if Stuart knew.

And when Hamilton took Madeline by the hand, took her to meet her new admirers, Annie watched. Watched as Madeline smiled. Glowed. Sipped her wine. Answered questions. Stood by her paintings as she was photographed. Annie thought. There she goes. My friend, moving on.

After ten they emerged on to the summer street. Lights, rustling taxis, scents – boozy wafts from pubs, garlic from an Italian restaurant across the road, fumes from passing cars – people laughing. And Madeline was high.

'Oh, don't you just love it? The noise, the business of being in the city. The movement.'

'Suppose,' said Annie. 'I don't really notice it. It just hums round me. I'm glad to get away.'

'I love it. I'd forgotten how much I love it. Are you coming to eat with Hamilton and me?'

Annie excused herself. She had to go home. Things to do. She had to phone Stuart.

'Oh, come on,' said Madeline, holding Annie's arm. 'Please. I want you there.'

Annie shook her head. 'Sorry, no. Have you called Stuart?'

'Tomorrow,' said Madeline. 'I'll do it tomorrow. Why won't you come?'

'You should call him now, tell him,' said Annie. And she thought, Tell her. Tell her now. But she didn't. The silence hung between them.

Madeline looked at her, sensed something. 'What?'

Tell her, tell her, Annie urged herself. Now, when she's got something else to hang on to. Hamilton came out, took Madeline's arm. 'Time for some food, girl,' he said. Looked at Annie. 'Coming?'

The moment passed. Annie shook her head.

'Oh, please,' said Madeline.

But Annie shook her head again. 'Things to do,' she said. 'Really. Sorry.' She turned and walked swiftly away. Heels clicking on the pavement. Cursing herself. Hating herself for betraying her friend. And for not seeing the worth, the uniqueness of Madeline's work, for all the sunshine hours she spent with Stuart, while Madeline was passionately pouring her dreams on to canvas.

Back home, she phoned Marglass House. Stuart answered, his voice thick with flu. He was depressed. More than depressed. A deep and black cloud had descended on him, cloaked him. He couldn't think. Saw only ruin around him. And no way forward. No way out. He thought he'd be clearing up rubble for ever. He'd stopped eating properly. He couldn't sleep. He never left the grounds, never went to the village. Spoke to nobody. He'd started to drink.

'I've been to Madeline's show,' Annie told him. 'You should have come along. It was wonderful.'

'I know,' said Stuart. Sounding flat. 'I've got so much to do. I don't feel so good.'

'Have you taken anything? Paracetamol?' she asked.

'Couldn't be bothered.'

'Are you still sleeping in the kitchen?'

'Yes.'

'Have you managed to clear up any of the mess?'

'Yeah. A bit. Got pissed off with it.'

'You sound drunk.'

'I am drunk.'

'Well, snap out of it. I'm coming up to see you. Don't move till I get there.'

A Potter and his Dog

Two in the morning when Annie arrived at Marglass House. She could see that Stuart had cleared the walled garden. Slates were in piles against the wall. The hallway and stairs to the kitchen had been cleaned. The layering of dust and grime vacuumed up, wiped away. But the sense of ruin, devastation remained. Stuart was in the kitchen, lying on his mattress. Unshaven, still grubby from working in the garden, he was red-nosed, watery-eyed, sorry for himself.

'You look awful,' said Annie.

'Well, thanks for that. He smiled. 'Drink?' He waved a bottle of wine at her.

'No thanks. Have you washed today?'

'No. Nor yesterday, now you mention it. It didn't seem necessary.'

'Not necessary? Why not?'

'Well, I was dirty yesterday, and I'm only going to get dirtier tomorrow. I thought I'd try and finish the clearing up of the garden, and that. Then I'd have a big wash. That seems the sensible thing to do.'

'You're drunk.'

'Something I do rather well, I think. Drink. That rhymes.' He giggled.

'Well, you've certainly cleared up a lot. Did Muriel and Donald help?'

'No, they scarpered off to Spain. They're not coming back.'

Annie let this sink in. 'So you are living here in this kitchen. In a house that is freezing cold. When there is a lovely cottage, that you own, yards away.'

'Yeah, now you mention it.'

'You're insane.'

'Annie, when I'm here, I lie on this mattress and dream of you.

341

But in my dreams you are a lot nicer to me than you're being now. I don't want to move in to Muriel and Donald's cottage. It's theirs. They did it up. It doesn't feel right.'

'It has a roof. I find having a roof one of life's necessities. Very handy. Especially when it rains.'

'I know. But I'm down here. And the rain's up there. It doesn't hit me.'

'It will,' she said. 'Get up off your arse and get down to that cottage now.' She glared at him. 'Right now. I mean it. If you think I'm spending the night with you in this smelly kitchen, when there's a warm bed and a bath down there, you are off your head.'

'If you put it like that,' said Stuart.

'I do.'

So Stuart moved into the cottage. And had to admit it was a lot more comfortable. Annie stayed for a couple of days before going home to do some house-hunting. They looked at one another when she told him that.

'You should move in here, with me,' Stuart said.

'You and Madeline?' said Annie.

And he looked away. 'I'll tell her. I will, I promise. When the moment's right.'

'I nearly told her the other night,' said Annie.

'No. Not then. Not when she's so happy.'

'I'll wait till she's unhappy, then.'

'No. When the moment's right.'

Annie said that the moment would never be right.

And Stuart said, 'Suppose.'

He watched Annie's car disappear down the drive, went inside. He slumped on the sofa thinking, Now what? He got up. Stared out of the window. Wandered through to the kitchen. Now what? He couldn't think. He went back to slump. And tomorrow, he thought, what'll I do, then? And the day after? No point in doing the garden. It was for sale. Like as not the new owners, whoever they might be, would take a JCB to it. Knock it all down.

So, he thought, what about the rest of my life? This was a new concept to him. He'd imagined himself an old man tending his vegetables and herbs. He'd been fond of this notion. Himself, nut brown, wise in the ways of growing things. He'd even, in his dreams, adopted a kind of rural accent, and a way of jerking his head, knowingly to the side and saying, 'Aye,' for this old man he was going to be one day. In fact, he'd thought that, come that time, he'd sport a beard, and maybe even buy a hat. A good hat, with a brim, but soft, so he could roll it up and put it in his pocket. He'd wear baggy corduroy pants, with braces. Striped braces, he thought, or maybe patterned. He liked the old man he was going to be.

He lay back on the sofa and toyed with notions. Go back to the city, get a job in marketing again. He wondered if his old employers would take him back, or give him a reference. He doubted that. Then he thought: Retrain. A teacher? Nah. A test pilot? Too old, now. He was working through being a market gardener or a botanist when he drifted off to sleep.

In the morning he walked to the village. He'd have a chat with Murchie, he thought. A drink at the Castle. If he was to be a man of leisure, he should enjoy it. He was walking down Main Street, thinking that he should get a dog. McCann had died years ago. A dog would be good. A friend, someone to talk. He had a notion for an Irish wolfhound. Murchie had a dog once, he remembered. He trained it to put logs on the fire, so he didn't have to get up and do it himself. 'Log, dog,' Murchie would say. And the dog would oblige. Stuart was thinking he could do that, when he met Freda.

'Well, young Stuart,' she said. 'Haven't seen you in a while.'

'Been clearing up,' he told her. Now that he was facing forty he quite liked being called young Stuart. Before that it had made him feel like a schoolboy.

'All finished?' she asked.

He shook his head. 'Nah. Given up on it. Marglass is up for sale, what's the point?'

'Exactly,' agreed Freda. 'You never know what someone new will want to do with the place. Best leave them to it. Tell you what I was thinking. I was thinking you could look after the pottery for me.'

'The pottery?' said Stuart. Becoming a potter hadn't been among last night's notions. But now he thought about it, why not?

'I hardly ever open the place these days. You could tend the shop. And you could make pots or whatever. If you fancy.'

He imagined himself working with clay, making things. The dog, which he was going to call Rufus, would lie quietly waiting for him to finish work. A swift pint at the Castle and home. This seemed like an excellent life to him. He could cycle, like Madeline had done. Rufus would trot along beside the bike. They'd do fine together. When he went into the Castle of an evening people would call, 'Hi, Stuart. Hi, Rufus.' He liked this new notion. And told Freda, 'Cool.'

'I can't pay you much, I hope you realise.'

'It's OK,' said Stuart. 'I've got somewhere to stay. I just need enough to pay a few bills and buy a bite to eat for Rufus and me.'

Freda wondered who the hell Rufus was. But said, 'Fine. That's settled, then.'

He started work at the pottery. And looked for an Irish wolfhound. He phoned a breeder in Dublin, and found, to his horror, what one would cost. First to buy, then to feed. He asked Freda for a raise.

But she said, 'You've only been here two days. And what have you sold?'

'Two postcards and a box of mints that says they're made locally. But actually they're made in Birmingham,' he told her. 'So I take it you don't see your way to increasing my salary.'

'You're not wrong there.' Freda said, and left him to his notions.

In the end he found a cross spaniel and border collie in a farm twenty miles away, and borrowed Ali's van to go get it. It was brown, hairy, with absurdly long ears and one eye blue, one eye brown. He fell in love with it. Though he did ask the farmer if it would grow big enough to lift logs.

'Depends on the log,' he was told.

And he was fine with that. Days, he worked in the pottery. Nights, he lay on the sofa, Rufus on his chest, drinking wine that he'd transported over several evenings from Marglass House. He'd used a wheel barrow and it had taken ten or more trips. But now his wine was in the store at the back of the house that had once been used for keeping game.

Weekends, Annie visited. He was happy. Except for several times a day and several more times in the middle of the night, when he thought about Madeline.

Everyone Suddenly Burst out Singing.
But Not in Unison

Madeline's departure from Marglass hadn't been sudden. She'd had several trips to Edinburgh whilst the paintings were being hung. The exhibition had been well received. Lyrical, funny, said one critic. Dreamlike, said another. This week's must-see, said someone else.

After that, Madeline returned to Marglass and worked at the Inverask Castle Hotel, manning reception, serving teas. She was removed from her success. And removed from the place she'd come back to. Removed from Stuart. Cycling to work, she'd stop, look round, think about her exhibition. Had that happened? Now, she wasn't sure. It seemed so far away. Long ago. Though it was only a week.

At work, her relationships changed. She'd catch people looking at her, wondering. What was going on in her head? People were still friendly. But she was no longer 'our Madeline'. Murchie had taken the cuttings from the newspapers. They'd been passed round. 'Madeline?' people in the bar had said. 'That Madeline?' It seemed unbelievable. They felt she'd, somehow, betrayed them. Maybe, she'd even been secretly laughing at them. Hadn't let them know what she could do.

'How could I have let them know, when I didn't know myself? I didn't know what I could do till I did it,' Madeline said to Freda.

'I have always known,' said Freda. 'I knew you'd come to yourself, one day. It's taken a while, though.'

Meantime, the paintings were packed and taken to Glasgow. Then to Manchester, Birmingham. Madeline went with them. Disappearing for a couple of days. Coming home again. Now her conversations with Stuart had changed. They slipped into memories. Indulged in moments of long ago, when, it seemed to them now, they had been happy. They'd go on nostalgia walks, pointing out special places. 'This is where we . . .' And, 'Over there, remember we . . .' 'Remember we were so knackered from working, and ate cheesecake in bed?' she said. They smiled. These reminiscences brought them closer than they had been in months. But Stuart was filled with sadness. He felt he'd held her back. All those years he'd seen her come and go to and from the Inverask Castle Hotel, waving goodbye, waiting for her to arrive home again, he'd been happy in his garden. But she had been frustrated, longing to paint. When they made love, it was even nostalgic. My, remember when we did it like that? There was a softness in the way they spoke to one another, a gentleness. As if they were both looking back to a time when they lived in the moment, enjoying everything about that moment, the sounds, scents and feel of it. And neither of them knew how to get back to being like that. Furthermore, at the time, neither of them had realised how happy they'd been. They'd let it go. Frittered away their closeness rather than building on it.

Then the exhibition moved to London. Madeline was invited to the opening.

'I won't go,' she said. 'I've had enough of it. They don't need me there.'

Stuart insisted she went. 'If you don't go, you'll always wonder about it. What it was like. Who you might have met. You have to go.'

She agreed with this and phoned Hamilton Foster to say she'd come to London. 'It'll only be a couple of days,' she told Stuart. But she handed in her notice at the hotel. It was time to go.

Stuart held her face in his hands, said he'd miss her. He thought to phone Annie. But felt that a bit devious, inviting his lover to the house, soon as Madeline was out of the way. Besides, Annie was busy looking for a new flat. He decided it best to leave her alone.

On the night before Madeline left, the bar at the Inverask was crowded. People crushed in to wish her well.

'What a success our arts festival has been,' said Murchie. 'A new talent uncovered.'

Freda agreed. 'We must get busy organising next year's.'

Madeline could not bring herself to mention the whole affair had been a washout. Few people had turned up. The flute recital had been cancelled, no tickets were sold. And the grand final night had been postponed due to the storm. People were too busy clearing up, and filling in insurance forms, to celebrate.

'What a triumph it was,' said Murchie. 'Madeline's thing could put us on the map. We could attract thousands next year.'

'We'll advertise nationally,' said Freda.

'What with?' asked Murchie. 'Who'll pay for that?'

'We'll use the proceeds from this year's triumph,' said Freda.

'We made eight pounds on the gate of the art exhibition. And three foreign coins.'

'We'll worry about that when the time comes,' enthused Freda.

They drank to that.

It was eight o'clock. They'd been drinking for some time. And saw an alcoholic night ahead. An hour later, George presented Madeline with the results of a swift whip-round. What to buy had caused some arguing.

'A new bike,' suggested Murchie. 'She's been needing that since she started here.'

'She'll not be needing a bike now,' said Freda. 'We should get her a lovely scarf.'

'Your idea of a lovely scarf might not be her idea of a lovely scarf,' George pointed out. 'A photo of us all at the bar, framed,' he suggested.

Everyone pooh-poohed that.

'A case,' said Ali. 'Bet you a hundred pounds she hasn't got a case.'

It seemed so obvious, everyone wondered why they hadn't thought of it.

'She might think since we're giving her that, we're glad to see her go,' said Murchie.

'We'll inscribe it. On the inside,' said Freda. ' "For when you come home." '

George made a speech as he handed over the gift. 'Years she's been with us. And when she came she knew nothing about the hotel trade. Now she's going, she still knows nothing. That's how good an artist she is.'

And everyone laughed.

'We'll be looking out for you, Madeline. We'll be watching for your face in art programmes. Following your every move. We'll all miss you.'

Madeline wanted to say she was only going for a couple of days. This was Tuesday. She'd be back Friday night. But didn't like to spoil the moment.

'And when we see your face in magazines, on the telly, we'll all be saying, "She was a friend of mine."'

Was? thought Madeline. I still will be. I'll be here. I'll be in the cottage. But she smiled and thanked everybody. And even shed a tear. It was touching.

Someone started to sing, 'He was a friend of mine,' a slow, maudlin, drunken whine substituting he for she. Others joined in. Whisky was downed. More whisky bought and downed. The song continued. But nobody was singing in time. Some people lingering on long notes, whilst others had moved on to the next verse. It was a din. A raucous alcohol-laden cacophony. A couple standing outside, beside their car, having come to the hotel hoping for a bite to eat, looked at one another, shook their heads. And drove off.

The party went on till three in the morning. Stuart and Madeline got home after four. At seven they were up and on their way to Glasgow in George's car. She kissed Stuart goodbye, said she'd see him soon and, clutching her new case, boarded the train to London. Hungover and tired, she slept all the way.

She stayed, at first, in a small hotel not far from Oxford Street. She'd imagined she'd have a view. But her bedroom looked out on to a brick wall. After the reception, she went back to it. Phoned Stuart. She was lonely.

'What was it like?' asked Stuart. 'Champagne?'

'Oh yes. And white wine laced with something. I drank too much. They don't seem to do that. Though I bet they all go home and get sloshed. Crack open the Jack Daniel's and the Silk Cut and indulge.'

'What did they say about your paintings?'

'They loved them. Dreamlike. Funny. Bloody quirky.'

But the evening had been fun. She'd been celebrated. Everyone knew her name. 'So you're Madeline Green.' And they'd look at her. Closely. What for? Madeline wondered. They can see the truth about me. I'm not really talented at all. I'm just me. Then, she thought, It's me. My clothes. She'd looked round at the other women. Some were dressed fabulously. Others were in jeans and boots and T-shirts. Some were dressed worse that she was, some better. No, she thought. I hit the middle ground there. My age. They're thinking: Didn't think she'd be *that* age. In the end she decided it was just her. She wasn't used to this. She identified with the women who were carrying round the trays of drinks.

The next day, she had lunch with Hamilton. He was in raptures. 'We sold a painting. The woman with the bird thumbs. Ten thousand.'

Madeline said, 'What? It isn't worth that. It only took a few days.'

'A few days and all your life.'

'Who bought it? Where do they live? Where is it going?'

'Somewhere outside Oxford,' Hamilton told her. 'It'll have a good home. Don't worry.'

He ordered a wild mushroom risotto, and Madeline said she'd have the same.

'So,' he said, 'what are you working on now?'

'Nothing,' she confessed. 'No studio. The roof blew off. Remember?'

'But you have to keep fluid. You can't stop now. We need more. No resting on your laurels, young lady.'

He found her some studio space in a converted warehouse in the East End. And let her use his flat till she found a place.

She phoned Stuart. 'I'll be staying a bit longer. I must work. I have a studio here now. There's no place there. I'll stay here till we get sorted out at Marglass.'

Stuart said, 'OK.' And he was missing her. And he didn't think he'd ever be sorted out at Marglass. He didn't think anybody would ever buy it.

'Rubbish,' said Madeline. 'It's in a great location. Just because it's got no roof is no reason for buyers not to like it.'

'I should have thought,' said Stuart, 'that it's a very good reason. In fact, having no roof I think is an excellent reason not to buy a property.' He sounded very drunk. 'Annie phoned. She's fine.'

That's why he's drunk, thought Madeline. He's pissed off because Annie phoned and it has reminded him that she has sold and he hasn't. 'Don't worry,' she said. 'Someone will come along. How are you enjoying working at the pottery?'

'Yeah. It's OK. I've started to make pots. Annie's coming up at the weekend.'

Madeline said, 'Good. She'll cheer you up.'

Hamilton thought it imperative she show new paintings. 'You are hot, right now. We have to keep the work coming.'

Madeline started her Marglass paintings. Sketches she would develop. Three people seen drinking, laughing uproariously as the roof of their huge grey building blew off. She put the library jigs down on canvas. And she drew herself cycling to work at the Inverask. A woman in a railway coat, weaving about the road, singing, as a white swan flew overhead. And again, herself returning to Marglass on the night of the storm. And time passed.

Madeline made friends. People who shared the same studio space, and people who knew the people who shared the same studio space. They were bright, funny, open and prone, like she was, to self-mockery.

'They're all younger than me,' she said to Hamilton.

'Are they?'

'Except for Stella, who's older.'

'Well, there you go. Not everyone is younger than you.'

'They seem, I don't know, happier than me. Or than I was at their age.'

He shrugged. 'More to do, probably.'

'They're so open about their lives.'

'They've just been doing what they want to do for longer.'

'No, it isn't that. Some of them are frustrated that nobody wants their work. And they're not all settled in relationships. They're confident. I don't remember being that. I suppose they've got more going for them.'

'What?' asked Hamilton. 'Clubs? Things, videos and stuff? Drugs?'

'No.' Shaking her head. 'There's always been clubs. And stuff. Not as sophisticated as now, but stuff. And there's always been drugs.'

'Sex, then,' said Hamilton.

'For heaven's sake, there's always been that. No.' She thought about this. 'I think they're just better at being young than I was. Damn.'

'Yes,' said Hamilton, agreeing. 'Damn.'

Madeline's favourite new person in her life was Stella. She worked as a PA in a small record company. Thus far Madeline had always imagined PAs to be tidy, besuited women, crisp of tone, organised in every facet of their own and other people's lives. Stella was large, wore T-shirts and jeans, was over forty, always losing things. 'Now, where did I put . . .?' she'd say. And, 'I'm sure I had a . . .' She laughed easily, often. She was comfortable.

'You should have a Stella,' Madeline told Hamilton when his PA bullied him into taking calls, answering his mail. 'I know,' he said. He could see the appeal.

Madeline liked Stella's easy manner. The way she'd knock on the door, then come in shouting, 'Hello.' And put on the kettle. Sit sideways on chairs, legs dangling over one arm. Tell silly stories at her own expense. Madeline liked that Stella had decided they'd be friends. It staved off her bouts of loneliness, missing Stuart. And it was reassuring, in a city full of strangers, to find one that liked her.

With Stella, she was invited to dinner parties. She went to bars. Thrumming busy places where she could hardly hear what anyone was saying for the buzz of conversation around her. And she loved it.

She phoned Stuart. 'How're you doing?'

'Fine. Annie's here.'

'Again,' said Madeline. 'Well, it's good you've got company.'

'Yeah,' said Stuart. 'She keeps me sane.'

Holding the receiver, Madeline smiled. Annie and Stuart. Her chums.

She worried that nobody would like her new work. She imagined people coming to view it and bursting out laughing. She imagined them saying how dreadful it was. She wrote criticism in her head. Juvenile. Absurd. Exactly what good art is not about. She sat up nights, in Hamilton's flat. Worrying. She started to smoke. It didn't help. In fact she hated it, and hated herself for doing it. But, somehow, the moment of reaching into the packet helped.

During the day when she was working, she was fine. It was the dark that brought the fear.

But, apart from the gnawing imaginings, she was enjoying herself. She met Stella and Stella's friends for lunch. They'd call her name, wave, as she approached. Embrace her. They never did that where she came from. It took a while to get the hang of the kissing thing. But soon she, too, was a kisser. 'Just the single cheek,' she told Stuart. 'Though some people do two. Mostly showbiz. Gallery people give you a peck several millimetres from your actual cheek. But other artists give you a smackeroonie dead centre. Actually, I like it. I must remember not to do it when I come back.'

Stuart pondered this, then told her Annie was staying for a few weeks. 'She's taken time off work. In fact she's thinking of giving up. After not getting her promotion. She's got nowhere to live. Now that the flat's sold. She gave a whack to Willie. He's got a new place. Somewhere near the centre. It's got a balcony. Anyway, she's here.' It all came out in a tumble.

Madeline thought perhaps he'd found another bottle of 1890 Bowmore. Or maybe he'd just been at the wine. 'That's wonderful,' she said. 'I don't like to think of you there alone.'

Hamilton sold Madeline's aubergine picture. 'Fifteen,' he said.

'Fifteen what?' said Madeline.

'Thousand,' he told her.

She sank into a chair. 'You're terrible. People can't pay that.'

'That's nothing to what you'll get in a couple of years. People pay a lot more than that for good art.'

'They're nuts,' said Madeline. 'You can get a good print at Habitat for about a tenner.'

And Hamilton told her he'd be grateful if she never mentioned that in public. And that people bought art as an investment, hoping its value would increase.

'Doesn't anyone just love art?' she asked.

'Of course they do. I do.' He loved the sketches of people whirling and jigging in a library, shelves and shelves of old books. 'On bikes,' he said. 'How odd. Where did you get the idea for that?'

'Just thought of it,' she said, shrugging. 'Just came into my head.' She thought if she told him the truth, he'd think her mad. And now, thinking about it, it seemed slightly mad. He asked if she was painting it. And she told him she was.

She phoned Stuart.

'Annie's still here,' he told her. 'She's painted the living room in the cottage.'

'Great,' said Madeline.

'Flo and the boys are staying with Willie, for the moment. So it's just Annie and me.'

'Great,' said Madeline.

'I made some pots,' he told her. 'Huge things for gardens. And I'm thinking of going into garden artefact things. Annie says it's a now market.'

'She's got great ideas,' said Madeline. 'She knows what's now.'

'Absolutely,' agreed Stuart. 'She comes into the pottery sometimes. She knows how to sell. I can't do that. I always back off if people aren't interested. But she can make them interested. We've sold over forty pots this week. I'll have to make more.'

'Fantastic,' said Madeline. 'I'm so pleased for you.'

'How're things with you?' he asked. He hoped, he always hoped, she'd tell him she'd met someone else. She wasn't coming back. He didn't want to break it off with her. Tell her about Annie. He hated confrontation. Wished all this worry, this deceit he was living, would fade quietly away.

'Your friend Annie and Stuart are alone together in the cottage?' said Stella. 'Doesn't that worry you?'

'No,' said Madeline. 'They're my friends. Chums. That's how it is. Annie's helping him paint the cottage. And with the pottery. Before that they did the garden together.'

'While you painted?'

'Yeah, and worked at the hotel.'

'Right,' said Stella slowly. Then looked at her, as if she was just a little bit simple.

Madeline rolled her mind round this implanted doubt about Stuart and Annie. 'Nah,' she shook her head. 'You don't understand. We're all friends. That's the way it is.'

And Stella said, 'If you say so.'

'No, really,' said Madeline. 'Stuart's wonderful. My friend, my soulmate. Right now. I'm here. And working. Well, in fact. I'm flying. I'm a kite. But Stuart's there for me, on the ground holding the string. Keeping me safe. He's like the very earth to me. I don't know what I'd do without him.'

And Stella looked suddenly solemn. 'If you say so.'

Conversations with Stella and her friends were often raunchy. People spoke sex. Sometimes, Madeline, who considered herself open, liberal, was surprised at how graphic they were. Of course, they'd spoken sex at the Inverask. But then, it had been available to Madeline, she thought nothing of it. Speaking constantly about sex, explicitly about sex, when going through an enforced celibacy was different. It made Madeline horny. She started to think about sex all the time. She found herself sighing. And longing. Lying alone in her bed nights, she dreamed of Stuart. Or at least parts of Stuart relevant to her current needs. She dreamed of sex.

'I haven't done that in years,' she told Stella. 'I feel like a teenager.'

Stella had laughed and said she'd be coming out in spots next. Erupting with unfulfilled hormones. 'You should nip home for a quick shag,' she'd said. 'Stuff the work. A girl has needs. In fact it would probably improve your output.'

Madeline laughed at this. Agreed. Got on with her work. But this new notion was with her. And would not go away.

At Marglass, Annie told Stuart she was pregnant. 'Four months. Four bloody months,' she said. 'Now will you tell Madeline?'

Night Swimming

At first, in London, Madeline was enamoured with the availability of shoes. Living so far from shops, getting them had been a problem. Clothes, she could buy mail order. Shoes needed to be tried on. She was a size five. But some size fives left room for two fingers behind her heel, and some nipped her toes. Now she could go out and feast herself on footwear. She went to the hairdresser. Something she hadn't done in years. Years and years, she thought, sitting in front of the mirror, swathed in black sheeting.

'Who's been cutting it?' asked her new hairdresser. Lifting strands of her hair. Letting it drop. Watching the line of the fall.

'Stuart,' said Madeline.

'What salon does he work for? He's a stylist, is he?'

'Oh yes,' said Madeline. 'He's with Marglass.'

'Who?' asked the hairdresser.

'Marglass. It's in the North.'

In the three months she'd been away, Madeline had restyled her look. Bought clothes. And she moved differently. Her old stride was back.

She phoned Stuart most days. She told him she loved him, and she'd be back soon. Every weekend, she'd think, I'll go back. But something would happen that kept her from going – a dinner party, a film she wanted to see at the NFT, a new exhibition, meeting friends for a drink or a coffee. She'd forgotten how much she loved city life. The movement of it, the thrum of it. The noise. Even the smells – food wafting from restaurants, and so many restaurants, pubs, fumes from taxis, she loved them all. She loved the shops. People sitting outside pubs, drinking. Everything about it, she loved.

She did not really know why, on a rainy evening in late September, she started not just thinking about Marglass House, but yearning to see it again. She was busy here, working. And wished she'd thought to enjoy her days of idleness more, when she had them. But this evening, window open, street sounds drifting in, she thought about the sea, the hills moving into the summer distance, like shadows. She thought about the late call of the curlew as it wheeled through the evening, a shrill almost lonely declaration of territory before it slept. She thought about lying in Marglass House with the sound of the sea rushing in through the open window. The smell of peat and ozone and open spaces.

She remembered nights making love to Stuart when the world was still outside. The smell of wood burning in the range in the morning. Walking through dew-soaked woods, Stuart's hand in hers. And she decided to go back. Maybe not to stay, but to see him again. Feel his face against hers. His hand on her body. Make love again. With the windows open, again.

Sex, she thought. That's what's driving me back. But what the hell? It's as good a reason as any. A better reason than most. She was filled with the need to be with Stuart again. She would just turn up at the cottage. A surprise. The joy of seeing one another again. They'd throw open their arms, and rush into an embrace. She imagined it. The joy and heat of it. It would be the best sex ever. Fabulous.

She boarded a plane to Glasgow at midday. Didn't bother with a bag. She had clothes at Marglass. She wanted to travel light. This was a homing instinct. This was urgent. This journey was all sex and hormones.

Two in the afternoon she was in a taxi from the airport to the station, barely able to sit still. She was burning desire. And at three she was on a train going north. After that the journey slowed. It was seven before she boarded the bus that would, in three hours, pass through Gideon. The four-mile walk from Gideon to Marglass took another hour. Dark, but she knew every pothole, every dip in the road, she'd travelled it so often. Every step that took her nearer to Marglass House and Stuart excited her. She quickened her pace. Sometimes, she ran.

At eleven o'clock that evening she walked down the drive to the house. She stood looking at it. Still there, looming in the moonlight. Still roofless.

Memories whirled back to her. The things she and Stuart had done. The walks, the games they'd played. The time they'd bought licorice sticks at Murchie's, after a long nostalgic conversation about distant times, sunnier days and sweets they'd eaten. They'd sat on the jetty in front of the shop, sucking their prized purchases. Comparing blackened tongues. Murchie had watched them, remarked to Freda how they reminded him of children. Lost in themselves.

'Yes,' said Freda. 'Will they survive when they come out of it and join the world?'

'Do you think they'll come out of it?' Murchie asked. 'They could stay like that for ever. Wrapped in each other. That's true love.'

'Nonsense,' snapped Freda. 'That's the idyll that precedes true love. The rapture. True love is what you are left with once the rapture is over. When you join the world again, and stay together.'

'You're an old cynic,' Murchie said.

And Freda had told him, nonsense. She was a woman who'd known love. And it had never once included sucking licorice on a jetty. Love is when the dream is over and life begins. She'd looked at them. 'These two are chums. Chums with sex. Nice if you can get it. But it won't last.'

Murchie had closed the shop and he and Freda had gone for a drink. For a few days the nature of love and definitions of true love had been discussed at the Castle. But no conclusions had been reached.

Madeline and Stuart, in their own world, thought licorice had changed. It didn't used to taste like this. 'Or, maybe, it's us that's changed. Our taste buds aren't what they used to be.' He'd sighed. 'Some things are best left in the past. Juvenile confectionery and Bay City Rollers records, for example.'

Madeline, standing in the night, staring at the old house, remembered the jigs in the library. The storm, the night the roof blew off. The slicing wind, and the rain and the centuries of dust reeling through the dark. What a night, she thought. And we all got blind drunk on whisky. I was there, I did all those things. Her old life seemed sweet. Tender. Precious. She was filled with the need to see Stuart again.

And now, look, Stuart's working at the pottery making trendy garden artefacts. And Annie's selling them all over the place. Great team they make, she thought. First they got the garden going. Then this. Walking down to the cottage she thought it funny how things worked out.

The cottage was in darkness. The door, like all doors round about, was unlocked. Even better, she thought. He's in bed. I can just climb in beside him. And wake him. And he will love me for that.

In the hall, she noticed her little ceramic tiger on the stand beside the phone. Smiled to it. 'Hello, tiger.' She looked in to the living room. It had been painted since Stuart took it over. Madeline saw Annie's hand in the decor. She made her way down the small narrow hall to the bedroom.

The night was warm. Annie was half out of the duvet. She was lying, where Madeline had planned to lie, beside Stuart. He was curled into her. Spooning. His hand on her stomach. Which was swelling slightly. Four months, Madeline thought.

She didn't know how long she stood watching them sleep. She was too numbed by hurt and shock to move. They looked peaceful, content. Beautiful, really, she thought. Rufus, the dog, was curled up at the foot of the bed, brown and hairy with absurd ears. It looked up, flapped its tail, and yawned.

Typical Stuart dog, Madeline told herself. Doesn't so much as bark when someone creeps into the bedroom. She turned and walked away. The dog yawned again, and went back to sleep.

Madeline picked up the tiger and left. She thought it suitable to leave this place as she'd arrived, with only a small ceramic tiger. It was over. There was no place for her here now. She walked down to the sea, where, for years, she'd gone swimming every morning. It was still. High tide. A huge white moon, casting silver paths on the water.

Madeline sat on the rocks, numbed. The pain of it was too much to bear. Annie and Stuart lying entwined. I've been a fool, she thought. Stella was right, I should've listened to her. She wondered if Annie and Stuart would ever have told her. If they'd known she was coming back, would they have pretended they weren't having an affair? And how long had it been going on? Months and months, she thought. Cradling herself. Rocking. I'm a kite. And he's holding the string. My earth. My life. A fool, me.

She remembered the night of the storm, how Annie had rushed to Stuart, to comfort him. And she'd thought then that it looked more passionate than cosy. But they'd all got so drunk, she'd forgotten about it.

Despair took her. She forgot about her new life, new friends. In this moment, there was only two lovers in that bed, where she ought to be. And the sea. She stripped off. A swim. Just me and the water and the moonlight. And the chill.

She sat on the rocks, and slipped into the water. At first, the cold bit into her. Hit her chest. She gasped. Swam. She remembered how she loved the water, the clean scent of it. The pure cool air that lay just above the surface. It soothed her. This was perfect. Night swimming. She moved through the water. Started to enjoy herself. She wondered why it was that as soon as she was floating, things didn't seem so bad. When she was swimming, swimming was all she thought about. Water, such a comfort. She struck out for the ocean. And past the bell-shaped rock.

'Don't swim past that rock,' Stuart had told her, years before when she first came here. 'The currents will get you.'

But she swam out. Where the waters were deep and merciless. It was so pleasant. Comforting. She swam.

She swam far past the rock. Wavelets hitting her face as she moved up the glisten on the water, the moon path. For a while it was glorious. She felt free. Surged on. It was easy. If she lay on her back, floating, she saw, above her, whole galaxies. When she eventually turned and looked back over the distance she'd covered, she was shocked to see how far she'd come. A panic welled within her. What the fuck am I doing? The warnings had been wise. She felt the currents pulling her, sucking her further and further out into the Atlantic. She couldn't get back. She struggled, pushed against the force that was taking her out. Heart beating wildly. Oh God.

Ali always checked his creels at high tide, whatever time it happened. He was heaving one up from the depth when he heard the cry. 'Stupid bastard thing to do.' And turned. Stared out across the water. He put his searchlight on, saw a small black head bobbing in the water. Started his engine and moved his boat towards it. He drew alongside Madeline. She grabbed the boat, pitching it towards her. Lifting herself up.

'Madeline?' said Ali. 'What the hell are you doing? Time of night is this to take a swim?'

She couldn't speak. Too shocked. Too cold. Too frightened. She reached out for him, gathered her strength and, finally, said, 'Please.'

He hauled her aboard.

She lay at the bottom of the boat, gasping and spitting. Her nose was running. Her teeth started to chitter, and there was nothing she could do to stop them. She was shaking with chill.

Ali took off his sweater and shoved it over her. Rubbing her. Warming her. 'Stupid fucking woman,' he was saying. 'Bloody idiot.'

Madeline shook, and coughed. And Ali kept holding her, moving heat back into her.

'What were you doing?'

'Taking a swim.' The words came out on a breath. Teeth chattering. She lay on the bottom of the boat. He loomed over her, and in the midst of her cold and trembling, she thought it strange. People looked so funny when you saw them upside down.

'I thought you were in London,' he said. Moving his hands over her feet, her legs. 'What were you doing way out here? You know not to swim so far out.'

'I know,' shivered Madeline. Swallowed water heaved out of her. She leaned over the side of the boat. Retching.

'Christ, girl,' said Ali. Holding her. Gazing out at the distance she'd come. 'You're lucky I was here.'

'I know.' She looked at him. Something was different. 'You've had your teeth fixed,' she said.

Ali stopped momentarily rubbing life into her and said, tapping his upper set, 'Yeah, porcelain caps. Pretty good.' Then, 'What the hell are you doing out here in the water?'

'I was taking a swim. I don't know. The water was just there. And I thought it'd be nice. Soothing.' She sat up, pulled the sweater on properly, hugging herself. Getting some heat into her bones, her blood.

Ali pulled a Thermos flask from a carrier bag and poured some boiling, sweet tea into the plastic cup. 'Here,' he said.

She thanked him, shaking, held the plastic cup to her lips, sipped the brew. 'Good,' nodding appreciation. 'I don't take sugar.'

'Jesus Christ, woman. I fucking save your life and you fucking sit there and fucking criticise my fucking tea.'

Madeline felt chastised. 'Sorry,' she said. Then to appease him, 'I like your teeth.'

He turned the boat, headed for shore. 'We better get you home before you freeze to death.'

'You're heading for the jetty,' Madeline protested. 'My clothes are on the rocks back there.' Pointing at a tiny distant bundle in the moonlight.

'Well, I can't get the boat in there. Too many rocks.'

Ali's cottage was sparse. He'd lived in it all his life. Was born in it. Both his parents were dead. But he saw no reason to move on. He liked this house. Though he'd emptied it. Now the living room contained a wood-burning stove, a sofa, shelves of CDs, a hi-fi and a computer. Both the sofa and the hi-fi looked expensive.

'This is nice . . .' Madeline looked round. She was wearing only Ali's sweater. And shivered. Was about to sit on the sofa. But Ali told her to get off his good upholstery with her wet bum. And fetched her some clothes. A pair of jeans and a sweatshirt. They were far too big. She didn't complain.

He poured her some whisky.

She said she didn't drink whisky, but took it anyway. 'I haven't drunk whisky since . . .' She decided that to tell him about the 1890 Bowmore was too embarrassing, '. . . the last time I drank whisky.'

'That sounds like you were about to tell me something and changed your mind.'

She nodded. Sat down. The warmth of the stove and the whisky mellowed her. She felt her face soften. The tension relax. The chill was easing.

'So why were you swimming out that far this time of night?' asked Ali.

'I came home to surprise Stuart and found him in bed with Annie. They must have been sleeping together for months. Months and months. I didn't know.' A tear slipped down her cheek.

'If you don't mind me saying, you go away for months and leave them together in that cottage. What did you think was happening?'

She looked at him. 'That's what Stella implied was going on.' She sipped her whisky. 'I just thought they were friends. I thought they just got along well. It never occurred to me.'

They sat. Saying nothing. But Ali thought Freda was right about Madeline. She seemed trapped in her own head. Fancy not thinking Stuart and Annie were sleeping together, he thought. Fancy not suspecting it.

Madeline pulled her legs up, sat clutching them. Chin on knees. Looking at the stove. The source of warmth. She started to shake. 'I'm sorry,' she said. 'I can't help it.'

'You're in shock,' he said.

'I'm sorry,' she said again. 'Really sorry.'

'What for?'

'Criticising your tea.'

'I'll forgive you.'

'I'm not sorry for that at all. I'm sorry for making a pest of myself. For this. For being here.'

'That's all right. I'll have something to talk about up at the Castle.'

'You're not going to tell, are you?'

'Well, I'll mean not to. I know you'd rather I didn't tell anyone about finding you miles out to sea. And naked. But it's such a good story. And I'll be there at the bar, and I'll have had a few. And I know I'll find myself telling it. It'll just come out.'

'Please,' she said, 'I'll do anything. Well, almost.'

'Do you know what I'd like? A painting. I could do with one over here,' pointing behind the sofa. 'No sea. No boats. No gulls. No cliffs. But anything else.'

Madeline nodded. 'I can do that.'

They sat. Ali put on a CD. Charlie Parker. A bluesy saxophone smoked through the room.

'That takes me back. Ted used to love jazz. I thought it was crap. But he said I'd grow into it.'

'Who is Ted?'

'My father. He died.'

'Didn't you call him Dad?'

She shook her head. 'Always Ted. My mother died when I was born. I never knew her. But Ted was lovely.' She paused. 'I'm sure he was lovely. He was drunk or stoned a lot of the time, I realise now. But, yes, he was lovely.'

'He sounds a bit irresponsible to me,' said Ali.

Madeline was tired. She was sitting talking. But she felt the only bit of her that was awake was her mouth. She gave in. 'Yes, he was irresponsible. I remember weekends when I was little, and he never dressed me. I spent the whole time in my pyjamas. I remember putting myself to bed. I remember coming into the living room late at night and he'd have passed out on the sofa. The lights would still be on. The television hissing in the corner. I don't think he ever got over my mother. But he was lovely. I believe that.'

'My father was a religious maniac. He didn't allow me to go out on Sundays, except to church twice a day. He didn't drink. No books in the house, except the Bible. If I did anything wrong, even as much as take a biscuit between meals, he'd beat me and tell me the wrath of God was on me and I'd go to Hell. He died fifteen years ago. I seriously hope that's where he went. I was so angry. Angry for years. I think your idea of keeping your old man lovely is a good idea. Wish I could.'

Madeline nodded and took his hand. They sat listening to Charlie Parker, palms pressed together in a moment of mutually misunderstanding their fathers.

'I have got to lie down,' said Madeline. 'It's been a day. A long journey. A shock. I'm knackered.'

'A duff attempt at suicide,' said Ali. 'You failed to mention that.'

'No, not that. The water was too tempting. I was just swimming because I was upset.' She sat, looking down at her glass. 'Thank you,' she said. 'You saved my life. I owe you.'

'The Chinese say if you save a person's life, you owe them.'

'In which case, do you have a spare bed?'

'No. Take my bed.'

'I can't do that. I've caused you too much trouble already.'

'Take it. I'll sleep here,' patting the sofa.

'No. I'll sleep on the sofa.'

'I'm telling you what to do. I am now responsible for the rest of your life. That's the Chinese rule. You sleep in my bed. And when you're up to it you'll go see Stuart and sort things out.'

This was not in Madeline's plans. She'd thought she'd just slip away. And never see Stuart or Annie again. Just ease herself from their lives. 'I don't think so,' she said.

'I do. You'll go make your peace with them. Then you'll get on the bus and never come back here again. You'll forget all about this.'

She shook her head. 'I'll never forget.'

'It'll slip away. Things do. But I'll be keeping an eye on you. It's my duty now. I'm looking forward to it. Bossing you around.' In truth, he thought it might be handy to know somebody in London. Somewhere to stay when he visited.

Madeline slept for twelve hours. Four in the afternoon she woke and had a moment of wondering where she was. But last night came back to her. The sea. The vastness of it. Endless water. The moment of utter panic when she realised she couldn't get back to shore. Ali pulling her into the boat. Yanking her up. The few seconds when she'd hung half in, half out, bum upwards. Oh God, she writhed. Her chittering and shaking. Nose running. Soaked. Oh God, no. I'm a fool, a stupid bloody fool.

She got up. Looked through the house for Ali. He wasn't there. Madeline looked out across at the pier. No boat. He'll be out checking his creels, she thought. I could slip away. Be gone. Never come back here. But no, she couldn't do that, her credit cards and return ticket were in her jeans, which were lying on the rocks beyond Marglass House. She bathed, washed her hair. Made herself coffee. And wondered what to do.

When Ali returned, he asked, 'You been to see Stuart yet?'

Madeline shook her head. 'I don't want to see him.'

'Well, you will. Come on.'

'Now? Don't you want something to eat first? I could make you a sandwich.'

'Now,' he said.

They drove up to Marglass House. Saturday evening, Stuart and Annie had just finished supper. Stuart had been at the pottery all day. Annie had spent some time looking for the ceramic tiger. The rocks by the shore hadn't occurred to her. Right now, as Madeline entered the kitchen, after knocking on the door and shouting, 'Anybody home?' they looked guilty. Neither could meet her eye.

Madeline and Ali each accepted a glass of wine. Sat down. Ali supposed he should go and leave them to it. But it was too interesting to miss. Besides, he felt he had a stake in Madeline's life now.

Madeline put her glass on the table. Twirled it. Watching the swirl of liquid. Said nothing. She didn't need to.

'Sorry,' said Annie, reaching over to touch Madeline's hand.

Madeline pulled it away. 'Why didn't you tell me?'

Annie caught Stuart's eye. A withering look. He shrugged. 'We didn't know how,' she said.

'You just open your mouth and say the words,' said Madeline. 'It's easy.'

'I wish it was,' said Stuart.

'How long?' Madeline wanted to know. 'Before I left?'

They nodded.

Madeline put her head in her arms. Tears. 'I'm a fool. A fool.'

Ali put his arm round her.

She shook it off. Turned on him. 'This is all your fault. You made me come here. If it wasn't for you I'd be on a plane by now.' The accusation was howled out. 'I didn't want to do this.'

Ali flinched. Held his open palm to his chest. 'Me? This has nothing to do with me.'

'You knew,' said Madeline, noticing the funny pitch her voice came out at. It cracked on the second word. She was staring at him, furiously. And realised she couldn't see him, for tears blurring her eyes.

'I guessed,' said Ali. 'Christ, Madeline, I save your life, and this is the thanks I get.'

'This has nothing to do with Ali,' said Annie. She turned to Ali, 'What do you mean, saved her life?'

'She was swimming towards America when I picked her up last night.'

'Madeline!' Stuart was shocked. 'How many times have I told you — . . .'

'What do you care? You're sleeping with Annie. She's having your baby.'

'I love her,' said Stuart. Which surprised him. He hadn't really mentioned this to her. She reached over and took his hand.

'I thought you loved me,' said Madeline.

'I do,' Stuart told her. 'Just not like that any more.' He reached over, laid his hand on Annie's little bulge. 'It just happened, Madeline.'

By now, Ali was telling Annie about finding Madeline in the sea. 'Stark naked,' he was saying, 'and shivering. Then she says, "I don't take sugar in my tea . . ." '

'Goodness,' said Annie, looking in alarm at Madeline.

Stuart looked sorrowfully across at Madeline, who had picked up a biscuit and was slowly chewing it, wiping her tears and nose with the sleeve of Ali's sweatshirt, which she was wearing. He smiled at her. She always made him smile. Sorry, he mouthed to her.

She nibbled the biscuit and said, 'I know.'

Later Annie and Madeline walked down to the shore to fetch Madeline's jeans.

'You weren't trying to do yourself in?' asked Annie.

'Don't be silly,' scoffed Madeline. 'I came to the cottage, saw you and Stuart in bed. All cuddled together. And I was gutted. So I came here. And there was the sea. So I went for a swim.'

Annie looked at her and said, 'Hmm.'

It was a perfect evening. Balmy. Madeline stuck her tongue out, tasting the air. 'A good vintage,' she said. 'Warm, slightly peaty with a hint of salt and ozone but with a slight autumnal aftertaste. Colder days are on the way.'

'But you won't be here to see them,' said Annie.

Madeline shook her head. 'No.'

They reached the rocks. Madeline stood looking at the sea. 'Doesn't it make you want to plunge in? Swim?'

Annie said, 'No. Definitely not. I hate swimming.'

Madeline turned to her. 'Actually, I understand about you and Stuart. When I think about it. Really think about it. It seems right. You two are right for each other. I don't know why I didn't see it. I imagined the pair of you sitting in the cottage talking about flowers and pots.'

'When we were actually shagging madly,' said Annie.

'Yes,' agreed Madeline.

They looked at each other. And despite themselves, desperately trying not to, sniggered.

'We shouldn't laugh,' said Annie.

'I know,' said Madeline. 'Well, I always knew you were a shite and a whore.'

'So you're a moocher. And, watch out for alarm farting.'

'Those were the days,' said Madeline. 'No, really, we shouldn't laugh.'

But they did. Till Annie spotted the tiger. 'Look. I've been searching for that everywhere.'

'I took it last night. After I saw you and Stuart in bed together. I thought it was fitting to leave with what I came with. A dramatic gesture.'

Annie said, 'I like that. Do you want it?'

Madeline said, 'Leave it. It looks happy there. Time to move on.'

Madeline collected her jeans. The two turned and walked back up the long grassy slope to the cottage. The tiger stood, shining slightly in the evening, a lonely thing. Still with that strange, bemused expression.

Madeline put her arm round Annie's shoulders. 'What a devious cow you are, Annie Borthwick.'

And Annie said, 'I know. It's lovely.'

A Strange Little Thing

with a Tale to Tell

In spring the next year Marglass House was bought by a hotel chain
that planned to turn it into a conference centre. Stuart used the
money to buy the pottery and extend the cottage. He had a daughter,
now. Jasmine Madeline McKinnon. He married Annie. Madeline
came to the wedding and stayed with Ali. She gave him a painting of
Charlie Parker. It was black and white, and had been inspired by old
photos in *A History of Jazz* she'd bought in a second-hand bookstore.
He hung it on the wall behind the sofa.

On her way North, she'd stopped at Edinburgh. And had persuaded Hamilton Foster to go with her to see her old landlord,
Maclean. 'He's got something of mine,' Madeline told him.

They went together to Maclean's office. The man had aged. But
he remembered Madeline.

'Miss Green,' he said. 'I never thought I'd see you again.'

Madeline told him stiffly that he had some things of hers. She
showed him her cheque and said he'd get it when he returned her
stuff. They went down to the storage vaults below his office. Large,
musty. Cluttered with cheap furniture that Madeline looked at with
horror. 'Ghastly. Burning's too good for it,' she said to Hamilton,
who looked alarmed.

Maclean looked about, saying he knew Madeline's things were
here, somewhere. Then spotted her old easel propped against a wall.
'Ah . . .'

'I only want the paintings,' said Madeline. 'You can keep the rest.
You can put that easel in some other flat and say it's worth thousands.'

Maclean was unmoved. 'Might just do that. Here we are.' He

handed Madeline a large sealed cardboard box. She gave him his money.

Outside, in the white Jaguar, Madeline ripped open the box. Everything was there. Her old paintings. Mrs Harkness and her bucket. Maclean collecting rent. And there was Ted's wedding ring. And his paintings. She smiled to see them. Held them to her. 'Mine, again.'

'Let's see,' said Hamilton.

Madeline handed them to him. 'My father did them. Aren't they wonderful?'

Hamilton didn't know what to say. 'Yes,' fearing if he said what he really thought, he'd hurt her feelings. 'They're vibrant. Um . . . what was he on?'

'He just did them for me when I was little,' said Madeline. Offended, but only slightly. She looked again at the paintings. Whorls of colour, splashes, small strange figures, waving, peering from tangled undergrowth. She looked again at Hamilton. 'I didn't know he was on anything, at the time. But I think now he was stoned most of my childhood.'

She took the paintings from Hamilton, looked at them. Breathed slowly out. 'Oh my.' She looked at Hamilton. A slow new truth creeping through her. 'They're awful, aren't they?'

He nodded.

'All my life I thought he was so gifted. His paintings so full of life. But his figures are wooden. And the colours. Just splashed on. Oh . . .' Madeline couldn't hide her dismay. She held the paintings to her. Said, 'Oh . . .' again. Then thought about Ted. And him singing Buddy Holly songs to her, and lifting her high to touch the ceiling with her fat baby fingers. And his ssshh plants. And walking about the living room conducting Mozart. And his moussaka. And his ladies. And driving through the dark that night, crying out, 'I don't know where the music ends, and the road begins.' She smiled. Turned to Hamilton. 'But he was lovely. Really he was. Ted was so lovely.'

'I expect he was,' said Hamilton. 'You're the one with the gift.'

Marglass was restored. New roof. New floors. New stairs. New everything. Except the bathrooms, which were too elaborate and fascinating to rip out. The grounds were replanted and the walled garden made productive again.

Stuart had toyed with the notion of applying for the job as head gardener. But Annie said, 'Wouldn't it upset you to have to work in your old garden when someone else owns it?'

Stuart thought it might. Especially since the pottery was at last showing a profit. Stuart's pots were becoming fashionable. Had been featured in the style section of a Sunday supplement.

'One notion at a time,' advised Annie. 'That's the way to go.'

On the day Marglass Hotel opened Mr and Mrs Namuto arrived from Japan. They'd come for the golf, and the whisky. After dinner they walked down to the shore. Stood looking out to sea. Mr Namuto spotted on the rocks, lying on its side, a tiny ceramic tiger with the strangest expression. He climbed down to get it. He and his wife held it, turned it over.

'What an odd thing to find here,' he said.

They wondered how it got there. Made up stories. It had fallen from a passing ship and been swept ashore. Someone had brought ashes of a lover to the sea in it. It was old, pirate's booty, suggested Mr Namuto.

But they agreed there was something alluring about the quizzical way it looked out at the world. And when they went home to Tokyo, the tiger went too. They put it on a shelf, alone.

Often they looked at it. Remembering where they'd found it. Still making up stories about it. They agreed however it got to a distant rocky shore, it was a strange little thing with a tale to tell.